Praise fo...

"Filled with originality, humor,
                                —New York Time:

"What a delight! This is enemies to lovers at its absolute finest, folks. DeLuca proves to be a master of creating characters you believe in and a story line to keep you totally engrossed. *Well Met* is a hilarious, swoony, and captivating romance—hands down our new favorite feel-good novel of the year."

                —New York Times bestselling author Christina Lauren

"A divinely entertaining romp. . . . The descriptions of him in his pirate gear, from the edges of his kohl-rimmed eyes to the deep V of his vests, down to his leather-clad legs . . . are likely to induce a thirst so wide and deep that you could sail a ship across it."

                                —Entertainment Weekly

"Jen DeLuca had me laughing out loud from the opening line. *Well Met* is fresh, fun, and the story I never knew I needed. I so wish I could grab a corset and live the wench life with Emily!"

                                —Alexa Martin, author of *Fumbled*

"I dare you not to want to travel to your nearest Renaissance Faire after reading the sweet, sexy, and smart *Well Met* . . . the kind of book that you want to live inside. Jen DeLuca is poised to become one of the freshest voices writing contemporary romance today."

                                —Kate Clayborn, author of *Best of Luck*

"DeLuca turns in an intelligent, sexy, and charming debut romance sure to resonate with Renaissance Faire enthusiasts and those looking for an upbeat, lighter read."   —Library Journal

"*Well Met* will especially appeal to readers who like bookstores, Renaissance Faire shenanigans, and nerdy English teachers wearing vests. DeLuca will have readers laughing all the way to the turkey leg vendor."   —Shelf Awareness

"Full of wit, hilarious banter, and swoon-worthy moments."
                                —Woman's World

ABOUT THE AUTHOR

Jen DeLuca was born and raised near Richmond, Virginia, but now lives in Arizona with her husband and a houseful of rescue pets. She loves latte-flavored lattes, Hokies football, and the Oxford comma. Her novels, *Well Met*, *Well Played*, and *Well Matched*, were inspired by her time volunteering as a pub wench with her local Renaissance Faire.

Also by Jen DeLuca

WELL MET

WELL PLAYED

WELL MATCHED

WELL TRAVELED

Well Played

Jen DeLuca

PENGUIN BOOKS

PENGUIN BOOKS

UK | USA | Canada | Ireland | Australia
India | New Zealand | South Africa

Penguin Books is part of the Penguin Random House group of companies
whose addresses can be found at global.penguinrandomhouse.com

First published in the United States of America by Berkley,
an imprint of Penguin Random House LLC 2020
First published in Great Britain by Penguin Books 2022

001

Printed and bound in Great Britain by Clays Ltd, Elcograf S.p.A.

The authorized representative in the EEA is Penguin Random House Ireland,
Morrison Chambers, 32 Nassau Street, Dublin D02 YH68

A CIP catalogue record for this book is available from the British Library

ISBN: 978-1-405-95651-2

www.greenpenguin.co.uk

MIX
Paper from
responsible sources
FSC® C018179

Penguin Random House is committed to a
sustainable future for our business, our readers
and our planet. This book is made from Forest
Stewardship Council® certified paper.

For Morgan

Who showed me that you don't need to be in the same
room—or even the same state—with someone to fall
in love with them. I'm so glad you made that first phone call.

One

It all started with a necklace.

A beautiful pendant, made of gleaming silver in the shape of a dragonfly, strung on a green silk cord. Its eyes were tiny crystals that caught the light, and the wings were a delicate filigree. I spotted it on the last day of the Willow Creek Renaissance Faire, while Emily—or Emma, since we were still in character—and I strolled the grounds. We were in our usual tavern wench costumes, with our personalities to match: a little louder, a little more brash and flirtatious than we were in real life. We stopped to interact with patrons—especially tiny ones dressed as knights or pirates—and we did a little surreptitious shopping as the vendors took one last chance to sell stock before packing it all up and moving to the next Faire on the circuit. That was when I saw the dragonfly, winking up at me from a jeweler's table.

"What d'you think, Emma, dear?" I held it up so we could both see it. I was wearing the pewter Celtic knot I'd gotten the summer before last, but my outfit needed a refresh. As the silver dragonfly rotated slowly at the end of its cord, its eyes flashed at me, whispering, *Yes. You need me.*

"Oh, Stacey, it's so pretty!" Emily clapped a hand over her mouth and turned wide eyes to me as she realized her errors. First, she'd called me by the wrong name, and second, she hadn't even made an attempt at her usual Faire accent. "Sorry," she said around a grin.

The vendor snorted. "It's all over but the shouting now. No one's going to notice you breaking character."

"I mean Beatrice, of course." To her credit, Emily slid back into character in a heartbeat. "Because that's your name. You truly deserve something new. I think it would do quite nicely."

"What's going on here?"

Now my wide eyes matched Emily's as we looked at each other in reaction to the stern voice behind us. Then we turned in unison to face Simon Graham, the Faire's organizer and Emily's boyfriend. He was still in costume as Captain Blackthorne the pirate: all black leather and roguish smile. But his forbidding tone was pure Simon the English Teacher, as though he'd already shaved his beard and cut his hair short as he did at the end of each Faire season.

So I scoffed at him, because a pirate and a tavern wench were roughly the same in the hierarchy of things, and out here he wasn't my boss. Not while we were in character. "Nothing wrong with a bit of shopping, Captain. Surely you wouldn't deprive your ladylove of a little indulgence."

"Oh, I don't need anything." Emily's hand went to the pendant she wore around her own neck—a deep blue crystal hanging from a silver chain. Simon had gotten it for her from one of the other vendors earlier this summer. "Why would I, when I have this?" Her eyes practically glowed when she looked at him, and I could tell she wasn't just talking about the necklace.

Simon raised an eyebrow, his stern expression melting away as though he had trouble maintaining it in front of Emily. "Quite right." He bent to brush a kiss across her mouth.

I coughed and glanced over at the vendor, who rolled her eyes good-naturedly in my direction. We probably had matching expressions. "Get thee a room," I muttered, and the vendor snorted in amusement. I fished in my belt pouch for the cash I carried to pay her for the dragonfly necklace. I didn't have anyone buying me gifts; I had to get my own. But I didn't mind. That way I was guaranteed to end up with something I liked.

Simon turned his attention back to me, and his brows drew together again. "Are you sure about that necklace, Stacey?" His voice was pitched low since he'd dropped the accent and his character. "It seems a little . . . elaborate for a tavern wench."

A flash of anger rose like bile in the back of my throat, and I swallowed hard against it. He was right, of course; the necklace didn't match my costume. Tavern wenches weren't high-class characters; my pewter Celtic knot was as fancy as I dared. But I'd inhabited this same character for six years now, and it was starting to chafe. I was tired of plain. Tired of settling.

My fist closed around the pendant, the dragonfly's wings digging into my palm. "Perhaps it's time for a change, then, Captain." I kept my voice light, almost teasing, so neither of them could see my irritation. This was a new revelation, and I wasn't quite ready to share it.

"She has a point," Emily said. "The taverns are mostly run by volunteers now, and you know I spent more time working on the Shakespeare skits with the kids than I did serving beer. Maybe the time for tavern wenches has come to an end, and Stacey and I can come up with different characters next summer."

"Perhaps." Simon shifted from one foot to the other as his Faire accent crept back. He didn't like change, especially when it came to Faire. But Emily looped her arm through his, bringing his focus to her again, and the smile returned to his face. "Perhaps," he said again. Fully back in character, his voice was pure pirate now, and he bussed Emily's temple. "For now though, I'm due on the chess field. Would you lasses care to join me?"

"The last human combat chess match of the year? I wouldn't miss it." Emily's devotion was adorable, especially since the chess match was as choreographed as the joust we'd just watched. Twice a day, Captain Blackthorne fought Marcus MacGregor, played by our friend Mitch—a giant of a man wearing little more than a kilt and knee-high boots and carrying a massive sword. And twice a day, Captain Blackthorne lost said fight. But Emily still cheered him on, every time. She was his biggest fan.

I wasn't in the mood to watch the chess. I'd seen it. Many, many times. "I'll walk around a bit more, if you'll forgive me." I was too restless. The last thing I wanted to do was stand still and watch a show I'd seen so often I could probably perform it myself.

Emily peered at me with shrewd eyes. "Everything all right, love?"

"Yes, yes." I waved her off. "I'd simply like to take in the scenery a little while longer."

"Of course." She squeezed my arm in goodbye as Simon doffed his hat and gave me a friendly bow. "Meet you at pub sing, then."

I had to laugh at that. Emily never made it up front for the farewell show of the day. But hope sprang eternal.

Alone now, I stowed my old necklace in my belt pouch, tied the green silk cord around my neck, and set off down the lane again, my long skirts kicking up dust—it had been a dry summer, and Faire lanes were made up mostly of dirt paths that cut through the woods. I took the long way around the perimeter of the site where we held Faire every year.

It was midafternoon and the sun was still high in the sky, but for me the sun was setting on the summer. There was something magical about the last day of Faire. Months of rehearsal and weeks of performance had come to an end, and it all culminated in this day. I always thought the sun coming through the trees looked a little brighter, since it was the last day I'd see it like that for another year. I wanted to catch it with my hands and hang on to it.

Many of the shows had finished, but I passed a children's magic act that was about halfway through its set, so I stopped to listen to the magician's patter for a few moments. The ax-throwing booth was still going strong, and I gave that a wide berth. What were we thinking, letting people who had no idea what they were doing fork over a few bucks to try and hit a target with a deadly weapon? The attendant didn't look too concerned, though, and he waved at me as I walked by. Multicolored banners hung from the trees, glowing in the sunlight as they blew gently in the breeze. A couple kids ran past me, headed for the lemonade stand. The sound of a tin whistle floated from somewhere nearby.

I ducked inside a booth displaying hand-tooled leather items, inhaling the heady scent. Inside, the wire-mesh walls were lined with leather goods of all kinds—vambraces and belt pouches, as well as modern-day accessories like belts and wallets.

"All handmade," the attendant said, not bothering with a

faked accent. She was my age, maybe a year or two older, but definitely not more than thirty. Her dark brown hair was pulled back in a long plait, and she wore low-key peasant garb: a long, dark green skirt and loose chemise, pulled in with a leather waist cincher.

"Do you make all this yourself?" I touched a soft blue back-pack made of buttery leather that hung on the end of one display.

"My husband and I do, yes." She bent down to scoop up a tod-dler in a long chemise with grubby bare feet. Even the kids dressed period here at Faire.

I pointed at the child. "Made that too, I assume."

She grinned in response and bounced the child on her hip, smoothing the babe's snarled hair. "Oh, yes. Though between you and me, the leatherwork's a lot easier. Do you have kids?"

"Oh, no." I shook my head hard. I didn't have a boyfriend. Kids weren't even on my radar.

She shrugged. "No rush, believe me." She turned to greet an-other patron who had ventured out of the sun and into the cool shade of the booth. As she walked away, she looked over her shoulder at me. "Anything you like, let me know. You'll get the Rennie discount: thirty percent off."

"Oh. Thanks." A warm feeling went through me at her words. Not at the discount, but at what it represented. She considered me one of them. As much a part of the crew as those who trav-eled the circuit with her. Even though I put a lot of effort into this Faire each summer, I'd never considered myself to be on the same level as the performers and the vendors who came through every year. They had their own culture, almost their own lan-guage, and I was just a local, on the outside looking in. After today these woods would be empty while the acts and vendors around me moved on to the next Faire, and it was a sharp pain to the heart. As if life were moving on without me, and I was being left behind. Sometimes I wished I was the one packing up and moving on. Sometimes I was tired of standing still.

I blew out a long breath, trying to chase those unsettled feelings away with it. Where had this come from? The Renaissance Faire had been my happy place since I was eighteen, but I didn't like the way I was feeling now. Had I outgrown the Faire? Or had it outgrown me?

I took one more glance at the blue backpack before making my way out of the booth. One necklace wasn't enough retail therapy to keep this melancholy at bay. Thirty percent off . . . I was going to have to come back for that.

I continued to wander the lanes with no conscious destination in mind, trying to get my thoughts in order, when my feet brought me to the Marlowe Stage. The Dueling Kilts' last set was about to begin. Perfect timing. I slipped into the back of the crowd, between a couple costumed vendors, right as the guys took the stage.

The Dueling Kilts were a trio of brothers—the MacLeans— who played Irish standards mixed with slightly naughty drinking songs, all on a hand drum, guitar, and fiddle. Their instruments were acoustic, their kilts hit just at the knee, and they were all very, very easy on the eyes. My eyes strayed, as they usually did, to the guitar player. Dex MacLean. The best eye candy at Faire. His red kilt was shot through with just enough dark green to keep him from looking like a stoplight, but it was still bright enough to draw attention. As though his powerful legs weren't doing that well enough on their own. The hem was a little ragged, and he wore it as casually as he'd wear a pair of jeans. Dex carried himself like a man who'd been born with plaid wrapped around his hips.

His off-white linen shirt did nothing to hide his broad, muscled shoulders, and he stomped one booted foot in time with the music he played. He shook his long dark hair out of his eyes as he turned to his compatriots, and his smile made something thud in my chest. Dex MacLean had been my favorite part of Faire for the past two summers. The man had a body like a Hemsworth, and I'd explored just about every inch of it. Just as he'd explored mine. He'd been clear from the start, of course. No strings. Just sex. I was fine with that. I wasn't looking to settle down anytime soon, and I didn't like Dex for his conversation. Again, body like a Hemsworth. What kind of fool would I be to pass that up?

After last summer, I'd been looking forward to a repeat of our sexual acrobatics this year, but things had turned out differently. He'd lost his phone over the winter and had apparently gotten a new number as well, so my initial texts had gone unanswered. We'd managed a night or two together, and it had been just as electric as ever. But the urgency hadn't been there as it had the summer before, and I wasn't disappointed when he didn't ask for my number again. I didn't volunteer it.

No strings, remember? The man wasn't relationship material.

So now I watched Dex play his last show on the last day of Faire with a curious mix of satisfaction, smugness, and regret. *I've had that*, the smug-and-satisfied side of my brain said. *But why hadn't I gone back for more?* I pushed down the latter thought, opting instead to appreciate what—and whom—I'd done.

Next to me, one of the vendors sighed. I recognized her; she sold tarot cards and crystals out of a booth shaped like a traveling wagon. She leaned over to the woman next to her. "So much pretty on one stage."

Her companion nodded. "Should be illegal, those legs. Thank God for kilts."

The tarot card seller sighed again. "Too bad he's such a man-whore."

"Really." The word slipped out before I could check it, and the two women turned to me with a conspiratorial grin. There was that feeling again, of being a Faire insider, with access to the best gossip.

"Oh, yeah." She leaned a little closer to me, and I did the same, as if she were about to share a secret. "I'm pretty sure he's got a girl at every Faire."

"Oh, he does," the other vendor said. "Wonder who it is here." She glanced around the audience as though she could identify Dex's Willow Creek hookup by some kind of secret symbol. A really satisfied smile, maybe. I bit hard on the inside of my cheek. If he was discreet enough to not blab about it, then I would be too.

"No idea," I said, pleased at how noncommittal my voice sounded.

"Lucky girl, though." The tarot vendor placed her hands on her belly, as if she were quelling butterflies that had gathered there. "I bet she had a hell of a summer." She snickered, the other vendor joined in, and I forced myself to do the same, even though my laugh was a little hollow.

At the end of the song the two women slipped out of the crowd and back to their booths. As the next song started, there was a touch on my elbow.

"Good morrow, milady Beatrice."

My attention slid away from Dex and to a different MacLean altogether. Daniel, Dex's cousin, managed the Dueling Kilts. He usually lingered somewhere in the back of the crowd like this, dressed in his uniform of a black T-shirt and black jeans. How the man managed to not die of heatstroke dressed like that in the middle of August, I'd never know.

"Well met, good sir." I bobbed a quick curtsy, still in character. Then I dropped the accent. "Faire's about over, you know. You can call me Stacey now."

Daniel's laugh was a quiet exhale. "I'll try and remember." He took off his black baseball cap and shook out his hair, and I was surprised anew at how red it was. Just long enough to fall into his eyes, his hair was usually obscured by the hat he wore all the time. "New necklace?" He raked his hair out of his eyes with one hand before settling the cap back on his head, eclipsing that bright hair again.

"Hmm? Oh. Yeah." My hand went to the dragonfly around my neck, the silver warm now from lying against my skin. "Just picked it up this afternoon."

"Looks nice." He raised a hand as though he was going to touch it, but he changed the movement to a gesture in the pendant's direction instead, shoving his hands in the front pockets of his jeans. "Means change."

"What?"

"The dragonfly." He nodded in the direction of my cleavage, current resting place of said dragonfly. "In a lot of cultures the dragonfly symbolizes change."

"Oh." I wasn't that deep, and for a moment I felt a little ashamed of that. But the hell with it. I shrugged. "To me, it symbolizes pretty." He laughed, a real laugh this time, and I couldn't help but remember that frisson of dissatisfaction that had seized me when I'd first picked it up. *Time for a change*, I'd said to Simon. Huh. Maybe this dragonfly knew what it was talking about.

I opened my mouth to tell Daniel about this, but he'd already turned his attention back to his cousins on the stage. Not for the first time, I contemplated the MacLean DNA. Dex and Daniel were both tall, but that was where the resemblance ended. Dex was dark, solid, and strong-muscled, a man who looked like he was about to rock your world in a dangerous way. Daniel was lean and fair, with bottle-green eyes to go with that red hair, and more of a swimmer's build than a bodybuilder's. Daniel looked less like he was about to rock your world and more like he knew exactly how you took your coffee and would bring it to you in bed with a soft smile just for you. While the Kilts played the Faire, Daniel stuck around to man their merchandising booth. It didn't seem like enough to keep him busy, but maybe Dex and the others required that much supervision.

Daniel was a comfortable, easy presence, but I always felt a little awkward around him, since I was pretty sure he knew all about Dex and me. There'd been that one night this summer when I'd run into Daniel at the hotel ice machine at two in the morning. There'd been no explaining that away.

Sure enough. "You . . . Um." Daniel cleared his throat, and I glanced over. His eyes were still on the stage, but his mouth twisted as he bit the inside of his cheek. "You know about Dex, right?"

I blinked. "Well, I'm familiar with him." Very familiar, but he probably wasn't looking for details.

He shook his head and leaned a shoulder against a tree, hands still shoved in the front pockets of his jeans. "I mean, you know he's . . ." He sighed and turned those green eyes my way. "You know he's kind of a player, right?"

"A wench at every Faire?" I raised my eyebrow, and his laugh in response was more of a snort. "I'd heard that." I sighed a dramatic sigh and looked back at the stage. "Guess I'm not as special as I thought."

I'd meant that as a joke, but Daniel didn't respond. I turned my head, expecting a knowing smirk on his face, but instead a flush crept up the back of his neck as he studied the ground. "I didn't say . . ." He cleared his throat and tried again. "I don't mean that you . . . I mean, you're . . ." Finally he sighed in exasperation and looked up at me again. "I don't want you to get hurt, that's all."

Oh. That. I waved an unconcerned hand. "Don't worry. I'm a big girl. I can handle it." It was my turn to blush at the words I'd just said. *Big girl.* My hands went to my waist, nipped in to a ridiculous degree by this corset I wore as part of my costume, as though I could push on my ribs and make myself even smaller. I wasn't one of those people who hated their body, but sometimes I was very conscious of the fact that I wasn't model-thin. That was one of the many reasons I loved being at Faire. Here, my voluptuousness was an asset: my chest looked incredible all hiked up like this, and the corset gave me an hourglass figure I could never achieve the rest of the year.

I cast around for something else to talk about. Anything. "So. Off to the next one, right? Are you going to the Maryland Ren Fest? I think just about everyone here hits that one since it starts next weekend."

He nodded. "Yep. It's so close by that it's a no-brainer. And it works out really well. We can try out new material here, where the audiences are smaller, and then hit up the big one next."

"Sure." I pressed my lips together. I knew this. I knew that our Faire was stupidly small potatoes compared to the Maryland Renaissance Festival, which was one of the biggest in the country. We weren't even in the same league. "I bet you're glad to see the back end of Willow Creek every year." I looked hard at the stage as rage bubbled in my chest. I loved this Faire. I loved this town. But that didn't mean that everyone did.

"Not at all." If Daniel had picked up on my reaction, he didn't say anything. When I glanced back to him he was looking at the stage too, not at me. "This is one of my favorite stops. Considering I travel about ten months a year, that's saying something." He paused, glancing at me quickly before looking back to the stage again. "I like it here."

And just like that, my lick of defensive anger dissolved, and relief swept through me like a cool breeze. "Yeah. Me too."

Onstage, the Dueling Kilts finished their set, and Dex lifted his chin in my direction. I'd already raised my hand in a wave when I caught Daniel doing an identical chin-raise in response. Ah. I turned the awkward half-wave into a too-casual check of my hair. Of course. Wench at every Faire. And Dex was done with both me and Willow Creek. On to the next one.

I shook off the sting of disappointment as I turned back to the lane, making my way up front for pub sing. We were down to the last hour or so in this year's Faire, and I was going to wring every possible moment out of it. Current feelings of frustration aside, these weeks in the woods were so much more fun, so much more interesting, than my real life.

I fiddled with my necklace again, tracing the dragonfly's wings between my fingers. Change, huh? Good luck with that, dragonfly. I'd lived in Willow Creek my whole life. Nothing changed around here.

I should have known better.

Dragonflies don't mess around.

Two

Ren Faire season was my favorite time of year. From tryouts in the late spring when we put the full cast of volunteers together, to weekend rehearsals spent learning songs and dances, enduring crash courses in history and etiquette, and practicing our accents, to finally the four weekends spent out in the woods at the Faire site through July and August, fully inhabiting our characters, Ren Faire season made me feel more alive. More vital. It was a life lived in full color, with music and laughter and oppressive summer heat and tight costumes.

So it stood to reason that those first couple weeks after Faire ended were my least favorite. Color leached out of life when I took my outfit to the cleaners and Beatrice the tavern wench was literally packed away for another year. Instead of looking forward to every weekend with excitement and slightly sore feet, all I had to look forward to now was another week at work. There was a bright side: being a receptionist at a dentist's office wasn't as flashy as being a tavern wench, but the clothes were certainly a lot more comfortable. I never understood why those of us on the business end of things had to wear the same scrubs as the hygienists, but they came in cute colors and it was like wearing pajamas to work, so I never complained.

But it was all so . . . blah. Just two short weeks ago I'd been running around in the woods in my costume, trading bawdy jokes with patrons, clapping along to music I only heard once a year. Karaoke at Jackson's had nothing on dirty drinking songs. But karaoke was all I had these days, so when Friday night rolled around I got ready to go out, as usual. Only I made the mistake of checking social media first.

So blessed to welcome Charlotte Abigail Hawthorne. 7 pounds, 3 ounces, perfect. We're both doing great! My best friend Candace looked great, anyway. A little sweaty, but she'd just pushed out a tiny human so that was to be forgiven. Charlotte looked mostly red and wrinkled, like a grumpy potato with hair. But I clicked "like" on the photo anyway and added a congratulatory comment: **Looking good, bestie!**, along with a heart-eyes emoji.

But was she my bestie? Candace Stojkovic and I had gone through every grade in school together, we'd cheered together, we'd graduated from high school together. But we'd lost touch after college, what with me staying here in Willow Creek and her marrying her college sweetheart and moving to Colorado. Thanks to the internet and social media we'd stayed in each other's lives, as much as we could, by clicking "like" on photos and tossing down witty comments. But that wasn't really "bestie" status anymore, was it? I'd become nothing more than a Facebook friend with my best friend. That . . . didn't feel good.

Enough. Time to go out.

I fastened the dragonfly necklace around my neck—the one bit of Faire I decided to keep as part of my daily life. All ready to go now, I took a selfie and put it up on Instagram: **Someone**

told me recently that dragonflies mean change. So here I go doing
something different tonight! JK I'm going to Jackson's as per usual.
#FridayNight

A couple likes popped up pretty quickly, but I examined the
pic with a critical eye. My roots were due for a touch-up: the
brown was really coming in, almost as dark as my eyes. My eyebrows made it clear that I wasn't a natural blonde, but there was
no need to be this blatant about it. The necklace looked nice,
though, and so did my smile. I'd always been known for my
smile, wide and open and happy, first in high school and then
later in college. It was a part of me, something I wore like a favorite pair of jeans. Even though sometimes it felt as false as a
push-up bra. Tonight it felt especially padded, but I kept it on
anyway. That was the Stacey everyone wanted to see, after all.
Ennui-filled Stacey was no fun, so I left her at home.

Jackson's was our local dive bar/hangout, the only real hangout in Willow Creek, actually, so I was guaranteed to see some
friends there. Sure enough, I found myself in a booth with my
Ren Faire compatriots, celebrating the end of another successful
season.

"Fine." Simon raised a bottle of beer to his lips. "I'll admit it.
Shortening the season from six weeks to four was a good idea."

"Told you." Emily nestled into his side and took a smug swig
of her own beer. "Fewer man-hours are required, we saved
money on the acts, and that cash goes right back in our pockets
for next year. That's what it's all about, remember?"

His brows drew together. "I've been doing this Faire since day
one. I think I know what it's all about."

I caught my breath. This was a touchy subject. Simon Graham
had started this Faire over a decade ago with his older brother,

Sean. We'd lost Sean to cancer a few years back, and ever since then Simon had grown more and more protective of everything having to do with Faire. Emily had shaken him out of that when they met last year. And while he'd finally been a little more open to change this year, to call Simon a micromanager was an understatement.

So my eyes darted from Simon over to Mitch Malone sitting next to me, who met my look and answered it with a roll of his eyes. Mitch had never had the patience for Simon and his darker moods, even when we were kids. He and Simon weren't the closest of friends, for all that they'd been working together for years to put on this Faire. In fact, the four of us represented most of the Faire's organizational committee.

I decided to venture a reply. "I think what Emily meant was—"

But Emily came to her own defense, lightly whacking Simon on the chest with the back of her hand before grinning at me. "He knows exactly what I meant."

"Wait a second." I put down my wineglass—I was the only one at the table not drinking beer, what a rebel—and reached across the booth for Emily's hand. When she'd smacked Simon, the light had flashed off a diamond ring I'd never seen her wear before. A diamond ring on her left hand. "What the hell is this?"

My voice came out a little shriller than I'd intended, and more than a few heads turned at the sound of me yelling at Emily. But I didn't care. I glared at her first, then Simon. I probably shouldn't glare at the thought of two of my closest friends getting engaged, but too bad. "Is this what I think it is?"

Emily's only reply was a giggle, and Simon's stern expression melted into a smile as he looked at Emily's hand in mine. "It is," he replied, and his smile widened, something I didn't think was physically possible. Simon didn't smile like that when he wasn't a pirate. "Emily agreed to marry me."

I squealed, and only the fact that I was sitting on the inside of the booth kept me from running around to hug them both. Launching myself across the table crossed my mind, but I managed to restrain myself.

"Well, hot damn! That's great, you two!" Mitch put down his beer bottle and stretched his arm across the table, offering Simon a fist bump. Simon was not a fist-bump guy, but he returned the gesture anyway.

Me, I stayed on topic. "When did this happen?" I examined her ring. It was a tidy, perfect diamond, nothing showy. Much like the man who had given it to her.

"Um . . ." Emily chewed on her bottom lip. "Monday afternoon."

"Monday?!" My response was practically a shriek. "That was four days ago!" I dropped her hand and sat back in the booth. "Were you planning on telling anyone?" It was inconvenient that I was so happy, because I really wanted to be mad at her for keeping this news from me. From all of us.

"Of course!" Emily looked chastened. "We were going to tell y'all tonight, actually. We . . . well . . ." She looked up at Simon, and they did that thing that couples do: communicating without words, just via facial expressions and a raised eyebrow. They looked married already.

"We were hoping we could ask the both of you for a huge favor." Simon cleared his throat, and Emily picked up on his train of thought.

"We want it to be a small wedding, and my big sister April is going to be my matron of honor. But Stacey, you've been my best friend since practically the day I moved here to Willow Creek. Would you be my other bridesmaid?"

"Of course!" I clapped my hands over my mouth, and tears shone in her eyes as our joy fed off each other. "Oh, Em, I couldn't be happier! This is going to be so great!"

"And. Um." Simon cleared his throat again and looked out into the bar, then up toward the ceiling, and then finally back to where Mitch and I sat across from him in the booth. "Well, as you know, Mitch, I don't have a brother anymore . . ." His voice faltered, and Emily covered his hand with one of hers, threading their fingers together. Her touch seemed to give him strength, although his smile had thinned. "So I wanted to ask if you would stand up with me as best man at our wedding."

Mitch's eyes were round. "Dude. Are you kidding?" That was all he said at first, and in the silence that followed, Simon deflated a little.

"No. I mean, I wasn't kidding. But . . ."

"Dude." He extended his hand again, but instead of a closed fist for a fist bump, it was open. Simon took it and the men shook hands, Mitch placing his second hand over their joined ones. "Of course I will," he finally said, his voice uncharacteristically serious. "It would be my absolute honor."

The two men smiled at each other, and I wished I could travel back in time to our high school days. Mitch had always been a larger-than-life blond jock type, a look that he played to great effect now every summer with his kilt and his claymore. Simon was the intellectual, smaller and slender, with dark hair and sharp eyes. He was a quiet, steady man who let his pirate side come out to play during Faire, transforming into a black-leather-clad rogue with a brash and outgoing demeanor that he never showed in real life. In high school, those two hadn't been friends. If I could tell teenage Simon and Mitch that they'd be having this conversation now, that they'd be sharing a beer and talking about one serving as the other's groomsman . . . well. Neither one of them would have believed me, and neither would have younger Stacey in her varsity cheerleader's uniform, big blonde ponytail bouncing down to her shoulders.

I twirled a lock of my hair—still blonde, but not in a ponytail—around my fingers and turned my attention back to Emily. "So," I said, "have you set a date yet? Next summer, maybe? We could do it at the Faire."

Emily's eyes brightened. "Yes!"

But Simon shook his head. "No."

She looked at him, a surprised laugh bubbling out of her mouth. "No? I figured a Faire-themed wedding was a given. You don't want . . . ?"

His head shake was even more emphatic. "No. I don't want to marry you in character. This isn't a joke. It's not . . ."

"Hey." She laid her hand over his. "No. It's not a joke."

"And it doesn't have to be in character," Mitch said.

"Right." I picked up on his train of thought. "We can skip the costumes. But the chess field would be a great place to set up a wedding. Out in the woods, it would be all . . . I dunno, pretty. Picturesque." I waved a hand; I wasn't great with words.

"Pastoral," Mitch supplied, and three pairs of wide eyes turned in his direction. He shrugged and took another swig of beer. "What, I have a vocabulary."

"Apparently." A smile played around Simon's mouth, but he tipped his bottle toward Mitch in a kind of salute. "You do make a good point. And we were thinking about an outdoor venue."

"Not to mention, this one would be free," Emily said. "Free is good. Bookstore managers aren't exactly millionaires."

Simon's nod was solemn. "Neither are English teachers."

"But I'm marrying you anyway." She kissed him, and her smile transferred to his face.

"Yeah!" I was getting into the idea now. "It can be in the evening. That way we could start setting it up after the last chess match. Have the reception while the sun's going down. It would be so pretty."

"Except for the mosquitos." Simon raised his eyebrows.

I waved a hand. "That's what those little citronella tiki torches are for."

"And you should get married on Sunday night," Mitch said. "That way we can party longer and not have to do Faire hungover."

"Priorities." Emily snorted. "I'll take that into consideration."

"Let me know what I can do to help," I said.

"Well, now that you mention it, how about brunch on Sunday? April's coming. I'm thinking waffles, mimosas, a silly number of wedding dress pictures?"

I had to laugh at that. "You have a Pinterest board already, don't you?"

"Guilty." But her grin said she felt anything but guilty. And who could blame her? I'd probably be just as excited if I were getting married.

The subject changed then, as we talked about the upcoming school year (Simon and Mitch both taught at Willow Creek High, so that was a popular topic), and other local gossip (we lived in a small town; gossip was what we did). But every once in a while, Emily moved her hand and light flashed off the diamond. Every once in a while, Simon looked down at her with a smile in his eyes. And every time, my heart overflowed with love for the two of them, which made total sense. Who wasn't happy for their friends when they found love?

But what didn't make sense was the thought that flashed through my mind—I'm gonna miss her. There was no reason for a thread of panic to grip my heart and make it race. Emily was right there, at the table across from me. She wasn't going anywhere. In fact, by marrying Simon she was settling down in Willow Creek for good. There wouldn't be any reason to miss her.

But my heart still raced all the way home until I pulled into my driveway, the same driveway I'd been pulling into since the day I got my driver's license. My parents lived in a four-bedroom, two-story house that was way too big for the three of us. Well, the two of them, now that I didn't live with them anymore. Technically.

My little apartment was a cozy nest. It ran the length and width of the two-car garage it was built over, with a small kitchen tucked in one corner and an enclosed three-quarter bathroom (no bubble baths for this girl) in another. My clothes lived in two freestanding wardrobes, and my queen-size bed was tucked in the eaves. I'd strung fairy lights on the wall that sloped above my bed, and their soft glow made it feel like I was sleeping inside a blanket fort. A pair of skylights in the kitchen area let in lots of natural light, and when it rained I loved falling asleep to the patter of the rain on the glass.

It was a great little place, and it was mine. I loved it. I told myself that a lot, and most of the time I even believed it.

I'd barely closed the door behind me and tossed my keys into the little dish by the door when my phone rang. Not my cell phone, which was silent in my bag, but the old-school landline attached to the wall in the kitchen. It didn't have caller ID, but

I knew who it was. There was only one person in my life who had the number.

"Hey, Mom."

"Hi, honey, I heard your car. Did you have dinner? We just finished eating, but I can fix you a plate."

"No. No, I'm fine. I ate when I was out." I slid my little leather backpack off my shoulders, the buttery blue leather bag I'd bought just as Faire had ended—I hadn't been kidding about the retail therapy—and dropped it onto my kitchen table. "I'm kind of tired; it's been a long day. I think I'll watch a little TV and turn in."

See? Semi-independence. Mom didn't call every night, but often enough to remind me that in some ways—in most ways—I still lived at home. I loved my parents, but it was getting old. Hell, I was getting old. I was almost twenty-seven, for God's sake.

That feeling of getting older without really being allowed to grow up lingered, and that feeling combined with the sight of Emily's engagement ring. *I'm gonna miss her.* Now that stray thought made sense. Getting married, becoming a wife. And what was I doing? Going out to Jackson's every Friday night and posting the same selfies on Instagram.

I needed to get a life.

I needed another glass of wine.

Ten minutes later I was in my pajamas and had flopped onto my old comfy couch with a second glass of wine. I powered up my laptop and hadn't even logged into Facebook before Benedick was purring in my lap.

Benedick. My main man. My one true love. Our favorite thing to do on a lazy Sunday was snuggle together and watch a movie. Superhero movies were his favorite, but he tolerated romantic comedies because I was the one who opened the cans around here.

And no, this did not make me a crazy cat lady. You needed at least three to qualify for crazy status, and I was a one-tuxedo-cat woman, ever since the day I'd found him in the parking lot after Faire three summers ago. I named him Benedick, after the hero of Shakespeare's *Much Ado About Nothing*, and I was his Beatrice. See? Who needed a diamond ring? Or a man looking at you adoringly over mozzarella sticks under the crappy light at Jackson's?

"Oh, shut up," I told myself, just loud enough to wake Benedick, who blinked at me reproachfully. I scritched behind his ears in apology as I scrolled through Facebook. But the more I scrolled, the more my mood darkened. Two of my sorority sisters had gotten married in the past six months, and three girls I'd grown up with had had babies. How had this happened? We'd all been allotted the same number of years, and they'd taken that time and built lives. Families. Meanwhile I was living in my parents' attic, working at a job that could replace me in five minutes if I got hit by a bus, with nothing going for me but a fat tuxedo cat—sorry, Benedick—and a half bottle of wine. Emily's little diamond ring flashed in my mind like a beacon, and I found myself fiddling with my dragonfly necklace again. Change. Bah.

"Screw you, dragonfly." I untied the cord and tossed the necklace onto my coffee table on my way to refill my wineglass. Looked like change was happening for everyone but me. When was the last time anything had changed in my life? Certainly not since college, and I didn't want to think about how long ago that was.

Back on the couch I took a healthy sip of wine and clicked

through to our Faire's private group page, filled with pics from not only the Faire that had just ended but also from years past. A warm glow filled my chest, which was only partially from the wine. Those few weeks of Faire every year were the best part about living in Willow Creek these days. I'd just put my wench's costume away for the winter, and I was already looking forward to taking it out again.

In one of the online albums, Emily and I grinned at the camera in a photo taken the summer before last, our arms around each other in our wench outfits. She'd been a complete newbie then but totally game, and by the end of the summer she'd become a real friend. *I'm gonna miss her.*

"Stop it," I said. "She's not going anywhere."

A couple more clicks, and I landed on a shot of the Dueling Kilts. One that was obviously taken at pub sing; Dex was framed by late afternoon sunlight streaming through the trees. God, he was gorgeous. I missed him.

That thought brought me up short. Did I really? Or did I miss the whole "friends with benefits" situation? That couldn't be it . . . we weren't friends. We'd gone out on what could loosely be considered a date a few times over the past two summers, and we'd hooked up more times than that, but we weren't friends. We'd hardly even talked this summer. Acquaintances with benefits? I should want a guy who wanted actual conversation with me. Who wanted to get to know me. Relationship material. Dex was relationship Teflon.

Besides, he had a girl at every Faire. For all I knew, he was with the next girl right this minute. I looked back at my laptop, at the photo I'd blown up to screen-size. Dex cradled his guitar, grinning at something just off camera, his dark eyes doing that crinkly thing at the edges that was somehow ridiculously sexy on guys. He'd smiled at me like that, and every time he did I was lost. Friends, acquaintances, whatever-you-wanted-to-call-it with benefits, he was the kind of guy who gave you his full attention when he was with you. I'd never asked for more . . . but what if I did? Would I stand out among the crowd? I'd stood out well enough for him here in Willow Creek, after all.

It was the photo that did it. That grin. Those crinkly eyes. What was he smiling at? I'd slept with the guy, but had no idea what made him laugh. And suddenly I really, really wanted to know.

Well, only one way to fix that.

The photo was tagged, so it was just a matter of a couple clicks to navigate to a private message screen. I put down my wine and started to type.

Yes. This was a great idea.

The next morning I woke up with a head full of hammers and I pulled the covers over my head. I was usually an early riser, and while the skylights were great for letting in natural light, they were hell on hangovers. I lay back on my pillows—as well as I could since Benedick took up most of the room there—and willed my head to stop pounding. That had been far too much wine last night.

Eventually I hauled myself out of bed and got some coffee started. Everything was so bright. I squinted against the early morning sunlight streaming down from the skylight over my whitewashed kitchen table, and I almost went looking for my sunglasses. Benedick abandoned my pillows to wind around my legs, reminding me to feed him.

Cat fed and aspirin acquired, I brought my coffee over to the couch before putting away the mostly empty wine bottle I'd left on the coffee table. At least Past Stacey had had the presence of mind to cork the thing. Especially since I'd left my laptop open next to it, and Benedick liked to roam at night. A knocked-over bottle of wine next to an open laptop would be a disaster . . .

Laptop.

The end of the night suddenly snapped into much clearer focus. That third—fourth?—glass of wine. An open private message screen.

Oh, no.

I practically fell onto the couch and woke up my laptop as fast as I could. "No. Nonononononono . . ." The word was a prayer under my breath as the screen came to life. Maybe in my drunken haze I'd forgotten to hit Send. Maybe my Wi-Fi had gone out and the message hadn't gone through. Maybe he hadn't seen it yet and I could delete it before he did.

No such luck. My screen blinked to life, and there it was. Wi-Fi fully connected, message sent. Even worse, it was marked as read. Crap. Who knew Dex was such an early riser? Certainly not me: our nights together had never evolved into sleepovers.

I pulled my mug over and took a long sip of my coffee. I barely felt the heat of it, as everything had gone numb. I didn't move, I didn't even want to blink. All I could do was read the message I'd sent my yearly hookup, well into last night's wine-drunk.

Hey!

This is Stacey Lindholm. Well, obviously you can tell that since my name is right here. Do you even know my last name? Well, you do now. That's kind of why I'm writing. Not about my name, who cares about that. But I realized that I don't know you. I mean of course I know you, I've known you for a few years now, right? And I guess I know more about

you than you do about me, since you just now learned my
last name and I already know yours.

So let's start with the basics.

What makes you laugh?

How do you take your coffee?

Do you like cats?

Do you miss me?

I should delete that last one. But I'm gonna let it stay up
there. Because with merlot you tell the truth.

So here's the truth. I miss you. I know I shouldn't, I know I
have no real reason to. But I'm already looking forward to
seeing you again next year, and that's eleven months away.
I'm not expecting you to do anything with this information,
other than just know it. Know that I miss you, and I wish we
had more than those few weekends a year to spend
together.

I hope you have a great run at the Maryland Ren Fest,
and the rest of the season. You travel so much, don't you? Do
you like traveling that much? See, something else I'd like to
know about you.

Take care,
Stacey

I groaned and leaned back against the cushions. This was
pretty bad, but after all that wine it could have been so much
worse. I thought about sending another message. Maybe I could
apologize for Past Stacey. For Drunk Stacey. But no. That would
just compound the awkwardness. Instead I closed my laptop and
finished my coffee. Nothing I could do now but wait for him to
respond.

Of course, it didn't occur to me until the next day that he might not respond at all.

Between Saturday morning and getting ready for brunch with Emily and April on Sunday, I checked my phone roughly a hundred times. It had been more than twenty-four hours since I'd sent that first regrettable message, and he hadn't answered. Relief mingled with disappointment, and I couldn't decide which emotion was stronger. No response meant not having to own up to my drunken words, and I was all for not being held accountable for my actions. But no response also meant that he wasn't interested, which, let's face it, sucked.

I sighed a long sigh, tied back my hair, and put on some pink lip gloss. This wasn't that big a heartbreak, after all. Nothing a little brunch couldn't cure.

I adored brunch. It was relaxing, a meal meant to be eaten over a good hour or two, savoring drinks and coffee and carbs in all forms. But brunch with Emily Parker was something else entirely. She had a paper planner already stuffed with printouts and brochures, and her tablet was on her Pinterest page of wedding dresses, which we flicked through while we waited for our waffles and eggs.

"Are you sure you don't want to get married in costume?" April shook a sugar packet into her coffee before stirring in the cream. "You'd look so cool as a pirate's bride."

Emily shook her head, not looking up from her tablet. "Simon vetoed that pretty much immediately."

"Too bad." April sighed dramatically. "Because that would have made Stacey and me your . . ." Her voice quavered, and when I looked over at her, she was having a hard time keeping a straight face. ". . . your bridesmateys." She barely got the word out before she sputtered into a laugh, and my own giggle burst out before I could check it.

Emily snorted a laugh of her own but shook her head. "You're the worst," she said around a grin. "Now, can we look at these dresses, please?"

"You've been engaged for like a week," I said, wonderingly. "How did you do all this?"

"I work fast." Emily flicked through her tablet before passing it to her older sister, April. "This one!"

April frowned at it. "You're too short for that."

I took a sip of coffee to cover my laugh, and Emily tsked at her sister. "I am not! Show Stacey; she'll back me up."

April passed me the tablet, and it was my turn to frown at the picture. It was a relatively traditional wedding gown, but April was right. The model in the photo was easily half a foot taller than Emily, if not more. Lots of lace, a train, and puffy sleeves . . . Em would be lost in a dress like that.

"Sorry, Em. I have to go with April on this one." Thankfully the waiter arrived with our mimosas to soften the blow, and I tipped mine to April in acknowledgment. "I mean it. It's very pretty, but you'll look like you're drowning in your grandma's linen closet if you wear that. You want . . ." I could imagine perfectly the kind of dress she should wear, but none of her choices matched the vision in my head. I set down my drink to head down a Pinterest rabbit hole, tapping and swiping and tapping again until I found a good approximation. "Something like this." I passed the tablet back to her. She peered at my choice, April leaning over her shoulder, and I chewed on my bottom lip and tried to read their faces.

Emily's face hardened at first, and my heart sank. But then she tilted her head, and the more she looked at the picture, the more her face softened. "You think? It doesn't look too . . . I dunno, casual?"

"Nope." I shook my head with no hesitation. "Think about it. You're getting married outside, so you don't want something that's going to drag all over the ground. Not to mention, it'll be what, July? August? The hottest time of the year. You don't want all those layers of fabric."

"I like the skirt." April gestured in an up-and-down zigzag motion. "It calls attention to the lace better than that other dress."

"I do like the lace." Emily bit her lip. "And the skirt is really cute."

"Exactly," I said. "The handkerchief hem shows off the lace better, and when it's in a couple layers like that it'll give you a fair amount of swish."

"Swish?" Em looked up at me now, her eyes twinkling. "Is that a technical term?"

"Sure is." I grinned back at her over the rim of my mimosa flute.

"Yeah, I think Stacey's right," April said. "But maybe more of a halter style up top, and keep the silhouette close. It looks like something . . ." She shrugged. "I dunno, like in a fairy tale. If you're getting married at the Ren Faire next summer, that's not a bad look to emulate, right?"

"And you have to have flowers in your hair," I said. "Like a flower crown. Or maybe a tiara would be better."

A smile played around Emily's mouth. "I like flowers. Good idea." As our food arrived she looked down at the picture again. When she tapped on it to save it to her board, I felt a surge of triumph.

"You're good at this," April said. She watched me carefully

while she took another sip of her mimosa. "You're one of those people who's been planning their wedding since they were four, aren't you?"

I had to laugh at that. "Hardly." Weddings weren't my thing. But clothes were. And I knew what looked good on people. To me it was automatic. One look at someone and I knew whether they should be wearing a ballerina or sweetheart neckline, a tea-length or a maxi skirt. It came together as a picture in my head, complete and sudden, like a snapshot. It was a talent that I didn't get to use a whole lot these days, so when I had the opportunity, I pounced on it.

"You *are* good at this, though," Emily said. "I mean, you picked out my costume last summer when I did the Faire for the first time too. Maybe you should dress me all the time."

I shrugged and tried to look casual, but that sense of triumph only increased, like victory trumpets sounding in my brain. "It's what I do. Or used to." Back in college. Back when I'd had a future. Bad memories surfaced, and that little surge of triumph fizzled and floated away.

"Well, I hope you still do," Emily said. "We have to decide on bridesmaid dresses, and besides, we're getting new outfits for next summer, remember? You know I'll need your help for that. Without you I'll keep calling a corset a bodice. Then I'll pick out something that's ten years out of date and Simon will probably call off the whole wedding in retaliation."

I didn't even try to suppress a giggle; Simon really was a perfectionist when it came to Faire. "Don't worry," I said as the food arrived. "I'll have your back."

"Thank God for that." Emily took a bite of her omelet before spearing some potatoes with her fork. "Okay. Now, flowers. Stacey, did you have a chance to ask your mom . . . ?"

"I did, and she wrote down the names of the florists she likes for you." I reached around for my little backpack, which was hanging on the back of my chair. I dug out a slip of paper and passed it across the table. "She also had thoughts on caterers. Of course, she has no idea what kind of food you want for the reception, so I think this is just a list of her favorite restaurants, but it's a start."

Emily nodded. "Great. I'll start making some calls next week. I was thinking something like . . ."

"Oh, Jesus Christ." April put down her fork. "We don't need to plan this entire wedding in one day, do we? This will probably be the thing we talk about the most for the next year or so, so can we just stick a sock in it for now and enjoy the morning?"

Emily blinked at her sister, a little startled, and I just smiled into my mimosa. April was definitely the more direct of the two sisters. I didn't know her all that well, but I found her bluntness to be refreshing. Too many people danced around what they wanted to say, myself included.

To my surprise, Emily didn't fight her. "Point taken. Sorry." She raised her glass to the two of us. "I promise I will do my best to not turn into a Bridezilla."

I toasted her back. "I'll hold you to that."

"Me too." April took a healthy sip of her own mimosa.

"Okay, then. New topic." Emily took another bite and turned to me. "Stace, what's new with you?"

"Nothing." The word came out a little harsher than I'd intended, and I focused hard on cutting into my waffles. *Nothing* pretty much summed it all up, didn't it? That unanswered Facebook message flashed through my mind, along with that fizzled-out reminder that I wasn't doing anything exciting with my life.

"Nothing?" Emily echoed. Her smile was still in place, but

her eyes looked quizzical. "That can't be right. You're always going out. You've always got stuff going on."

For a split second I imagined telling her. Telling them both how my life had stalled out. Saying, *I need to get my shit together. I've been doing nothing but existing for the past few years, working an uninteresting job and going to happy hour and karaoke nights like that's all I want out of life. Because it's all I've got.* I pictured filling them in on Drunk Stacey and her laptop a couple nights ago, but I couldn't decide if they would be amused or horrified.

But I wasn't ready to share any of that. It was all too messy, too complicated, to be able to fill her in over one brunch. So instead I put my smile back on. Fixed it in place so I could hide behind it. That was the Stacey that had been invited to this brunch. "That's me," I said, as I forked up a bite of waffle. "Always something going on."

"I detect sarcasm," April said.

Emily snorted. "That's because you're the master of it." April pretended to look offended, but instead just grinned into her drink.

"Maybe a little," I conceded. My smile slipped a fraction, but I pushed it back in place. "I think I'm still in that post-Faire letdown, you know? Eleven more months till it starts up again."

"Counting down already?" Emily rolled her eyes with a smile. "You're as bad as Simon."

I shrugged. "When you grow up doing it, you look forward to it, you know?"

"I can see that." She nodded and nibbled at her toast. "Not to mention that guy. I bet you look forward to him too, huh?" She raised her eyebrows at me suggestively.

"What guy?" I felt a guilty tingle across the back of my neck. I thought Dex and I had been more subtle than that.

"That guy you were seeing over the summer. And last summer too." She frowned. "Is it the same guy? You kept sneaking off to see him. Someone from Faire, right?"

"Ooh." April leaned forward, her eyes eager. "What guy?"

Emily pointed at her sister with a piece of bacon. "I thought you didn't like gossip."

"This isn't gossip," she said mildly. "This is girl talk. Very different." She turned back to me. "So who's the guy?"

I took another bite of my waffle to stall for time. "I don't know about . . . Who are you talking about?" My heart pounded in my throat, making it hard to swallow. How did she know?

"Stacey." Emily put down her fork and looked me square in the eye. "Don't play coy with me. You sent me texts. With little fire emojis. And something else . . . eggplants or something."

"Oh," I said. My heart calmed down. "Yeah." I'd forgotten about that. It had been a particularly long, particularly . . . creative night with Dex. And Emily had been going through a rough patch, so I'd sent her a string of dirty emojis to cheer her up. I was nice that way. But now it came back to bite me in the ass.

"Yeah," Emily echoed, her eyes shrewd. "And if you think I didn't notice how sometimes you practically ran out of Faire at the end of the day and came in the next morning looking suspiciously tired yet happy . . ." She trailed off, obviously forgetting the beginning of that extremely long sentence. "Well, I noticed," she finally said.

"Right." I pretended that my memory had been jogged, as if Dex and our sporadic hookups hadn't been sitting in the forefront of my mind for the past few days. "It was nothing," I said. "At least nothing that lasted." I hated the note of regret that colored those words. I wasn't going to see Dex for eleven months, and since he hadn't answered my message it seemed unlikely that we'd be picking up where we left off. I should just write him off for good at this point.

"Do you wish it had?" Emily's eyes searched mine, a flicker of sympathy in them.

I didn't want sympathy. "Nope." The Stacey Smile was back in place, but it didn't feel as much like a mask this time. The sting had started to wear off the rejection, and maybe in a day or two I'd even be able to forget I'd sent it. I could delete the one-sided attempt at conversation and pretend it had never happened. Sure, it might be a little awkward when next summer's Faire came around. I was already sad at the prospect of losing my summertime hookup. But it was probably all for the best. Wine-drunk Stacey had gotten everything off her chest, and now I could cross Dex off as any kind of prospect. Not that he'd ever been a legitimate one in the first place.

One mimosa wasn't enough to untangle all these conflicting feelings. But I kept my smile in place and I didn't order a second one. Alcohol had gotten me into this mess, after all. Moderation was the way forward.

I'd just pulled into the driveway after brunch, my belly full of waffles and my brain full of whirling thoughts, when my phone pinged in my bag. I pulled it out while I bumped the car door closed with my hip. Before we left the restaurant, April had invited me to her neighborhood book club, but she'd forgotten which book they were reading. Emily had promised to text me with the title when she opened up the bookstore after brunch.

Before I could read Emily's text my phone lit up with a second notification, and I froze in place three steps up the staircase.

Emily's text was there, but I didn't register it. All my attention was focused on the instant message icon below it, along with the first few words: **I have to say first that getting your message the other night was such a surprise. But . . .**

Jesus Christ, phone. *That's* where you chose to cut off the preview? Despite the heat of early afternoon, I went cold all over. Tingles spread from the back of my neck down my arms, every little hair standing at attention, while my entire consciousness focused on that one little word on my phone screen. But.

I'd been resigned to him not writing back. Not hearing back from him was a rejection, sure, but it was a passive one. This message, with its "but," was going to be a much more active kind of rejection, and I didn't know if I could handle it. Oh, God, I didn't want a message from Dex cataloging my many faults, but here it was. I'd messed up big-time.

I didn't want to open the message, but if I ignored it, that little (1) icon would bug me for the rest of my life. I considered throwing my phone away entirely. Getting a new number. Maybe a new identity while I was at it. People did it all the time in movies. How hard could it be?

Instead, I sank down to sit on the stairs leading up to my apartment, certain my legs wouldn't carry me up to the top until I ripped off the Band-Aid and opened the message. I drew in a long, slow breath and clicked on the message before I let myself change my mind.

I have to say first that getting your message last night was such a surprise. But it was probably the best, most welcome surprise I've had since I can remember.

"Oh my God." I leaned back against the railing and let relief

wash over me. That was a good "but" after all. I pressed one hand
to my chest, trying to calm my racing heart, and kept reading.

> For one thing, I'm glad you finally told me your full name.
> After knowing each other for so long, you'd think I'd know it
> already. I guess it just never came up, huh?
>
> On to the more important things:
>
> Lots of things make me laugh. My cousin doing
> something stupid, which happens almost daily, so that's good
> news for me. Japanese cat videos. Dogs wearing sweaters. I
> don't know why on that last one. They just usually look so
> bewildered by the whole idea of wearing clothes that it
> makes me laugh.
>
> No sugar, but a good dollop of cream. I mean a GOOD
> dollop. Several dollops, actually. So much that I almost have
> to put my coffee in the microwave to make it hot again.
>
> I love cats. See above re: Japanese cat videos. I've never
> had one myself, but they've always fascinated me. They're
> these perfect little predators, yet we let them curl up
> on our laps like they wouldn't eat our faces if we died
> in the night. Hmm, that got morbid. They're also really
> soft, and I hear that sometimes they let you pet their bellies.
> I like that.
>
> And Stacey, I do miss you. More than I should. More than
> I have any right to, for someone who's not really in your life.
> For all the time we spend on the road (and to answer that
> question, it's a lot; we're on the road more than we're home,
> and that's really only for a month or two around the
> holidays), I'll tell you here and now that your smile is
> something I look forward to seeing every summer. And now
> I'm looking forward to seeing it more.

I'm between shows right now, so I have to run. I don't
have time to come up with questions to ask you, so how
about this: Tell me something. Something I don't know about
you. Which, let's face it, is just about everything.

That long, slow breath escaped in a whoosh as I read over
Dex's words. I read his message twice, and the cold feeling that
had enveloped me was quickly replaced with heat. My cheeks
burned, and I put one palm to my face in an effort to cool them.

He missed me too. Well. That certainly changed things. I
didn't hesitate, didn't even go all the way up the stairs into my
apartment. My thumbs flew over my phone's keyboard as I composed a quick message back.

Dex,

I owe you an apology. For the past couple summers we'd
said that there was nothing more to us than what we did in
bed (NOT THAT I'M COMPLAINING ABOUT THOSE
THINGS). I thought you were never interested in getting to
know me. I thought that all you were looking for was ... well,
what we were already doing.

And here we were missing each other. I guess that's what
I get for not speaking up sooner. But you could have too, you
know. Though I guess you just did.

Have a great show today. Or shows. It's early in the day still.

Something you don't know about me: I told you my last
name, but you still don't know my first name. Here's a hint:
it's not Stacey.

Stacey (or am I?)

Before I could lose my nerve, I hit Send. Always leave them wanting more, right?

My legs only shook a little as I pulled myself to my feet and up the stairs to my place. He missed me. He loved my smile. I traced the wings on my dragonfly necklace with one hand as I unlocked my door. "Change," I whispered to myself. That's what I'd been looking for, after all. Maybe these messages were the first step toward making that happen. Toward finally moving forward and getting a life of my own.

Four

A *watched pot never* boils, and a watched phone never . . . lights up with a text. Something like that. I was never good with metaphors. The point was, Dex didn't message me back right away, and I was almost mad at myself for thinking he would. He'd said he was between shows, hadn't he? I needed to get a grip.

I was so caught up in waiting for Dex to message me that it took a good hour and a half to remember that Emily had texted me too. **Have extra copies of April's book club book if you want to come pick one up!** I'd just seen her at brunch, but the only other thing I had to do today was laundry, and that could wait. Besides, going to see Em would distract me from my darkened phone and its lack of notifications, so I grabbed my keys and headed downtown to Read It & Weep, the bookstore Emily managed.

"Sorry," she said, as she handed the book across the counter. "Apparently her friends are in a depressing, World War II phase right now."

"That's okay, I'm just in it for the snacks. April did say there were snacks, right?" I frowned at the book. How much would I have to pay for a book that, let's face it, I was only going to pretend to enjoy reading?

Emily nodded at it. "Half price, by the way. That's a used copy."

Okay, that made it less painful.

"I guess I can't talk them into reading something fun, huh?" I fished my wallet out of my backpack and handed over my debit card.

"Probably not. They seem determined to read 'important' books." Emily shrugged. "But you make a good point. I'm lining up selections for the store's book club soon. I'll make sure to pick . . ." She thought for a moment. "Well, books that are less depressing than this."

"Good call." I watched Emily run my card through. "So any more thoughts on the wedding dress?" I'd only seen Em a handful of hours ago, but who was I kidding? Of course she had more thoughts.

"Yes, but on my honor as a non-Bridezilla I will not subject you to them." She grinned as she handed me back my card and receipt. "I'll hold it to once a week."

I snorted. "You will not."

"Okay, maybe twice."

"Mmmhmm." I tucked the receipt between the pages of Depressing World War II Book. "How about you add me to your Pinterest board, and I'll get a notification whenever you see something cool. Then we can discuss."

"Deal. As long as you contribute to it too. Your eye is much better than mine."

I ducked my head down to slip the book into my backpack, but I couldn't keep the smile off my face. As compliments went, it wasn't exactly effusive, but it lifted my spirits to be appreciated. Noticed. "Of course. Send me your thoughts on bridesmaid dresses and I'll get to work."

On the way home I had to swing through the Starbucks drive-through. Pumpkin Spice Latte season started a little earlier every year, and I was a sucker for it. Once I got home I positioned the Starbucks cup on my coffee table, moved Benedick out of the way twice, and took a picture. The coffee was mostly gone, and what was left was cold and supersweet, but that didn't matter for the photo. Then I cross-posted it to Instagram and Facebook because I was a multitasker when it came to my social media:

First #PSL of the season! Anyone care to guess how many I'll consume this year? Last year was 15, which I believe was a new record. Let me know what you think! Winner gets absolutely nothing, but I get lots of pumpkin spice deliciousness. Happy Fall!

Happy fall, ha. It was barely September and still as hot as midsummer outside. But if it was PSL season, it was officially fall. I tossed my phone onto the couch and ran a load of laundry. The washer and dryer lived in the garage, so I shared the use of them with my folks. Mom usually did laundry during the week, and it was my turn on the weekends.

My PSL post had become a silly thing I did every year, and my friends liked to both guess how many times I'd manage to stop at a Starbucks in the next couple months and make fun of me for doing so. The ribbing didn't bother me; it was part of the fun.

Once I got back upstairs, my phone was lit up like a Christmas tree. I made myself put my laundry away before I settled on the couch with my phone, scrolling through the notifications.

Thirteen!

Seriously, how can you drink those things? So gross.

Stacey (which apparently isn't even your name wtf??), let's take this private, okay? I'd rather . . .

Thirty-seven!

Twenty-five and diabetes.

Wait. I scrolled back up. That third one wasn't a comment on my coffee post. I opened the notification, and my instant message app came up.

Stacey (which apparently isn't even your name wtf??), let's take this private, okay? I'd rather communicate with you off the public page. Either email or text, I don't mind. But no matter what, please write me back ASAP and tell me what your real name is. You've been Stacey in my mind for quite a while now. I have some catching up to do. -D

Public page?

Oh, no.

For the first time I looked at the profile Dex was messaging me from. I hadn't paid attention before, because Drunk Stacey had started all this. Drunk Stacey had clicked on the tagged picture and messaged Dex without a second thought. But that crucial second thought might have allowed me to notice that I hadn't sent that message to a private profile. Nope. I'd messaged the Dueling Kilts' fanpage.

Jesus. Anyone could have seen that message. His brothers could have seen it. *Daniel* could have seen it. That combined with that ice machine run at the hotel . . .

Man, I'd really dodged a bullet there. Relief made me a little giddy, and I clicked back to the message, where he'd left his email address and phone number. Well. That was a good sign, wasn't it? I added both into my contacts before switching to my laptop. The explanation of my name was going to take a full-size keyboard. I decided to use email. It was early in the relationship, or whatever you wanted to call this, and texting felt far too intimate.

To: Dex MacLean
From: Stacey Lindholm
Date: September 3, 4:47 p.m.
Subject: My Real Name

So.

I'm what you might call a miracle baby. My parents wanted kids from the second they got married, but had trouble conceiving. They tried all the old wives' tale ways of conception, but no luck, and medical intervention was way too expensive for them. They applied to be adoptive parents and were put on some kind of waiting list. While they were waiting, they got a letter from my grandmother. My mom's great-aunt, someone Mom hardly even knew, had died and left my parents a pretty big sum of money, but she earmarked it for my parents to try IVF. So they did, and eventually I came along. My mother felt like she had to name me after their benefactor, even though she was a distant family member that she didn't really know. A nice gesture, right?

Well, let me tell you, Anastasia isn't the most fun name to go through the first grade with. I've been Stacey to everyone who knows me since I was six years old. So I can be Stacey to you too.

There. Now it's your turn. Tell me something about you.

His answer came more quickly than I expected. I wasn't used to refreshing my email as constantly as the notifications that came through on my phone, so it wasn't until almost bedtime that I checked my email again and saw that he'd answered within a few hours. I curled up on my bed, with its fairy lights switched on, and read.

To: Stacey Lindholm
From: Dex MacLean
Date: September 3, 7:56 p.m.
Subject: Re: My Real Name

Something about me. I'm really not used to talking about myself all that much. People don't usually ask. I mean, the most interesting thing about me is what you already know: what I do for a living. I love it. The travel. Meeting new people, and basically living out of a couple duffel bags and a backpack. But it's sort of one of those blessing-and-a-curse situations. Sometimes I miss home. And what's weird is that I'm not sure that I know where home IS. I mean, there's our family home, where I crash in the basement for the couple months a year that we're back up there. But that's not MY home. That was childhood-me's home. Teenage-me, even. But adult me? I feel like a guest in the place where I grew up, and that's a strange feeling. I'm starting to suspect that I don't really have a home, and I'm not sure how I feel about that.

Sometimes I wonder how much longer I can do this. This life on the road. Don't get me wrong, I love it. There's something compelling about not having a fixed address, and not being tied down to things like mortgages and car payments. But sometimes meeting new people sucks. I'm a friendly guy, that's not the issue. But I miss familiarity. I miss people who know me for more than a couple weeks at a stretch.

Then again, I get a little twitchy during those couple months every year that I'm home in Michigan. Restless. Then I'm packing and unpacking my shit, wondering if I can travel leaner, lighter, during the next round of faires. So maybe I don't want that down-home kind of life as much as I think.

Am I wrong, Anastasia? There must be a reason that you stayed in a small town like Willow Creek. Tell me what I'm missing about small-town life. Besides you. Which, let's face it, might be reason enough to convince *me*.

Well.

My heart pounded at those last couple sentences. I couldn't believe this. Dex MacLean, who had a new wench at every faire, missed *me*. He thought I would be a reason to settle in one town. I flipped back to the tagged picture of him from our Faire, which

I had downloaded to my laptop. I took my time savoring him. His smile, free and open and just a little naughty. The strong column of his throat and hint of chest disappearing into the loose linen shirt. Strong corded forearms; long, nimble fingers coaxing music from his guitar.

I studied his face with the new knowledge of this email I'd received, and I felt a twinge of guilt. I'd severely misjudged him, thinking he was just a fun piece of man candy for a couple weeks. No, Dex was the complete package: gorgeous as hell, but smart and sensitive at the same time. Why hadn't he shown me this side of him when we were together?

Maybe it was my fault. Maybe I hadn't let him in until I'd sent that first message. But he'd certainly let me know that it wasn't too late.

Good job, Drunk Stacey. Maybe you didn't screw up so badly after all.

Five

To: Dex MacLean
From: Stacey Lindholm
Date: September 4, 7:37 p.m.
Subject: Re: Re: My Real Name

I didn't exactly stay in Willow Creek by choice. Some of us choose to settle in small towns; some of us have settling in small towns thrust upon us.

Let me back up.

When I graduated from college with a degree in fashion merchandising, I was so excited. I had a future. A job: my advisor had, by way of a well-worded recommendation letter, paved the way to an entry-level job in New York with one of the bigger department stores. A place to live: okay, it was with three roommates, and I was relatively sure that my future bedroom had originally been a closet, but it was in New York. I was on my way to everything I'd ever wanted. Independence. Excitement. My life was about to begin.

I only had one more carload of stuff to move to New York when Mom had her first heart attack.

I didn't even get to start the job. I put them off, and for a few weeks they were even nice about it. But when Mom ended up needing surgery—the scary kind, with words like "bypass" and "quadruple"—those weeks stretched into months. I couldn't imagine trying to start a new life and a new job away from home while worrying about Mom and her recovery. The job offer disintegrated. My New York roommates found someone else to sleep in their closet. I got the message: you're not going anywhere.

It's not all bad, but I think one reason it seems so compelling to you is because it's a novelty. Something you don't experience. Because if you lived it, if you were born and raised in a nowhere place like Willow Creek, you would think very, very differently.

I'll admit that it's kind of nice to be where everyone knows you. But at the same time, everyone knows you. Did you go through that rebellious teenage phase? I'm sure you did, you have that look. Not me. Imagine trying to pull some shenanigans when not only are you risking arrest, you're risking your mother knowing what's going on before the cops do. Believe me, overprotective moms are scarier than the prospect of getting arrested.

Also, I'm not sure how I feel about you calling me Anastasia. Literally no one calls me that. Except for teachers on the first day of school, which was a while back.

"What are you working on, honey?"

"Nothing," I said automatically, and closed my laptop before she could see the screen. I looked up as Mom came into the kitchen and immediately snapped into diagnosis mode. I'd become very observant these last few years when it came to my mother and her health. She'd looked fine earlier when I'd come down to the house to have dinner with my parents—her meatloaf was not to be missed. But now her eyes looked fatigued, and her complexion had a dull cast to it that I didn't like at all. "You okay? You look tired."

"Thanks." Her eyebrows went up. "Just what every woman wants to hear."

I tsked at her. "You know what I mean, Mom. Did you overdo it today?"

"I've had a couple rough nights." She ducked into the pantry and came out with a bag of microwave popcorn. "Nothing worth worrying about."

"Rough nights?" My voice was sharper than I'd intended, but she couldn't just wave off something like that. "What do you mean?"

"I mean I've had a little insomnia, that's all. Cut it out. I'm fine. You're as bad as your father." After starting the popcorn, she came over and kissed the top of my head as if I were seven—in her eyes I probably still was. She nodded at the still-closed laptop. "So what are you working on?"

"Nothing. Just . . . just an email." I felt my cheeks heat with guilt, as though she somehow knew I'd been writing about her. I tried to come up with something, anything, to change the subject. "I'm going to the grocery store tomorrow after work if you need anything."

"Some more milk would be great, if you're going to be there anyway."

"Sure." Behind me, little pops started coming from the microwave, quickly followed by the smell of hot salt and fake butter. I traced the edge of my laptop with my index finger, itching to open it and finish my email, but I couldn't do it while Mom was in the room. When I looked up again, she was digging through her purse on the kitchen counter and extended a twenty-dollar bill in my direction.

"Here you go," she said. "For the milk."

"Are you kidding?" I shook my head. "Okay, first of all, milk does not cost twenty dollars. Second, I just mooched dinner off you. I think we can call it even."

"Just take it, will you? I know you're trying to save your money, Stacey. You're still paying student loans, not to mention rent and your car . . ."

"My car is paid off, and you hardly charge any rent at all." And I'd insisted on paying rent in the first place, back when I'd made the decision to stay. Back when Mom's mobility had been limited and Dad had looked lost: Mom was his compass, and he didn't know how he'd get by without her. The rent was a pittance, but it made me feel a little less like I still lived with my parents.

The microwave beeped, and Mom popped open the door. "Grab the bowl for me, will you?"

I didn't have to ask which one; the popcorn bowl lived on top of the fridge. I stretched onto my toes and fished it down, handing it to her. Mom smiled at me, and I had to admit that she really did look okay. I was worrying too much. But every time I looked at her, I couldn't help but remember how she'd looked in the hospital: small and pale, hooked up to machines that beeped and kept her alive. Every time I wondered what I'd been thinking, sticking around for so long, I'd think of her so tiny in that hospital bed, and no, I didn't regret staying home. Even if it really did mean I'd blown my chance to get out of this town and start a life of my own.

"I meant to ask," Mom said. "Did you give your friend those lists?"

"I did, and she said thanks. She's already getting a big head start on this wedding." That was an understatement, and I rolled my eyes, my patented grin back on my face.

Mom clucked her tongue at me. "It's a lot to plan, Stacey. You'll see someday."

Yeah, maybe if marrying my cat became legal one of these days. But out loud I said, "I'm sure you're right. No pressure, though, right, Mom?"

"No, honey. No pressure. You'll find the right guy when it's the right time." A slightly awkward silence followed, because honestly, when would the right time be? Ever since I'd made the decision to stay home, my parents had lived by the mantra of "take your time." It was nice that they liked me being around and were in no hurry for me to strike out on my own. But every once in a while, I wondered if taking my time should be taking this long.

Finally, Mom cleared her throat and held up the bowl of popcorn. "Want to watch a movie before bed?"

I did. I really did, but I shook my head. "I joined this book club, and I need to read this before next Thursday." I pulled the Depressing World War II Book out of my bag and waved it at her.

She took it from my hand and frowned at the cover. "Hmm."

She flipped it over and read the back before handing it back to me. "You need to be in a better book club. That looks depressing."

"You're not wrong." I sighed. "Emily said she's picking out more fun books for the store's book club. Maybe I should just join that one instead."

Mom shrugged. "You could do both, you know. But let me know if you do the fun one. I'd be up for that."

"You got it." I looked at the book once more, then at the bowl of popcorn Mom still held. I tossed the book to the table. "Screw it. Let's watch a movie." Who needed a life, when you could spend your evenings watching rom-coms with your mother?

Oh, God, I needed a life.

After the movie I left through the kitchen on my way to the garage and the stairs to my apartment, stopping to grab my laptop and my backpack from where I'd left them on the table. Upstairs and in bed, I opened my laptop and Mom's twenty-dollar bill fluttered out from inside it.

"Dammit, Mom." I sighed. But I folded the bill and stuck it under my phone. I started to reread the email I'd composed at my parents' kitchen table, but it made my skin prickle. Should I be telling him all this? In my experience, people didn't want to hear this kind of stuff. They wanted Fun Stacey. The cheerleader, the one who commented with heart-eyes emojis on the pics of your children, the one who was eager to help pick out bridesmaid dresses. These days I was more comfortable sharing a duet on karaoke night at Jackson's than sharing my innermost thoughts. And I was really bad at karaoke.

But he'd asked, hadn't he? I hit Send before I could change my mind. Maybe I was sharing too much information and he wouldn't like this Stacey. But there was only one way to find out.

Turned out Dex was a TMI kind of guy.

I got ready for bed, and as I went to move my laptop, the screen sprang to life, and there was an email waiting for me.

To: Stacey Lindholm
From: Dex MacLean
Date: September 4, 9:52 p.m.
Subject: Re: Re: Re: My Real Name

I'm so sorry about what you've been through with your mom, but for what it's worth, I would have done the same thing. I mean, you're talking to a guy who travels with family year-round. Family's important, and when the chips are down there's nothing I wouldn't do for mine. Sounds like you're the same way.

That said, you make a good point about small towns and overprotective moms. I guess I can't blame you there. But I can't blame your mom either. Can you? Not that I'm taking her side, but you said it yourself: Miracle Baby. I take it you're an only child too? That makes it worse, I'd think. With siblings you have someone else to blame shit on.

Oh, and too bad, Anastasia. You can't give me a name that feels like music in my mouth and not expect me to revel in it. The name fits you.

I closed my laptop with a snap and pushed it away from me as though it had burned me. I sucked in a breath and it tasted like sweet relief; had I forgotten to breathe those last few moments, reading that my name felt like music? Who *was* this guy?

How could this be the same person who hadn't even said good-bye at the end of Faire this season?

Benedick crawled into my lap, his front feet kneading the blankets that had been warmed by the laptop. I stroked one hand down his back, over and over, absorbing his purr and letting it calm me. When I closed my eyes those words were imprinted on the backs of my eyelids . . . *a name that feels like music in my mouth* . . . but the more that Benedick snuggled into me and I scritched behind his ears, the easier I could breathe.

"Well," I finally said to the cat, "I said I needed a life. Maybe that's what's happening now."

The next morning I woke with that phrase in my head again—*a name that feels like music in my mouth*—and I suppressed a delicious shiver. Overnight my thoughts regarding Dex had apparently untangled themselves just fine, and I couldn't keep a silly grin off my face as I got ready for work.

At least at work I wouldn't be tempted to check my phone every fifteen seconds; personal cell phones weren't allowed, so I kept mine zipped up in my bag during the day. I itched to talk to someone about this, about the incredibly hot guy who *missed me*, but as friendly as I was with my coworkers, I wasn't friends with any of them on any kind of personal level. We were grab-lunch-together friends. Go-to-happy-hour friends, at most. Not dissect-every-bit-of-your-new-potential-love-life friends.

It was a slow morning, and by ten I was already perusing the deli menu, wondering if it was too soon to order lunch. The Reuben on the menu made me think of Emily; that was her favorite. She was probably the closest thing I had to a bestie, a *real* bestie, these days. She'd asked me to be her bridesmaid, right? So she at least saw me as more than a happy hour and Ren Faire friend. Maybe Emily would want to hear about this new development. Did a couple emails that made me tingle count as a love life worth sharing with your bestie?

I could figure that out later. But for now, when I ordered my turkey and Brie panini from the deli, I also ordered a Reuben for Emily. The deli was just down the street from the bookstore, and I could use a little girl time.

Sure enough, when I got to Read It & Weep with my bags full of sandwiches and chips, Emily was behind the counter frowning at something on her laptop. The bell over the door chimed as I opened it, and she looked up, startled, her frown melting into a smile.

"Is there a Reuben in there?"

"Of course there is." I handed her one of the bags and she handed me a bottle of water before we settled into one of the tables at the back of the bookstore, where Emily and Chris, the owner, had carved out a little café area. Emily made a mean vanilla latte and Chris's lemon squares were to die for, so the space was put to good use.

"What brings you by?" Emily unwrapped her sandwich with all the glee of a kid on Christmas morning; she really did love a good Reuben.

I opened my mouth to answer her but took a bite of my own sandwich instead, stalling for time. "What, I can't just bring you a sandwich for no reason?" My voice was light, breezy. Typical—chickening out again. "Maybe I like the company."

"Hmm." She narrowed her eyes at me as she chewed but didn't press further. Her eyes lit up and she reached for her bag. "You know, I was going to email you tonight. I found a couple really cool ideas for a cake that I think would—"

"Mom and I are going to join your book club." It was rude, I knew. So rude to interrupt Emily. But wedding talk made me think of Faire, which made me think of that email last night from Dex. And as much as I wanted to spill everything, part of me wanted to keep this new side of him all to myself. So what better than a new topic entirely, pulled directly out of my ass?

"Book club?" Emily shook her head. "But you just joined a book club."

"Yes, and that book is already depressing the hell out of me. You promised more fun books, right?"

"Well, yeah . . ." But Emily still looked skeptical. "Are you quitting April's book club then? I think she was excited that you were joining up."

I narrowed my eyes. "I can read two whole books in a month, you know." How much of an airhead did she think I was?

But Emily's expression softened, and she tsked at me. "Of course you can. I didn't mean that. And your mom wants to join up too?"

I shrugged. "She said she did."

"Cool. I'll add you to the list when I go back up front. I'm sending out an email blast later this week with next month's book selection. Third Thursday of the month, is that okay?"

"Perfect." I had nothing going on, and Mom never went out at night so she should be free.

"Excellent." She went back to her beloved sandwich. "We'll need the people, so I'm glad you two are coming. Chris'll be heading back to Florida soon with nary a care in the world."

"I heard that." Chris, the store's owner and our ersatz Queen Elizabeth at Faire, appeared from the back room, but she didn't look particularly annoyed. She looked at the two of us with an indulgent smile. Part of her was probably still Queen, and we her benevolent subjects.

"You know what I mean." Emily turned in her chair to watch Chris get her own lunch out of the café fridge. "It's not like we have a million people in book club. Once your daughter goes back to school, and then you leave for Florida, there's a notice-able drop in membership."

"There's plenty to keep you busy." Chris approached our little table, and we scooted over to make room. "The writing group still meets twice a month, and you have to keep an eye on them to make sure they don't get too rowdy. Not to mention your Shakespeare reading night with the high school kids. You still doing that?"

Emily considered the question while she nibbled on her sandwich. "Probably. I should pick a play and see if the kids want to do it again."

"Oh, right," I said. "I forgot you did that." Emily was an un-abashed Shakespeare nerd, and she'd started a read-along of some of his works that had been well attended by the junior and senior high school students who volunteered at Faire. Most of the kids, in fact, were in Simon's advanced placement English class. Simon and Emily really were ridiculously perfect for each other.

"Like I said. Plenty to keep you busy." Chris took the lid off her Tupperware and started fluffing through her salad with a fork. For all that Chris owned the bookstore, and had for years, she seemed perfectly happy to leave the running of it to Emily these days. And why not? Em was really good at it. And Chris had more important things to worry about.

"How's your mom doing? Any better?" I didn't know a lot about strokes, but I knew they could be tricky to recover from.

But Chris's smile was unconcerned. "She's fine. As well as can be expected, anyway. Not any better, not any worse. But I think it helps for me to be with her." She shrugged. "Better that than assisted living."

I didn't have anything helpful to say, so I just nodded and popped the last of my sandwich into my mouth.

But Emily's mind was still on the store as she turned back to me. "Okay. So with you and your mom joining book club, maybe you can help me brainstorm titles, since Chris is off to Florida in October."

Chris snorted. "Just one more month till I'm back in the land of alligators and mosquitos." For the past couple years Chris had split her time between Maryland and Florida in the winter, taking care of her mother in both locations. It seemed like a hell of a sacrifice, but I would probably have done the same thing.

"And hurricanes." I nodded solemnly while I checked the time on my phone. My lunch break was about over; I needed to think about getting back to work.

Chris chuckled as I got to my feet and collected the lunch trash into one of the bags I'd brought. "Hurricane season's about over by the time I get there. That's the best part of Florida, at least: the winters. Don't have to worry about getting snowed in anywhere."

Emily groaned. "Don't start. Your emails all last winter were bad enough, mocking us for freezing our asses off up here."

I threw the both of them a wave over my shoulder as I headed back to work. I checked my phone again on the walk back, but my notifications were all but empty. Just a couple comments on an Instagram picture I'd posted of Benedick over the weekend. He'd been especially cute, snoozing in a patch of sun, and frankly it should have gotten more attention than it did. But there was never any telling what the internet liked. I shoved my phone back into my backpack with a frown. I'd been hoping for another message from Dex; now that we were messaging, and our conversations were getting deep, I wanted more from him.

It wasn't until I was about halfway through the afternoon that I realized he'd been the last one to send an email. It was my turn to write to him. I almost slapped my palm against my forehead in the middle of scheduling an annual cleaning, but quickly got my mind back on task and filled out the reminder card. Then I impatiently counted down the minutes until the end of the day. After work I stopped for another Pumpkin Spice Latte (number four of the season so far) and sat at a table with my phone to reread his last email before answering it.

To: Dex MacLean
From: Stacey Lindholm
Date: September 5, 5:44 p.m.
Subject: Re: Re: Re: Re: My Real Name

Oh, yes, I'm an only child. I know I mentioned the whole IVF thing, but I don't think I mentioned that Mom was almost forty when I was born. That's the other part of me being a miracle baby. I think I was also her last-chance baby. No more kids after me, so they got to take allllll their parenting issues out on me. It's fun.

I'm kidding, it's really fine. My parents are great, and they're ridiculously supportive of me. And I'd do anything for them. Which is one of the reasons I still live in Willow Creek. We've been a team of three my whole life, and I wouldn't have it any other way.

Also, you're wrong. Anastasia was a fancy Russian princess who met a gruesome end. There's nothing about that that fits a small-town girl like me.

Inexplicably, tears filled my eyes when I typed that last sentence. What the hell was I doing? My friends were making real, tangible plans with their lives, while I was getting caught up in this weird fantasy spun from words and pixels on a screen. I was supposed to be getting a life, something real, and instead I was fixating on this online flirtation, letting it fill my mind and my heart.

I hit Send and clicked out of my email app before I could think any more about it. Enough of this distraction. Time to go home and feed the cat. Time to turn my attention to my real life, instead of whatever game Dex and I were playing. I needed to get my head on straight. Stop living my life online.

Of course, the problem was my online life was much more exciting than my real one. I needed to do something about that.

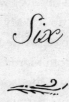

Six

As it turned out, I was only human, and the lure of my on-line life was too great to be ignored. There was an email waiting for me before I went to sleep that night, and every time I answered, Dex wrote back again. Despite my initial reluctance, my heart thrilled every time there was a new message. It was my own personal shot of dopamine, I looked forward to it every day, and he never let me down.

After a couple weeks I started to notice his patterns. He usually wrote to me late at night, after shows were done for the day. I thought about his "wench at every faire" reputation, and it was all I could do to not ask about them. Was he still picking up new conquests at every stop? Was he having flings and then writing to me every night after they left? Or worse, after they'd gone to sleep? I imagined beautiful women, sated and happy, sleeping soundly in his bed while his face was bathed with the blue light from his laptop or phone as he wrote yet another email to me.

But I didn't ask. I probably could have at first, but as days became weeks, Chris left for Florida with her mother, and Pumpkin Spice Latte season gave way to peppermint mochas, it became harder and harder to bring it up. How could I? In the middle of deep conversations about fears we'd had as kids, was I supposed to slip in, "Hey, forgot to ask, but are you still banging your way across the country?"

So I buried that one important question I feared the answer to, and concentrated on more pertinent things instead.

To: Dex MacLean
From: Stacey Lindholm
Date: November 15, 10:47 p.m.
Subject: PSL Final Tally!

Fourteen. I had fourteen Pumpkin Spice Lattes this year. My sorority sister Monica guessed thirteen, so I sent her a Starbucks gift card as a prize. In my head she's still nineteen—well, we both are, dyeing our hair pink for breast cancer awareness. She's a psychiatrist now, officially much smarter than me. How did that happen?

Sometimes I think about time, and what we do with it. I turned twenty-seven last month, so I'm inching closer to thirty, and what am I even doing with my life? I look at my friends on Facebook. Friends from high school who grew up and moved away. Friends from college who went on to brilliant careers. At one point we were all in the same place; we theoretically got the same basic start in life. I look at what they've accomplished. And then I look at me. Part of me thinks that I really screwed up by staying here. But when my mom got sick all my priorities shifted.

Here's what I won't tell Mom, though. It was like that first heart attack jump-started her into getting old. What an awful thing to think, right? I mean, my parents have always been old. Older, at least. Mom was thirty-eight when I was born. She was in her forties when I started school, while all my friends' moms were much younger. So it's something that I'm used to. But then she had that heart attack. I can't tell you how . . . old she looked in that hospital bed. That was the thing that got me. My mom, who'd always been the strongest person I knew, the person I went to with every single problem of my life, was suddenly this frail little thing that I wanted to swaddle in bubble wrap.

Now that she's better I could get on with my life, of course. Start that fashion merchandising career that I'd intended. But an internship in New York at twenty-seven is a lot different than an internship at twenty-two. Those connections dried up long ago, and I have no idea how to find new ones. Not to mention, every time I think of leaving I think of my mom in the hospital and how helpless she looked. What if it happens again? What if it's worse, and I'm not here? I mean, yeah, Dad's here, and he took great care of her before. But he's not getting any younger either. I feel like I should be close by. I love them so much, and they love me.

You know, love songs say crap like "love will set you free," but lately I've been thinking that love is more like a cage. The most beautiful cage, with gold filigree and diamonds on the bars. But a cage nonetheless.

To: Stacey Lindholm
From: Dex MacLean
Date: November 16, 01:30 a.m.
Subject: Re: PSL Final Tally!

Checking my email isn't something I usually do on faire weekends. There's so much going on here at the grounds that email is usually a "during the week" thing. But I have to say that I like this new habit of writing to you before I go to sleep. It's the perfect way to end my day.

Fourteen is a lot of pumpkin spice lattes. Is there maybe a support group you can join?

I had to think about that for a minute: love is a cage. I think you're on to something, but at the same time the idea makes me sad. Something as glorious and powerful as love shouldn't make you feel caged in. I wonder if what you're seeing as a cage is obligation instead of love. They can look the same, especially when it comes to family. It's hard to break free from that, and some people never do. Says the guy who tours the country with his extended family on the Ren Faire circuit for a living.

You sound like you feel trapped, and it's totally understandable. I can also relate. Not just because this particular stop is a much smaller Faire that doesn't provide hotel rooms. And that's fine: we have an RV that we can camp in, and in a pinch I sleep in the back of my truck. But this part of North Carolina had an unexpected cold front, so camping wasn't as pleasant as it usually is. It's the last weekend here, though, before we move further south, so I'll survive.

But for how much longer? Like you, I've been thinking
more and more about the passage of time lately. And
wondering how much longer I can live this lifestyle. I'm not
twenty-one anymore, when traveling the country and
sleeping in the back of a pickup was an adventure. But now
that I'm thirty-one (hitting thirty wasn't as painful as I
anticipated, BTW, you'll do just fine), I'm more likely to wake
up with a backache, and insist on contracts at festivals that
include hotel rooms. No more of these small-time places that
want us to just work for tips. We've been doing this too long
for that.

And then my mind circles back to How Much Longer? I
know guys, performers on this circuit, who've been doing the
same gigs for years. Decades. Is that how we're going to end
up? Are all of the guys going to want to keep this going that
long? I mean, at some point, we're going to have to make a
real living, right? At least one of us is going to get married
and want to stop traveling. And it's not like we have health
insurance, or any kind of retirement savings. Or a roof over
our heads that doesn't belong to family. This nomadic life
can be great, but sometimes it feels like I'm speeding toward
a cliff that's just getting closer and closer. Sometimes I wish I
had a safety net.

Hmm. That got kind of deep, and kind of down, which
isn't how I want to feel when I write to you. So it's up to you,
Anastasia. Cheer me up. Tell me what you're doing on this
lazy Sunday.

To: Dex MacLean
From: Stacey Lindholm
Date: November 16, 1:43 p.m.
Subject: Re: Re: PSL Final Tally!

Lazy Sundays are my favorite thing in the world, actually.
Right now I'm on my laptop in my parents' living room, about
to watch a movie with my mother. She has a weakness for
romantic comedies. If this is part of being in that cage, I
don't mind it so much.

Shut your mouth about PSLs. They make me happy. No
support group needed, thank you very much.

Obligation, huh? You may be on to something there.
You're right, it's tricky when it comes to family. Sometimes
I wish

"Stacey?"

I jumped at the sound of Mom's voice and closed my laptop.
"Yeah, Mom." I put my laptop on the coffee table and got off the
living room couch. "You need me to get the popcorn bowl?"

"You know it. Come in here, Tall Girl."

I had to laugh. I'd outgrown my mother by about an inch
when I hit the tenth grade, but I'd stopped growing not long
after that, topping out around five foot five. In no way did that
make me a tall girl.

But I went into the kitchen anyway. "You could put the bowl
somewhere else, you know." I stretched on my toes to tease at the
edge of it until I'd moved it far enough off the top of the fridge
for it to tumble into my hands. "Somewhere you can reach."

She shrugged and got the bag of popcorn out of the microwave. "Why do I need do that when I have you?"

"True." I nodded slowly, trying to keep my expression neutral. There it was. She didn't mean anything by it. She didn't know about the email conversation I'd just been having. But just the same I felt myself nudging against the bars of that golden cage. "But you might not always."

"What do you mean?" Mom raised her eyebrows. "You going somewhere?"

She had me there. "No . . ." I hated how heavy my heart felt in my chest when I said that. "But I might, you know." It was a small thing: the tiniest of pushes against those golden bars. At least it was a start.

"Of course. But no rush, honey. Take your time. And until then, you can get the popcorn bowl down for me." She patted my cheek as only a mother could as she took the bowl from my hands.

Take my time. Right. What did I expect?

Back in the living room, I moved my laptop off the coffee table while Mom picked up the remote. "Working on anything important?" She nodded toward my laptop as she pointed the remote at the television.

"That? No." I glanced at my laptop. "Just some wedding stuff for Emily." The lie slipped easily from my mouth, and my heart pounded. I didn't lie to my mother. I never had. But what was I supposed to say? *I'm bitching about you to a guy I used to bang but who is now a long-distance pen pal that I spill my secrets to?*

If she noticed my lie, she didn't say. "She's so on top of everything, isn't she?" She settled back onto the couch next to me, scrolling through the movie selections. "She runs that book club of hers with an iron fist."

The thought of Emily distracted me from my anxiety and even made me laugh. "That's putting it mildly. I think her lists have lists."

I picked up the popcorn and put it between us on the couch. I could finish that email later.

Seven

Birds flew south for the winter, and apparently so did Renaissance faire performers. I'd never paid attention to the Faire
circuit as an entity; it was just something I did every summer in
my hometown. But since Dex and I had started—well, whatever
you wanted to call what we were doing; I wasn't sure I wanted to
define it—I checked in on the Kilts' fanpage on a regular basis,
and it became clear that our Faire was just one stop among many.
One small dot on a path that wound through the eastern United
States, snaking through several states, sometimes ducking out
toward the Midwest before coming back to the East Coast again.
And as the weather grew colder and the holidays grew closer, that
path moved farther and farther south, culminating in Florida just
before Thanksgiving. After that they went home to Michigan
through the new year, and then it was back down to Florida,
where the whole thing went in reverse: Faires in the South as the
path headed northward again and the weather warmed up.

Following their progress down to Florida, combined with

Dex's emails about his daily life—so different from mine—lit a fire in the back of my mind. Not a raging fire. Not even an especially bright or urgent one. More of a flickering candle flame, but it combined with that odd feeling of being left behind when Faire had ended this past summer. And together, that flickering light and that sense of yearning made me want something new. A life on the road. A life somewhere other than here.

But, as usual, I let that candle and those feelings flicker out and then I went back to work on Monday as though they'd never existed.

After Dex and the rest of the Kilts went home for the holidays, his emails came less often, which I tried not to take too personally. He was back with friends and family, after all; he probably didn't need his online pen pal as much while he wasn't on the road. But as Christmas slid into New Year's Eve, the lack of emails showed me how much I'd made them part of my life. Made Dex part of my life. And I wondered if that had been a mistake. If he was just someone else who would move beyond me.

But I masked the feeling and sent him an email before I left to go out on New Year's Eve. In the spirit of Auld Lang Syne and all that.

To: Dex MacLean
From: Stacey Lindholm
Date: December 31, 9:32 p.m.
Subject: Happy New Year

I've always thought that New Year's Eve had a special sort of energy to it. Saying goodbye to the old, worn-out year, and

looking forward to the promise of a bright new one. Like
sliding into a bed with fresh, clean sheets on it. It's not an
energy that lasts. By February most people have forgotten
the New Year's resolutions they've made. I've stopped
writing them down, myself—I hate the feeling of not living up
to my own expectations.

I'm off to a New Year's Eve party at Jackson's with a
bunch of friends. It's a cold night, but I don't think we're
getting snow. I hope that you're safe and warm this New
Year's Eve, and I hope that you have a very happy New Year.
I'm glad I've gotten to know you better these past few
months.

There. Friendly, but not too friendly. If he really was back-
ing off our little online relationship, I didn't want to look too
clingy. I slipped my phone into my clutch on my way out the
door, but once I got to Jackson's I tried really hard to not check
it. Which meant I tapped the email icon every five minutes or
so. I frowned at my email inbox, empty of new messages, until
Mitch took my phone out of my hand and put a shot glass in it
instead.

"Hey, give that back." I made a weak attempt to take my
phone, but Mitch was something like twice my height and just
held it over his head. I wasn't getting it back until he was ready
to give it.

"Nope. Not till you've done a shot with me. And then a shot
with Park over there." He nodded over to where Emily leaned
against the bar. She saw us looking at her and waved, a grin
spreading over her face.

"When did Emily get here?" I tossed back the shot—vodka, so
there weren't any accompaniments like salt or limes to contend

with. I only coughed a little as it went down, warming me from the inside out.

"About three checks of your phone ago." He took the empty shot glass away and handed me a bottle of beer as a chaser. His face darkened slightly, which was an odd look for the world's most cheerful guy. "You getting stood up or something?"

"No. Nothing like that." I wasn't about to explain my odd online relationship in the middle of a crowded bar on what was supposed to be the most festive night of the year.

"Hmm." Mitch looked me over critically and handed me back my phone. "Well, come on. That shot was just a warm-up. Come join the party. But let me know whose ass I need to kick later, okay?"

"You got it." I turned off my phone and stuck it back in my purse. Screw it. Dex wasn't writing me back tonight. He was probably out celebrating New Year's Eve, just as I was. Except he wasn't wasting the whole night staring at his phone.

Enough. I took a swig from my beer and clung to the back of Mitch's shirt as he led us through the tight crowd. Funny how I'd had such a crush on Mitch when we were in high school. But now I was grateful that the crush had dissipated, replaced by a big-brotherly feeling. I truly believed that if someone hurt me, Mitch would hunt the guy down and make him regret it. And then get me drunk to help me forget. Of course, he'd do it with beer and tequila, never remembering that I liked wine better. It was the thought that counted.

Sure enough, when we got to Emily's side of the bar, her sister April was there next to her, lining up shot glasses and lime wedges.

"Not too many," Emily cautioned. "Tequila is not my friend."

"Tequila is nobody's friend," April said as she handed each of us a lime wedge. "That's the point."

Mitch scoffed. "It's one shot. That's all."

Emily squinted at him. "Since when is it only one shot with you?"

"She has a point." Simon appeared on the other side of Emily, two longneck beers in his hand. He passed one over to Emily and kept the other for himself. "I don't think I've ever seen you stop at one."

"It's New Year's Eve!" Mitch protested. "If you can't let loose on New Year's Eve, when can you?"

"I agree with Mitch," I said, my usual bright smile back in place. I punctuated the statement by reaching for one of the shot glasses and the saltshaker and lime. Lick it, slam it, suck it. "Nothing wrong with saying goodbye to the old year."

"I agree." Emily followed suit, chasing the liquor with a swig of beer. "It's been a pretty good year, after all. It deserves to go out in style." She fiddled with the diamond ring on her left hand and stole a glance up at her fiancé. They exchanged a smile so intimate that I felt I was intruding by seeing it.

Bah. I nudged away my beer bottle and reached for another shot of tequila. So what if I didn't have anyone to kiss at midnight. I wasn't the only one. April and I clinked shot glasses and knocked them back together.

"I meant to say . . ." April leaned on the bar in my direction, and I leaned toward her in response, because it was getting kind of loud in here. "I'm so glad you joined book club. Sorry the books are so depressing, though."

I waved a hand. "It's okay. I'm one of those 'history shouldn't be forgotten' kind of people."

"Oh, me too." April nodded earnestly, probably a little too earnestly, but we were both a couple shots in at this point. "Totally. But I'm also one of those 'let's read something fun after a long day of work' kind of people."

"Well, you should join Emily's book club then." I motioned between Emily and myself. "We're reading fun books. Didn't Emily tell you?"

April considered it, her head bobbing left and right on the end of her neck. Finally the bob became a nod, followed by a head shake. "I don't know. You think this town is big enough for two book clubs?"

That was a valid question, considering that Emily's book club still didn't have a ton of members. But tequila made me optimistic. "It's been great so far. They can have the depressing, important books. We read the fun ones with sex in them."

A laugh escaped April's mouth, a loud guffaw that I wouldn't have expected from her. She clapped a hand over her mouth to contain the sound, but her eyes grinned at me. "Now that . . ." She trailed off. ". . . That is something I can get behind. I mean, if that's the only way I can get any, I'm in."

"I hear that." I grinned, a little harder than was necessary, but again, tequila. "Go to the store. Emily will hook you up with the book."

"I can't believe she didn't tell me about it. Em, why didn't you tell me about the sexy book club?" She glanced over her shoulder, and I stifled a giggle. Emily's arms were around Simon's neck and he had her backed up against the bar, his hands low on her hips. She fiddled with the hair at the nape of his neck, and they didn't have eyes for anyone else. There was no way Emily was thinking about book clubs, sexy or not.

My instinct was to avert my eyes, that feeling of being an intruder on someone else's happiness coming back to the forefront. April obviously felt no such desire. Instead she whacked her little sister on the arm. "Get a room, you two! You do know you're out in public, right?"

Simon backed away a step, a flush climbing up his neck as he ran a hand through his hair. He at least had the grace to look a little mortified, but Emily just rolled her eyes and whacked April right back with a grin.

"Nothing wrong with kissing my fiancé at midnight," she said.

"It's not midnight." I handed her a shot glass.

"That's right, it's eleven forty-seven, so keep it in your pants for another thirteen minutes." But April was smiling through her admonition, and we three girls did one more shot together for good measure.

Ooof. That was four shots in a very short amount of time, and with the way my fingers and toes were tingling, I was feeling the effects pretty quickly. I ordered a glass of water and squeezed two lime wedges into it. The alcohol had taken hold, and my muscles felt loose. I took slow sips of water as the room got just swimmy enough for me to feel good. A little silly. A lot happy. Happy New Year.

I'd taken an Uber to the bar, and I took another one home. Good planning ahead, Past Stacey. After another glass of water with a couple aspirin to stave off tomorrow's hangover, I crawled into bed, switching on my fairy lights so I could see enough to plug in my phone. When it blinked to life, there was a notification. An email.

To: Stacey Lindholm

From: Dex MacLean

Date: January 1, 12:32 a.m.

Subject: Re: Happy New Year

I hope that you managed to stay warm, and that you didn't get any snow while you were out tonight. I like to think of you as being as safe and warm as you wished I was. And I am. There are usually bars to hit up and parties to attend, but I ended up staying in tonight. Long talks with family ended up being a good way to say goodbye to this old year.

And now I'm sending you an email to say hello to the new year. Start as you mean to go on. I hope you had a great time out with friends, and that there was someone there to kiss you at midnight since it can't be me.

I thought about getting my laptop, but it was on the other side of my apartment and I was tucked in bed with Benedick purring in my lap. So instead I pecked out a response on my phone.

To: Dex MacLean

From: Stacey Lindholm

Date: January 1, 1:13 a.m.

Subject: Re: Re: Happy New Year

It was a great evening, thank you. A smidge too much tequila but that's how a lot of these nights go. No one at the bar worthy of kissing, but I gave Benedick a smooch and he didn't seem to mind.

A response came almost immediately.

To: Stacey Lindholm
From: Dex MacLean
Date: January 1, 1:16 a.m.
Subject: Re: Re: Re: Happy New Year

I take it back. I don't know if I want someone there kissing you. Who the hell is Benedick, and why did his mother name him after a Shakespeare character? I can't believe this. You're out there getting kissed while I rang in the new year at the kitchen table with my uncle Morty.

A warm glow bloomed through my skin, almost as intense as the tequila buzz that had subsided about a half hour ago. Dex was jealous. This was wonderful.

I flipped to my camera and scooped up a sleepy Benedick. He barely moved as I took a selfie of the two of us, me planting a kiss onto his fluffy head. He'd lived with me long enough that he was used to me demanding photos; sometimes he even seemed to enjoy his little bursts of Instagram fame. If a cat knew what Instagram was. I deposited him back into my lap, where he purred and snuggled into my belly as I cropped the photo, brightening it since the fairy lights were kind of dark. I started to switch back to my email, but after a moment's hesitation, closed out of the email and opened up my contacts instead. I'd never sent Dex a text before, because texting had felt too intimate. I wasn't sure if it was the lingering tequila, the lateness of the hour, or the buoyant knowledge that a man who looked like Dex was actually upset that someone else might have been kissing me. Whatever it was, I was feeling intimate. Besides, pictures from phones sent better via text than email. So I selected his number and attached the picture to a text.

Meet Benedick. He's an excellent kisser. Or kissee, really.

I held my breath as I hit Send. Was he even anywhere near his phone? He could have been emailing me from a laptop. Maybe he wouldn't get it till morning. But no: the message was marked "read" almost immediately, followed by those dots that indicated he was texting back.

Of course. Benedick to your Beatrice. Okay, I'll allow it.

A slow smile spread across my face, and the warm glow intensified. He remembered my Faire name. Maybe I wasn't just another wench in another town to him.

He sent another text: **Much cuter than my date.** Followed by a photo of a tall glass of beer. Something dark.

I approve of your date as well, I texted back. **Though there's plenty to be jealous of there too, you know.**

Oh really? How so?

I caught my breath as I realized what I'd texted. I'd been thinking about that tall glass. His mouth on its edge, the tip of his tongue licking foam off his lips. And I'd been jealous. Of a glass of beer. Maybe this was getting a little too intimate. But what the hell.

I wish I could have kissed you at midnight. Is that a bad thing to wish? My fingers were uncertain on the keys, and it took two tries to send the text. Was that too much? It shouldn't be; I'd slept with the man, for God's sake. But our emails over the past few months felt more intimate than anything I'd shared in his bed. I'd been getting to know the man he was inside, not just how he liked to have sex. Through our emails, I felt like I'd met him for the first time all over again. But while we'd shared the secrets of our hearts, we hadn't talked attraction, either from our past encounters or the new intimacy blooming between us. Kissing him now would feel like kissing him for the first time, and I ached for it.

My last text was delivered, then it was read. Then my phone was silent, and dread swirled in the pit of my stomach. I'd gone too far. I'd ruined it. But then the dots came.

No.

No? I scrunched up my face as I read those words. What the hell did that mean?

But he wasn't done. More dots.

That's a perfect wish. Because I wish it too. More than anything.

My breath caught. Oh thank God.

He was still typing. **Times like this, especially when it's late at night, I think about you more than I probably should. Think about how your hair would feel between my fingers. Think about how your lips would taste. Your mouth. Those are the things I think about when it's this late at night, when my mind goes crazy with wondering and wanting.**

I pressed my palms to my suddenly very warm cheeks and kicked my legs out from under the blankets, disturbing the cat.

When had this room gotten so warm? But if he could confess those things, so could I. I dug my phone out from the blankets to see he hadn't finished. **Sorry. Probably shouldn't have texted all that. Maybe had one beer too many.**

I giggled as my thumbs flew over the keyboard. **A couple tequilas too many over here, but that's okay. I know what you mean. I was just thinking how new this all feels, getting to know you this way. And how much I want you to kiss me for the first time all over again.**

There was a longer pause before he answered. **I want that too. More than you know. Good night, Anastasia. Happy New Year.**

Happy New Year, Dex.

I went to sleep with a smile on my face and a purring cat curled around my head. This new year was starting off pretty damn well.

Eight

J*anuary brought enough* snow that some days I had to leave for work a good fifteen minutes earlier so I could scrape off the car and warm it up. On those days I didn't have time for my mother to call when I was on my way out the door. Which was, of course, exactly when the landline on my wall rang. Mom's direct line to me when she wanted to talk.

"Ugh, Mom!" I tried to let out all the frustration in that one growl under my breath before I picked up the phone so she wouldn't hear it in my voice. She knew my schedule; this was not a good time to talk. I blew out all the negativity and picked up the receiver.

"Hey, Mom." There. My voice was nice and light and breezy. Typical Stacey. "I'm on my way to work, can't really talk. Can I drop by tonight?"

"Hey, Princess." I froze at the sound of my dad's voice. He never called; he wasn't a phone guy. We usually communicated by him telling Mom to tell me something, and me telling her what to tell him back. So his voice on the phone was the first alarm bell in my head. The second was the hesitant, tired way he spoke. He'd said only two words, but he sounded just like he had the day he'd called me from the hospital, that first time that Mom had . . .

"Dad? What's wrong? Is everything okay?" Forming words was harder than usual. My mouth didn't seem to want to work right.

"Everything's fine. We're at the hospital—"

I dropped my backpack purse to the floor, and I was lucky I didn't fumble the phone as well. "If you're at the hospital, everything is not fine. Is it Mom?"

"Yes, but don't worry. She wasn't feeling right last night, so we went to the emergency room. They took her right in, and—"

"Last night?" I screeched. "And you're just calling me now?" I started mentally flicking through the schedule at work. Was it a full day? How screwed would they be if I called in, and how much did I care? Not too much, I decided, and not at all.

"You know your mother." Dad's voice broke through my scrambling thoughts. "She wouldn't let me call you until morning. She didn't want you to worry."

"Okay, but I'm worried now. Look, let me call in to work real quick, and I can be at the hospital in about fifteen minutes."

"No, no. Don't do that, your mother will kill me. I wasn't supposed to call you till they've finished running tests. Just go to work, and keep your phone on you if you can, okay? I know you're not supposed to . . ."

"Oh, the hell with that," I said. "I'll keep my phone in my pocket, and they can fire me if they don't like it. You call me the second you hear something, okay?"

I barely remembered the drive to work. My mind was five years in the past, replaying that first phone call from my dad from the emergency room. He'd tried to downplay Mom's condition and his worry, but that time he hadn't stopped me from joining him at the hospital. That itself was what made me go to work that day. Mom never wanted me to worry, but Dad had a hard time going through this stuff alone. We'd clocked lots of hours together, side by side in waiting rooms. Once Mom was okay we went back to basically talking through her, but during a crisis he needed me.

So the fact that he didn't need me today was encouraging. But I still took my phone out of my backpack when I got to work and turned it to vibrate. I was about to slip it into my pocket when instead I unlocked it. Before I had a chance to think about it, I sent a text to Dex. **Mom's in the hospital.** I wasn't sure why I did it; we didn't usually text during the day. Our time was at night. But I felt like I had to tell someone, and no one else in my immediate circle knew my history with my mom's health. Not on the level that I'd told Dex about it. So I sent that text and then slipped my phone into my pocket.

Almost immediately it vibrated and I dug it out, expecting it to be Dad with an update. But to my surprise, it was Dex. **Oh shit. Is she okay?**

I don't know yet, I responded. **Dad's going to update me as soon as he knows. I'm at work.** I winced as I hit Send. When I wrote it out like that, I looked like a real jerk. Why had I gone to work today? I should have been with my parents.

But Dex's response didn't judge me. **I'm sure he'll let you know something soon. I'd tell you not to worry, but of course you're worried. Let me know if you need distraction.**

I'll definitely need distraction. Just no dick pics, okay?

Ha! Not exactly my style.

I blinked at that. Dick pics were a hundred percent Dex's style. In fact, I was frankly surprised that he had never sent me one. Or any other picture of himself or some other lickable part of his body. Now that we'd adopted text messages as our major form of communication, I had figured it was only a matter of time. After all, this was the guy who'd sent me more than one **U up?** text the first summer we'd hooked up. Maybe he really had changed.

I put my purse in its drawer, and before I opened the office for the day I ducked in to see the office manager. Lindsay and I had been cheerleaders together at Willow Creek High, and while we hadn't been besties, she was the one who'd hooked me up with this job when I'd needed one. And sure, in some ways it was weird to have an old high school classmate essentially be my boss. But she was also a friend, and I knew I could count on her on a day like this.

As usual, she was the first one here, so I wasn't surprised to see her already behind her computer, frowning at something on her screen.

"Hey." I kept my voice low so she wouldn't jump out of her chair, and I flashed her a weak smile when she looked up. "Real quick, I need to keep my phone out today." I took it out of my pocket and waved it in illustration. "My mom's . . . uh, she's . . ." To my surprise, I couldn't say it out loud. I could text that she was in the hospital, but saying the words out loud made it more real.

As it turned out, I didn't need to say anything. "Oh, God, yes, of course." Her brow furrowed in concern. "Is she . . . Is she gonna be okay?" There was that good thing about small towns. I didn't have to explain. Everyone just knew.

She'd already risen to her feet with her Concerned Face on, which just made me revert back to my usual smile. The one that said *Nothing's wrong! Everything's great! Nothing to see here!* "Oh, she's going to be fine," I said in the sunniest voice I could manage. "I'm just waiting for Dad to call, and he gets worried if he can't get hold of me right away, you know?"

Lindsay nodded slowly and sat back down. "Well, don't worry about it. If Dr. Cochran says anything, I'll take care of it. And when your dad calls, if you need some privacy, feel free to come in here. I think I'm the only one with a door that shuts."

And that way she'd be the first to know what was going on. But that was the trade-off, wasn't it?

I went to unlock the front door, fully expecting to spend the morning on pins and needles while I waited for a call from my dad. I knew it would be a while before I heard from him—hospitals were notoriously slow—but that was a good thing, right? If there was something seriously wrong with Mom, they'd move a lot faster, and Dad would have called by now. It was all well and good that Mom didn't want me to worry, but we were past that now.

My phone first buzzed about fifteen minutes after we opened for the day. My heart leapt into my throat at the vibration against my hip, but it only buzzed once, so it was a text, not a phone call. If Dad was barely a phone call guy, he definitely wasn't a texting guy. When the lobby was quiet I slipped my phone out of my pocket to see a picture of a Starbucks drink, something iced and so pale I wondered if there had ever been any coffee in there at all. **It's not pumpkin spice**, the accompanying text said, **but I told you I take a lot of cream.**

The picture and its caption made me smile. **You're not kidding**, I texted back. **Did you just get a cup of milk with some ice in it?** His response was a shrug emoji, and when nothing else was forthcoming, I put my phone away, turning my attention back to the mother and daughter who had come in for a yearly checkup.

My phone buzzed again about twenty minutes later. Another text. Another picture, this time of a pony dressed up as a unicorn. **Meant to send you this over the weekend! I met this unicorn at the faire we're currently working. He says he wants to come to Willow Creek soon.**

I sucked in an excited breath, because while on the outside I was twenty-seven and mature as hell, on the inside I was still a nine-year-old who squealed at the sight of a unicorn. **Simon would love that,** I responded. **Send me that unicorn's digits and I'll put him in touch with someone who can make that happen!**

It'll probably be people you'll be dealing with, not the unicorn. Unicorns don't have thumbs and have a hard time operating a smartphone.

Well, have his people contact my people, then. I grinned as I hit Send and put my phone away again.

The rest of the morning went like that—a text a couple times an hour from Dex, with a random thought or a meme he pulled off the internet. It hit me, after the fourth or fifth innocuous text, that not once did he ask if I'd heard from my dad or how my mom was doing. He was distracting me, just as he'd promised. He was also making me accustomed to the feel of my phone vibrating in my pocket, so by the time my dad finally called, a little before lunchtime, I didn't jump out of my skin the way I would have if my phone had been silent all morning.

"She's fine," he said without preamble. "Indigestion, can you believe it?"

"Are you kidding?" Lindsay had already left for lunch, so I

ducked into her office and left the door cracked so I could still keep an eye on the lobby. I'd already switched the phones over to the answering machine; it was only five minutes early, no one would notice.

"Your mother said the same thing," he said. "But it's true. She's got a prescription for an antacid and we're following up with an ear, nose, and throat guy later this week. It's got nothing to do with her heart. She's fine."

It took a few frantic heartbeats for his words to sink in, and while they did, I'd taken a seat in one of the little chairs in front of Lindsay's desk, my knees shaking too much to keep me upright. "She's fine," I echoed.

"Well, she's cranky as hell and I'm taking her home for a nap. But otherwise, yes."

I blew out a long, relieved breath, and my shoulders relaxed for the first time since he'd called that morning. "Thanks, Dad. Just . . . I was so . . ." My throat closed, and I had to cough hard before I could speak again. "It was just so much like last time. When—"

"I know." His voice was as somber as mine. "I know, Princess. But she's fine. It's not like last time at all."

"Okay." A few more breaths, and I was breathing normally again. "How about I pick up something for dinner tonight? I can be home about six or so."

"Oh, that would be great. Thanks, honey."

I managed to keep it together until we hung up, then the leftover adrenaline coursed through me, making me shake and my breath turn into barely-there sobs. She was okay. Mom was okay. But my mind was full of memories of that first frantic trip to the hospital, finding Dad in the waiting room, seeing Mom hooked up to machines . . .

But that was then. This was now. And she was fine this time.

I pushed to my feet and nudged the office door the rest of the way open. Lunchtime, but I wasn't sure if I could eat. My emotions had been on a roller coaster this morning, and my stomach felt jumpy from it all. But I got my purse out of its drawer and locked the front door behind me on the way out. Getting out of the office would be good for me, at the very least.

I took my phone out of my pocket and let my feet carry me blindly down the sidewalk to the deli. I had one more text to send.

> All good with Mom. Thanks for keeping me company this morning. It helped more than you'll ever know.

It didn't take long for him to text back. **I'm glad I could be there. Well, not THERE. But you know what I mean.**

A smile flickered over my face. It had been a tough morning, but I'd smiled more than I'd expected to. And that was all thanks to the man I was texting. **This was the next best thing. This would have been a tough day if I'd been all alone.**

> You'll never be alone. Not if I have anything to say about it.

I wanted to hug the phone to my chest, but even I knew that would look a little weird. Instead I went to slide it into my bag when it chimed again. **Wait. Did that sound stalkery? I promise I'm not a creep.**

I snorted. **You're definitely not a creep. I'll let it slide.**

Thank God. But he was still typing. **I have to get back to work now, but I'm glad your mom is doing all right.**

Me too, I texted back. I put my phone in my bag and pushed open the door of the deli. I wasn't hungry now, but I would be later tonight. And so would my parents. I put in an order for three large sandwiches and a vat of chicken soup that I could pick up on my way home from work. By the time I got back to work for the afternoon, it felt more like a regular workday. I'd see my parents tonight, as I did almost every night, and no one would be hooked up to anything. Everything was back to normal. I was relieved.

But I was frustrated too. My brow furrowed at that realization. And at the realization that those texts with Dex this morning, as innocuous as they were, had been the best part of my day. They'd been a glimpse at another life, and now they were gone, and my regular life faded back to gray. I felt the bars of that golden cage closing in on me. Again.

I had no one to blame but myself. Hadn't I chosen this cage? Willingly walked into it and locked the door behind me? I didn't know what it would take to finally break out of it.

But that wasn't worth thinking about now. Not after a day like this. My parents needed me, so golden cage it was. At least for a while.

Nine

Now that Dex and I had added texting to our communications, our relationship had leveled up. Every notification was a hit of adrenaline to my system. Every ping on my phone felt like a kiss.

As winter melted into spring, I tried telling myself it was no big deal. The relationship was still just words on the screen, no matter the format. It didn't get me a date on Friday nights, or someone to kiss on Valentine's Day. So really, how much of an impact were these conversations having on my life?

Those more rational thoughts still didn't stop me from clinging to my phone like a lifeline, my heart thrilling with every text notification. But it wasn't a problem. I kept my phone on silent and in my purse while I was at work, because my job was boring enough and the temptation would be too great. Outside work, I was discreet. I didn't check my phone too much, and hardly anyone noticed.

At least, that's what I thought.

At the bridal shop, while April and I waited for Emily to try on another dress, I slid my phone out of my backpack, even though it was ten thirty in the morning and I'd already read the late-night email Dex had sent the night before. The nights were for emails—longer and more introspective, sometimes a little sexy—while the daytime was for quick text messages. He hadn't texted yet today, and while he sometimes checked in with me between shows, the weekends were his busier time, so I usually didn't hear from him until the evening. Nothing wrong with a quick peek, though, just to make sure . . .

"Okay, that's it." April plucked the phone out of my hand.

"Gimme that." I reached for it, but she leaned back in her chair, stretching her arm as far away from me as possible.

"Nope. This is an intervention."

I scowled and crossed my arms over my chest. "I don't need an intervention. I need my phone back." My hands already felt empty, as if I were missing a couple fingers. Tension twitched along the back of my neck. What if there was a text? What if he'd just sent me a text and it was on the screen right now, and I couldn't see it? I wanted my phone back. I needed my phone back.

Huh. Maybe April had a point.

I huffed out a breath and adjusted the scarf around my pony-tail. My hair had turned out weird today. I'd been nervous while I was getting ready, and every section I hit with the curling iron fell at the wrong angle. So I'd caught the whole thing back into a low pony and tied a filmy scarf around it, so it all looked like it had been done on purpose.

The nervous feeling had only increased when we got to the shop. Emily had picked out options, both for her and for us, and we were there to see the finalists for her wedding dress. The shop had hooked us up: we were settled in a private alcove in comfortable chairs, drinking fizzy water with lime slices while Emily fiddled around in the dressing room. Super relaxing. Except I felt like a bundle of live wires. Hence the crazy phone checking. Just knowing that Dex was out there thinking about me made me feel better. More centered.

But he wasn't going to text me anytime soon. Saturdays were performance days, and I had more important things to think about anyway.

"Fine." I opened my backpack and held it out to her. "Consider me reformed. No more phone, I promise." April dropped my phone into my bag, and I cinched it shut.

"Is everything okay?" She peered at me with concern in her eyes.

"I don't know." I blew out a breath and looked toward the dressing room. "I haven't felt good about any of these dresses that Em's showing us, so I'm a little worried about . . ."

"No, I mean, is everything okay with you?" April tilted her head. "Just . . . you're checking your phone a lot lately. I've noticed it at book club, and just now too. Even back on New Year's Eve. Is something up? Something with your mom? I know she's been sick . . ."

Maybe I hadn't been as discreet as I thought. "No," I said. "Mom's fine. Everything's fine. Just, you know, social media." I waved a hand in what I hoped was an unconcerned gesture, pasting my bright smile back on my face. "Can't stop checking my notifications. It's a sickness."

"Pfft. You kids and your Instagram." She took a sip of her fizzy water and shot me a crooked smile and I relaxed, glad to be off the hook.

Just then, Emily came out in dress number three.

The first dress she'd showed us had made her look like a ballerina in a child's jewelry box, and not in a good way. She'd been swallowed up by all the tulle, and the whole thing had been Too Much. The second dress had been the opposite extreme: sleek and fitted. It looked fantastic on her, but she didn't look like a bride. She looked like someone on the way to an overly formal business meeting.

But dress number three, much like Goldilocks and Baby Bear's chair, was Just Right.

I remembered that first day when Emily, April, and I had talked dresses. Passing Emily's tablet back and forth over brunch, pulling up photos of ideas. The dress Emily wore now was the perfect amalgam of our thoughts that first mimosa-fueled morning. The top was halter style, fitted and embroidered with transparent sequins that caught the light perfectly. The skirt was made up of layers of tulle and lace, but she didn't disappear into them the way she had in the first dress. This skirt poofed out just enough, falling in soft points around her legs, giving the appearance of a full-length dress without the weight of fabric or bulkiness that would normally come from so many layers. She looked perfect for an outdoor wedding at a Renaissance faire.

April obviously agreed with me. "Yes!" She surged out of her chair, still holding on to her glass of fizzy water. "Oh, yeah, kiddo. This is the one!" She paced a slow circle around her sister, and Emily's eyebrows rose at me in a question while April was behind her.

"You think?" Her question was a response to April, but she directed the words toward me.

"Absolutely!" I said. "I love it. In fact, I'm pretty sure now that you were trolling us with those first two dresses."

"Oh, yeah, Emily. Those other two were shit. Just shit."

Emily barked out a laugh. "No, go ahead, April. Tell me what you really think." She shot me a wide-eyed look, but I couldn't back her up.

"Sorry, Em. But I agree with your sister on this one. This is obviously the winner. The other two were just awful."

"Fine." She threw up her hands and tried to look annoyed, but her wide smile gave her away. She ran her hands over the bodice of the dress, down to her waist, fluffing the tulle in the skirt. When she looked back up at me, her eyes were shot through with worry. "I really do like this. You think Simon will . . . ?"

"Simon's gonna swallow his tongue when he sees you in this." I nodded solemnly.

"For real," April echoed.

Emily flushed pink, and when her smile turned slightly wicked, I knew she was already thinking ahead to her wedding day. Maybe even the wedding night. Nope. I wasn't going there.

She twirled for us one more time, then went back into the dressing room, emerging a few minutes later in her jeans and T-shirt. Fashion show was over, apparently.

"Next!" She clapped her hands together while, behind her, our assigned shop attendant cleared the dressing room of rejected wedding gowns. "April, your dress is in there. The green. Stacey, you're after April."

I kept a smile on my face while my anxiety spiked. This was exactly what I was nervous about. I wasn't terribly self-conscious about my body. It was mine and it was healthy, even if it was a little rounder than the glossy women's magazines said it should be. I knew how to dress myself, and I knew what looked good on me.

But that didn't mean Emily knew. She was tiny. She was thin. In her wedding dress, once we put a crown of flowers on her head, she would look like a fairy princess. Her sister was built much the same, so Emily wouldn't have any problem finding something that would work on her. But on my completely different body type? This could be a disaster. Sure, I'd given her input on dress ideas—our shared Pinterest board was impressive. But I hadn't seen any of her real choices before today. Those first two wedding gowns had been garbage, so I didn't trust her taste anymore. What was she making us wear?

Sure enough, a few minutes later April came out of the dressing room looking like a model. Well, a model who was a foot too short to actually walk a runway, with no shoes on, and still wearing the baseball cap she'd worn to the shop.

"Seriously?" Emily plucked the hat from her sister's head, and April snatched it back.

"I'm not wearing it in the wedding, calm down." She stuffed her hair back inside her hat, threading it through the back, then smoothed her hands down the dress. "This works. I mean, we have to take it in, but they'll do that, right?"

Take it in. I'd never had that problem. I tried not to roll my eyes while I surveyed April's dress. Then I pursed my lips and turned to Emily. "You were trolling us with those first two dresses. I knew it." April's dress was a riff on Emily's gown: simpler lines and in pastel green, but the same lacy handkerchief hem, this time with a sleeveless, high-necked bodice that called attention to April's well-toned arms.

Emily grinned. "Okay, maybe a little. But I wanted to be sure, you know?" She nudged me. "Your dress is in there too. The pink. Go try it on; I can't wait to see."

I didn't want to. April's dress looked perfect on her, but if I wore it I'd look like a sausage in a too-small casing. My boobs would distort the lace, and the high-neck sleeveless cut would make my very not-toned arms look like Christmas hams. But I trudged into the dressing room anyway, because that was what you did for best friends. You wore awful dresses and your biggest smile while they got married.

Inside the dress was waiting for me. A perfect soft pink, but I couldn't tell much about the shape of it from how it draped off the hanger. I stepped into the dress and pulled it up over my hips. It cleared them, and I blew out a sigh of relief. One hurdle down. One to go: getting it zipped up.

As I stuck my arms through the sleeve holes, I realized there was far too much fabric for this to be a high-necked dress like April's, or a halter-top like Emily's. I got the dress settled on my shoulders and reached behind me for the zipper. It went up a little more than halfway but stopped under my shoulder blades. No amount of jumping around the dressing room and stretching my arms behind me would get it to go up the rest of the way. Finally I gave up and turned back to the full-length mirror.

I looked amazing. Well, there was still the issue of the dress not zipping up all the way, so it distorted the way the neckline fell, but otherwise it looked like it was made for me. The draped neck was both revealing and modest all at once, and the dress was topped off with fluttery cap sleeves. The pale pink was the perfect shade: warm against my skin, it made me look brighter somehow, the way a good blush brings dimension to your cheeks. My dress was different from the others, but it looked the same too: all three dresses had the coordinating handkerchief hem. Modern dresses with almost period detail. Appropriate.

I was in love with this dress. If only it fit. My emotions were all over the place as I joined the other two outside, where Emily and April both proceeded to coo over my dress.

"But it doesn't fit." I turned around to show them how it was only zipped halfway up.

"You just can't reach it. Here . . ." April stepped up behind me to try the zipper, but it only went up another inch or two. Embarrassment rushed through me in a hot wave, and my insides clenched in a full-body cringe. I opened my mouth to apologize, but Emily dismissed it with an impatient wave.

"Bridal dress sizes are bullshit. We'll order it bigger and have them take it in at the waist."

"Exactly," April said. "They're gonna have to alter mine too, so it's no big deal."

My cringe eased at not only her words, but her nonchalant attitude about it. Like fog disappearing when the sun came out, my discomfort dissolved. They were right. Dresses got altered all the time. There was no shame in ordering a few sizes up and making it fit. I was so used to the inconvenience of being plus-sized that apologizing for it was second nature. But like April said, it wasn't a big deal. I'd been the one building it up inside my head, and that was all on me.

I turned back to the mirror and looked at the three of us. Emily back in her civilian clothes, April in her bridesmaid dress and baseball cap, and me in my dress that barely held me in. But I put those things aside and saw how April and I coordinated. I pictured Emily's dress in the mix. The three of us outdoors, in the woods at twilight. We'd look like a maypole. We'd look like summertime. It was going to be a gorgeous wedding.

I was practiced in the art of the mirror selfie. And "art" was absolutely the word to describe it. There was a specific technique to holding the phone, so you both got yourself completely in-frame and didn't block anything important. Don't look at the phone with a furrowed brow or a did-I-get-the-shot expression. Look relaxed, smile confidently into the mirror, and just delete and try again if the shot didn't work out. I'd deleted a lot of shots when I'd first started taking pics. But now, jokes about my Instagram addiction aside, it had made me really good at the mirror selfie.

So, back in the dressing room, before I took off the bridesmaid's dress I snapped a couple pics, and when I got home I contemplated putting them up on Instagram. I hadn't posted a selfie in a while, and maybe the people who followed my feed would like a break from pictures of my cat. But would it spoil the surprise? What if Simon happened upon the photo? He'd have a clue to what Emily would look like, and that wouldn't be good at all. No, I should keep the selfie off social media.

But what was the point of taking a selfie if you didn't share it with anyone? Besides, there was only one person whose reaction I was after. I pulled up my text chain with Dex and sent him the pic.

I saw his response a half hour later, after I put together a salad for dinner. **Very nice. New work outfit?**

Ha, I wrote back, though I blinked back disappointment as I did so. I wanted him to lose his mind when he saw me in that dress, the way I pictured Simon would when he saw Emily. **Bridesmaid dress for this summer.**

Are you sure you wanna wear that?

The bottom dropped out of my stomach. I scrolled back up to look at the picture again. I'd made an effort to arrange the neck so the draped fabric fell perfectly, the way it would when it fit and I could zip it up all the way. I loved that dress. I looked nice in it. Or I would, once it fit. **What's wrong with it?**

Seems rude, outshining the bride. That's all.

Oh, he was good.

Before I could respond, he sent another text. **This must be the year for weddings. My old college roommate is getting married in June. Not too long before we head back in your direction.**

Then you'll be going to two weddings this summer, I replied. **If you want to, that is. This one's happening at Faire.**

Oh, I want to. You think I'd miss seeing you looking like that in person?

A grin crawled up my face, and I pressed one hand to my cheek, which had gotten awfully warm.

He texted again. **You don't know what I'd give for the chance to dance with you in that dress.**

My grin dipped a little. It was a nice sentiment, but it seemed so . . . pessimistic. As though he thought the chance of actually getting that dance was unlikely. **You think I'd turn you down? You have to know I'm a pretty sure thing here.**

He took a long time to reply. Longer than he really should have. **LOL of course.**

He didn't elaborate, and I didn't ask him to. Something about his "LOL" rang false. I couldn't explain how I understood that via text, but I did. Dex had never been an LOL kind of guy, so to use it now felt like a brush-off.

I'd always known, of course, that when Faire rolled around and we saw each other face-to-face and in the flesh again, things might change a little. We knew each other so much better than we had last summer, but we hadn't talked. Hadn't touched. We would have to reconcile all the things we'd said via email and text with seeing each other in the flesh. Would all this flirting translate into a real relationship once he came back to town? Or would the sensitive, intellectual Dex I'd gotten to know over the past few months be subsumed by the swaggering hottie I'd hooked up with the two previous summers? Even after all this time, it was hard to believe that they were the same man.

My finger hovered over his number, and not for the first time I thought about calling him. It would be so simple. One tap, and I could hear his voice. But I didn't. I'd never taken that step, and neither had he. We were keeping that final bit of distance between us, no matter how intimate our conversations.

So I clicked my phone off without calling him. Summer was almost here. Almost time for Faire sign-ups, and for the cast of the Willow Creek Renaissance Faire to be assembled once again. Before I knew it, it would be July. Faire would open, and Emily and Simon would get married.

And I'd see Dex again. For better or for worse.

Ten

My *phone dinged* with a text one Tuesday night in April while I was unloading the dishwasher, and I dove for it with embarrassing eagerness. I was disappointed to see that the text was from Simon Graham and not from Dex, and then I was disappointed in myself for being disappointed.

> **Sign-ups for Faire are Saturday at 10. Can I count on you to help out as usual?**

Of course, I texted back immediately. **Wouldn't miss it!**

> **Thank you. You're great at recruiting the adults.**

I know. I couldn't hide my smirk as I tapped out my reply. **I got Emily on board a couple years ago, after all.** I'd been the one to shove a clipboard in her hands and gently break it to her that if her niece Caitlin wanted to be in the cast, then Emily had to be too. The rule was barely enforced, but to my surprise Emily hadn't dropped out, as most well-meaning parents did. She'd been dedicated, and after some initial clashes of personality with Simon, she'd become pretty dedicated to him too.

You did, Simon texted back. There was a pause as he kept typing. **Been meaning to thank you for that.**

I grinned at my phone. Simon was not an effusive guy; for him that was practically a squee. **See you Saturday morning. I'll be there an hour early.**

I was true to my word. I met Simon at Willow Creek High School—our alma mater and his employer—bright and early that Saturday morning. He unlocked the building and turned on the lights in the auditorium, and I sorted out stacks of forms, attaching them to clipboards. Before long, the first wave of kids started showing up for tryouts.

Tryouts. Auditions. Sign-ups. This whole process was a little of each, which is why we never called it by one name. Our cast was made up largely of high school kids, and we vetted them for whatever talent they had, which meant listening to a lot of questionably sung madrigals. Our dance captain was a volunteer from the local ballet school; she led aspiring dancers through some simple figures and would let Simon know later which kids had promise. Students who had participated in the past were a shoo-in if they wanted to do the same thing the next year. Adults who wanted to participate had a much easier time of it; we always wanted more adult volunteers, so if you could fill out a form and were even halfway willing to learn an accent, you were in.

I stationed myself at the top of the house in the auditorium, handing forms out to kids and adults alike as they came in. Emily joined me a few minutes after ten.

"There you are," I said. "I thought you'd come in with Simon." She shook her head. "I swung by to pick up Cait." She indicated down at the front of the auditorium, where I immediately spotted Caitlin by her brown, curly hair—so much like Emily's you could tell they were related. She leaned against the edge of the stage, talking to Simon. Emily shook her head. "She's such a suck-up."

"What do you mean?"

"I think she's got a little bit of a crush on Simon—excuse me, on Mr. G—but she won't admit it to me."

"Oh, really?"

She shrugged. "I could be wrong. May not be a crush so much as her seeing him as a means to getting into a better college. She's been all about that college prep this past year."

"Well, that's good, right? She'll be a senior, time to start applying to schools."

"Oh, absolutely. But soon I'm going to have to break it to her that she won't be in Simon's class next year."

"She won't?" Simon taught advanced placement English to juniors and seniors. "I thought her grades were good."

"They're great. She's a smart kid. Like her mom."

"And her aunt." I nudged her with my shoulder, and Emily smiled in thanks for the compliment.

"But once Simon and I get married this summer, he'll be family. And he doesn't want anyone to think he's favoring her for any reason."

"Ahhhhh." I blew out the word as a sigh. "Well, that sucks."

"Yeah." She shrugged. "I just need to make her see that there's an upside to him being family. I foresee a lot of private tutoring sessions at the dining room table."

I considered that. "Well, if she really has a crush, then she'll like that more."

"I can only hope so. She's been talking about Simon's college prep English class since, oh, I don't know, the first day I met Simon. Two years ago."

"And thought he was a prick." If Emily thought I was ever going to let her live that down, she was wrong.

She nodded, a rueful smile twisting her face. "Well, he was kind of a prick."

"Uh-huh." I handed forms to some more kids who walked through the door, offered one to a mother who put up defensive hands before shaking her head and sitting down in the back of the auditorium. "Good turnout this year." I still remembered the days when kids were strong-armed into participating; Simon's big brother had been in charge back then, and he'd been particularly good at begging. These days we had more high school kids volunteering than we could use; we had actually started turning some of them away the past couple years. Amazing. Sean would have been proud. I made a mental note to mention that to Simon later.

Emily scanned the crowd of kids. "Caitlin wants to sing this year, so she's been practicing." She threw me a sideways glance. "Didn't you used to sing? Before your tavern wench days?"

"Sure did. Lots of summers of madrigals." I smiled at the memory. I'd been active in glee club in high school, so it had been a no-brainer for me to go in that direction. I'd spent my first summers at Faire singing in five-part harmony with four other girls. The Gilded Lilies, we were called, all five of us dressed in identical yellow dresses, like some kind of Renaissance-themed Von Trapp kids. As the older girls aged out and stopped doing Faire, younger girls took their place. I switched over to being a wench sometime during college, and by then the original four girls I'd sung with had all moved away. But the Lilies lived on. The girls seemed younger every year, but maybe that was just me getting older. The dresses, however, were still yellow and weren't flattering on anyone.

I eyed Caitlin. She'd look good in yellow. "She should go for it." This would be her third year doing Faire, and she was a rising senior. She wouldn't have to worry about being turned away. And after all, at this point she was also family. Simon might not want to show favoritism in his classes, but he had no such scruples when it came to Faire.

All in all, sign-ups went extremely well. Plenty of kids, and I was even able to persuade a few new parents to take part. We had a cast in place, and once school let out in June, rehearsals would begin in earnest. Before long, we'd be spending our Saturdays at the high school for the yearly rehearsals for life as a Faire volunteer. For the returning cast members, these Saturdays were mostly a refresher, but for the newbies they would be a crash course in Elizabethan history.

Of course, I was also excited about Faire for a different reason. Text messages with Dex were practically a nightly occurrence these days, and the closer we got to the summer, the more inadequate they became. There'd been more than one night that I'd almost hit that Call button on my phone, desperate to hear his voice. Something always kept me from doing it, but knowing that Faire was on the horizon, and that I'd be seeing him soon, kept me anticipating his return like a kid waiting for Santa Claus. But with more kissing.

Meanwhile, the planning for Simon and Emily's wedding had started to ramp up as well. There was lots going on, and more and more often we met a couple evenings a week at April's house, which became command central for both wedding planning and Faire organization. April had lodged a protest at first, saying that she had nothing to do with Faire, but it was halfhearted and we kept showing up anyway. She must not have minded that much, because somehow there was always a family-style dinner waiting for us on those nights: a huge tray of baked ziti and salad or a shepherd's pie. Caitlin joined us some nights around her mother's big dining room table, usually engrossed in homework since finals were coming up for her, but also giving us a unique, teenage perspective on high school gossip, especially when it concerned kids who were participating in Faire. I kept a close eye on her, especially when she asked Simon for help with her homework, but I didn't detect any real signs of a crush. Her interest in her future uncle seemed to be purely academically motivated, which had to be a relief to Emily.

One night, Caitlin looked up at me from across the dining room table. "Emily said you used to sing too, right?"

"Sure did." I shot her a grin as I slipped my phone into my bag. It was too early in the evening for Dex to be getting in touch anyway. "Let me know if you want any help rehearsing. It's been years since I was a Lily, but those songs are still stuck in my head."

She nodded eagerly. "That would be awesome, thanks." She peered at me a little closer, and I wondered if I had something on my face. "You really like doing Faire, huh?"

"Guilty," I said with a smile. "I've been doing it since I was your age. Probably my favorite part of the summer."

"Well, it's not like there's a whole lot else to do around here." Her voice had a grumble in it, and I could see her point. Willow Creek wasn't exactly a metropolis. I was about to turn back to my list again, but Caitlin wasn't done. She tilted her head to look at me, looking so much like a younger version of her aunt Emily that I had to bite down on my smile. "Is that why you're here?"

"Well . . ." I shrugged. "I mean, I'm helping more with wedding stuff than Faire stuff, but it's kind of all hands on deck, you know? You should be careful; they'll put you to work next."

"Nope, I have to study," she said cheerfully. "But I mean, is that why you haven't left Willow Creek? Because you like doing Faire?"

"Oh." I looked down at the papers in front of me. I wasn't sure how to answer that question.

"I mean, Mr. G and Coach Malone grew up here, but they teach at the high school. But, like, you could work in a dentist's office anywhere, right? So did you stick around here to do Faire?"

"They have faires other places too, you know." I hated how defensive I sounded. Why was I arguing with a teenager? I fought to not cross my arms over my chest. Instead I slapped my patented Stacey Smile back on my face. "But, yeah. Maybe I like this one."

"And maybe you're being rude, kiddo." April appeared in the doorway between the kitchen and the dining room. "You don't just ask someone why they live where they do. Maybe it's none of your business."

Caitlin opened her mouth and then shut it again, her face reddening. "Sorry," she mumbled, throwing a look in my direction.

"Hey, it's cool." My defensiveness faded. She was a kid. It was okay to ask questions. I picked up my pen again. "Let me know when you want help with those songs. I'll teach you some of the ones you're too young for, and you can sing 'em in the tavern when Simon isn't looking."

"Yeah?" Her eyes lit up.

"No," April said from the doorway, in unison with Simon from the other end of the table. But Caitlin and I grinned at each other in solidarity, all awkwardness forgotten.

April shook her head and leaned against the doorjamb, swirling some red wine in her glass. "When am I getting my dining room back?"

On my left, Mitch shrugged and reached for another slice of pizza; he'd contributed dinner tonight, which meant takeout. "Well, Faire's in July, and so's the wedding, so . . ."

"July," I chimed in, my attention back on the invitation list. Emily and April had been sending them out in their free time in groups of ten or fifteen, and someone needed to make sure none of the names had fallen through the cracks. And since I'd been the one to point that out, that someone had become me. It was going well, though; most of the invites had been sent out, and I could probably get the last of them addressed in the next few days. RSVPs were already starting to come back too, so that was my next task.

"July." April sighed. "Great." But when I looked up she dropped a quick wink at me, and I caught the ghost of a smile that she camouflaged with a sip of her wine.

"I know. I'm sorry." Emily's sigh was a more genuinely aggrieved echo of her sister's. "Getting married at Faire seemed like a really good idea last fall, didn't it?"

"Hey," I said, "it's still a great idea. The wedding is going to be fantastic."

"I know." Emily sighed. "Everything's happening so fast now, though. All the prep, along with Faire rehearsals every weekend, and there's still a lot to plan . . ."

"For the wedding or for Faire?" April asked.

"Yes." Emily nodded. "Both." Her eyes were wide, and her chin trembled a little. Oh, man, she wasn't kidding around. She was overwhelmed. I'd never seen a problem that Emily couldn't plan her way out of. This was serious.

I put down my pen and grasped her arm, getting her attention. "We'll get it done," I said. "Don't worry."

"We will," April said. "And it's all going to happen at my dining room table."

"Oh, whatever." Emily's snark was coming back as she glanced up at her sister. "It's not like you throw any dinner parties anyway."

"I might." April took another sip of wine, but her eyes laughed at us over the glass. I knew her well enough by now to know that our book clubs were as social as she got. Odds were good that she'd never thrown a party in this house, and wasn't likely to do so anytime soon.

"You won't." Emily picked up her own glass of wine. "And that's what you get for having the biggest dining room table." She was back to joking around; she was going to be okay.

"Plus you're a better cook than I am," Mitch said.

April snorted. "I can see that, considering your contribution tonight."

He shrugged again. "Some people are good at cooking. I'm really good at picking up takeout."

"Everyone's good at something," Simon said absently from the other end of the table. He frowned at his laptop before looking up at Mitch. "Speaking of which, how are the acts coming?" Simon was holding down the Faire-planning end of things while Emily took care of the wedding stuff. They were a list-making power couple.

"It's getting there," Mitch said. "There are a few that I still have to confirm, and a good seventy-five percent still have to send in their contracts, but I'm sure it'll work out fine. It always does, right?"

"Well, yes." Simon's frown didn't go away. In fact, the crease between his eyebrows deepened. "But not without effort. You'll be able to stay on top of it, right?"

"Well . . ." Mitch rubbed the back of his neck. "Here's the thing. Baseball season is winding down, but I'm pretty sure we've got a shot at State this year. I've really got to concentrate on my guys right now. I mean, I'll do what I can, but . . ."

Simon sighed. "Okay." His eyes sharpened and he pinched the bridge of his nose; he was thinking hard. "Okay," he said again. "I suppose I can take that part over, so you can . . ."

"No, you can't." Emily's eyes were just as sharp. Bridezilla or not, the closer it got to go time, the more stressed out she'd become.

So I jumped in, to try and diffuse some of her tension. "What about Chris?" As the words came out of my mouth I realized that she should be here. Didn't she help organize Faire every year?

But Simon and Emily shook their heads in tandem. "She's still in Florida," Emily said. "With her mom." She clicked through the calendar app on her phone. "She comes back in June, so she can help with rehearsals at least."

Mitch sucked in a breath. "Yeah, I need someone to take this over before then."

"Okay," Simon said. "I'll see if I can . . ."

"Oh, no, you don't," Emily said. "You have wedding stuff to do. We're meeting with the bakery soon, and we still have a million little things to decide on. Like, you know, what you're wearing."

"I've got a kilt you can borrow," Mitch said cheerfully. Emily snorted, and even Simon cracked a smile.

"No one's checking out my knees at my wedding," he said.

"I'll do it," I said.

Simon raised an eyebrow. "What, check out my knees?"

"They're not that great," Emily tsked. "Sorry, hon. Your strength really lies in your leather pants." She looked thoughtful. "Are you sure you don't want to get married as Captain Blackthorne? My mom would love to see you in that hat."

"No." Simon's voice was stern, but his eyes warmed as he looked at his fiancée. "I'm not getting married dressed as a pirate. That's final."

I couldn't believe this. They'd all completely lost the thread of the conversation. Was this Opposite Day? How was I the only one who cared about Faire right now? "What I meant was, I'll do the entertainment stuff." I looked over at Mitch. "It's just down to confirmation, right?"

"Yep," Mitch said. "Almost everyone's booked, like I said. Once we get the contracts, it's just a matter of confirming rooms for the ones who need them and sending them their confirmations. We have a deal with a couple hotels and split the cost with the performers fifty-fifty. And it's not even that many. Most of these guys camp in RVs. It's just a few that use the hotel."

"I know that," I said. I probably said it a little too quickly, but I was pretty familiar with at least one of the hotels, and at least one of the acts who took advantage of our offer of rooms. A thrill had started taking hold in my chest the moment I'd volunteered for this. It didn't make sense: Dex had nothing to do with contracts and hotel reservations. His cousin Daniel was the one who handled that minutiae. But there was still a part of me that was excited to see the Kilts listed as performers. Confirmation that he was coming back into my life. My real life.

If Mitch noticed my uncharacteristic eagerness, he didn't say. "Yeah, so that's basically it. You think you can handle it?"

I waved a hand. "No problem. Do you have a list of what you're still waiting for?"

"Yep. Here . . ." He pulled his phone out of the pocket of his jeans and sent me a text, judging from the answering beep that came from my phone in my bag hanging on the chair behind me. "That's the password to the email account; just about everything is in there. I've got a spreadsheet with everything else. I'll email that to you tonight."

"That sounds perfect." I wasn't sure why I was so impressed at Mitch being that organized. It was easy to think of him being the fun guy who shoved tequila shots in my direction at Jackson's, but the man coached football in the fall and baseball in the spring. Of course he was organized.

"You sure you don't mind?" Simon's words were careful, but I caught the meaning behind them. He knew, Emily knew, hell, probably Mitch knew, that I wasn't exactly stellar when it came to organization and planning. It was a weakness, and something I wanted to get better at. I was great at big-picture stuff, and I could tell when things were going wrong, but details overwhelmed me. I wasn't great at figuring out what puzzle pieces I needed to make that big picture happen.

But that wasn't the case here. I had the big picture, and Mitch had all the puzzle pieces for me. I just needed to put them together.

"I don't mind," I said. "It'll be fun."

And it was fun, for a little while.

When I got home that night I downloaded Mitch's spreadsheet to my laptop, and created a folder with all the other paperwork he'd sent. I logged on to the Faire's business email account and sent out reminders to the acts that hadn't confirmed. Easy.

A warm thrill went through me when I saw that Dueling Kilts had already confirmed for the summer. Dex. I couldn't wait to see him again, and that time was coming up so soon now.

Over the next couple weeks the last confirmations trickled in, and we had a full complement of acts for the summer. A few signed contracts were still outstanding, but most of them had come via email, so I wasn't too concerned yet. Plenty of time.

When I left work one Friday in early June, there were two notifications on my phone. The first was a text from Mitch, saying that the last two contracts had been mailed to him, and to meet him at Jackson's for happy hour and he'd pass them along. It sounded like a thinly veiled request for a drinking buddy, but what the hell. I didn't have any plans.

The second notification was a short message from Dex, which I waited to read until I got to the bar. I wanted to savor it with my Friday night glass of wine while I waited for Mitch to show up.

To: Stacey Lindholm
From: Dex MacLean
Date: June 5, 4:37 p.m.
Subject: Weekend

A rare weekend off! This hardly ever happens. And what am I doing? Sitting here in a bar on my own. The other guys are off doing their own thing, and I couldn't be bothered tonight. All I can think about is you. Which feels ... strange, don't you think? It's been months since I've seen you, and I'm not even sure that you ...

I'm not going to finish that thought. But I'm not going to delete it either. I'm just going to hit Send. July will be here before we know it.

That all sounded so vague, and almost ominous. I sipped my rosé and took a look around Jackson's. No Mitch yet. I suppressed a sigh and ordered some mozzarella sticks. I never wanted to hear him complain about women taking too long to get ready for anything. I switched from email to text and tapped out a message to Dex.

What a coincidence. I'm alone at a bar myself right now. What do you like to drink when you're drinking alone?

He wrote back right away. **I don't know if I like the thought of you drinking alone. I'm about halfway through a pint of Guinness right now. You?**

I shuddered. **Ugh. That stuff is too thick. You don't drink it, you chew it. No, thank you.**

Ha, he replied, **dark beer is definitely not something you chug. But it's my thing. Every new town, as soon as I check into the hotel, I head for the nearest bar and order the darkest beer they have. Usually it's a Guinness and that's fine, but sometimes I get surprised by a craft stout. Not so much refreshing as comforting. Really nice after a long drive. I sip it really slowly and center my brain, focusing on the shows ahead.**

No shows this weekend, I texted back. **What are you focusing on now?**

The future.

I frowned. That was a vague reply. But before I could ask for clarification he changed the subject. **But you didn't answer my question. What are you drinking there, alone?**

My mozzarella sticks arrived, and I took another sip of wine. Still no Mitch. **Rosé, I responded. That's *my* thing, I guess. Part of the whole basic white girl aesthetic that I embrace. Can't help it. I'm a blonde. I love mimosas, Pumpkin Spice Lattes, and my rose-gold iPhone. But I have some standards: no UGG boots and I'm terrible at yoga.**

His answer came quickly. **There are a lot of words I'd use to describe you. Basic isn't one of them.**

"Hey, there you are."

I started at the sound of Mitch's voice and almost dropped my phone onto the bar. "Here I am," I said back, a little irritated. "Hiding from you right here at the bar ten feet from the front door."

"Funny." Mitch took one of my mozzarella sticks and ordered a beer before sliding a folder with the contracts in my direction. "Who you texting? Big date tonight?"

I snorted as I tucked the folder and my phone into my bag. "Hardly. The hottest date I've had lately is the battery-powered one I have waiting for me at home." Of all my friends, Mitch would appreciate a vibrator joke the most.

I was right. He laughed out loud and slapped the bar with the flat of his hand. "Nice!"

His appreciation of the joke made me smile. Same old Mitch. He was another one who'd never left town, just like me. But unlike me, I wasn't sure that he'd ever tried. I watched him polish off the other half of the purloined mozzarella stick and take a swig of beer before I spoke again. "Mitch," I asked, "do you ever wish you'd left home?" I wasn't sure where this change in subject had come from, but texting with Dex always made me feel a little wistful. A little lonely. A little stuck. Was I the only townie who regretted staying behind?

His expression turned thoughtful, an odd look for him. "Not really," he finally said. "I never really thought about it, if you want to know the truth. I like it here, my family's here, and I've got a pretty good thing going. Other people are destined for bigger things in bigger cities. But not me. Besides . . ." He shrugged. "If I weren't here, who'd get the baseball team to State? Simon?"

I scoffed and reached for my wineglass. "Yeah, that would be a no."

"Exactly. I'm needed here." His tone was that of a world-weary general who couldn't desert his troops. He peered at me over his pint glass. "I always thought you'd get out of here though."

"You did?" I had no idea that Mitch had ever given me more than a trivial amount of thought.

"Yeah. I remember you in school. You were pretty driven." His lips curved up in a nostalgic smile. "Cute too."

Hello. "Now you tell me!" I put my glass down. I couldn't believe this. "I had the biggest crush on you in high school, you know. Well, I'm sure you do know. Most girls did, right? You were the football hero."

Mitch tried to look modest, but he failed miserably. Just like when we were kids, he was born to preen. "Well, someone had to take over for Sean Graham once he graduated. I still can't believe that Simon wasn't an athlete like his brother, you know? What a waste."

"Simon ran track," I protested.

Mitch scoffed. "Simon read books. Nerd."

I rolled my eyes with a smile. "Whatever."

He rolled his eyes back. "I almost asked you out a couple times senior year, you know."

"What?" My jaw sagged. "You've got to be kidding me. I was way younger than you!"

"Well, yeah. That's one reason why I didn't. But you'd also just made varsity and wore that cute little cheerleading skirt on game days, so I was conflicted. I mean, sure, you were just a sopho-more, but your legs, man . . ." He gave a wolf whistle that made me tingle with embarrassed pride and brought our bartender over so we could order another round.

"I can't believe you're just telling me this now," I grumbled as I crunched down on another mozzarella stick. "High school would have been a lot more fun."

"Tell me about it." Mitch's sigh was belabored as he took my last mozzarella stick. "We would have absolutely rocked prom."

I stole an appraising glance at him as we got our second round of drinks, and I reached deep inside for the high school girl that I knew still lived inside me. That girl who would have shanked someone for five seconds of attention from Mitch Malone. But she lay dormant now, and any wild crush on Mitch had been replaced with affection. Once I'd gotten to know him, the real Mitch that lay beneath the gorgeous exterior, he'd become more like a big brother, a good friend, and wasn't that better in the long run anyway?

When it was time to go and we settled our tabs, it struck me that the way I felt about Mitch was a lot like how I felt about Dex. While I certainly appreciated the outer package and had nothing to complain about there, it was that inner layer, the one he'd been showing me in his emails and texts, that really inter-ested me. These past summers, it had been that Hemsworth-like body and nothing else. But I'd learned so much about him over the last few months that I realized it was his words I was attracted to now, and who he was inside. His Hemsworthiness didn't matter to me anymore.

That was . . . That was a revelation. He was states away—I actually wasn't sure what state he was in at the moment—but I needed to let him know. But not via text. Not from a bar. I had to get to my laptop. I couldn't tap all this out on my phone.

Eleven

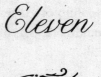

To: Dex MacLean

From: Stacey Lindholm

Date: June 5, 9:47 p.m.

Subject: Revelation (no, not the Bible)

I realized something tonight. I realized that I'm in deep
with you. I guess that should be obvious, considering
how much I look forward to every email and text. But
that's what I'm trying to say here. It's your words. Parts of me
have forgotten your touch, your face. But it doesn't
matter at all. It's you that I miss. You've shared so
much of yourself with me through these messages that
what you look like doesn't even enter into the equation
anymore.

Is that strange? I know you're proud of the way you look.
And you absolutely should be—don't get me wrong. But it's
just . . . that doesn't matter to me anymore.

And now that I've typed this all out, it doesn't seem like as much of a Deep Thought as it felt like it was in my head. Hopefully you know what I mean.

To: Stacey Lindholm
From: Dex MacLean
Date: June 6, 1:13 a.m.
Subject: Re: Revelation (no, not the Bible)

I do know what you mean. And it's a much deeper thought than you realize.

Anastasia, there are things I need to say to you. Things I need to say in person. Words on a screen aren't good enough. Even Skyping with you wouldn't be enough. I need to see your face. Be in the same room with you, breathe the same air. Maybe even touch your hand, if you'll allow it after you hear what I have to say.

I'm going to be completely honest, it's a conversation I'm a little afraid to have. But it's necessary. Our stop at Willow Creek can't come soon enough. At the same time, I don't want this to end. Our emails. Our texts. Getting to know you this way feels so much more honest than through the masks we wear on a day-to-day basis. That seems counterintuitive, doesn't it? Face-to-face communication should be more honest, while we can hide behind words on the internet. But here we are.

Dex's email woke me up more than the mug of coffee in front of me that next morning. *Things I need to say to you . . .* His words squeezed my heart, and I couldn't take a good deep breath. What did he need to say, and why he was afraid to say it? Now I was afraid too.

But I didn't have time to think about it the way I wanted to. It was Saturday morning. A Faire rehearsal morning. Chris had returned from Florida and was here to wrangle the kids, but she'd asked that I come and help out. It wasn't my usual gig—I'd been a tavern wench for years now—but it was nice to be helpful in another way. So off I went.

Taking over Faire planning for Mitch turned out to be a lot of work, but it was work that I was good at. I spent most evenings after work behind my laptop at my little kitchen table. Now that I'd been emailing with Dex for so long and knew some of the ins and outs of the lives of the traveling performers, I knew that our accommodations were some of the best they got on the circuit. I considered bringing it up with Simon; surely he'd like to know if there was a way that we could be saving money on running things. But Dex had spoken of staying in campgrounds when hotels weren't available or affordable, and Willow Creek didn't have anything like a campground anywhere nearby. So hotel rooms it was.

Organizing the rooms was a complex affair. First, I figured out how many rooms each act needed, then I worked to Tetris everyone into the blocks of rooms at each hotel. Once that was done, I logged into the Faire's email account and started sending emails to the managers of each act with confirmation numbers and directions. Mitch had never signed any of the emails since it was just from a generic business account, so I didn't bother letting anyone know that the person handling things had changed. It wasn't likely they'd care; we were all part of the Faire's organizational committee. I did add a note to all the confirmations, letting them know that Simon and Emily's wedding would be the second weekend of Faire, and anyone who was performing that weekend was welcome to join the festivities. Most of these people had been working with Simon and this Faire since the beginning, and I figured they would want to know.

Simon checked in on my progress a few times when I'd first taken over, but once he saw that I had it all under control he was able to let go and let me handle it. And not a moment too soon; Emily basically swooped in and took him away to finalize their wedding plans. He had enough to do without needing to micro-manage me. And from Simon, there was no higher compliment than not needing to be micromanaged. That made me feel good. I was doing something right.

Meanwhile, Mitch's baseball team did indeed make it to State, which he told us all in a badly spelled group text that appeared to have been sent after more than one beer. But what the hell. He and his boys had worked hard for that victory, and he deserved a chance to savor it. April's congratulatory response corrected his misspellings. His reply was a middle finger emoji.

When school let out later in June, Mitch's time freed up, but Emily and Simon's was nonexistent. Mitch offered to take the booking assignments back from me, but I was almost done with them, so he went back to planning a bachelor party for Simon. I didn't want to imagine the kind of shenanigans that would pass for a bachelor party in Mitch's mind, so I did my best to not think about that at all.

By early July, the summer progressed from pleasantly warm to oh-my-God-it's-hot, just in time to go to the Faire site and help with the main prep. We spent two weekends placing benches and painting sets.

"Okay, this is what I don't understand." Emily opened the cans of paint while I taped out lines on the wooden information booth in the shape of a Tudor-style thatched cottage. "We painted a bunch of stuff last year. And the year before that. Why are there new things to build and paint every year?"

I stepped back and checked my handiwork. The wide masking tape was in a Y-shape. Last weekend, we'd painted this booth dark brown. Today, we'd paint the booth with a textured paint to look like stucco with the tape marks on; then once the paint dried we could take off the tape, and the darker color underneath would look like the timbers of a Tudor-style house. We'd get a couple kids to climb ladders and paint the roof to look like a thatched cottage. Easy. At least, easy when you've been doing stuff like this for a decade or so.

Satisfied with how the tape looked, I turned my attention to Emily's question. "It's all about what needs to be refreshed. I think the booth we used last year was from when we'd first started. We reuse the benches every year, but some of them get broken during each Faire, so they have to be replaced."

"Yeah, but the stages . . . we have to rebuild the stages every year too." She stirred the paint while she thought. "But I guess they would look pretty crappy if they were left out all winter."

I nodded. "Weather isn't kind to wood."

"There should be a better way, though. I'll talk to Simon about it." She handed me a paint roller, and we got started on the first coat of primer. It would dry fast in this heat, and we would be able to get the cream-colored faux stucco done by the end of the day.

I had to laugh at her. "Don't you and Simon have enough going on right now without worrying about that?"

"Well . . ." She stretched up on her toes but still couldn't reach the top of the booth. I wasn't much taller than she was; we were definitely going to need to grab some assistants. Tall ones. "Yeah," she finally admitted. "I guess we have enough on our plate right now."

"Mmm-hmm." I refrained from an I-told-you-so and we painted in silence for a few minutes. "Anything you want to talk about?" I finally asked. "Wedding-wise?"

"No." Her denial was tentative. I didn't push her in the lie. Instead I concentrated on coating the roller with more paint and attacking the next wall. We were good enough friends by now that she knew she could confide in me. But we were also good enough friends that I knew she talked about things when she was ready.

I didn't have to wait long. "It's getting away from me." Her voice was quiet. "Between work, and Faire, and the wedding . . ." She sighed. I raised my eyebrows in response but didn't speak; she wasn't done yet. "It's too much," she finally said. "I don't know how it's all going to happen, and Simon isn't any help. He—"

"Okay," I said. "Take a breath." I stretched on my toes and rolled paint as far as I could reach. "You know how Simon is about Faire. It takes over his life this time of year, right?" I didn't look over at her to see her nod; I knew she was doing it. Faire wasn't Simon's true love the way it had been before Emily had come into his life, but it was still an all-consuming project. And all the help in the world, from Emily and Mitch and me, wasn't going to change that. Simon was a make-lists-in-his-sleep kind of guy, and he always had been. I knew that. Emily knew that. At least I hoped she did, since she was about to marry the guy.

"Of course." Her voice was shaky, but her nod was firm. "And I'm fine with that. There's just a lot still to finish up. Lots of little things, you know? And April's busy, so . . ."

"You have another bridesmaid, you know." I pointed exaggeratedly at myself, slopping a little paint on my tank top as I did. Thank goodness I'd worn old clothes today.

"Yes. I do know that." She threw me a side-eye, and I felt a little surge of triumph. She wasn't freaking out anymore; she was back to her snarky self. "But I also know that you've been busy, doing all that stuff for Mitch."

I waved a hand. "I'm just about done with that. A few more emails to send tonight; that's it. So lay it on me. What do you need?"

"It's mostly just little stuff." She started rolling paint on the booth again, her mind back on our task. "I haven't looked at the seating chart since the last RSVPs came in, so I need to make sure everyone's accounted for. Stuff like that."

"So you're really doing a seating chart?" I kept my voice as neutral as possible. I wasn't criticizing. I was observing. "Even though we're going to be out in the woods?"

"There are still going to be tables," she said. "And people want to know where to sit, believe me. I went to this wedding once where they wanted it to be all casual. 'Sit wherever you want,' they said. Well, it was chaos." She shook her head. "Simon hates chaos."

Emily hated chaos too, but I wasn't going to say it. "Give it to me," I said. "Is it on paper or spreadsheets?"

"Paper." She sighed. "I should have done a spreadsheet; it would have been easier. But it's too late now."

"No kidding," I said, not really sure which of her statements I was agreeing to. Both, really. I'd become a bit of an expert on spreadsheets since I'd been helping Mitch coordinate everything for Faire. "But either way, it doesn't matter. You want me to look at them for you?"

"God, yes," she said. "That would be fantastic. Do you think you could come over tomorrow to pick them up? I can't even look at them anymore."

"Of course." As we finished up the painting, I thought that no one was going to be happier to see the back end of this wedding than Emily. Just so she wouldn't have to think about it 24/7 anymore. The girl liked to plan things, but this was getting ridiculous.

Later that afternoon, Emily and I parted ways in the grassy lot in front of the Faire grounds, with plans for me to go to her place in the morning for coffee and to pick up the seating charts. She already looked happier; the furrow between her brows had smoothed out, and while her smile was still tired, it was genuine. "Thanks, Stacey." She paused with the driver's side door of her Jeep open. "I know this isn't exactly your thing."

"Helping out friends has always been my thing." I tried to not sound defensive. Everyone in town, Emily included, seemed to think that I was a ditz. And maybe I encouraged that reputation, with the blonde dye job and the propensity to hit happy hour. I could have changed people's perceptions if I'd put my mind to it. But then again, maybe I couldn't. Maybe I was doomed to be the basic white girl in everyone's lives.

Oh, well. It could certainly be worse.

Once home, I took a long, hot shower to scrub off the last traces of woods and paint. Faire opened next weekend, and while Simon was rounding up a few of the older kids to finish up painting and other final details tomorrow, my workdays out in the woods were over. Until it was time to wear a corset, of course. My hair was still wet as I settled onto the couch with my laptop and my cat. Benedick kneaded my thigh as I logged into the

Faire's email address, wishing I were wearing body armor instead of yoga pants. I needed to trim his claws.

"Spa day for you soon, buddy." I dropped a kiss on his head and gave his chin a scritch as the email page loaded. Several new emails, mostly confirming my confirmation, and I wondered if I should respond to them. Confirming their confirmation of my confirmation? It could be a never-ending circle if I wasn't careful. So instead I opened each email and logged the responses carefully on the spreadsheet, in the final column. Later tonight I'd send the completed spreadsheet to Simon, and the last i's would be dotted and t's crossed. Just in time. That would make him happy.

Most everyone acknowledged the upcoming wedding, which was nice. Simon and Emily met at Faire, they fought at Faire, and they fell in love at Faire. Getting married at Faire and celebrating with so many people who loved them was exactly what they deserved. So each email expressing excitement at the wedding made me smile a little wider.

Until.

The last email was from Daniel MacLean, confirming the reservations I'd made for the Dueling Kilts. Two rooms, and the rest would camp in their RV.

"Daniel." A smile crept up my face as I said his name aloud. After all these months of getting closer to Dex, I felt that I was part of this group in a weird way. Part of the family. Which was why the final paragraph of Daniel's email stopped my breath.

Congratulations to Simon and Emily! This must be the year for weddings. My old college roommate got married a couple weeks ago in late June. Looking forward to

celebrating with all of you when we head back in your
direction.

I'd read those words before, and they'd made me smile. Now
my smile was quashed, my pulse sped up, and a tingle spread
across the back of my neck, sending gooseflesh down my arms.
I picked up my phone from the coffee table and scrolled back to
the day I'd been trying on wedding dresses. It took a while; Dex
and I texted a lot. But there it was. . . . *Must be the year for weddings . . .
old college roommate . . . married in June . . . head back in your direction.*

There were only two scenarios here that would explain what
I had just read. One: Dex and Daniel MacLean were cousins. So
it was possible that they used similar syntax, especially in writing. It was also possible, but a little less likely, that they both had
an old college roommate getting married in June.

Or.

Or.

No.

My eyes flicked back to my laptop, to the email from Daniel
that was still up. To the signature that was appended to the end,
that included his cell phone number. By now I couldn't breathe;
my hands shook as I fumbled with my phone, tapping the little
icon that brought up the details of Dex's contact info. His email
address, which I'd entered into my laptop as "Dex MacLean,"
that we'd been communicating through all this time. His
cell phone number, which showed up as Dex on my phone . . .
because I'd put it in there that way. My eyes went back and forth,
from laptop to phone, and there was no denying it. The number
was the same.

All these months, when I'd been texting, emailing, and falling in love with Dex MacLean, the man on the other side of the screen was his cousin. Daniel.

What.

The.

Fuck.

What the fuck.

I wasn't one for the F-bomb usually, but as I paced around my tiny apartment, those three words kept echoing in my head, in time with my footfalls.

What.

The.

Fuck.

It only got worse when my phone chimed with a text an hour later. A text from Dex . . . or Daniel. Or whoever the hell. Of course: it was about this time every night that his day ended and he texted me to say hello. I cleared the notification from my screen without reading the text, and then I did the unthinkable. I powered my phone off and tossed it onto my bed.

"Fuck you," I snarled at the phone. Or possibly at Daniel Mac-Lean. It was so hard to tell. Benedick darted under the couch at the sound of my voice, and who could blame him. I wanted to hide from my own anger. Tears stung my eyes, and it was hard to draw a good deep breath. "Fuck you!" Now that I'd gotten a taste for the word, I couldn't stop saying it. I wanted to scream it until my throat was raw.

So much for a relaxing night in. I was too angry to sleep, and too keyed up to do anything relaxing. After the third lap of my small apartment, pacing off my nervous energy, I stopped to straighten up my little bookcase. Then I cleared the clutter off my kitchen table. A couple laps later I dug out the broom and dustpan. By one in the morning my place sparkled, and I'd exhausted myself. Just as I fell facedown into bed, sinking into sleep, I remembered I'd told Emily I'd drop by her place for that wedding stuff. Ugh. I fumbled in the blankets for my phone and turned it on.

More texts from Liar MacLean:

Hope you're having a great . . .

In a few days we'll be on the road to Maryland. I think . . .

Wow, you must be busy this Saturday night. Usually you . . .

Stacey, is everything okay? Text me back when you . . .

Nope, nope, nope, and nope.

I cleared all the notifications with stabby fingers, leaving the texts unread. Then I set my alarm and pulled the covers over my head. I'd talk to Emily about all this tomorrow, I thought, as everything faded around the edges again and sleep crept in. Maybe some good old-fashioned girl talk could help me solve this.

If I got any more text notifications that night, I slept through them. Which was what they deserved.

In retrospect, I probably got to Emily's place a little earlier than I should have the next morning. But I'd bolted awake around six, unable to get back to sleep. I'd been dressed and ready to go soon after sunrise, and she'd never actually specified a time. It wasn't until I pounded on her door and she opened it wearing her bath-robe and a blinking, sleepy expression that it hit me. A little af-ter eight on a Sunday morning was too early to show up with my laptop and anger in tow.

But because she was the Best Friend Ever, she didn't slam the door in my face. Instead she opened the door wide. "Coffee?"

"Yes, please." As I stepped inside, the scent of freshly brewed coffee hit me, so at least I hadn't gotten her out of bed with my early morning visit. Emily's place wasn't much bigger than mine, though it was a real honest-to-God apartment, and not a studio space over a garage. As she bustled in the kitchen with coffee mugs and creamer and whatever else, I plonked my laptop on her dining table and woke it up.

"Here." Emily passed a mug across the table to me. "Have you even had breakfast yet? Let me drink this and I'll get those seat-ing charts for you . . ." Her voice trailed off as she took in my laptop and my thunderous expression. "What's up? You're not just here for the seating charts, are you?"

"Look at this." I turned the laptop around so the screen faced her.

Emily squinted at the screen and took a sip of coffee. "What am I looking at, exactly?"

"This email." I tapped my fingernail on the screen in empha-sis. "Look."

"What, the one from Daniel MacLean?" She tilted her head and read it over again, while I was pretty sure steam was coming out of my ears. "Oh, he's looking forward to coming to the wed-ding. That's so nice of him to say so. I've always liked—"

"What about Daniel MacLean?" Simon emerged from the bedroom, and I tried not to do a double take. It hadn't even oc-curred to me that he'd be here, but they were engaged. Of course they'd have sleepovers. I'd never seen Simon first thing in the morning, and I'd certainly never seen him this rumpled, in sleep pants and a stretched-out T-shirt. He ran a hand through his hair, settling it, but he still looked roguish; with a week before Faire opened, his pirate beard and hairstyle were in full effect. But the concerned look he shot our way was less carefree pirate and more worried Faire organizer. "Is something wrong with the Kilts?"

Emily shook her head. "They're confirmed, at least according to this email. But I'm obviously missing something." She looked up at me quizzically. "What am I missing, Stace?"

"Okay, you read that email. Now look at this." I took the laptop back and hit a few keys, bringing up a screenshot of Dex's text message—the one about his roommate's wedding—before flipping it back in her direction.

"Huh. Well, that's weird. That text pretty much says the same thing."

"Exactly. And this phone number"—I handed her my phone, with Dex/Daniel's contact screen showing—"matches this phone number." I alt-tabbed back to the email, with Daniel's electronic signature. "So they were written by the same guy, wouldn't you say?" My voice was judge, jury, and executioner.

"Oh, yeah, definitely. But why are you texting with Daniel MacLean? I didn't realize you knew him that well."

"And why would he tell you the same thing twice?" Simon frowned and leaned against the archway leading to the kitchen. "He's not forgetful like that."

She looked down at her mug. "This isn't decaf, is it? Because I don't think it's working."

"Because . . ." And now I saw the problem with keeping this whole thing with Dex a secret. It was going to take forever to bring Emily up to speed on why I was so pissed off. I sighed. "Okay. Remember last summer? You asked me about . . ." Emotion overwhelmed me for a moment, and I had to clear my throat. This was harder than I thought it would be. "You asked me who I'd been seeing? The mystery guy?"

"Ohhhhhh." Emily's eyes lit up at the promise of early morning gossip. "Why, yes. I do remember that." Emily rested her chin on her hands, settling in for my story.

"I don't think you need me for this." Simon threw up defensive hands and went into the kitchen in search of coffee. I gave him a thin smile of appreciation that he didn't see, then I turned back to Emily and, for the first time, spilled the whole story. Of being so lonely I couldn't handle it anymore. Of drinking one glass of wine too many and sending that first message to Dex. His response. Our emails. Texts. And realizing last night that it had all been a lie.

"So . . ." While I'd been talking Emily refilled our coffee mugs, and now she sat down again, staring hard at my laptop. "All this time you thought it was Dex, but it was Daniel writing to you instead?"

"Exactly." I nodded emphatically.

"Are you kidding me?" I jumped at Simon's voice, harsher, angrier than I was used to hearing. He was back, leaning against the archway again, his own mug of coffee in his hands. "What kind of *Cyrano de Bergerac* bullshit is that?"

Emily clucked her tongue and turned in her chair. "I don't know about that," she said.

"Of course it is!" He gestured to my laptop. "Look, I've known the Dueling Kilts for years. They've played the Faire since . . . well, I think since the first year we started hiring outside acts. And they're great guys. But there's no way that Dex MacLean could string together a coherent sentence, much less an elaborate email."

"Hey." I felt a lick of defensive anger for the hottie I'd hooked up with. But then I thought about it and, well, Simon wasn't wrong. Hadn't I thought something similar when I'd first started hearing from Dex? Daniel? Who-the-hell-ever? "Okay, yeah," I said. "That's fair."

Simon's smile wasn't unkind as he finished his point. "Which means he got Daniel to write those emails for him. And that's classic Cyrano."

"Yeah, but what about the texts?" Emily picked up my phone and waved it at him. "Daniel was using his own phone number. You think Dex was standing over his shoulder, telling him what to say?"

"He could have been."

"I don't think so. Besides, in the original play, Cyrano and Christian were both in love with Roxane, but Cyrano sacrificed his chance to be with her because he thought she loved Christian more. But we don't know if that's the case here. Maybe Daniel . . ."

"What the hell is wrong with you two?" I closed my laptop with a snap and took my phone back from Emily. "You're both nerds, you know that? In this century we don't go straight for a Cyrano reference. We call it catfishing."

Simon snorted, and Emily bit down on her bottom lip, but amusement danced in her eyes. "Well, yeah. That's true. But Simon does have a point."

"Of course I do." He blew across the top of his mug before taking a sip.

I narrowed my eyes at him. "Don't you have sets to finish painting?"

His eyes flew up to the clock on the microwave. "Shit." He set down the mug and headed back to the bedroom.

"You're fine!" Emily called after him. "You don't have to be there for a half hour at least." Then she turned back to me, continuing as though we hadn't been interrupted. "I guess it could be a Cyrano situation if it happened the way Simon suggested. If Dex enlisted Daniel to be his mouthpiece, and if Daniel is also interested in you. Do you think he is?"

"I don't . . . I don't know." All these months I'd been thinking about Dex, but now I let myself remember his cousin. Daniel, long and lean, those bright green eyes, his red hair caught back in that black baseball cap he always wore backward. Calm and steady where Dex was brash and bold. He'd always sought me out to say hi during Faire. He noticed when I got a new necklace. He wanted to make sure Dex wasn't breaking my heart. Now that I thought about it, thought about Daniel, his personality matched our communications better than Dex's ever did. How could I have missed it? But then again, how could I have known that my previous interactions with Daniel had led to the kinds of feelings he'd expressed over the past few months, those words I'd taken into my heart as I read them snuggled in bed under the fairy lights?

"But if he isn't into you, maybe he was just helping Dex express how he really felt?" Emily drummed her fingernails against the side of her mug while she thought. "So the real question is, whose heart is in the words you've been getting? No." She snapped her fingers. "Which one do you want it to be? That's the real question. Because then you'll know what to do when you find out which one it really is."

"Yeah." I sighed and let my head drop onto the table. The more I talked about it, the worse I felt. Who did I want to be behind the words?

"Should I call Daniel?" I looked up to see Simon coming out of the bedroom again, dressed in old clothes suitable for painting and carrying a pair of battered running shoes.

"What?" The thought horrified me. "No. Why?"

He sat down on the couch and started putting his shoes on. "We can revoke their contract. Tell him we don't need them this year. I don't like that they were jerking you around like that." His voice was casual, but the way he kept his eyes down, focused hard on his shoelaces, told me what a hard thing this was for him to offer. This Faire was one of the most important things in Simon's life, and the Dueling Kilts was a long-term act. Firing them for no reason wouldn't go over well; word traveled fast on the Faire circuit. But Simon was willing to risk our Faire's reputation for the sake of standing up to someone who had broken my heart. I'd known Simon for most of my life, and he'd always been a friend, but it wasn't until this moment that I realized just how good a friend he was.

"No," I said. My heart wasn't broken. It was just a little bruised. I wasn't down for the count yet. "It's okay." I took my laptop back and snapped it closed. "I can handle this."

"You sure?" Emily raised her eyebrows.

"Yep. I have a plan."

Having a plan, I soon realized, and implementing said plan were two different things. I didn't want to tip my hand too early, so once I got home from Emily's I sent Dex—Daniel, whoever—a quick text. **Sorry. Faire prep in overdrive around here, so I'm crazy busy. Talk to you soon!** I even included a smiley-face emoji so he wouldn't get suspicious. His answer came back relatively quickly—**I can only imagine! Hope they're not overworking you!**—and was easy enough to respond to with a couple happy-looking emojis without saying too much.

I couldn't put my plan into action until Friday, when Faire was about to begin, so I had to spend the week going about my life as though nothing had happened. I wasn't sure how long I could stay neutrally pleasant when Dex—Daniel?—emailed or texted, but he made it easy on me by going dark most of the week. I got a couple good morning/good night texts, and I responded so he wouldn't suspect that my perspective on his messages had changed, but other than that I didn't hear much from him.

That, to me, was a tick in the "It's Definitely Daniel" column. Dex wouldn't have anything to hide. In fact, he'd be looking forward to seeing me again with this new, richer relationship. Daniel, however, would most likely be filled with anxiety, knowing that the jig was about to be up.

But what jig? Wasn't that the question, as Emily had said? Now that I was all but assured that Daniel was the one on the other side of the screen, I still didn't know why.

The week seemed to take about a thousand years. Emily and I exchanged a lot of texts that week too. She offered more than once to help me face the MacLeans to figure all this out, and while the show of support warmed my heart, I ultimately told her that I needed to do this alone. This whole thing was so bizarre, and had the potential for so much humiliation, that I wasn't sure if I'd be able to go through with confronting anyone if I had an audience.

Okay, if you're sure, she'd finally texted on Thursday night. **But you need to tell me EVERYTHING Saturday morning!**

I promise, I responded. Wouldn't that be a fun way to kick off Faire season? But she meant well, and there was the very real danger of me needing a shoulder to cry on.

Thursday night my tavern wench costume came out of its trunk and I hung it over the front of my wardrobe. All my accessories were together—I'd put them all away at the end of last summer, where else would they be? I'd gotten a new pair of boots a few weeks ago, and I'd worn them enough that they were broken in and comfortable. (I'd made the mistake once of wearing a brand-new pair of shoes the first day of Faire. When I spent that first night putting Band-Aids on all of my blisters, I vowed to never do that again.)

The last thing I did was get my dragonfly necklace out of my jewelry box. I looked from its sparkly crystal eyes to my wench's costume and frowned. Simon had been right—the two really didn't match. Emily and I had talked about getting new costumes, and she'd even pinged me to look at a few contenders on our shared Pinterest board sometime in the spring. With everything else going on, it hadn't been a top priority for either one of us, but rather something we'd get to when we had time. And then we'd run out of time, and here I was with the same costume as always.

"So much for change." But I tucked the dragonfly into my belt pouch anyway, along with the hair ties and pins for my hair. Let Simon complain about it once I put it on. I didn't care.

One of the best things about work was that the office closed at noon on Fridays in the summer, but that Friday even those few hours crawled by at an excruciating pace. But then finally, finally, it was time to clock out, and I could get ready. At home, I switched my office scrubs for a soft pink sundress and kitten-heeled sandals and took extra care with my hair, styling it so it fell in soft waves around my shoulders. I stepped back and looked at myself in the full-length mirror and nodded solemnly. I looked good, and that was important for this plan. My phone chimed with a text, and my pulse spiked as I looked down at it. But I'd been expecting this text. It was time. I scooped up Benedick and gave him a kiss before I left. I needed luck to pull this off.

My hands shook on the steering wheel, and I took a few calming breaths when I reached the parking lot of the hotel. I slicked on my favorite pink lip gloss and checked my hair one more time in the rearview mirror before I got out of the car. My heels clicked on the pavement, then on the tiles of the lobby, and those clicks sounded like the stride of a powerful woman, which gave me confidence. I needed confidence right now.

I walked toward the check-in desk and waved at Julian, who was on the evening shift. He took his cell phone out of his pocket and waved it at me in a salute. There was that everyone-knowing-everyone advantage to living in a small town again. Julian and I had been in every class together since preschool, and I'd long since forgiven him for putting glue in my hair in the first grade. And now he'd grown up and gotten married, and he and his husband had stayed here in Willow Creek, where Julian worked at the hotel. He was our point of contact for the block of rooms we got here for the Faire performers, so we'd been emailing back and forth a lot lately.

He also knew when the performers had arrived and checked in to the hotel. So he could text me and let me know. And then I could come over here. That had been the first part of the plan.

The second part of the plan was waiting in the lobby, leaning on the check-in desk, scrolling through his phone. Black jeans, black T-shirt, black baseball cap covering a shock of red hair. My heels clicked their way toward Daniel, and my heart thudded harder with each step.

He looked up as I approached, and the molecules inside my body shifted when his eyes met mine. Part two of this plan was getting Daniel to admit that he'd been the one writing to me all this time, and that he wasn't doing it as some kind of mouthpiece for Dex. Until this moment I hadn't been sure how I'd wanted this conversation to go. Somewhere, down in the deepest part of my primitive lizard brain, I'd known that it hadn't been Dex that I'd been getting to know all these months, and even more importantly, I hadn't wanted it to be.

I wanted it to be Daniel.

But one step at a time.

"Stacey, hey." Daniel's voice was light, casual, and it gave me pause. This wasn't the attitude of someone who knew that he was caught.

"Hi, Daniel." My voice matched his for casualness, and I have myself a mental high-five. "What are you hanging out in the lobby for?"

"Oh. Some kind of mix-up with the rooms. The guy said he was working on it." He glanced down at his phone, then over at Julian, who busied himself at his monitor, pointedly not looking at us.

"Hmmm." I nodded, as though I hadn't orchestrated the whole thing. "That's weird." It wasn't weird. Julian was stalling Daniel, just as I'd asked him to. "But I'm glad to see you. I've been wanting to talk to you."

"To me?" His eyes lit up with interest as he stowed his phone in his back pocket. He was still acting way too casual, and I wanted more than anything to trip him up.

"Sure," I said. "After all these months, you know. All those emails, all the things we've said to each other. It's nice to finally see you face to face."

"Me? No." There was a glimmer of something in his eyes, but he blinked it away fast. He was good. But he couldn't hide the flush that crept up the back of his neck, which I saw as he turned his head to the side, away from me, to study the terrible artwork on the far wall. "No," he said again. "You mean Dex."

"Do I?" My eyes narrowed as I studied him. Even though I was confronting him with the truth, he was still denying it. He still wanted to nudge me toward his cousin. Was he just Dex's mouthpiece after all?

"Well, yeah. You've been . . ." He glanced up at the ceiling now, and he swallowed hard. The casualness was gone from his expression, and he was starting to struggle. "You've been communicating with Dex. At least, that's what he . . ."

"You know what, you're right." I shook my head with a hollow chuckle. "Silly me. Do you know where he . . . Never mind." I dug in my bag now for my phone. "I have his number. I can just call him."

"No!" Daniel took a step toward me, his hands raised, his eyes wide, and I knew I had him. Better yet, he knew I had him. But he still tried to keep up the pretense. "No, don't. I . . . uh, I think he's driving. You should probably . . ."

"Oh, I'm sure it's fine. Let me just . . ." I pulled up my contacts and hit the green button next to Dex's name. That green button I'd never had the nerve to hit, all these months. Then I watched the blood drain from Daniel's face as his back pocket began to ring.

I raised an eyebrow. "Well? Aren't you going to answer it?"

He pressed his lips together hard before making a sigh of defeat. Then he pulled his phone out of his back pocket, still ringing, my name on the display. He hit the red button on his phone at the same time I did on mine.

"I think we need to talk." All the playfulness was gone from my voice, and he nodded.

"I think we should." His voice was hushed, defeated.

"Why don't you finish checking in," I said. I glanced over at Julian, who winked at me and brandished a key card like it was a winning ace. "I think everything's straightened out now. I'll be in the bar; you can meet me there."

"Okay." Daniel had the look of someone who realized he'd been set up, but knew that he didn't have the right to complain. "Yeah. I'm gonna need a beer."

· · ·

The hotel wasn't anything fancy: one of those low-budget chain affairs, but it had a little restaurant connected to it. Not even a restaurant: more of a glorified bar with a burgers-and-sandwiches menu, but the important thing was that it had Guinness on tap. That was part three of the plan.

The clicking of my heels faded into the general noise of the bar, and I settled myself on a stool where I had a good view of the entrance. I ordered a glass of rosé for me and a pint of Guinness for him. And then I waited. Now that I knew that Daniel was the man on the other end of the phone, I knew his drink order. He'd told me weeks ago. He hadn't been referring to this particular night, and he'd been making me believe he was someone else, but I knew his plans. I knew his routines. I knew him.

I just wasn't a hundred percent certain who he actually was, or how much of what he told me was the real him. So the Guinness was a test.

It didn't take him long; I was only a few sips into my wine before he walked through the door, and I sucked in a breath. I'd been so busy analyzing his expression in the lobby, looking for truth in his eyes, that I hadn't really looked at him.

I did now.

He looked tired. Which, of course, made sense because he'd probably been driving the better part of the day, and all of our drama aside, his mind was probably on the first day of Faire tomorrow. His face was pale, made paler by that uniform of black T-shirt and black jeans he always wore, and there was the shadow of a couple days' stubble on his cheeks. He was so different from his cousin, the kind of guy who spent quality time in the gym counting reps. There was nothing about Daniel that was showy, except maybe his hair. His build spoke of subtle, lean strength born from years of hauling around equipment and living on the road. Arms that didn't advertise their muscles, but they would be there when needed. The kind of guy who could catch me if I fell.

The more I looked at him, the more I remembered all the words we'd shared over the months. And the more I fell.

I really, really hoped he would be there to catch me.

He'd taken off the baseball cap, and his red-gold hair hung low over his brow. He shook it out of his eyes, scanning the bar for an empty seat, and since I was watching him, I saw the moment when he found me. I waved, my fingers wiggling in his direction, and while a smile played around his lips, his expression was wary as he approached, his long legs eating up the distance between us in a few strides. What kind of recalibration was his brain making? Was he mentally cataloging our emails, working on getting his story straight? Was the Guinness thing even true?

He settled on the stool next to me and slid a hand toward the glass of Guinness. "You remembered."

I blew out a breath. That, almost more than the ringing phone in the lobby, was all the confirmation I needed. He was the one. "Darkest beer you can find at the closest bar. That was you, right?"

"That's me." He lifted the pint glass, took a sip, and closed his eyes in pleasure. "Oh, that's perfect." He set the glass down and he turned to me. Neither of us spoke at first; his eyes ate me up like I was an appetizer. I'd forgotten how his eyes were almost translucent, like the smoothest sea glass. "It's so good to see you," he finally said. "I mean, really see you." His voice was hushed, reverent, and I almost forgot how angry and betrayed I'd felt all week. Because despite everything, it was good to see him too.

After all these months of nothing but words on screens, his physical closeness was almost too much to take.

But then I remembered that sad, sick feeling of being lied to. Of being deceived for months. Happy to see each other or not, we had to clear the air first. That was my plan. Clear the air, then kissing. Hopefully.

"So." I pushed my wineglass away. "First things first. Has it been you? This whole time?"

"Yes." He answered immediately, and I respected that. No more lying. "I run the Kilts' fanpage. That first message from you that came in . . . I thought it was for me. So I wrote you back. I didn't realize until you wrote again that . . . that you thought I was Dex." He blinked hard, his mouth twisted, and my immediate instinct was to soothe him. Someone in distress made me itchy, and nothing eased that itch like saying and doing whatever I could to make that distress go away. But I resisted the urge. I was the one who'd been deceived here. Wasn't I in distress too?

"And you never thought to correct me?" I blew out a frustrated breath. "What were you thinking?"

"I wasn't." He gave a helpless shrug of his shoulders. "I wasn't thinking."

"Uh-uh." I narrowed my eyes and crossed my arms over my chest. "Try again, buddy. I'm gonna need a better answer than that."

"I don't know if I have one." He took another sip from his glass, his eyes trained on the bottles above the bar. He wasn't avoiding my eyes, though. He was thinking. "You were talking to me," he finally said, his eyes still focused elsewhere. "Noticing me. I mean, sure, you thought I was someone else. And I knew I should come clean. But if I did, it would all stop. So I didn't."

"But you said . . . A few weeks back, you said there were things you needed to say, that you were afraid to say. That you needed to say them in person. So"—I waved a hand, indicating the space between us—"here we are. In the same room. Breathing the same air. What did you need to say?"

I watched the tip of his tongue peek out to lick a drop of beer from his lower lip. Heat surged through me in a wave. I wanted to lean in. I wanted to nibble on his lower lip. I wondered how he'd taste, all dark beer and warm skin. But no. We weren't anywhere near nibbling yet.

A slightly shuddering sigh escaped him. "You're right." This whole conversation he'd been looking down at the bar, or up at the bottles that lined the top shelves, almost everywhere but at me. But now he pushed away his glass too—no distractions—and turned on his stool to face me. "You're right," he said again. "I did say that. And the conversation I was afraid of is the one we're having right now. Stacey, I . . ." His voice caught, and he spared one sidelong glance at his beer, but turned back to me. "I still remember the first day I saw you, here at this Faire. I don't remember what you said, but I remember your smile, and as far as I was concerned, that was it. You were it. But I'm . . . you know, me." There was that awkward laugh again.

"And what's wrong with you?" I asked gently. A little defensively, even. Despite my anger, a protective feeling for Daniel had started to bloom in my chest, and I didn't want anyone saying anything mean about him. Even Daniel himself.

"Nothing," he said quickly. "I mean, my self-esteem is fine and all. But put me next to my cousin—any of them—and it's no contest."

I opened my mouth to protest, but closed it again. Okay, he had a point. If the members of the Dueling Kilts resembled varsity football stars, Daniel was the AV club geek of the group. Not necessarily unattractive on his own, but not the one that your eye fell on first when he was in a group.

"And my cousin won that contest. Didn't he?" His voice was grave. "I don't know how long you two have been . . . well, is *together* the right word?"

I had to snort at his description. "No. No, it's really not." Certainly not now that I knew that Dex hadn't been anywhere near a computer or a cell phone to compose any of those messages I'd read in my nest of a bed under the soft fairy lights.

"I hoped not," he said. "Not just for my sake, but . . ." He cleared his throat, shifted on his barstool. "I saw you that night last summer. Here at the hotel, at the ice machine."

"Yeah. I saw you too." My face heated with remembered embarrassment. The ice bucket had been cold in my hands, and my instinct had been to duck behind the rough stucco pillar so that Daniel wouldn't see me. It was as though I'd known even then that Dex wasn't the one I wanted to be with, and that Daniel's good opinion was one worth keeping. Why hadn't I listened to my instincts? I should have chucked that ice bucket and gone home that night.

Silence settled over us as we sipped our drinks.

"I knew it wouldn't last," Daniel finally said, and I could barely hear him over the general noise of the bar. "You said 'Happy New Year, Dex.'" He shook his head. "Dex. By then we'd talked so much, and shared so much, that I'd let myself forget that you thought you were talking to him, and not me. I didn't know what to say."

"You could have started with 'By the way, this isn't Dex.' That might have been a good beginning."

"Yeah?" He raised his eyebrows. "And how would that conversation have gone, both of us slightly drunk at one in the morning on New Year's Day?"

Anger still blazed through me, but I had to admit he had a point. "There were plenty of sober opportunities to set me straight. You should have told me."

"I know." He tilted his head back, draining the last of his beer, and pushed the glass away. "I should have done a lot of things. For what it's worth, Stacey, I'm sorry. I never meant to hurt you." He reached for me, his hand halfway to my arm, but something in my eyes must have made him halt the movement.

"No." I put my hands up. This was all confusing enough. If he touched me it would only be worse. He'd hurt me, but he was also the one I wanted to comfort me. "I trusted you." Tears sprang to my eyes, but I blinked them back. They weren't part of this conversation. "I told you things that . . ." I bit down hard on my bottom lip. "Do you have any idea how much you meant to me? How much it meant to have someone to talk to? Really talk to for a change? You were . . ." I swallowed hard. Those damn tears weren't going away, and that made me angrier. Which made me tear up more. I hated this.

"I know," he said again, his eyes large and sorrowful. "I wish I could fix this."

I shook my head. Most of my anger at him had burned away with my tears, leaving me frustrated and not a little bit sad. "I wish you could too."

"Yeah." I thought he was going to say something else, but instead he stood up, his barstool making a scraping noise as he pushed it back. He took his wallet out of his back pocket and laid a couple bills on the bar in between us, placing his empty glass on top. "I'm so sorry," he said again. But his eyes weren't sorry.

They ate me up again, and this time I was the main course and dessert all wrapped into one. His eyes were gorging themselves on me, as though he knew he'd never get this chance again, and I didn't like the way that made me feel.

Before I could say anything else he was gone, threading his way through the Friday night crowd that had formed while we'd been talking at the bar. And that's when his eyes made sense. He hadn't just been saying sorry. He'd been saying goodbye.

Well, crap.

At first I just stared at the empty space he left behind. The empty beer glass, my mostly full wineglass, the cash to pay for both. The air between us was clear, but there would be no kissing tonight. Maybe not ever.

So much for my plan.

Thirteen

The Willow Creek Renaissance Faire had been a part of me—and I'd been part of it—for a decade now, and from the beginning the first day of Faire felt like magic. It was opening night of a play, the first day of school, and the beginning of the best summer vacation all rolled into one. The grounds were ready. The performers were in town, and vendors were set up with otherworldly wares. And while every year brought some new faces into the mix, for the most part the performers and vendors were the same each time, so it was like a reunion of familiar faces.

But on this opening day I woke up without that same sense of joy I always experienced. I tried to push away my frustration, remind myself that Faire was my happy place. My happy time. But would it still be, knowing that Daniel would be there too? Were we about to start four weekends of elaborately avoiding each other? Faire wasn't that big.

The sun had just crested the trees when I parked my car in our grassy lot in the back of the Faire grounds. I didn't get out right away; instead I watched the early morning sunlight through the trees. I'd thought about texting Daniel a couple times last night, and at least three times this morning, but I hadn't known what to say. He hadn't texted me either.

"Ugh, enough," I finally chastised myself. I locked my phone in my glove compartment. I wasn't going to need it for a while. I'd put on most of my costume at home: the underdress and overskirt of my wench's outfit, along with my new boots; all I had to do was get wrangled into my corset, pull back my hair, and put on my necklace. As I tripped my way down to the Hollow that first early morning to finish getting ready, I passed the leathersmith's booth and she flagged me down.

"How did that backpack work out for you?"

"Oh, it's wonderful!" I was so pleased she'd remembered selling it to me last summer. It had been an impulse buy to assuage my sadness at the end of the season, but it had become one of my favorite souvenirs. Every time I looked at it and used it, I was reminded of these trees, and how I felt during these weeks. It reminded me that this was my favorite time of the year, every year.

But this time . . . Daniel's presence lurked at the edges, like storm clouds waiting to blot out the summer sun. All I'd wanted was to clear the air between us, and maybe move forward, but instead he'd just . . . walked away. I'd started at least three texts to Emily last night about the whole thing when I'd gotten home but had erased them all. I'd see her this morning, and talking was better than texting when it came to things like this.

Now that I was alongside my castmates, I pulled my hair up and tied a kerchief over it so it looked oh-so-carefully casual. Then I loosened the strings on my corset as far as they'd go and went looking for Emily. Once she strapped me in, my transfor-

mation into Beatrice the seventeenth-century tavern wench
would be complete. I'd missed Beatrice, and I was looking forward to being her again.

Em was five minutes late, which for her was right on time.
How she managed to do that while living with a control freak of
a fiancé was beyond me, but there you were. It was also possible
that Simon slept on the Faire grounds once it was this time of
year . . . he was pretty attached to it. The idea of the fastidious
Simon living in a tent was so ridiculous that the smile was still
on my face when Emily found me. But when I saw her my smile
fell. I'd been looking all over for her blue and white wench's
costume, but here she was with an underskirt the color of deep
wine, and the dress over it a dark black. The corset she'd fastened
around her middle was a dark wine color the same shade as her
underskirt. She'd gone and changed her costume, and here I was
in the same old thing.

Why was everyone else able to seek out change while I let
everything remain the same?

But before I could ask her about her new outfit, she hurried
over to me and grabbed my arms. "Did you talk to him? How did
it go?"

I blinked as my brain switched topics. "Daniel? Oh, yeah." I
folded my arms over my chest. "I talked to him last night when
he got into town." My flat tone of voice did a pretty good job of
letting her know how that went.

"Ohhh." Her eyebrows climbed her forehead as she drew the
word out. "It really was Daniel writing to you all this time?" I
gave her a tight nod, and her hopeful expression faded quickly.
"So I take it things didn't go well?"

"No. Not at all." I filled her in on what had happened the
night before. How I had hoped that after Daniel and I had talked,

there would be a fresh start between us. A new beginning. But his response had been an apology and a closed door. An ending.

"But it's okay," I said after I'd brought her up to speed. I tried to give her a helpless, *what are you gonna do?* shrug and my usual smile, but neither one of them really fit right.

And Emily wasn't buying it for a second. "But he's been writing to you for months. *Months.* You've been getting to know each other better than anyone else, right? And the second he's confronted with the truth, he just throws up his hands all 'Welp, you caught me'? That's it?"

"Well . . ." When she put it like that . . .

"You'd think he'd try to fight for you. At least a little." She shook her head. "That's disappointing."

"I guess he didn't want to." A sense of loss swept through me, which was strange. How could I lose what had never been mine? But despite everything, I didn't want to believe that this was it. That after all these months, what Daniel and I had had together was over, as if it had never happened. That didn't seem right either.

My shrug and smile were slightly more successful this time. It was long past time to change the subject. "Anyway. I have two questions for you."

"Okay, shoot." She turned her back to me. "Tighten me up?"

"First off, when did you get this outfit?" I started at the top, working my way to the middle of the corset, pulling on the laces until the corset was fully closed in the back and the dress underneath was completely covered.

"A week or two ago." She threw a quizzical glance over her shoulder. "I sent the link to you, remember?"

"Well, yeah, but I didn't know you'd actually ordered it." I tugged on the laces from the bottom of the corset and moved up, meeting in the middle and tying it off. "Okay, the other question. Did Simon approve it?"

"Do you think I gave him a choice?" She grinned and turned back around, and something in my expression made her face fall a little. "I'm sorry. I really thought you knew I was getting a new outfit. I thought you were too."

I shrugged as she started gathering the black overdress up, pinning it up at her hip as I'd taught her to do during her first year of Faire so that the deep red skirt underneath showed. "It's okay," I said. "I've been a little preoccupied lately." That was putting it mildly.

"What do you think?" Her expression was uncertain as she shifted around in the new outfit, which was understandable. It was a departure from her wench's outfit, that was for sure. The corset was tighter, the colors were bolder.

But she looked great in it. I smiled. "I think you look like a pirate's bride. So that's fitting."

"That was the plan. You should have seen his face when it came in the mail."

"You're going to give that poor boy a heart attack before he's thirty." I wrapped my loosened corset around my rib cage and fastened it down the front before turning so Emily could lace me up.

"Eh, he's fine." She pulled on the strings, and the breath whooshed out of my body. Not only because she'd tightened my corset, but because I spotted Daniel across the way. He looked like his normal self, the one I'd seen every summer: black jeans and black T-shirt, red hair under that black baseball cap. He held a clear takeout cup of iced coffee in one hand, the beverage pale with milk.

In an instant, I flashed back to that awful day earlier this year, when my mother had been in the hospital and I'd been so scared. He'd kept me distracted, starting with a picture of his coffee order, the same kind of coffee he held now. That was who Daniel was. Not a creepy catfisher, looking to take advantage. He was the guy who'd gotten me through that terrifying day, sending me silly memes to make me laugh when I'd been at my worst. He cared about me, the way no one else had in a long time. He was . . .

He was talking to Simon, whose face was like thunder.

"Oh, crap." I said the words on an exhale.

"Did I pull too tight?" Emily froze behind me, the laces of my corset still in her hands. "I'm sorry, this seemed about right, but give me a sec, I can loosen . . ."

"No." I put my hands on my waist, tracing the familiar dip and curve that came with putting on this outfit. Wearing these clothes, changing my body's shape, really helped me get into character as someone else. "No, I'm good, you can tie it."

"You sure?" But Emily tied the strings into a firm knot that would last the day. "So what was the 'oh crap' for . . ." Her voice trailed off as her gaze followed mine. Daniel and Simon were deep in conversation, Daniel gesturing while Simon finished buttoning his vest and started adjusting the cuffs of his pirate's shirt. "Oh," Emily said. "Crap."

"Exactly." I glanced over my shoulder to make sure Emily was done with my corset before I stepped away from her. "Do you know what they're talking about?"

She shrugged. "I'm marrying the guy, but I still can't read his mind. He's been pretty pissed about how upset you were last weekend, though. Should we save him from Simon or let him fend for himself?"

I was more inclined toward the latter and opened my mouth to tell her so, but my better nature won out. "Let's go save him."

We'd made it only a few steps when I skidded to a halt, dragging Emily to a stop as well. "What the hell . . . ?" She turned to me.

"On second thought, let's don't." Because Dex had joined the two of them, and I thought my heart was going to beat right out of my chest. A tight corset, plus the guy I'd hooked up with the past two summers, plus the guy who'd been wooing me by email while pretending to be someone else the whole time? I suddenly couldn't breathe. Couldn't speak.

It hadn't even occurred to me that, now that I'd straightened things out with Daniel, I would have to straighten things out with Dex too. I'd been his wench with benefits for a couple summers now. How soon was he going to expect me to jump back into his hotel bed again? Was he expecting it at all? Was two summers a pattern? God. I didn't want anything to do with anyone named MacLean. Not now. Not yet. Maybe not ever.

So like a coward I spun on my heel, hiked up my skirts, and hurried away, Emily trailing after me. It was official. My excitement for the first day of Faire had been replaced by a low-level anxiety that took up residence in my gut. And that made me angry. I'd looked forward to this day, to these four weeks, all year, and now I'd ruined it for myself over a guy.

Well, the hell with that. I wasn't going to let Daniel MacLean take Faire away from me. I just needed to get away from him long enough to think.

Once again, Emily earned her Best Friend status by following me on my mad scramble up the hill out of the Hollow, catching up to me when I stopped at the top of the hill to lean against a tree and attempt to catch my breath.

"Hey. Come on." She settled her hands on my shoulders, making me look her in the eyes. "Don't think about any of that shit right now. Let Stacey deal with it later. You're not Stacey right now."

"I'm not." My voice was a slight wheeze—I was still getting used to being back in the corset—and my words came out close to a question.

"Of course you aren't. Look around. Out here there's no emails, no texts. No guys lying to you about who they are. It's time to be Beatrice now."

I let her words settle in my brain, and when I was calm enough I took her advice. I looked around, at the sunlight filtering through the trees. At the vendors lined up on either side of the dusty lane under our feet. The multicolored banners fluttering in the treetops. I concentrated on the quiet sounds of the Renaissance Faire waking up for the day. Just like that, some of the anxiety dissolved, and my shoulders felt lighter. "You're right, Emma. Of course." I slipped into both Beatrice's accent and Emily's Faire name as easily as putting on a comfy pair of fuzzy socks. I bumped her shoulder with mine and gave her hand a grateful squeeze. "They're waiting for us at the tavern. We should get started."

The path to our tavern was like the road home. Our volunteers were waiting for us, and had already done most of the work of setting up for the day. Emily and I pitched in, putting the wine bottles in ice and making sure the beer coolers were stocked up. But soon Emily put her hands on her hips and frowned.

"Those tables aren't right . . ." she said under her breath. This was her third summer here, and her third summer with this obsession: figuring out the right configuration of tables, stools, and benches that would look the most inviting and would persuade patrons to linger and get that second drink. It was all about selling refreshments, which raised more money.

"Em, it's fine." Jamie, one of our head volunteers, had gotten used to Emily's trying to change things around, even though he'd been with us almost as long as I had and knew more about running the tavern than probably all of us put together. But he tolerated her ideas with good-natured patience. Because what did it hurt, really, if Emily wanted to move a few tables around? The girl was getting married in a week. She probably had some nervous energy to burn off.

And what better place to burn off energy than outside, under the trees and bright midsummer sunshine of a Renaissance faire? There was plenty to do to keep us both distracted. We pitched in with the volunteers, serving beer and wine. We flirted with patrons and counted it as a victory when we could elicit a blush. We strolled the dusty lanes together, stopping to take in parts of shows, cheering loudly for each one and helping draw patrons in when we happened upon a show that was about to start. Last summer Emily and I had transitioned from being strictly tavern wenches—glorified bartenders in uncomfortable costumes—to serving as local color. And being local color was fun, in a way that being an overworked bartender was not.

While we stopped off more than once at the human chess match—Simon's domain—so that Emily could visit her fiancé, we gave a wide berth to the Marlowe Stage, where the Dueling Kilts were set up. In fact, Emily made a point of shooting a squinty side-eye in the direction of their stage, and I suddenly became very interested in the trees on the other side of the lane.

I didn't want to see the Dueling Kilts play. I didn't want to see Dex, and I sure didn't want to see Daniel.

But the universe didn't care about that. Later that day, while I took the long way around on my way to the front stage and the first pub sing of the year, I ran almost smack into Daniel, coming from the opposite direction, *away* from pub sing.

For a couple heartbeats we just stared at each other, a little startled. "Sorry . . ." I started to say.

"No, I'm sorry," he said. "I know you like pub sing, so I was . . ." He jerked a thumb over his shoulder, where the banners at the front gate were visible.

"You were avoiding pub sing." I nodded. "Avoiding me."

"Not avoiding. Giving you space." He shoved his hands in the front pockets of his jeans, his shoulders hunched as though trying to make himself smaller, to take up less of said space. "Sorry," he said again.

I wanted to sigh a huge sigh, but I was still strapped into a corset, and this time of year sighs were something that happened after hours. Was this how all this was going to go? I couldn't do four weeks of the both of us skulking around, hoping to avoid each other.

"C'mere." I hooked a hand around Daniel's arm and pulled him back the way I'd come, down the lane and against the flow of traffic. There weren't any more shows happening on this side of Faire, and the day was almost over, so there was only a trickle of patrons around us.

He followed me without complaint, and I ducked into an almost-alcove made up of a small grouping of young trees. He took a deep breath when I turned to face him. "Listen . . ."

But I wasn't going to let him speak. It was my turn. "No, you listen." I tightened my grip on his arm, and he made no attempt to pull free. He raised his eyebrows in a question, and I had trouble forming words. How dare he look so damned sincere, after everything I'd learned about him. How dare his eyes look so welcoming. How dare I want to forgive absolutely everything and start over again with him.

"Tell me something," I finally said, stepping closer to him, as though I wanted to tell him a secret. Screw personal space. It didn't apply right now.

"Anything." He shifted his weight forward, bringing himself even closer. This close, I could see a sprinkling of freckles across his nose, and I idly hoped that he wore enough sunscreen.

But I forced myself back on topic. "Why did you do it? Why did you lie about who you were?"

He seemed to expect this question. "You were happy," he said simply. "And I wanted you to stay that way." He shrugged, his expression helpless. "I knew you didn't want me, not really, but if I could keep talking to you and keep you happy . . ." He trailed off with another shrug.

Damn. That was a pretty good answer. I forced my brain back on task. "Was it . . ." I cleared my throat. It was hard to speak with his eyes looking all green at me like that. "Was that the only lie? Or was it all . . . ?" I couldn't finish that sentence. The thought of everything he said being fake was too much to contemplate. I tried one more time. "Was any of it real? The words, I mean. Did Dex tell you to say those things, or . . . ?"

"No." His eyes sharpened, chips of glass instead of green fire. "Dex had nothing to do with anything I ever wrote to you. I . . . Stacey . . ."

"Anastasia," I corrected him. A smile danced around the corners of his mouth.

"Anastasia." My full name was a soft breath, and utterly delicious when he said it out loud. "Everything I said . . . every email, every text. Those were all me. I promise. I know it was . . ." He swallowed, and I tried to not watch the movement of his throat with any interest. "I know it was a pretty big lie, but I swear it was the only one."

"Promise?" I asked, and he nodded. "No more lies?" I searched his eyes and saw nothing but honesty in them.

"No more lies," he echoed. "I promise. If I could take it all back, I would, believe me. I'd figure out a way to do it right instead."

"No," I said. Despite the past few days, I wouldn't want to take back our words. The way he'd made me feel. That terrible day he'd gotten me through.

Besides, when I'd reminded him that my name was Anastasia, I'd already decided to forgive him, hadn't I?

So after another search of his eyes, I nodded slowly. "Okay." My breath escaped my body with that one word, and with it went the tension, the doubt I'd been feeling.

"Okay . . . okay, what?" His expression was guarded, as if he didn't dare to hope.

"Maybe we could . . . I don't know. Start over or something?"

"Yeah?" His eyebrows shot up and a genuine smile blossomed across his face, crinkling the edges of his eyes. "I think I'd like that."

"Me too." My breath stalled in my lungs in a way that had nothing to do with my corset as his hand came up to touch the side of my face, tracing my cheekbone with his fingertips. His touch felt better than anything I could have imagined. I reached up to lay a hand on his shoulder, warm under his T-shirt. He caught his breath, and his hand curled under my chin, tipping my face up to his.

"Anastasia." His voice was hushed, my name reverent. "I'd

really, really like to kiss you. Would that . . ." He swallowed hard and bent down a fraction. "Would that be . . ."

"Okay." I rose slowly up onto my toes, smiling.

"Okay." The word was said against my mouth as his lips finally met mine: a kiss that was months in the making.

His kiss was a soft brush of lips and a rough scratch of stubble, almost over before it began, and I stretched up farther on my toes to keep his mouth right there where I wanted it.

Daniel made it clear from the start that he was nothing like Dex. If Dex had kissed me out in the open at Faire like that . . . well, he never would have kissed me in public like that, first of all. The closest we'd ever come to any kind of PDA was outside the door of his hotel room, and we were in his room and up against the wall within thirty seconds. Everything with him had been down and dirty and in the dark, and there was a part of me back then that had really responded to that.

But Daniel was different. He wasn't down and dirty. His kisses were sweet, closed-mouthed, and achingly conscious of the fact that we were in public. If someone had walked by or thrown us a second glance, he would have stepped away from me immediately. But no one did, and after a few moments of soft, exploratory kisses that made my toes curl in my boots, he pulled away, just far enough to brush my cheek with his mouth.

"Why don't you come by tonight, after you're done here?"

"Oh." My heart sank, and in an instant the promise in those kisses melted away like a sugar cube in the rain. Of course. There was the down and dirty. He knew the arrangement I'd had with Dex for the past couple summers, and now he was looking for his turn. I didn't like the way that made me feel. Cheap. Like I was being passed around from one cousin to the other. No, I didn't like that at all.

It must have shown on my face, because Daniel's eyes went wide and he looked chastened. "Stacey." He moved toward me again, his hand cupping my elbow. It was a comforting touch, though I didn't want it to be. I should have wanted to brush him away, not lean into him. "I'm not my cousin." He caught my chin again and ducked down, catching my eyes with his. "Look at me. I need you to understand that."

"I do," I said, but I didn't sound convincing even to myself.

"No," he said, "you don't. But you will. Please, come over tonight. Room 212. Okay?"

I didn't want to be a cheap hookup to Daniel. But he'd just given me the sweetest kisses of my life, which deserved to be taken into account. Which was why I ultimately nodded. "Room 212. Okay."

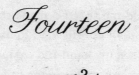

Fourteen

I *almost talked myself* out of it.

I went home after Faire and took a long, hot shower. I dried my hair and snuggled with Benedick for a few minutes. I put on a cute dress. I took it off and pulled on yoga pants and a T-shirt. I put on makeup. I took it off. I was stalling.

My phone remained silent, something I wasn't used to these days. I'd grown used to those nightly check-ins from Dex . . . no, from Daniel. When I'd gotten home from the bar last night I'd changed Dex's name in my phone to Daniel's, but I was still working on reordering my thinking when it came to this whole mess. But he didn't send any texts. He didn't ask if I was coming or not. He was giving me space, as he'd said this afternoon.

But I wasn't sure if I wanted that space. I wasn't sure what I wanted next with him. As I checked my phone for the fourth time since I'd gotten home, I realized that I missed him. I wanted to hear from him. And he was waiting, more patiently than I could have ever expected, for me to take what we'd had all these months off-line and into real life.

I kissed Benedick on the top of his head, plopped him on the couch, and grabbed my keys. I'd stalled long enough.

It didn't take long to drive to the hotel, and before I could think too hard about it I was knocking on the door of his room. The relieved, almost overjoyed look on Daniel's face when he opened the door told me that I'd made the right decision. He wasn't looking for a hookup. He was looking for me.

"You came!" He took my hand and led me inside. The genuine surprise in his voice almost made me sad; obviously he hadn't thought me showing up was a sure thing. Dex had never thought I wouldn't show up. Or maybe he just hadn't cared.

"Of course I did." He didn't need to know how long I'd dithered at my place. I could just let him think that it always took me this long to shower and throw on glorified pajamas and minimal makeup.

He bent to kiss my cheek, his lips skimming over my skin, and I turned my head, catching his mouth with mine and turning it into a real kiss. He accepted it with a sigh, and his hand tightened around mine for a split second before letting go, dropping to rest at my waist. I let him pull me into him, enjoying the way we seemed to fit well together despite our height difference. My heart swelled, and suddenly I couldn't recall why I'd been so unsure about all this. Sure, we needed to get used to each other, but Daniel and I had more in common than Dex and I ever had. Even if Daniel was after a quick hookup as Dex had been, a month with this guy would be so much better than any relationship I'd had lately. What was so bad about that?

Besides, his mouth was warm on mine, his lips soft. I'd never had a more comfortable kiss, and I wanted to stay there forever. But my stomach growled, and I broke off with an awkward laugh and pressed a hand to my belly. "Sorry, I forgot to . . ." I trailed off as I realized that his room smelled *delicious*. For the first time, I looked past him into the hotel room. The television was on, the sound muted, and the table by the window was covered in Chinese takeout cartons.

"Forgot to eat dinner? Good." He nodded toward the table.

I wandered over to the buffet he had set out. Lo mein, deep-fried something with neon-red sweet-and-sour sauce, a whole carton full of egg rolls, another of dumplings, and pepper steak swimming in brown sauce. "I mean, I'm hungry, but I don't know if I can eat all this."

"I'd be impressed as hell if you did. But don't worry. I know a few guys down the hall who'll finish all this in a heartbeat."

"Oh?" I raised my eyebrows. "Are we having company?"

"Nope." His hand went back to my waist, a small show of possessiveness that I didn't mind a bit. "They can have leftovers tomorrow morning. That's what the mini-fridge is for."

"Breakfast of champions." I glanced up at him, and the humor that danced in his eyes was an echo of my smile.

"Exactly," he said. "These guys are not picky. Now, come on, grab something to eat. They were just about to renovate the bathroom when you got here." He nodded toward the television.

"What?" My gaze flew to the muted television, which was tuned to one of those endlessly similar cable shows about people renovating houses. "Oh my God, I love these shows."

Daniel nodded. "I remember."

"You . . . remember?" My brow furrowed. He sounded so certain, as if it was something we did all the time that had become a familiar routine. Takeout Chinese and . . .

Then memory sparked, and a slow smile spread over my face.

"You remember." It had been a throwaway email one night, when the hour was so late I'd forgotten what I'd typed until he replied to it. But I'd confessed one of my favorite guilty pleasures. Take-out Chinese and home renovation shows on cable. Something about lo mein going great with schadenfreude.

"Of course I do," he said. "I remember all of it." He shrugged. "But you weren't specific as to what kind of Chinese food you liked."

"So you got all of it."

He chuckled. "Something like that."

This night wasn't turning out at all like I'd expected, and I couldn't have been happier about it. When I'd come to this hotel to spend the night with Dex, there had been little conversation. Acrobatic sex, sure. But no real conversation. Now, Daniel and I propped ourselves up with pillows in his bed, our legs stretched out in front of us, passing the lo mein and dumpling cartons back and forth, digging into them with chopsticks while we heckled the married couple with more money than sense on the television.

"Really?" I yelled. "You have a quarter of a million dollars to renovate a Philadelphia row house, and that's the cheap garbage tile you pick for the bathroom?"

"They have to make up for the money they spent replacing those hardwood floors somehow." Daniel crunched into an egg-roll.

I tsked and shook my head. "They could have refinished the original ones for half that, easily."

"Oh, yeah?" He bumped my shoulder with his. "Refinish a lot of floors, do you?"

"I watch a lot of TV where other people refinish a lot of floors. I think that makes me an expert."

He considered that. "Close enough. I'll accept that."

I slurped up one more bite of noodles while the couple on the screen bickered about the color of the shower tile. Their marriage wasn't going to last beyond the renovation of that house. "I wonder what it's like," I finally said.

"I think the green would have looked better, but that's not the hill I want to die on."

"No . . ." I passed the lo mein carton to him. "I mean having a space like that. My place would fit in their kitchen, you know? I watch shows like this and wonder what it would be like to live that kind of life. Where you have an amazing space like that, and the money to make it exactly what you want."

On the television, the show segued into one about an even richer, even more nonsensical couple trying to decide which private island they wanted to buy. "I don't know," I said. "It seems like a lot of work. A lot of responsibility."

"The island? Definitely."

"Any of it." I shrugged.

"Hmm." Daniel leaned to the side, placing the empty lo mein carton on the nightstand. "No idea," he finally said. "I mean there's the RV, but we rotate who sleeps there, so it's not really mine. The biggest space I've ever had that's all mine is my pickup truck. It's nice and all, but it's mostly decorated in last month's fast-food wrappers."

I snickered at that, but looked at him thoughtfully as I finished off the last dumpling. "Yeah, you're not exactly a putting-down-roots kind of guy, are you?"

"Not really." He leaned back on his pillows, and I watched the flicker of the television screen in his eyes. "We're here for the next month, and that's probably the closest thing I have to putting down roots these days."

Right. He'd only be here for four weeks while the Kilts performed at Faire. But that month stretched before the two of us like a deserted highway, long and winding. Plenty of time. Why think about it right now? That was in the future. For now he was here, and that was all that mattered.

"How does that work exactly?" I echoed his position, reclining on my side of his bed, my shoulders and head cushioned on my pillows but turned toward him. "I helped organize stuff this year, and I know we only cover the hotel for the weekends y'all perform for us."

"True." He nodded against the pillows at his head. "We pay for the rooms during the week. This is a great central location, near DC and northern Virginia, so I'm able to book the guys into bars for shows at least two nights each week." He shrugged. "It's kind of like downtime, before we do the Maryland one. They can rehearse, I can get paperwork done."

"Sounds glamorous."

He snorted. "Oh, yeah. You have no idea."

The private island purchase wasn't going well for our friends on the reality show. One island was perfect, but the mansion on it needed work. Another island was substandard, as private islands went, but the house was perfect. As for me, I was full of food and contentment, slowly growing sleepy as the mega-rich couple prepared to spend more money than I'd ever make in my lifetime. Before long I'd moved closer to Daniel, seeking out his warmth, and dozed a little with my head on his shoulder. His arm went around me, his fingertips stroking slowly up and down my upper arm. There was no expectation of anything physical. He hadn't even kissed me since I'd first arrived.

It was the best date I'd been on in years.

. . .

The next morning, while I was bustling around getting ready for day two of Faire, my phone buzzed from where it was charging on my kitchen counter. I nudged Benedick away from my cream cheese—covered bagel on the way to my phone.

"Not yours," I chided. But my annoyance at the cat trying to steal my breakfast faded as I picked up my phone.

Good morning! Thanks for coming over last night.

I licked cream cheese off my thumb before typing a response. **Feed me lo mein and I'm yours forever.**

Is that all it takes? Score.

I grinned around another sip of coffee. **Just leave the sweet-and-sour where it belongs next time. In the trash.**

That got me a couple laughing emojis in response. **Well, the guys appreciated it when they got back from the bars, so I got to be a provider for everyone last night.**

Lucky you. But bringing the rest of the band into the conversation brought Dex into the room, into our burgeoning relationship, and I didn't like the way that made me feel. I wasn't the kind of person who regretted much. My philosophy was more "What's done is done, let's move on." But for the first time in my life, I wished I'd never hooked up with Dex. Because what was happening with Daniel felt so much more real, so much more substantial that I didn't want the memory of my fling with his cousin getting in the way.

So I changed the subject. **Are we back to this now? Words on a screen?**

I don't think I'd say we're *back* to this. How about "in addition." Because I love your words on my screen, and I don't know that I'd want to give them up.

Fair enough, I texted back. I love your words on my screen too. The words looked intimate when I typed them out, like a confession. I reminded myself not to read too much into it. He wasn't saying he loved me, he was saying he loved our exchanges. Our communication. There was a difference, and it was far too soon for anything deeper.

Or was it? Another text from him popped up on my phone while I was thinking. But here's the great thing. Not only are we texting good morning, but I also get to see you. In person. It's like a dream come true.

Whew. So much for not reading too much into it. I like your dreams, I typed. My eyes flicked up to the top of my screen, and I yelped. Speaking of seeing me, I need to get going if I'm going to be on time. Who was I kidding? Being on time was already out of the question. Time to shoot for not being embarrassingly late. I let my phone clatter to the table as I abandoned the last few bites of my bagel, much to Benedick's delight, to finish getting ready for the day. I grabbed the outer layers of my costume and dashed out the door in little more than my chemise and my boots. I could finish getting dressed at the Hollow.

The good thing about having worked at this Faire since almost the beginning was that putting on the outer layers of my costume was second nature to me. I was ready in a flash, and right when I'd started looking for Emily to cinch me into my corset, she was looking for me for the same reason.

"You know, I was thinking," Emily said.

"Thinking what? Ooof!" A sharp tug on the corset strings

from Emily had me almost losing my balance, and I groped in front of me for one of the posts that held up the stage's canopy, much like Scarlett O'Hara holding on to the bedpost. "Warn a girl, will you?"

"Sorry." She didn't sound sorry. "How long have you had this outfit, anyway?"

I shrugged, bracing myself as Emily tugged again. "A few years. Why?"

"Well, I was thinking we should go shopping this morning."

"This morning?" I looked over my shoulder at her. "We kind of have a Ren Faire to work, remember? Besides, I'm not going to the mall dressed like this."

"Funny." She gave my strings a sharp tug, more in rebuke than anything else. "I meant here, before the gates open. I just . . ." There were a few more small tugs as she evened everything up and tied the strings off. Then she sighed. "You were right. We were going to plan new costumes together. And I went and did it without you. I'm so sorry." She sounded on the verge of tears, as if she thought she'd betrayed our friendship, and that broke my heart.

"Oh, Em. That's okay." And it was. Sure, I'd felt a little stab of hurt yesterday, but in the grand scheme of things it was no big deal. We both had a lot going on. Weddings and long-distance maybe-relationships. And since I'd spent the better part of last night snuggled against Daniel watching bad television, it would have taken a lot to upset me today.

But it still meant something that she wanted to make it up to me. I looked down at my ensemble, really studying it as I adjusted the way my chemise lay under the corset. The movements were automatic after spending so many summers adjusting the same outfit. Maybe Emily had a point. And far be it from me to discourage someone who wanted to go shopping. I looked back up at her, her eyebrows raised in a question, and I grinned at her. "Let's go shopping."

"Yay!" She grabbed my arm and we slipped away from the rest of the cast, still getting dressed and ready for the day, and hurried up the hill to the vendors. They were already set up, after all, and wouldn't mind making an early sale.

"What do you think?" Emily took a blue flowing underdress off the rack and held it up to me.

I shook my head. "With my hair? I'd look like Alice on her way to Wonderland."

"Good point." She replaced the dress and started hunting through the rack. "Who do you want to be?"

I had to laugh. "That's the question, isn't it?" But my hand went to my belt pouch, and I drew out the dragonfly necklace I'd bought the summer before. There was my answer. I wanted to wear something that was deserving of the sparkle in that dragonfly's eyes. Something that matched the thrill I'd felt yesterday when Daniel had kissed me. "Something to match this."

Emily's smile widened. Maybe she remembered the moment I'd bought it too. "Good call." She stuck the blue dress back on the rack and rummaged around, while I moved to look at corsets. There were ones in all different sizes and shapes, underbust and overbust styles, as well as simple waist cinchers. I dismissed the cinchers and underbust corsets out of hand: not enough support. I had far too much bosom to go braless, and if I was going to cinch myself into a corset, I shouldn't have to deal with underwires too. That was just cruel.

"Here you go." Emily was back with another dress, and as soon as I saw it, I knew it was a winner. Flowing, gauzy fabric in a color that could only be described as marigold: bright orangey-yellow that would make me look like a blazing sunset come to life. I looked from the dress back to the display of corsets, and reached immediately for a green and brown brocade bodice that was a similar shape to the one I'd stuck Emily in her first couple seasons at Faire. Perfect.

"No," Emily said. "Are you sure about that?" She looked disappointed by my choice. "You wear greens and browns now. Isn't this about getting you something different?"

"This is different," I said. I reached behind me for my corset strings and pulled, undoing all the hard work Emily had done just a few minutes ago. "You'll see. I know what I'm doing." I took the dress from her and the vendor showed me back to the dressing area, a little space roped off and draped with fabric. On the way I grabbed an overskirt in a matching brown.

"No!" Emily howled. "Come on! I picked out that gorgeous dress and you're just going to cover it up with brown!"

"Oh my God, will you just trust me for five minutes?" I laughed all the way to the dressing area, and once inside I shimmied out of my longtime tavern wench outfit and pulled the sunburst-colored dress over my head. Skirt next, then I shrugged into the bodice and started the work of lacing it up. It was so much easier wearing a costume that laced up the front. I should have done this years ago.

While I was getting dressed, the vendor and Emily were making small talk on the other side of the curtain.

"Wedding's coming up soon now, isn't it?"

"Yep!" Emily's voice was high and chirpy, a sign that nerves were taking over. "A week from today."

"And everyone's okay with the wedding day being on Sunday? I mean, obviously it works best for all of us, but your family and everyone? It's not the most conventional day for a wedding."

"I'm getting married at a Renaissance faire," Emily said. "I think conventional left the building a long time ago."

I had the bodice laced up; now I bent over to adjust everything before I gave it a final tightening up. "Has Simon told you where you're going on your honeymoon yet?" I tossed the question over the curtain in an effort to change the subject. Maybe reminding her that all of this planning came with a nice vacation at the end would help.

It didn't help. "Nope!" The chirpiness in her voice only increased. "All I know is that we're leaving right after the last day of Faire. He said he'll tell me what to pack a couple days in advance."

"Wow. That must be killing you." I tied off the bodice and ran my hands down my sides. The elaborate brocade felt downright decadent after so many years of wearing simple tavern wench clothes.

"You have no idea." Emily sighed. "But I'm trying to be chill about it, let Simon have his fun."

"That's awfully nice of you." I refastened my brown leather belt around my waist and tied the dragonfly around my neck. "I know how much you like to . . . Wait a second."

"What?"

I pushed the curtain open to glare at her. I wanted to cross my arms over my chest, but the bodice had hiked up the girls sufficiently enough that they were an obstacle. I settled for putting my hands on my hips. "I'm a project, aren't I?"

Emily's eyes went wide. "Holy crap, Stace. That looks amazing. You're right, I'll trust you in all wardrobe-related decisions from now on."

"Don't change the subject." I pointed a finger at her in accusation, but I was smiling too much to look truly angry.

"What do you mean?" Her brow furrowed. "A . . . a project?"

"That's what I said. The wedding's all planned. You've already rearranged the tavern for the summer, so you don't have anything left to fix up. Except me." I gestured down at my outfit. "So here you are, fixing me."

"No," Emily said. "That's silly. Why would I . . ." But she closed her mouth with a snap, her eyes wide as realization took hold. "Well, hell. I made you into a project, didn't I?"

"Sure did." But as I turned to the full-length mirror, I realized that I didn't care. I looked great. The brown overskirt made the green in the bodice pop, and once I'd gathered it up on the sides, the marigold in the underdress practically blazed to life against the green and brown. The whole thing looked like the sun setting behind the trees, just the way I'd pictured it in my head.

Behind me in the mirror, Emily smiled. "You look like a wood nymph."

I made a noncommittal hmm at that and turned to look at my reflection from the side. Bodices didn't pull in quite as much as corsets, so my shape in this new outfit was a little different. "Do nymphs come this round?"

"If they're in a Rubens painting, they do." Her smile widened at me in the mirror, and I had to laugh. "We should get you a pair of wings."

"Ooh, yes," said the vendor. She pointed down the lane. "About two spaces down that way, I saw yesterday that she was selling wings. You'd look great."

I shook my head with a laugh. "I'd take someone's eye out."
But I liked this outfit. Emily was right; I did look like a wood
nymph. Which was fitting, considering how much I loved spending time in these woods every year. This was definitely an outfit
worthy of the dragonfly.

I paid for my new outfit while the vendor bundled up my old
wench's clothes and promised to keep them until closing gate. I
felt lighter as I started my day, as though I really had donned the
wings that Emily had suggested.

We split up to check on our taverns; while Emily peeled off
to the tavern by the chess field, I headed up the lane to where
the food court section was, to the auxiliary tavern we'd set up
last summer. They'd just about finished setting up when I got
there, and I was immediately waved away. It was odd to not be
needed, and as I turned to go back down the lane again, I realized I didn't have anywhere to be. It was an unsettling feeling.
The front gates had just opened, and I put on my best smile as
I greeted patrons, addressing them as lords and ladies and directing them to the shows that started the earliest. It didn't take
long for my smile to feel like the real thing, and for the joy of
the day to fully take hold. I was in the woods, after all, and
it was Faire season. And I had someone I wanted to say good
morning to.

The glade in front of the Marlowe Stage was quiet, since the
Dueling Kilts' first set wasn't for another hour or so. I'd picked
my way halfway across the rows of empty benches before I noticed Dex, perched center stage on a stool, tuning an acoustic
guitar. He was talking to Daniel, who was sitting on the lip of
the low stage, his long legs stretched out in front of him and
crossed at the ankles. I stopped short when I saw them. Dex and
I still hadn't exchanged one word yet this summer, and I wasn't

sure what to say to him. Obviously our yearly hookup wasn't going to happen. Did he know that already? Did he know about Daniel and me? Did he care?

Both men looked up as I approached, and I squared my shoulders. Too late to run away now. Time to face the MacLeans.

Fifteen

H ey." *Daniel's voice* was a cool drink of water on a summer's day. I felt better the moment he spoke. I looked from him to Dex. How had it taken me so long to realize who had really been writing to me? Now that I knew the truth it seemed ludicrous that I'd ever thought otherwise.

Dex nodded at me. "Stace. What's up?" He got up from his stool and gave me a quick up-and-down appraisal. "You look different. Change your hair?"

Daniel's snort was barely audible, and as his eyes met mine, I pressed my lips together to hide my smile. "She changed her whole costume." His gaze roamed over me, from my pinned-up hair to my long, full skirts. I basked in his appreciative look like a flower soaking up the summer sun.

"Oh." Dex shrugged, clearly losing interest in the conversation. Probably because it wasn't about him. "Looks good." The words were a compliment, but there wasn't a lot of power behind them. He held the guitar by its neck, letting it dangle carelessly.

He was comfortable with the instrument, treating it as an extension of his arm. "Where the hell is Freddy, anyway? He's late."

"Getting his drums out of the truck. Todd's with him." Daniel looked away from me and frowned as he checked his phone. "They're not late yet. Not technically. They should be here in a sec."

Dex shrugged again. "I'll go find them." He handed the guitar to Daniel.

"Make sure you call him Freddy a few more times. You know he loves that."

Dex hopped down off the stage, and without another word to either of us, he was gone. I watched him leave, amazed. This time last year I'd lusted after that man with every fiber of my being. Now, while I could still appreciate him in an aesthetic sense, none of my fibers wanted anything to do with him.

Instead I turned back to Daniel, and all those fibers went on alert, saying, *Yes. We want this one.* Before I could speak he spoke first, his nod a little more formal, in keeping with the setting. "Milady Beatrice. Good morrow." His accent wasn't bad, but then again the man lived at Renaissance faires. It was to be expected.

"Good morrow, sir." I bobbed a little curtsy at him and we shared a warm smile, a place made just for the two of us. "So," I said. "Freddy?"

He rolled his eyes as he stowed his phone in his back pocket. "Frederick. Dex's baby brother. He plays the hand drum and is never, ever on time. Also, he absolutely hates being called Freddy."

"So Dex does it as much as possible." I nodded sagely.

"Exactly." He squinted down at me. "Are you sure you're an only child? You seem to have a good grasp of sibling dynamics."

"Just me, as far as I know." I grinned back, but something about my voice felt hollow. Like we were making awkward small talk.

His gaze roamed over me, that peaceful smile still on his face. "Sorry," he said after a second. He took my hand, threading our fingers together. "It's just so nice to see you. And to talk to you in person, instead of typing out the things I want to say."

I laughed because I'd been thinking much the same thing. "It's weird, though, right? I worry that I don't sound smart enough in person. When I'm sending you an email I have time to think about what I want to say, as opposed to just babbling. You can't backspace conversation." And here I was babbling, proving my point.

"Well, if it makes you feel better, we can go back to that." He pulled his phone out of his pocket and waved it at me for emphasis. "We can stand here and text each other."

"Nope." I wagged a finger at him. "No phones at Faire, remember? Simon would have my head if I pulled out a phone while I'm in costume."

"Hmmm, good point. But those rules don't apply to me. I can still text you as much as I want. All day long." He glanced down at his phone, and his smile vanished. "Okay, now Frederick really is late. I should go find those yahoos."

"So this is what you do all day? Wrangle those guys?" It hadn't seemed like much of a task, but now that I was standing here with him I could see that Daniel was clearly the brains in the family, and his life consisted of herding cats. Hot-looking cats in kilts. There were worse ways to spend a life, but being the sole grown-up in the group had to be exhausting.

"Yep." He spread his arms in illustration as we headed up the lane together. "Welcome to my life."

I couldn't help but smile as we parted at a fork in the lane:

him toward the parking lot to find his musicians, and me back toward the chess field tavern to find Emily. The more I learned about his life, the more I liked it. And if I'd had a choice, I would have gladly followed him.

I thought I'd miss my phone more than I did. Every summer, I got in the habit of locking my phone in my glove compartment when I got to Faire. Some people carried their phones with them, either in a belt pouch or in the bottom of a basket, always turned off. But I knew the temptation to pull it out would be too great for me, so I didn't bring it inside at all. My hands usually felt empty those first couple days. I fully expected it to be worse this summer, since I'd grown more and more attached to my phone over the past year. How many times had my friends kidded me about it, or flat-out threatened to stage an intervention? But now that I was here, strolling the grounds in my new costume, trying to figure out who this new Beatrice character might be if she wasn't a plain tavern wench, my need for my phone faded away quickly. It didn't belong here.

It helped, of course, that the main reason for my recent phone addiction was right there, all day, close enough to touch. If I missed him, I could just slip over to the Marlowe Stage and say hi. So I indulged myself a few times over the course of the day, and from the way his face lit up whenever he saw me, he was as glad to see me as I was to see him.

Bringing our relationship out of cyberspace and into real space took a little getting used to, but I couldn't deny the thrill that went up my spine now every time Daniel's eyes caught mine. He wasn't conventionally attractive, the way Dex was. Daniel wasn't Hemsworth-esque in the least. But his glass-green eyes shone whenever he looked at me, and my skin heated up whenever his hand brushed mine. There was something so genuine in his smile that echoed the sincerity in the words we'd exchanged all this time. Last year he'd just been a casual friend, someone I'd looked forward to saying hi to every time he came through town. Now we were only two days into this year's Faire, and he was already the best part of the season.

I learned really, really fast that there was more to life than Hemsworthiness.

I dropped by the Marlowe Stage at the end of the day once pub sing was over, but Daniel was talking to his cousins, and they all seemed very focused. I didn't want to interrupt that, so I slipped out the way I'd come in. I knew how to get hold of him, after all. Sure enough, by the time I got to my car and retrieved my phone, it was lit up with texts. Based on the time stamps, Daniel had sent them throughout the day, the way he'd threatened to.

I really love your new costume. You look so good in bright colors.

Dex has called Frederick "Freddy" six times already this morning. I think he may be going for a record.

Okay, this isn't nearly as fun when you aren't allowed to have your phone. I'm doing all the texting in the relationship these days.

But I've gotten to see you twice already, so I suppose it's a fair trade-off.

Freddy tally: eleven. I predict a wrestling match in the parking lot after Faire.

Twelve Freddys now (Freddies?), and he's threatening to quit
the band. Do you know how to play drums?

I'm going to need to have a band meeting with these guys
after Faire today. I really wanted to see you tonight, but it
looks like that's going to be delayed. Let me know what your
schedule is like this week. Dinner sometime?

Hurry up and get your phone, will you? I haven't gotten a text
from you all day.

My giggle expanded into a full-on laugh as I read through all
the messages, my car getting hotter and hotter as I realized I hadn't
turned it on yet and the air-conditioning wasn't running. I was still
laced into my costume, even. Texts from Daniel rated above oxy-
gen, apparently. I remedied that, starting the engine and cranking
the air as cold as it would go before loosening my bodice. I took a
good, deep breath as my fingers flew over my phone's keyboard.

You KNOW I can't have my phone during the day. I told
you that.

I do not know how to play drums. Don't you? I bet you'd look
great in that kilt. You're taller than Freddy though, it'd be a
miniskirt on you. Hmm. I could be into that.

Sunday night after Faire is Jackson's night! Come out and sing
karaoke with us! I'll be there for a bit, text me if you think you
can make it.

I have book club on Thursday night, but otherwise I'm free.

You're going to Simon and Emily's wedding next weekend, right?

Once I'd sufficiently blown up his phone in retaliation, I put my car in gear. Time to go home, shower off, feed the cat, and get a pizza at Jackson's. I couldn't keep the grin off my face. I loved this time of year: the camaraderie, the long days, the nights out where every Sunday night felt like a cast party. Having Daniel be part of it now made it that much better.

Seven nights, six days, four workdays, three after-work evenings with Daniel, and one girls' night out/half-assed bachelorette party with Emily and April later, it was Sunday of the second weekend of Faire. Simon and Emily's wedding day. Or wedding evening, since there was still a day of Faire to get through first.

I woke up early the day of the wedding, but I was still running late somehow, so when my landline rang, I groaned out loud. I was half-dressed for my morning at Faire and juggling all the stuff I'd need to turn into a bridesmaid later that day. I loved my mom more than just about anything, but I really didn't have time to talk to her right now.

But I was a good daughter, so I pushed all that annoyance down and picked up the phone. "Morning, Mom!"

"Oh, good morning, honey." Mom sounded pleasantly surprised that it was my voice on the other end of the line. How many people did she think lived up here? "I was just wondering if you needed any help getting ready."

I blinked. "For Faire?" I looked down at myself, clad in my bright orange underdress. I'd drive to Faire in that and put on the rest when I got there. What did Mom need to help me with? "No, I'm good. I've been doing this a while, you know."

"Not for Faire." She tsked at me. "For the wedding. Time's going to be tight today, isn't it?"

I let out a sigh. "Oh, you have no idea." Simon's head would have exploded if we'd skipped Faire that day, but we did manage to talk him into letting those of us in the wedding party, himself included, leave in the midafternoon to get changed and ready for the wedding. We all had two very different costumes in store for us over the course of the day, and it was a lot to get ready for. "But I think I have a handle on everything. We're getting ready at April's house, and the limo is picking us up from there to take us back to Faire for the wedding. But I'll see you there, right?"

"Of course you will. Your father and I wouldn't miss it." Mom had been so pleased to get Emily's invitation. They'd become friendly ever since Mom had joined the book club at Read It & Weep. I had the feeling that Emily's relationship with her own mother was a little on the frosty side, so she'd really connected with mine. I didn't mind sharing Mom, especially with someone I loved as much as Emily. She would have been fun to have as a sister growing up.

After hanging up, I finished throwing my makeup and hair stuff into an overnight bag—my hairdryer and curling iron took up a lot of room—and reached for the garment bag that contained my bridesmaid dress and shoes. It took two trips down the stairs to my car to get everything loaded in the back. Bridesmaid stuff first, then Faire stuff.

That day at Faire was . . . well, it was weird. Mitch kicked Simon off the chess match, citing a ridiculous number of nerves on the part of the groom-to-be, so Simon roamed the grounds instead in character as the pirate captain, interacting with guests. Since it was bad luck for the groom to see the bride before the wedding, I had my work cut out for me. Emily and I usually split up to check on the taverns throughout the day, but today I stuck to Emily like a shadow, always looking out for a pirate in black leather and a big feathered hat. We took a lot of detours that day, checking out the shows we'd never seen before.

"We hired these guys? On purpose? And Simon approved it?" Emily shook her head in wonder as we watched the mud show wrap up. A couple well-built guys doing some bizarre cross between a comedy routine and mud wrestling. We watched mostly in morbid fascination, but the act seemed to go over well with the crowd, even the ones who were getting spattered with mud.

"I think Mitch was responsible for this one," I said. "I don't think I talked to them at all. He probably snuck it by Chris when Simon wasn't paying attention."

"Yeah, but when is Simon not paying attention?" Emily's giggle was high-pitched, nervous. Her mind was only half on our conversation. I looked over her shoulder and spotted the man himself, way down the lane facing the other direction. He was probably going toward the joust. Which meant we were going the other way.

"Come on." I steered her toward the main tavern, where Jamie flagged us down.

"Yeah, so the caterers got here early."

Emily sucked in a breath. "What time is it?" She reached for Jamie's wrist to look at his watch. "It's only two forty-five! They're not supposed to be here until four!"

"Which is why I said they're early." Jamie was the most unflappable person I'd ever known. Emily looked like she was about to burst a blood vessel, and it didn't bother him a bit. "Don't worry about it. I talked to them and they're coming back in a couple hours. Look at it this way—you'd rather they got here early than late, right?"

"Or not at all." I bumped Emily's shoulder with mine. "More importantly, we have to get the hell outta here." We were on a tight schedule. Faire ended at five, technically, though pub sing started up front about four thirty. Once the last human chess match of the day was over and people started filtering toward the front, we had a team coming in to set up chairs on the chess field and an archway at one end in time for the wedding at six thirty. Meanwhile, Em and I had to get going to transform into a bridesmaid and a bride. She didn't need to be worrying about caterers and whether or not they'd set up in time. She had to worry about looking beautiful and marrying the man she loved.

And it was my job to keep her on task. Emily was normally great at that, but she was operating with maybe half a brain today, and that was a generous estimate. "Time to go get pretty," I said.

She blinked at me, her eyes a little wild, and yeah, we were going to need to break into the champagne a little early. My girl here needed a drink. "Okay," she said.

"You okay to drive?" Jamie peered at her. "You look a little freaked out."

"I can drive you," I said. "We can leave your Jeep here for now."

"No." Emily shook her head. "I mean yes. No, I'm not freaked out, and yes, I'm okay to drive."

"Then let's go. I'll follow you over to April's place." I tugged on her arm. I was doing a lot of arm tugging and directing today, and this constant vigilance had me on edge too. I'd been so focused on keeping Emily away from Simon that I'd hardly been in character at all today. I loved being Beatrice, and I'd been cheated out of a day to be her. Oh, well. We still had two more weekends of Faire. It wasn't over yet.

Back at April's house I was a little more in my comfort zone. Emily and I had practiced her wedding hairstyle a couple times already, and it was easy enough. A simple updo, with tendrils of her natural curls escaping around her temples, and a delicate crown of pale pink silk flowers on top of it all. I took my time until her hair was perfect, while April supervised.

"Wow, that looks great. You need to do mine next." She refilled Emily's champagne flute.

"No." Emily tried to move it out of the way, but April steadied her hand and kept pouring.

"Yes. Don't worry, I'm not going to let you get hammered. You just need to relax a little."

"I'm plenty relaxed."

"Uh-huh. You're about to snap that champagne flute in half."

"April's right." I waved her out of the chair she was in. "Go. Sit over there, drink your booze and chill for a minute while I do April's hair." I hadn't realized that I would be doing April's hair too, but her requesting it was an offer of friendship that I realized in that moment I'd been craving. So I settled her at the dressing table and our eyes met in the mirror. "Same updo?"

"Same updo." She nodded and looked up at me in the mirror, her eyes a little uncertain. "You have time, right? I probably should've asked instead of just assuming . . ."

"Ah, hush up." I gathered April's hair in my hands. It was a little longer than Emily's, but the curls were the same. "This won't take any time at all."

Once April's hair was done, I attacked my own. I had no natural curl to speak of, so I wielded my curling iron like a weapon until my hair had twice the body it normally did and cascaded in loose blonde curls down below my shoulders. Then I pinned it up and threaded a few pale pink flowers into it here and there. April had some loose flowers in her hair too—green to match her dress. Only the bride got a bona fide flower crown at this Faire wedding.

There was something incongruous about arriving to Faire in a gray stretch limo as the last patrons were leaving for the day. The tires crunched over the gravel in the parking lot and several heads turned, trying to peer through the tinted windows.

"You ready?" April leaned across the seat and laid a hand over her sister's wrist. Emily had been looking out the window the whole ride over, not saying a word. She'd been a big ball of stress all day, but now she turned to us with sparkling eyes and an easy smile. Her nerves were gone. Yes. She was ready.

She let out a deep breath as the limo driver opened the door. "Let's do this."

Sixteen

W e'd had a wedding rehearsal, of course. One evening last week we'd met up at the Faire site to run through where everything was going to happen and where we'd need to stand. But going through the motions and marking our places didn't give an accurate picture of what it was going to be like. How dream-like it was going to be, the three of us in our fluttery white and pastel dresses with flowers in our hair, heading down the main lane of Faire to marry Emily to Simon. Modern dresses with period details in this pastoral setting (yes, Mitch had been right about that word) made it hard to determine exactly what century we were in.

A couple dozen yards away from the chess field, Emily's father was waiting for us, standing in the middle of the lane in a dark gray suit with his hands folded in front of him. I'd met him earlier this week at the rehearsal dinner but hadn't talked to him much. He seemed quiet, almost stern, but now his expression melted when he saw us.

"Hey there, Sprite." He stepped forward and bent to kiss Emily's cheek. "You look beautiful."

She blinked back tears as she practically glowed up at him. "Thank you, Daddy."

April cleared her throat, and Mr. Parker looked shamefaced for a moment as he glanced over at April and me. "Of course, you girls look great too."

"Yes, we do," April agreed cheerfully. "Now let's get Emily married."

"Good idea." He offered the bride his arm. "Are you ready for this? I like Simon fine, but you never know. Maybe he's a jerk. You're sure about this guy, right?"

Emily's eyes widened in horror. "Of course I'm sure, Dad! What the hell kind of question is that?"

He smirked. "Just making sure." He caught my eye and ushered me forward. "You first, I think."

"Yep. It's all me." From where we stood I could hear the music coming from the chess field, a string quartet made up of some of Willow Creek High's music students. It was time.

I set off down the lane by myself, and when the chess field was in sight I slowed to a languid stroll more suited for walking down a wedding aisle. It was easy to smile and look the part of a joyful bridesmaid, because that was exactly how I felt inside. The field that hosted our human combat chess match every weekend of Faire had been transformed. The giant chess board was still visible in its grass-and-white squares that covered the field. But those squares were covered with rows of wooden folding chairs with an aisle running down the middle. At one end of the field was a white wicker archway, and as I got closer I could see Simon and Mitch up there, waiting with the officiant.

As my foot hit the white vinyl runner, people turned in their seats to watch me process down the aisle. My eyes immediately caught on a figure sitting on the groom's side, smack-dab in the middle of a row. A figure whose vivid auburn hair was a direct contrast to the all-black outfit he was wearing. Daniel's polite smile widened into something more genuine when he saw me, and I didn't know what shone in my eyes to put that smile on his face, but I was glad it did. I'd forgotten how vivid his hair was when it wasn't hidden under a baseball cap. Now it was combed back from his face, and a little damp from a late-afternoon post-Faire shower. He'd shaved before the wedding, too. I wanted to climb over the people sitting between him and me. I wanted to settle into his lap and run my hand down that smooth cheek. Instead, I shot him a playful wink, and he laughed without making a sound.

I got to my place at the front of the aisle and turned. April was about halfway down the aisle herself, while Emily and her father were just visible, still on the lane. I looked from them back to Simon. At first glance he looked calm, but that was only a thin veneer. I'd known him long enough to know that the man was about to come out of his skin. There was a wild look in his eyes, a muscle jumped in his cheek from his tightened jaw, and his hands were clasped together in front of him so hard his fingertips had turned red. The early evening sun flashed off the silver hoop earring in his ear, and seeing it made me smile. For all that he had insisted he wouldn't get married in costume— and he wasn't, his dark gray suit with a matching striped vest beneath was all Simon—he'd brought that little piece of Captain Blackthorne to the wedding.

Of course, there were a lot of pieces of Faire at this wedding. Venue aside, Mitch stood there in his dark gray suit jacket and a green kilt, wearing a proud smirk. Had Simon really approved that? Seemed unlikely. Out in the crowd, roughly a quarter of the attendees were Faire performers, most of them still in costume. Leather jerkins and long skirts mingled with neckties and flowered dresses worn by family members and in-town friends.

The music changed as Emily and her father came down the aisle. Simon sucked in a sharp breath, and Mitch nudged him. "Look at her." His voice was a whisper, but it carried to those of us in the wedding party. I was pretty sure Simon couldn't have spoken even if he wanted to, but that was okay. He didn't need to. He gripped his hands tighter—could a man break his own fingers that way?—and his gaze sharpened to a laser-point as he watched his bride's approach. As for Emily, she looked beatific; I'd never seen someone smile with their whole being before. Even the flowers she carried looked happy.

What would it be like to look forward to your future with such unbridled joy? Without thinking, my gaze flicked over to Daniel, and when he turned his head to catch my eye at the same time, I felt a stirring of that same kind of joy deep in my chest. I could blame it on the setting, sure, but I had a feeling it was all Daniel.

The wedding ceremony was like a dream, a pleasant one that I couldn't fully recall after it was over, but it left me with a glowing feeling. My memory was reduced to snapshots, images of moments. Emily and Simon joining hands, looking like they'd been waiting their whole lives for that moment. April wiping a surreptitious tear during the vows. Caitlin reading a romantic Shakespearean sonnet that made Emily blush and Simon's hand tighten around hers. The most perfect, sweetest of kisses as they were pronounced husband and wife.

After the wedding, while we took an endless series of

wedding-party photos, the chairs were repositioned and the chess field became the reception hall, with tables and chairs set around the edges and a makeshift dance floor in the middle. The caterers set up little stations of appetizers, the string quartet gave way to a deejay with a sound system, and before long everyone was chatting and eating. I was released from all the posed wedding photo–taking to find Daniel waiting for me with a plate of finger food—chicken wings, stuffed mushrooms, assorted canapés—along with a plastic glass of champagne.

"God bless you." I couldn't decide what I wanted to attack first, but the fact that I had hardly eaten a bite all day made me practically snatch the plate out of his hand. "Are we sharing this?"

"Nope, this is all yours. I ate my share while I was waiting for you." He ushered me to a seat at a nearby table and picked up the beer he'd left there. "You haven't eaten today, have you? You hardly eat during a normal Faire day, and with all of this going on, I figured . . ." He shrugged, and there was that feeling again. That easy, familiar feeling that we'd been together for a few years and not a couple weeks. He knew my habits and the things I liked. He knew *me*.

I sank gratefully into a chair and took a healthy sip of champagne. My role in this wedding was over. Now I could relax and enjoy myself. No longer a bridesmaid, now just a wedding guest. Thank God.

The food wasn't particularly Faire-themed, which was probably a good thing. The more conventional wedding guests wouldn't have gone for a dinner of giant turkey legs, mead, and funnel cakes. Instead it was an assortment of finger foods, like tapas, but in large enough quantities to guarantee that no one would go hungry. Once the guests were full of food, the toasts began, and we raised our glasses again and again, saying lots of

"Huzzahs!" to the happy couple before they took the floor for the first dance.

"Come on." Daniel popped one last mini-meatball in his mouth and wiped his hands on a napkin before he stood and extended a hand to me, his eyebrows raised in a question. "Dance with me?"

As if I'd say no to that. I let him pull me to my feet and onto the makeshift dance floor, moving to a sweet, slow song.

"So, tell me." I laid a hand on his broadcloth-covered chest, relishing the way the muscles tightened under my hand. "Do you own any clothes that aren't black?" In black dress trousers and a black button-down shirt with a black tie, he looked like a dressed-up version of the clothes he wore every day.

"Hey," he said, but his protest had no real heat to it. He covered my hand with his, keeping it over his heart. "It's an easy color to wear. Everything matches that way."

I considered that. "One of these days I want to see you in a pink shirt."

He barked out a laugh. "With my hair? No, thank you." He shook his head, and the aforementioned hair fell into his eyes. I reached up to brush it off his forehead, and his eyes softened in reaction to my touch. "I'm really not a pink-shirt kind of guy. Besides . . ." He ran a hand up my back and then over my shoulder, the soft fabric of the sleeve of my dress sliding between his fingers like water. "You wear enough color for the both of us."

The both of us. I loved the way that sounded.

The sun sank lower in the sky and a slight chill crept into the evening, just enough to take the worst of the heat off the day. Daniel and I took a break from the dancing to split a slice of white wedding cake, and I watched Simon and Emily mingle among the guests on the other side of the chess field.

"They look so happy." I'd had a couple glasses of champagne and some cake by now, so I wasn't exactly grouchy myself. I leaned back, pillowing my head in the hollow of Daniel's shoulder, and his arm went around me as though we did this all the time. I wished we could do this all the time. Why did the summer have to end?

Nope. Not thinking about that yet. Instead I turned my attention back to the newlyweds and sighed. What I wouldn't give to have someone look at me the way Simon looked at Emily. With his entire soul in his eyes. Out of nowhere I remembered how I'd felt at the end of last summer. The restless melancholy, the sense that I didn't have my shit together, that had led me to send that first drunken message to the man who turned out to be Daniel. It had all been spurred by the news of Simon and Emily's engagement, and the feeling that I needed to build a life of my own.

Then I felt a touch on my arm, and I turned my head to see Daniel staring down at me, and oh my God. He was looking at me the way Simon looked at Emily. When I looked in his eyes, I didn't feel restless. I didn't feel melancholy. A lot had changed for me in a year. He skimmed his fingertips up my arm and to my shoulder, leaving little electric tingles in the wake of his touch. My breath caught in my lungs, and I was lost in the endless green of his eyes.

"Hey, you." My voice was hushed, barely more than a whisper of breath, but a smile played over his mouth. He'd heard me.

"Hi." He caught a lock of my hair, winding the strands between his fingers. He bent closer and my eyes slid closed as I waited for his mouth to close over mine.

And that was when a raindrop splashed directly onto the middle of my forehead.

I started, my eyes flying open, and Daniel turned to look up at the sky as I touched the water that had hit me. "Is that rain?" Above us the sky had grown dark, much darker than it should be this time of evening; there should have been at least another half hour or so of daylight. But now a breeze kicked up, and there was a subtle rumble of thunder in the distance.

"Yep," he said. "That's rain. Shit."

I hadn't checked the forecast that day, but I wasn't exactly surprised. Summer thunderstorms were common, especially when the day had been as warm as this one. "At least it waited till the wedding was over."

"Mostly." Stray raindrops started falling faster, and in moments they'd coalesced into a steady drizzle. Soon it would be a downpour. Daniel tugged me to my feet and we ducked beneath a large tree that provided some shelter. But that rumble of thunder in the distance meant lightning, so we couldn't stay there. All around us the party was breaking up quickly. The music shut off abruptly as a couple volunteers, Mitch included, helped the deejay break down his equipment. Wedding guests started running for their cars. Meanwhile, Emily's parents, April, and Caitlin gathered the wedding presents in tablecloths, pulling them away like Santa Claus with sacks of presents. In minutes, the wedding reception was all but over, abruptly called on account of rain. The only two who hadn't gotten the memo were Simon and Emily themselves, still on the chess field dance floor, with eyes only for each other.

"Get out of the rain, you idiots!" I yelled, and Emily flicked her eyes to me, waving me off with a laugh before turning her attention back to her new husband, who smiled down into her eyes as though he couldn't feel the rain.

Well, I'd tried. I reached inside the pocket of my dress for my keys, and then I remembered. I had keys but . . . "I don't have my car." It was at April's house, because I'd come here in the limo. I'd intended to hitch a ride home with my parents, but apparently I'd forgotten to share that plan with them; they'd left after the cake was cut.

"Come on." Daniel looked up at the sky again. "It's just going to get worse. I'll take you home."

"You sure?" But we were already running in the rain, our hands clasped together and him pulling me along toward the performers' parking lot.

He hazarded one glance over his shoulder, a skeptical look on his face. "Of course I'm sure. You think I'd leave you stranded?"

No. If there was one thing I knew for sure about Daniel, he wouldn't leave me stranded.

"It's just up ahead." I leaned forward in the passenger seat of Daniel's pickup as he navigated us through the rain and onto my street. "Third house on the left. With the light on."

"Got it." He swung into my driveway. "Wow. I have to say I'm impressed."

"Impressed?" I looked at the rain-soaked driveway, then back at him again.

"Yeah." He pulled to a stop and for a moment we both sat there, windshield wipers throwing rain from one side of the windshield to the other, staring at my parents' completely unimpressive house. "I had no idea receptionists in dental offices made so much. That's a pretty nice house you've got there."

"What?" My laugh echoed in the cab of his truck, louder than I'd intended it to be. "No. No, this isn't my house. You know that."

"What?" He turned in his seat to look at me. "You said third house on the left. This isn't your house?"

"No. I mean, yes. I mean . . ." I huffed. "I don't live in *there.*" I pointed to the side of the garage, to the stairs that led to the door of my apartment. "I live up there. You knew that. From my emails." Hadn't I explained my whole apartment-over-the-garage situation to him?

"Up those rickety stairs? No. You're not going up those stairs in the rain."

I clucked my tongue and unfastened my seatbelt. "Oh, yes, I am. I do it all the time."

"Not in those little shoes, you don't. You're going to slip."

"I'm not going to slip." He was right, but there was no way I'd admit it. The wood plank stairs were soaking wet by now, and these sandals had no tread on the bottoms. I could absolutely break my neck trying to prove him wrong.

"Come on." He unclicked his own seatbelt and turned off the truck. The windshield wipers slammed to a halt and the truck cab filled up with silence from the sudden lack of engine noise. "I'll help you up the stairs."

I scoffed. "What are you going to do, fireman-carry me up there? You'll get a hernia and we'll both fall."

He sighed a long-suffering sigh. We really hadn't been together long enough for him to be this annoyed with me. "No, but I can walk behind you and make sure you don't slip."

I sighed in response and peered up toward my door. So close and yet so far. I'd hoped that while we were bickering the rain would stop, but no such luck. Water covered the windshield now, blurring the streetlights. Lightning lit up the sky, closely followed by a crack of thunder.

"Storm's getting worse." Daniel didn't sound accusatory; he was just making an observation. But I frowned anyway.

"Okay." I took a fortifying breath. "Let's do this." Another deep breath, and I threw open the door to his truck and darted out into the storm. I shrieked as the cold water pelted down on me, and as I ran to the stairs I heard Daniel's startled shout as he followed me, getting just as wet as I was. And sure enough, on the third step up my foot slipped out from under me on the wet wood. A squeak erupted from my mouth as I started to fall, but Daniel was there. He caught me with his hands on my hips, steadying me until I had a good grasp on the handrail, and then we both pounded up the stairs. I dug for my keys and the rain fell harder just to spite me.

"Fine, you were right!" I shouted to be heard above the storm as I fished my keys out of my pocket. "I would have fallen on the stairs!"

"I can gloat later!" he yelled back. "Open the door!"

I turned the key in the lock and pushed, and we practically fell into my apartment like something out of a French farce. He slammed the door behind us, and the noise of the hard-falling rain was cut off like a switch had been thrown. For a few moments all I could hear was our breath, hard and a little labored from our mad dash up the stairs. I turned around, raking my disheveled hair out of my eyes, and looked up at Daniel, leaning back against my door. He was so tall in this tiny space, but it wasn't an imposing presence. He was a mess, soaking wet, looking as bedraggled as I felt, and a helpless laugh bubbled out of me. He joined in almost immediately, his laugh more a loud rush of breath, and as it died out I noticed the rain was coming down even harder, the water pinging off the skylights above us. Another noise too: a faint chirrup from the vicinity of the couch.

"Oh." Daniel pushed his hair out of his eyes, raking it straight back before taking a step forward. "This must be Benedick. Your true love." He reached out his other hand, but Benedick looked at him with startled eyes before zipping away toward the bathroom.

I tried not to laugh at the hurt in his eyes when he looked back at me. "That's right. I forgot you're not a cat person."

"I never said that. I said I've never had one. There's a difference."

"Well, it shows." But I kept my voice kind. "Cats startle pretty easily. He doesn't know you, and with you looming over him like that—"

"I don't loom."

"You're ten feet tall, of course you loom. Not to mention you're soaking wet." So was I. And with the air conditioner running I was also freezing. I suppressed a shiver.

"Oh." He looked down at himself, plucking his wet shirt away from his chest with a sigh. "Well, there is that."

I ducked into the bathroom for towels and to check on Benedick, who glared at me from behind the toilet. When I caught sight of myself in the mirror, I tried not to scream. I'd worked so hard on my hair, and now the carefully pinned-up curls listed to the side like a drunken wedding cake, flowers poking out haphazardly. And the less said about my supposedly waterproof mascara, the better. When I came back out, Daniel was back to leaning on the front door, his expression unsure.

"I should probably . . ." He jerked a thumb over his shoulder, toward the downpour outside, and my heart fell into my stomach. It was only his uncertain expression that kept me from despairing completely. He didn't want to go. He was just giving me an excuse to kick him out if I didn't want him there.

I didn't take it. "Don't be silly." I handed him a towel as thunder rumbled outside. "You can't go back out in that. It should let up soon. Stay."

Seventeen

The *word hung* in the air between us, and I was afraid to breathe, to make any sound that would erase it. Daniel reached for the towel but I didn't let go, so when he tugged on it, he pulled me closer to him. He ran a thumb under my makeup-smudged eyes before stroking my hair. "You're wet." His voice had dropped an octave, and a shiver ran through me that had nothing to do with the cold.

I wanted to snicker. I'd been hanging out with Mitch for too long, because my first instinct was to respond with a dirty joke. But Daniel had let go of the towel to take my face between his hands, and I remembered he'd been about to kiss me at the wedding reception before the rain interrupted us.

There was nothing to interrupt us now. His kiss was a greeting, an affirmation, a confirmation that he was meant to be here at this very moment. No perfectly-broken-in pair of jeans had felt as comfortable, as right, as his mouth felt on mine.

But comfortable didn't last long. The heat in his kiss chased away the chill of being caught in the rain. I let my mouth open under his as he began to press, to explore, and before I knew what was happening he had turned us, so now my back was against the door and he pressed against me, crowding into me, and I didn't mind it a bit. I let the towel fall to the floor as I reached for him. The skin of his neck was cold against my palms but warmed up fast, and the wet hair at the base of his skull slicked between my fingers.

"Stacey." My name was a whisper, a prayer on his lips. His fingertips traced a tingling trail down the side of my throat. He pulled back to catch my gaze with his, and whatever he read in my eyes must have been encouraging since he bent to me again, catching my mouth in a quick, searching kiss as if he couldn't bear to be away. Then his mouth dropped to my neck, nuzzling just under my jaw, and my blood raced in response.

I stretched onto my toes to get closer to him, and he stooped a little, his hands cupping my hips. We were dealing with a definite height difference here, but I could work with that. I'd climb him if I had to. I just needed to be closer to him. From the way Daniel's touch had turned from caressing to grasping, he was feeling the same way. He leaned into me, pressing me against the door, almost lifting me against it, and I could feel myself melt against the hard lines of his body.

And then my landline rang, and it was like being doused with a bucket of ice water. I groaned and let my head fall back, thudding onto the door behind me. "Mom."

"If you're thinking about your mom right now, I'm doing this wrong." But he smiled against my neck and slowly, slowly released his grip on me. The loss was devastating, but my phone was still ringing.

"On the phone." I lightly pushed at his chest with my fingertip and he stepped back. I got to the phone on its fourth ring, thank God. I didn't have an answering machine hooked up and Mom was tenacious; she'd just let it keep ringing till I answered. Or worse: she'd give up and come looking for me.

"Hey, Mom." I blew out a breath and tried to slow my racing heart. I sounded pretty calm for someone who was just making out fifteen seconds ago.

"Oh, hi, honey." There was Mom's usual mild surprise that it was my voice on the other end of the line. "How was the wedding?"

I had to laugh at that. "The wedding was great, Mom. You were there." But even as I laughed, alarm bells went off in the back of my mind. None of her health issues had ever been neurological. Could this be a new thing?

Mom scoffed. "Well, of course I was. Emily was a beautiful bride. I hope Simon appreciates her."

"Oh, I'm pretty sure he does." The alarm bells faded a little, replaced by impatience. The last thing I wanted to do right now was rehash Emily's wedding. I loved her, and I loved my mother, but there was a much bigger priority in the room right now. A priority that was well over six feet tall and was the best kisser I'd ever experienced. So why were we having this conversation? Why now?

"I meant how was the wedding for you? We left early. Did it start raining before it was over?"

"It did! I'm glad you got home before it started. It came on kind of sudden."

"Well, I hope you had a good time before it got rained out. I saw you dancing with that tall fellow. Who is he?"

"Oh . . ." I looked over at Daniel, who had his back to me; it looked like he was adjusting the front of his pants. The thought of what was in those pants, and what this damn phone call had interrupted, sent heat coursing through me, and I needed to not be thinking about that while talking to my mother. "That was Daniel." He turned to me when I spoke his name, his eyes wide with alarm that I might hand him the phone. I smirked at his discomfort and waved him off; he responded with a shake of his head, scooping the forgotten towel from the floor. "He's . . ." *He's standing right here. He was about to bang me against that door, so if we could get off the phone, that would be great, thanks, Mom.*

"Well, I won't keep you." It was as though she'd read my mind, and I had to fight to not breathe a sigh of relief. "I just heard you come home and wanted to make sure you didn't get too wet out there."

"Oh, I'm soaked." Was I ever. I winced at my choice of words but plowed on ahead. "It's raining like crazy. But I'm okay. Thanks, Mom." As we hung up the phone, though, I realized that it wasn't raining like crazy. Not anymore. Rain still skittered off the skylight, but not nearly as hard as it had before. Ugh. No. I wanted the bad weather back. I wanted Daniel trapped in here with me, with no choice but to stay. I couldn't believe Mom had brought our momentum to a grinding halt.

I turned back to Daniel with a sheepish smile. "Sorry. Um. So that's the ugly truth."

He raised his eyebrows. "What ugly truth?"

"That I live with my parents." I spread my arms in defeat. "You are now welcome to flee in terror."

He made a show of looking around the living area, then walking past me into the kitchen. "I don't see them here," he said. "Are they both in the bathroom?"

I rolled my eyes. "No."

"Under your bed? Kind of a tight fit under there."

"No," I said again, but this time with a laugh in my voice.

"Then I don't see the problem." He shrugged. "You live *near* your parents. You're parents-adjacent. I knew that already, remember? You're close with your parents."

"Literally." But it was a sorry attempt at a joke, and in this moment I felt disappointed in myself. Here I was, twenty-seven years old, living steps away from my mother, who called to make sure I had gotten out of the rain on my own. Some adult I was.

He shrugged again and glanced up toward the skylight. I did the same, gauging the state of the weather outside. Was he looking for an out? I braced myself, waiting for his goodbye. But then he looked at me and I caught my breath. The heat hadn't left his eyes, and he held out a hand to me. No, he held out the towel.

"C'mere," he said. "Your hair's still soaking wet." His voice was hushed, and it was obvious that he wasn't just offering to dry my hair. But I went along with the pretense, reaching for the pins in my hair as I approached him, little silk flowers scattering in my wake.

"So no fleeing in terror?" I finger-combed my hair as it tumbled down around my shoulders, and Daniel caught his breath, his eyes darkening.

"Not even a little." The towel went right back to the floor again as he reached for me. I reached for him right back, and we kissed all the way to my bed under the eaves, unzipping and unbuttoning as we went.

"We really need to get you out of these wet clothes." Daniel pushed my dress to my waist, and I shimmied the rest of the way out of it, kicking it away. "Your mother was very concerned about you. You could catch your death, you know."

"Mmm, oh yes. Catch my death in July." I let his tie flutter to the floor and tugged his shirt out of his waistband.

"I'm a little bit serious, though." He stroked one hand up my side, around the dip of my waist and to the fullness of my breast, taking a slow journey around my curves. "Your skin really is cold."

"Warm me up, then." My voice was husky with invitation, and from the way he pulled me close and kissed me harder, it was an invitation he was eager to accept. I finished with the buttons on his shirt and squeaked a little as I slid my arms around his chest. "You should talk," I said. "You're cold too."

"Warm me up, then." His words were an echo of mine, and a surprised laugh sprung from me. He shrugged out of his shirt and went to work on the hooks on my longline bra while walking me backward toward the bed.

"I'm impressed," I said, as he popped the hooks open one by one down my chest in a steady rhythm. "These things can be tricky."

"Probably easier to get out of than into." The last hook popped free and we both sighed: me with relief as the loosened garment fell away from my body, and him with something that looked a little bit like worship. My instinct was to cross my arms over myself: my soft middle wasn't something I displayed all that often, and the first time with a new partner was always a little nerve-wracking. But there was nothing in Daniel's eyes that showed distaste. Instead he reached a tentative hand toward me, curving it around my waist, his fingertips tracing a line up my skin from my waist to just under my breasts. He sucked in a breath that was less aroused than concerned.

"Does that hurt?"

"What . . . ?" I ran a hand up my rib cage, feeling the indentations left behind by the boning in the bra. Ah. He'd been tracing a literal line up my body. "Maybe a little," I said. "Nothing to worry about. I'm used to it. Especially this time of year. Lots of corsetry in my life in the summertime."

He huffed out a laugh, which turned into a sigh as I caught his hand and moved it up. He got the message quick. His palm was rough against the underside of my breast, his thumb circling a rapidly tightening nipple. His touch was electric, but it wasn't enough. I needed his mouth, his lips, his tongue on my skin. I wanted everything from him. But I forced myself to take my time, running a hand across his taut stomach and then up his chest, loving the way his muscles flexed under my touch. Up and up, tracing the line of his breastbone and curving around his neck, before I drew his head back down, meeting his mouth with mine. His hands tightened on me, breast and hip, and I swallowed the groan that came from his throat. We moved together in perfect concert, toeing off our shoes and sinking onto my bed.

Which squeaked under us.

Kind of loudly.

I ignored it and ran my hands up Daniel's back; his skin was no longer cold under my hands. He braced his hands on either side of my head and rolled his hips to mine, aligning our bodies. He rocked against me, hard, and I gasped. The only thing between us were his pants and my underwear, but that was still too many clothes. I ran my fingers down the dip of his spine—he shivered and kissed me harder—and made quick work of his belt and the button and zipper on his pants. He bucked his hips as I reached inside for him.

"Jesus, Stacey . . ." He was huge in my hand, hard and hot, and I didn't mean to tease but I couldn't help mapping his size and girth with my fingers. The heat of him, the size of him, I couldn't get enough, and it didn't take long for mapping to become stroking, in a slow glide from base to the tip. His breath came hard in his chest, shuddering in his lungs, and I couldn't keep the grin from my face as he rocked against me, thrusting gently into my hand in a steady rhythm. He felt good. This felt good. This was . . .

. . . loud. When had my bed become so damn squeaky?

Daniel stilled his movements and pushed himself up on his hands, looking down at me.

"So. Um . . ." There was that laugh again, that quiet one that was like a rush of breath.

He looked up at the wall behind my head, as if he could find something important there, then looked back down at me. "I don't know about this." He pushed himself off me, away from me, and I missed his weight immediately. Everything felt cold without his skin touching mine.

"Okay . . . ?" I hated how small my voice sounded. How defeated. He'd undressed me a few minutes ago, but this was the first moment I felt naked. But it didn't take long for defeat to dissolve into anger. Frustration, even.

"So what's the problem?" I pulled at the blanket I kept folded at the end of my bed, tugging it around my chest as I sat up to face Daniel, who was sitting on the other side of the bed, as far away from me as he could get.

"Problem? No . . ." He shook his head and reached for me, but I shrugged away from his touch.

"Then why did you . . ." Frustration mounted and I surged to my feet, wrapping the blanket around me like a kind of toga.

What exactly had I misread here? Him dry-humping me into the mattress, or the helpless sound he'd made when I had his dick in my hand? But asking him why he didn't want me anymore was mortifying. "You changed your mind," I finally said.

"What? No, I didn't."

"Yes, you did." I folded my arms over my chest, partially in annoyance and partially to help keep my blanket-toga in place. "You stopped"—I waved a hand, indicating the space between us—"all this."

"Because your parents are on the other side of that wall, and your bed won't shut the hell up." He nodded his head back toward the wall behind him. "Shouldn't we be a little . . . quieter?"

All my anger and hurt feelings melted away, replaced by . . . I wasn't sure what. Maybe still a little bit of anger. Definitely some frustration. But mostly relief. "Are you serious?" I threw up my hands. "My old bedroom is on the other side of that wall. All that's in there now is a treadmill, and believe me, they never use it."

"Are you sure?" He looked over his shoulder, as though my mother might materialize through the wall and ask him his intentions.

I rolled my eyes. "Yes, I'm sure."

"Okay, then." Doubt cleared from his face, replaced with a slow smile as he turned back to me. "Then why are you all the way over there, and wearing a bedspread?"

"Maybe I look good in this bedspread." But I took his outstretched hand and let him pull me back to where he was on the bed. He bracketed my body between his spread knees, tilting his head back to look up at me, and whoo boy, there was a throat I wanted to nibble on. So I did.

"God, Stacey, you feel . . ." His hand tightened around mine, and his other hand went into my tumbled-down hair. He swallowed hard, and I felt the movement against my lips. "You feel better than I ever imagined you would."

I smiled against his neck. "You imagined me?"

"For months. You have to know I did." He pulled away to take my mouth with his again, and I felt his kiss all the way down to my toes. I moved closer to him, crawling into his lap and letting the bedspread fall from my shoulders.

"I wish I had." I rocked against him, the friction of my panties and his pants between us both delicious and frustrating. "I wish I'd known it was you, all that time." That was the one regret I had in all of this. Not so much that he'd lied: we were past that now. But that I hadn't known the truth. A fine line there—but now that I knew the man behind the words, I wished I'd always known. I wished I could have fantasized about the right man all this time. Because the man in my arms right now was better than Dex had ever been. Better than anyone I could have ever imagined.

"I'm sorry." He cradled my face in his hands, pressing his forehead to mine. I was drowning in the ocean of his green eyes searching mine. "I'm so sorry. I should have . . ."

"No, it's okay." I punctuated the words with another kiss. "I know why you did."

"No, but . . ." He sighed, his breath ghosting across my lips. "It's so stupid. All of it. But . . . I'm not my cousin. I don't know what kind of moves that guy has, but he obviously knows what he's doing with women. And I didn't know how to break it to you that I wasn't . . ."

"Shhhh." It was my turn to cradle his face in my hands. I let my thumbs trace over his cheekbones, trying to soothe whatever ache inside him made him feel he wasn't good enough.

"I knew you'd be disappointed, and I kept telling myself that I needed to come clean. I just didn't know how to . . ."

"I know." I dropped a kiss on his cheek, his mouth, his chin. The past was behind us. All I wanted to do now was look forward. "I don't care about his moves. He's not here. You're the only one I see."

"Yeah?" But his hand was back in my hair, his other stroking down my back, urging me closer with a gentle pull. I scooted a little closer in his lap, and we both drew in a breath at the contact.

"Do that again." He moaned the words into my mouth, tilting his hips up in a slow grind against me, and why were we still wearing so many clothes? We had to do something about that.

"I think it's time you show me your moves," I said.

"You think so, huh?" His hand tightened in my hair, holding my head just where he wanted to kiss me more thoroughly. His tongue glided against mine, drinking me in, and I gave as good as I got. I let my hands wander up his chest, learning the planes of his body, the sprinkling of coarse, dark red hair against my palms, and the heat of his skin. His other hand smoothed around the dip of my waist before sliding into the back of my panties, cupping my behind and pulling me more firmly into his lap. A lap that was . . . well, firm. Extremely so.

Before long he lay back in the bed, taking me with him. My breasts were crushed against his chest, and I wanted us to be that close everywhere. He was easing my underwear over my hips, and my hands slid down between us, returning to his open pants. I eased up onto my knees, straddling his hips, alternately rocking over him and wrestling his pants down. Finally. Time to . . .

He broke off our kiss with another quiet laugh. "Seriously. What is wrong with your bed?"

"Nothing!" But he wasn't wrong. The springs let out a little squeak of protest every time we moved, and the more into it we got, the more . . . rhythmic the squeaking became.

He looked up at me, laughter in his eyes and his hand still down the back of my underwear. "You've never noticed how noisy your bed is?"

"Well, no." He was still hard beneath me and I squirmed on him, making him catch his breath. "I guess Benedick and I don't move around much when we're sleeping."

"Well, I'm planning to move around with you quite a bit."

"So you keep promising. Will you shut up about my bed already?"

"Hold on." He slid an arm around my back, and took a firmer grip on my hip.

"What are you—oooh!"

Without warning, he sat up, taking me with him, and from there got to his feet, wrapping my legs around his hips. I locked my arms around his neck to help hoist myself up his body while he took me . . . where?

"What are you doing?" I couldn't keep the giggle out of my voice. I wanted to protest that I was too heavy to be carried, but he didn't seem to have any trouble. The blanket from my bed was still tangled between us and he took it with him, dragging it behind us like the train of a wedding gown.

"Getting away from that bed before your mother comes storming up here."

"Oh my God!" My giggle blossomed into a full-on laugh. I would have smacked him on the shoulder but I also didn't want him to drop me. "Will you stop worrying about my mother already? My parents can't hear anything that goes on up here."

He didn't look convinced, although humor danced in his eyes. "Promise?" He dipped me back, lowering me to my couch.

"Promise," I said. But I couldn't resist. "I mean, unless you're doing laundry or something. We're right above the garage."

He looked alarmed. "What if she decides to do laundry?"

"This late at night?" I shook my head. "Now, shush." I reached for him, and he sank to his knees in front of the couch. He didn't kiss me, though, not yet. Instead he pushed gently on my shoulders, laying me back against the couch cushions before tugging my panties down my legs and off. He pulled the blanket away gently, as if he were unwrapping a Christmas present.

"Let me look at you. Please."

I drew a nervous breath, exceedingly conscious that he was not seeing me at the best angle. I looked better lying flat, not in this half-reclining state. But I couldn't say no to him. I couldn't deny the shine in his eyes, the wonder in his gaze as his fingertips glided up my thighs, encouraging them to part for him. Oh, God, he was going to touch me. Finally. And it was going to devastate me. My eyes fell closed and my breath shuddered out of me as his fingers started exploring, fondling, stroking.

"Holy shit." His voice was weak, little more than a whisper. I forced my eyes open to see him watching my face. "You're the most beautiful . . ." He slid a finger inside me, then two, in then out slowly, every move deliberate yet gentle. Taking his time. Savoring. Meanwhile, I wasn't sure I'd survive the night. My hips heaved up to meet his touch and my breasts felt swollen, heavy.

I wanted to feel his touch everywhere. I cupped them in my hands, my nipples hard against my palms, not as good as his hands on me but the best I could get for now, and Daniel groaned.

"God, yeah. Keep doing that. Touch yourself for me." His thumb slid up, hooking over that most sensitive part of me, almost sending me over the edge, and I bit my lip hard to keep from crying out. All joking aside, screaming in ecstasy in what was technically still my parents' house wasn't something I wanted to do. But Daniel was making it extremely difficult. He slid an arm around my back again, pulling me to sit up, to perch on the edge of the couch, while he knelt up against me, his hand still busy between my legs, his mouth on the side of my neck.

"You're so wet." His voice was a low growl in my ear, and his words sent a thrill through me, making me clench around his fingers. "And tight . . . Is this how you're going to feel? God, I want you so bad, but I can't stop."

"Don't stop," I gasped. "Don't you dare stop." I wound my arms around his shoulders, holding on, trusting him, while I rode his hand shamelessly. It was too much. All of my senses were full of him, but it wasn't enough. I wanted more. I needed him. I reached down, pushing at his unfastened pants that hung low around his hips, but he shook his head.

"Not yet. This is for you. All for you." His teeth sank gently into my earlobe, tugging, then his tongue soothed the bite. "I've imagined how you'd look, how you'd feel . . . let me see this. Let me see you. Let me feel you. Please."

The combination of his words, his voice, his touch, it was too much. Too much to take, and soon I was clutching his shoulders, fingernails digging in, as I gasped and my body shook in his arms. His mouth covered mine, taking my cries into himself, swallowing them. It took somewhere between a few moments and forever for me to come back to myself, and I sagged against him, my head dropping to his shoulder.

"Now?" I asked. My voice was a plaintive whine, but I was too satisfied to care. "Now will you take your pants off?"

His laugh was an explosion of breath in my ear. "Oh, gladly."

I expected him to stand up, or to push me back down onto the couch again. Instead he moved backward, sitting, then lying flat on the area rug beneath him, pulling me with him. I spilled down beside him in a tangle of limbs.

"Are you kidding me?" I pushed up on my elbows and watched lasciviously as he stood and finally, finally, finished the job I'd started on his pants roughly a million years ago. My breath escaped my body in a long whoosh as his pants hit the floor, and it was all I could do to keep teasing him. "You really have something against my bed, don't you?"

"What?" He tossed his wallet down near my head before kneeling down next to me again. "This rug is great. I've always wanted to make love on a pink fake fur rug with sparkles on it."

"Hey, I love this rug. I take a lot of Instagram photos on this rug." Though maybe not anytime in the near future, after what was apparently about to happen on this rug. I'd probably need to clean it first.

"Anyway, your bed is ridiculous, and I'm just fine here." He crawled up my body, caging me in his arms to claim a kiss. So much heat. So much bare skin, soft and hard and hot against mine. "As long as I'm with you, I'm fine anywhere." His arms tightened around me and he rolled us, stretching his long, long legs under me and pulling me firmly on top of him. "Come here," he said. "I'll be your bed."

"Mmm. Best bed ever." How could one person's skin feel so right against mine? I wound my legs around his and relished the feel of his body under mine. He was long, lean, and hard where I was short and soft, but somehow we fit. Everything about him fit everything about me.

Well, almost everything. There was one thing we hadn't tried the fit of yet. And I couldn't wait any longer. I reached down between us, taking him back into my hand again, and the breath rushed out of his lungs. He was harder, hotter than he'd been before, throbbing in my hand as I stroked him, and I stole a glance up toward the bathroom, and the box of condoms that I knew was in my medicine cabinet. So far away. I hadn't trained Benedick how to bring me things, and that was super inconvenient right now. Where was a Harry Potter spell when you needed it? *Accio prophylactic!*

"Wait." He reached above his head for his wallet, fumbling with it. "Here, wait. I've got . . ." A ridiculous number of business cards spilled to the floor before he finally produced a condom and pressed it into my hand.

"Ohthankgod." The words exploded out of me in a sigh, and I wasted no time in sheathing him up. I watched his eyes as I sank down onto him—they were dark now, deep, dark green and so very hot—and my own eyes fluttered in reaction to the stretch of him inside me. I caught my breath and he caught my hands, balancing me, as I took him in a little at a time. I could feel him everywhere, but it still wasn't enough. I wanted more.

Beneath me, Daniel let out a strangled moan. His eyes slid closed as his head dropped back, the cords of his neck taut. I needed to taste that throat so I did, leaning down, laving his pulse with my tongue while his hands urged my hips to move, to ride him. "Please." The word tore itself from his chest. "Please, you've got to . . ."

So I did. Being on top wasn't my forte—talk about an unflattering angle, right?—but I persevered. I pushed up with my hands on his chest for balance, keeping my movements teasingly slow, and watched him slowly lose his mind underneath me. It was a beautiful sight. Maybe there was something to unflattering angles after all.

Soon Daniel took over, steadying me with firm hands on my hips, his fingertips making divots in my skin. He moved my body the way he wanted it, thrusting up into me, and it was just on the right side of pain. "Please," he said again. It seemed to be all he could say. I curled a hand on his chest, my nails scratching lightly, and he sucked in a hiss of a breath. His eyes opened and he gazed up at me, the green of his eyes almost eclipsed by dark pupils. I wanted to drown in him, in the way he looked at me.

"Now." One hand on my hip slid inward, down to where we were joined, hooking, stroking. "Now. Give me . . ."

I couldn't hear him anymore. I could barely see him. All I knew was the pleasure streaking through me in bright waves. Too bright. Too much. I shuddered above him and he pulled me down, his mouth finding mine, closing over mine, and there was nothing but mouths and tongues, thrusts and moans and shivers and his skin against mine.

Afterward, we lay together on that fake fur rug, and he wrapped his arms around me as though he'd never let me go. Long minutes passed as I nestled my head into the hollow of his shoulder and sighed in pure contentment.

"You should probably stay." I had just enough energy to turn my head and lay a kiss on his throat. "The storm still sounds re-

ally bad out there." The rain had stopped a while back; my skylight had gone silent and the moon had even come out around
the time of my second orgasm.

"Mmmm," he murmured in agreement. "I don't think I want
to drive in this. You're right."

Eventually, we made it to the bed. Daniel didn't say another
word about the bedsprings.

Eighteen

My *stomach was* warm when I woke up, which wasn't a surprise. More often than not, Benedick joined me in bed, nestling into my belly as I slept on my side, making himself my little spoon.

But this morning felt different. I was warmer, not just from the fuzzy warmth of the cat. I felt warm all over. As I reached for Benedick, stroking his fur with sleepy, half-awake movements, an arm tightened around my waist. I came fully awake and aware: Daniel was curled around my back, holding me to him in much the same way Benedick was nestled into me. I had both a big and a little spoon, and I was safe and secure in this cocoon of warmth.

Too bad I had to pee.

After extricating myself, to an admonishing chirrup from Benedick and a sleepy protest from Daniel, I came back from the bathroom to find that Benedick had found another spot to sleep: on Daniel's pillow.

"I think he likes me." He reached up to rub between

Benedick's ears, and the cat closed his eyes in sleepy pleasure. Daniel watched the cat for a moment, then turned his attention back to me.

"He's not the only one." I took his outstretched hand and let him pull me back into bed and tuck the blankets around us both. Morning light streamed in through the skylight in my kitchen, but by unspoken agreement, we refused to believe it was morning.

"Any plans today?"

"Hmmm. Besides this?" I grinned as his arms tightened around me. Could we just spend the day like this? Sure, we'd have to eat at some point, but that's what takeout was for, right?

"Wait," Daniel said. "It's Monday. Don't you have to go to work?"

I shook my head. "I take Mondays off during Faire."

"Good thinking. And they don't mind?" He pushed a lock of my hair off my shoulder, letting his fingertips linger on my skin.

"Nope." It was hard to concentrate on answering his question when his mouth replaced his fingertips, working his way slowly up to where my neck met my shoulder. "I cover for people other times . . . like Christmas and . . ." Oh, who cared about my vacation schedule when Daniel's mouth was on my skin? How could I make this last forever?

I was still pondering this question an hour or so later, after he'd borrowed both my shower and a new toothbrush from my medicine cabinet. He looked so good, wearing yesterday's clothes, his auburn hair wet and combed back, sitting at my dinette table drinking coffee out of one of my pink mugs. He looked like he belonged in my life. I didn't want to think about Faire ending, and him moving on to the next town.

Daniel peered out my front window, down to where his truck

was still parked in the driveway. "Think your mom is up doing laundry yet?"

I snorted. For a grown man, he was really worried about my mother. "Probably not. Are you that worried about the walk of shame you have to do to your truck?"

"Not really." He went to refill his coffee mug, then moved to the fridge for the milk. He wasn't lying; he took a ridiculous amount of milk in his coffee. "As walks of shame go, this one seems pretty mild. It's what, about thirty feet?" But there was concern in his eyes when he turned to me. "Why, do you think I should be worried?"

"Honestly, she probably didn't even notice you were here." I blew across the surface of my own coffee before taking a sip. I was lying. Mom had to have seen Daniel's truck in the driveway when she got up this morning. I was impressed with her restraint, really. I'd fully expected her to call by now. But Daniel looked so worried about parental confrontation that I didn't want to worry him.

He checked his watch and groaned. "I probably should head back."

"Are you sure?" I pouted theatrically, and he grinned in response.

"Sadly, yes. I have some paperwork I was putting off till this morning." He took my hand, tugging me over to sit next to him, threading our fingers together. "If I'd known I'd be *here* this morning, I would've made other plans."

"Well, you know where I live now. You're welcome here anytime." I loved Daniel in my space. He was tall, and he took up a lot of said space, but he also fit. We fit. I loved that.

My landline rang about thirty seconds after the sound of Daniel's truck had faded, and I imagined my mother peering out the window, waiting to pounce. I was so glad she hadn't pounced on poor Daniel.

"Did your friend leave already? I was going to see if you wanted to bring him down for breakfast."

"Um . . ." My heart raced, as if I'd been caught. I'm twenty-seven, I reminded myself. I'm too old to be grounded by my mother. Out loud I said, "Yeah, he left. Sorry. I didn't realize you wanted to make him pancakes." An image of the look on Daniel's face if I'd invited him downstairs for breakfast popped into my head, and I had to swallow hard against the giggle in my throat.

"Well, don't be silly, Stacey. I wasn't going to make him pancakes."

"What then, eggs?" I took a sip of my coffee.

"I'll have you know I made your father a frittata this morning. It turned out great, and if you're going to be a smart mouth you can't have any." She sounded so prim that I couldn't hold back my laugh this time. "Anyway." There was a smile in her voice too. "What are you doing today?"

"I don't know. I need to do laundry at some point, but other than that I think I might just take it easy. Yesterday was a pretty long day, with the wedding and all." Followed by bringing Daniel home with me last night and . . . My mind was suddenly filled with the memory of Daniel waking me up sometime in the night with his mouth on my skin, me making a run for the condoms in the medicine cabinet, crawling back to bed in the dark, his body pulsing against mine, into mine, softly as he reminded me that we had to be quiet, so quiet . . . I shook my head hard as I remembered I was talking to my mother, and I forced a yawn instead. "I'm pretty beat today." This was not a lie. I was sore in places I didn't know could be sore.

"Well, if you're not going to need the washer right away, I may get some laundry out of the way this morning."

"Yeah, Mom, of course. It's your washer, after all. I can do mine after dinner." Why was she asking me permission when it was her house, her appliances? Low-level annoyance churned in me, a response that made no sense.

That annoyance stayed with me after we hung up, and I couldn't make sense of it, nor could I make it go away, so instead I spent the day putting my life back in order. I took an Uber over to April's place to pick up my car. I straightened up my place, which, considering its size, took about a half hour. I took a spin through social media on my phone, uploading some of the pics I took at the wedding, but even the little hearts of social media attention left me feeling restless. I played with Benedick, but as the afternoon got warm he abandoned me and my feather on a string for a nap on the couch.

Maybe he had the right idea. I settled down beside him with a cup of tea, a few of the chocolate chip cookies Mom had made a couple days ago, and our Fun Book Club selection. Our meeting was coming up, and since I'd be leading it in Emily's absence due to her honeymoon, I should probably read the damn thing. I tucked my feet under me and let one hand rest on Benedick, who purred in his sleep as I rubbed behind his ears. Now would have been a good time for that rainstorm we'd had last night, but I made do with the quiet, sunny afternoon, reading a good book with my cat curled up by my side.

A few chapters in, I glanced down at my phone on the arm of the couch, which had lit up with notifications. I swiped it awake, and the first thing I saw were some tagged pictures of me at the wedding, dancing with Daniel. The first shot was of the two of us from the side, me laughing at something he'd said, him smiling down at me. The second shot was of me from behind, and I scowled a little at it. Not a good angle at all. My finger hovered over the picture, about to untag myself from it, but I hesitated. Sure, the angle wasn't the best, and my face wasn't even visible. But there was something about the way Daniel's large hands cradled my back, something about the way he looked down at me as though he'd never want anything else in his life, that made me want to claim that moment, preserve it.

Last night with him had been perfect, in every single way. I wanted to tag every second of it with our names.

In some ways it was weird that my relationship with Daniel became so intense so fast. I wasn't usually the kind of girl to sleep with a guy so soon into a relationship—Dex aside, but let's be real, I'd never thought of him as a *relationship* when we were having sex—but those months of emails and texts had laid so much groundwork. Now that we'd gotten used to seeing each other in person, we could skip the awkward small talk portion of things and go straight into being . . . well, not in *love*. We weren't using that word. Not yet. But we were definitely together.

Daniel fit into my life like a puzzle piece I didn't realize had been missing. There were the same good-morning texts and late-night chat sessions. But there were also the flowers he sent to my work on Wednesday, and the pizza I had delivered to his hotel room Thursday night while we spent the night binging on bad reality television.

The week flew by, and before I knew it, it was time to get back in costume for the weekend.

"Beatrice. A word?" Simon called my name—my Faire name—

as we were just about to leave the Hollow to go up the hill to start the next Saturday at Faire.

Emily and I both turned at his approach, and to my surprise he seemed more interested in me than in his new wife.

I inclined my head. "Captain," I said in my Beatrice voice. "What is your will?" Emily raised her eyebrows next to me; she wanted to know too.

"I need you today."

"Captain!" My grin was wide and flirtatious, and it only got wider as Simon looked increasingly uncomfortable. "I'm flattered, sir, I truly am. But I have it on good authority that you are newly wed to this good lass here. Therefore, any needing should be in her direction, aye?"

"Indeed." Emily put her hands on her hips and tried to look offended, but amusement danced in her eyes. "Tired of me already, good husband?"

"That's not . . ." He swept off his hat—a black leather monstrosity with a large red feather that had been part of his costume since the early days—and raked a hand through his hair before glaring at the both of us. "That's not what I meant and you know it." He'd dropped the accent, which surprised me. That wasn't like him.

"Do we?" Emily's smile widened, and he scowled in response, stepping a little closer, his attention all on Emily now.

"I've a mind to take you home right this moment, and let you know just how very *not tired* of you I am." The accent was back, and his voice was a growl. Whoa. He and Emily had always been flirty in character, and later as their real selves, but this was a little more . . . intense than I was used to seeing from him.

Emily's eyes flared, then she laughed and shoved him away

with one hand planted in the middle of his chest. "Off with you," she said in her Faire accent. "Beatrice and I have much to do today."

Simon had fallen back a step when she pushed him, but now he stepped back to us again, hat still in his hand. "I actually really do need to talk to you a second, Stacey," he said, his voice all Simon-the-Faire-organizer once again.

Oh. This was actually serious, and not just character banter. "Sure, Simon," I said. "What's up?"

He shifted his hat from one hand to the other and ran a hand through his hair again, stealing a glance over his shoulder. "Any chance I can get you to sing with the Lilies today?"

I blinked. Of all the favors I had expected, this was the least of them. "Well. I mean, I haven't sung since, what, college?" When I'd turned twenty-one I'd shed the Gilded Lilies costume as fast as I could, trading that yellow dress for a wench's costume. It had felt like a rite of passage—being an adult at last. That summer Simon's older brother Sean had dubbed me Beatrice, a name that I still held on to in his honor.

"Not true," he countered. "You spent a lot of time practicing with Caitlin during rehearsals. I heard you with her at April's house."

"Okay, but that doesn't count." I shook my head. "Why do you need me?"

Simon didn't answer; he just looked at me and waited for me to get there. And I did, a moment or two later. "Oh." I put my hands on my hips. "I told you."

"You did." He had the grace to at least look at little shame-faced.

"I told you." I all but shook my finger at him. "I told you that Dahlia would flake on you." Dahlia Martin had been the best singer we'd had try out, and since she was a college student she had that little bit of extra maturity that meant she could lead the Lilies' rehearsals with minimal supervision. But I'd had a chat with Ms. Howe, who was still teaching and directing the chorus at Willow Creek High, about our crop of Gilded Lilies this year. While she'd approved of the talent we'd chosen, she had warned me that Dahlia in particular was likely to lose interest and stop showing up after a couple weekends.

And here we were. Simon held up a defensive hand. "You're right. But she's a strong singer. I had to give her a chance."

"So what happened?"

"Well, she didn't show up this morning. I figured she was just running late, but she texted a few minutes ago that she couldn't come today. Like she's calling in sick to work. Like . . ." Simon clenched his jaw, and there went that muscle in his cheek again. Poor guy. We all had his back these days, but there were still the occasional moments like this, where it seemed like he carried the whole Faire on his shoulders.

I sighed. Fine. "But I'm not exactly a teenager anymore. Aren't the Lilies supposed to be a group of sisters?"

"Oh, never mind that," he said. "You know the songs, that's what's important. You can be their—"

"Watch it." I put my hands on my hips and narrowed my eyes.

"Their much more beautiful older sister?" His eyes turned pleading, and I had to laugh. He relaxed a little when I did; he knew I was giving in.

"Their really, really young mom?" Emily supplied.

"Their fun aunt?" I suggested.

"There you go." Simon shrugged. "Work with that."

I looked across the tent, where the remaining Gilded Lilies, four high school girls, milled around and played with the rib-

bons on the front of their yellow dresses. "I don't have that outfit anymore," I said. One of those girls was probably wearing the
exact dress I'd worn a few years back. We recycled costumes a lot
around here. "And even if I did, I wouldn't have time to go home
and change. Opening gate is in like twenty minutes."

"You look fine." Simon waved a hand at my newer, more
wood-nymphy outfit. "I mean, that orange is in the same color
family, basically, right? It's good enough."

"Good enough?" My eyes went wide. I never thought I'd hear
Simon say *good enough* about anything when it came to his pre-
cious Faire. "Wow. Marriage has changed you."

Emily snorted from beside me, and a slow smile came over
Simon's face. "Maybe it has," he said. Could just a smile be TMI?
It made me want to get a room. If only to get away from those two.

"Fine," I said. "I'll be a Lily."

Simon blew out a sigh of relief and settled his pirate hat back
on his head. "Thank you."

I wasn't done. "But just for today. Figure something out for
tomorrow, and next week." I'd had very important plans of doing the bare minimum today so I could hang out and play at the
Faire with Daniel, so I was not pleased that those plans were
getting shunted to tomorrow.

"I promise." Simon held up his hands. "I'll go to Dahlia's
house myself tomorrow morning, stuff her into her costume,
and drag her here if necessary."

"I one hundred percent believe that," Emily deadpanned
while I snickered.

Daniel chose that moment to join us; I saw him over Simon's
shoulder, walking up to our little group. Something must have
shown in my face because Simon turned around just as Daniel
walked up.

"Hey, good morning." Daniel inclined his head toward Simon in greeting, but his expression was careful. He met my eyes and raised his eyebrows a fraction. The message was clear: were we public with our relationship? Canoodling at a wedding was one thing, but day-to-day was something else. This was my town, and these were my people. He'd follow my lead in this.

Well, the hell with that. I stepped up to his side and rose onto my toes, skating a hand around his ribs to steady myself. With me on my toes he only had to bend a little to kiss me, and thankfully he took the hint, brushing his lips over mine. "Morning," I said around a smile. We were public. We were public as hell.

Simon coughed. "Morning, Daniel. Everything okay with the Kilts?" Emily elbowed him, and he gave her a *what the hell did I do?* look.

"He's not here on business," Emily said, and I pressed my lips together hard to keep from laughing.

Simon blinked at Daniel and me, then closed his mouth with a snap. "Right. Of course." He shook his head. "I knew that."

"It's okay, Captain," I said. "You've been a little busy."

"Running Faire, getting married . . ." Daniel laid his hand on the small of my back as he spoke, further cementing the public nature of our relationship. "You've got a lot going on." I felt the heat of his skin through the layers of my costume, and I instinctively leaned into him and his warmth. His hand curved around my back to rest on my waist.

"True." Simon adjusted his hat as Emily grasped his arm to pull him up the hill. "Speaking of which, I need to get up front. Beatrice." He touched his fingertips to his hat. "Thanks again."

"Of course." I waved him off. After they were gone, Daniel turned to me.

"So." He leaned down for another kiss, a better one than that quick "people are watching" peck he had given me earlier. His hands explored the defined dip and curve created by the bodice I wore. "You ready for today? I'm thinking we need to hit the ax-throwing first. It seems to get busy quick. Lot of bloodthirsty people in your town."

I sighed. "I have to take a rain check." I filled him in on the missing Lily situation, and how my plans for the day had changed.

"Wait. You sing?" A slow grin came over his face. "You never told me that."

"I used to sing. Today should be interesting. Wait." My heart sank as something occurred to me. "I don't even know what part Dahlia sings. Oh, God, I hope she isn't the soprano." I pressed my hands to my bodice-flattened belly, where butterflies had started to churn.

"You'll be great." He slid an arm around my back and held me close, his lips pressed to my forehead in a comforting kiss. "Don't worry, okay? You've got this. I can't wait to hear you."

A nervous laugh bubbled out of me. "Oh, you don't have to watch us. In fact, please don't."

But he shook his head. "No chance I'm missing this." He laughed at my defeated groan. "Now go on. Marshal your troops."

"Yeah." I squared my shoulders. The girls were waiting, after all. One more kiss from Daniel, and I went to join the Gilded Lilies. They were still milling around, looking bored and a little lost now that the morning's meeting was over and everyone else had moved toward their places for opening gate.

"Hey, Stacey." Caitlin waved as I approached. "So, Dahlia's not here. I told Mr. G, and he told us to wait here." Her face scrunched up in confusion. "But gate's like really soon. We need to do something, right?"

"It's okay," I said. "Dahlia told Simon she can't be here today." I stopped short when I realized that Caitlin wasn't the only one of the Lilies that I knew. "Sydney?"

"Hey, Stacey." She gave me a little wave and tugged on the bodice of her dress. "It's Syd now, actually."

"Oh. Of course," The last time I'd seen Sydney Stojkovic she'd been five years old, sitting in the back of the minivan when Mr. Stojkovic picked Candace and me up from one cheerleading competition or another. Now she was in high school. Time really was passing by too fast.

"Hey," I said, still trying to get my mind around Syd not needing a car seat anymore. Then I got my mind back on topic. "So you all know, obviously, that Dahlia's out today."

Syd rolled her eyes. "Dahlia got a new girlfriend a couple weeks ago. Betcha that's where she is."

"Probably." I brushed that off. "The good news is, I used to do this, so I'll sing with you all." I wasn't sure how this announcement would go over, and I reminded myself that I'd been cool when I was younger, dammit. I'd been a cheerleader. These girls would have been lucky to hang out with me then. Surely they could get through a day with adult-me without rolling their eyes.

Thankfully, Caitlin was on my side. "Oh, that's really good!" She nodded vigorously before turning to the others. "Stacey helped me learn the songs this year. And she's an alto, like Dahlia."

Thank God. I tried to not make my relief too visible.

Syd nodded, but her eyes focused behind me. "Who was that guy you were with just now?"

"Hmm?" I turned around to see Daniel disappearing up the hill, and I took a second to appreciate the way he looked in a pair of jeans. Denim was really underrated for what it could do for a man's . . . assets.

"That's her boyfriend," Caitlin said with authority. She was enjoying the fact that she knew me better than the other girls did. Maybe there was something to this Fun Aunt role after all.

"Is he?" Syd raised her eyebrows at me. "He's cute."

"Yeah." I smiled. "I think so."

It turned out Simon was right. I did know all the songs the Gilded Lilies performed. Those practice sessions I'd had with Caitlin had been practice for me too. I just hadn't known it. Performing with the girls was like riding a bike, but it was a surreal experience. Like those dreams where you're suddenly back in high school and it's finals week, but you haven't gone to class all year. Performing was familiar, but it wasn't quite the same. When I'd been a Gilded Lily, we hadn't had set performance times; we'd just strolled the lanes of the Faire and sung a song or two as we went, adding color to the whole day. Now we were actual performers, setting up mostly on a small stage toward the front of the Faire, near the gate. We hustled to get up there before gate opened, and by the time the first patrons came in we were midway through the first verse of "Greensleeves," our voices in perfect harmony. The girls were good singers, and I realized almost immediately how much I'd missed winding my voice around others in soaring harmonies. Yep, just like riding a bike. It was even fun. My irritation at not spending the day with Daniel faded, and I let myself relax into the music.

We performed short sets of four or five songs each, leaving us time to wander the lanes. I fell into the role, turning my character of Beatrice into the unlikely guardian of a quartet of sisters. I stopped patrons as they walked, asking the men if they were eligible bachelors. "Would you be interested in a bride? I desperately need to get these girls married off and out of my hair—er,

I mean, I want to have their futures secured. Of course that's what I meant! So are you eligible?" I purposely targeted some obviously married men, who usually laughed and hid behind their wives. Once in a while we found a small clearing or a stage where a show wasn't taking place, and we performed a song or two. Small crowds gathered whenever we did, and though I kept a wary eye out for a black-clad redhead, so far Daniel hadn't seen any of our performances. I couldn't decide whether to be relieved or disappointed.

By midafternoon we found ourselves near the Marlowe Stage, roughly twenty minutes before the Kilts' next show. The guys were nowhere to be seen, and the benches for the audience were mostly empty, except for a few people here and there taking a break in the shade. Perfect. We could do a couple songs and be on our way before they got back.

I led the girls up onto the stage. "Have we done 'Drunken Sailor' yet?" I couldn't remember if I'd practiced that one with Caitlin or not, but it was a standard. The girls should know it.

Syd gave a slow shake of her head. "That's . . . That's not one that we do."

"Yeah." Caitlin nodded emphatically, her eyes wide. "It's about drinking. We're too young for that."

I felt a jolt in my stomach. Oh no. Was I corrupting the youth? Simon was going to kill me.

But Janine, the tallest Lily and our highest soprano, broke the mood with a giggle. "They're messing with you. We did that song a bunch in rehearsals."

Caitlin rolled her eyes. "Yeah, but Mr. G said we can't do it. Too adult."

"Well, this isn't a performance." I gestured out into the audience, where three people had left and the last two were sitting with their backs to us, clearly not interested. "And Mr. G isn't here to boss us around, okay? It's just for fun."

Unselfconsciously, I launched into the song:

What shall we do with a drunken sailor,
What shall we do with a drunken sailor,
What shall we do with a drunken sailor,
Early in the morning?

The rest of the girls had joined in with me by the second line, and we started the refrain together:

Weigh heigh and up she rises
Weigh heigh and up she rises
Weigh heigh and up she rises
Early in the morning

By the time we'd finished, we weren't alone. A handful of patrons had settled in the back, giving us a smattering of applause. Meanwhile, the men of the Dueling Kilts, trailed at a slight distance by Daniel with a drink in his hand, had come back to reclaim their stage, and looked amused to find it taken over by a bunch of girls.

"Don't let us stop you." Dex had his guitar slung over his back, and now he swung it forward and picked out the melody, nodding at us to keep going.

So we did, and soon Frederick and Todd got their instruments from the small backstage area and joined in. Verses of "Drunken Sailor" were tricky, because the song was hundreds of years old and had probably a million verses. But we started with the standards:

> Chuck him in the longboat till he's sober
> Chuck him in the longboat till he's sober
> Chuck him in the longboat till he's sober
> Early in the morning
>
> Shave his belly with a rusty razor

("Ouch," said Syd, and we all laughed.)

> Shave his belly with a rusty razor
> Shave his belly with a rusty razor
> Early in the morning

During a round of "*weigh heigh and up she rises*" I hopped off the stage to where Daniel sat in the empty second row, his legs stretched out on the bench in front of him.

"What's that?" I took the small plastic cup out of his hand and sniffed the pale liquid inside. "Mead?" I made a face and handed it back to him.

"Yep. Got it from your tavern." He took a sip. "You don't like mead? You should. It's sweet, like that wine you drink."

I shook my head. "It's too thick, like that beer you drink." He laughed as I went back onto the stage with the girls.

"Now the great thing about this song," Dex said to the girls while he continued to play the melody line, "is that it's so old, people just keep making up new verses, and as long as they fit the meter, it works. It's good for audience participation–type stuff, you know?" The girls nodded, eyes wide, soaking in the man-candy that was Dex MacLean, as though they hadn't told me ten minutes ago that they shouldn't be singing this song at all.

"Like . . . like what?" Janine asked.

"Well . . ." Dex finished the final bars of the verse and started them over again. Frederick jumped back in with a flourish of his hand drum.

"Like . . ." Frederick pointed at Todd, on the fiddle. "Put him on *stage and make him tap-dance!*"

We all laughed, but Todd did an impressive time-step in his stompy boots, and the girls joined in:

Put him on stage and make him tap-dance
Put him on stage and make him tap-dance
Early in the morning!

Syd jumped in next: "Make him listen to eighties music!" That one was even better, and we turned it into a verse:

Make him listen to eighties music
Make him listen to eighties music
Make him listen to eighties music
Early in the morning!

By now the girls were all laughing, and we were all clapping along with the music, our voices harmonizing with the Kilts, and I was almost sorry when we did one more round of the *"weigh heigh and up she rises"* refrain to end the song. The guys were grinning, the girls were giggling, and the audience that had gathered for the Kilts' next show gave us an enthusiastic round of applause. Great. We'd become their opening act. Hopefully Simon wouldn't find out about this.

Daniel stood up from his place in the second row, tossing back the last swallow of his drink. "I hate to break this up, guys, but we've got a show to get ready for." From the look on his face, he really did hate being the voice of reason. But it was about time for the guys to do their set. Which meant we should get back to our little stage up front for a set of our own.

We bid the guys goodbye, and I gathered the girls like a mama hen with her chicks, shooing them off the stage and up the center aisle. Daniel was there when I got to the lip of the stage, offering a hand to help me hop down. But when my feet were back on the dirt he didn't let go. Instead his hand tightened on mine and he tugged me a step closer.

"I'll see you later, right?"

I grinned up at him. "Of course you will. Early in the morning?" I pronounced the word the way it was in the song: *earl-eye*.

He shook his head. A hint of a wicked smile played around his lips, and his eyes held a glimmer of heat. "There's no way I'm waiting that long." He bent to brush his mouth over mine right there in front of everyone, and oh yeah, we were definitely public now.

The taste of mead wasn't so bad that time.

Nineteen

I'd *meant to* catch up with Daniel at pub sing, but once the Gilded Lilies had finished their final set of the day, I felt obligated to stay with the girls as they got out of their costumes down at the Hollow. Caitlin stayed with me since Emily was her ride, and by the time we got back to the front of the Faire it was over for the day. Pub sing had just ended, and patrons were filtering out through the front gate. I went over to the Marlowe Stage, but it was empty too. Not a MacLean in sight. When I got to my car I checked my phone, but there wasn't a text from him either. Then again, he knew I didn't keep my phone on me, so I tried not to read too much into that. He knew where I lived— he'd probably be by later.

But by the time I'd taken a long, hot shower and gotten into my most comfortable yoga pants, I realized that he hadn't actually said he'd come by. I'd just assumed he'd come over tonight, but "sooner than earl-eye in the morning" wasn't exactly a concrete plan. I checked my phone to make sure he hadn't called while I was in the shower. Nothing. Hmm. I twisted my hair up and put water on the stove for some pasta for dinner.

"Is he ghosting us, Benedick?" It seemed unlikely, but it was also weird to not hear from him. The cat didn't answer, opting instead to wash his butt. Great. Helpful.

Just as the water started to bubble on the stove, there was a knock at my door. The sound was loud, echoing through my quiet apartment and shattering the thoughts that had started to spiral in my head. I hurried to open the door.

"There you are." I leaned on the doorjamb and tried to look casual, as if I hadn't been checking my phone every fifteen seconds for a text from him.

"Here I am." He bent to kiss me, a real kiss this time, one that didn't need to stay all polite and closed-mouthed in front of witnesses, and any residual annoyance I may have had flew out of my brain. "I was going to text you like I always do," he said when we came up for air, "but I thought, why do that when I can see you instead." Daniel took in my yoga-pants-and-messy-bun ensemble and grinned. "I was going to see if you wanted to get dinner somewhere, but you look pretty settled in . . ." His eyes widened as he took a sniff of the air. "Not to mention that whatever you have in here smells delicious."

I pulled the door wide and ushered him inside. "It's just spaghetti. I threw sauce and meatballs in the slow cooker this morning, and there's tons of it. Come on in and have dinner."

"Yes, please." He followed me into the kitchen, where I threw some salt into the boiling water, followed by the pasta. I pulled down another plate for Daniel and dinner was an intimate affair, not so much because of the romantic ambience but because my dinette table was really, really small. But we barely noticed as we worked our way through a carb-laden dinner of pasta and about four pitchers of ice water. Faire could dehydrate a person.

Daniel refilled our glasses and added another slice of lemon to his before leaning back in his chair with a happy sigh. "I can't tell you the last time I had something home-cooked. Probably not since the holidays?"

I scoffed, though I couldn't help smiling at the praise. "This was hardly homemade. Frozen meatballs and sauce?"

"Still better than takeout." He raised his plastic tumbler to me, and I clinked it with mine.

"Come over anytime." I meant it. Daniel could move in, for all I cared. Squeaky bed and all.

Daniel was mid-sip when his cell phone rang, a custom ringtone that sounded like Celtic fiddles. He groaned and reached for his back pocket. "Dex."

My heart thudded at the name, but I brushed past it. "You need to take it?"

"Yeah. He probably forgot how to . . . I don't know. Order a pizza on his own or something. Be right back." He answered the call on his way out the front door. "Hey, man, what do you need? . . . No, I'm out . . . I don't know when I'll be back . . ." He shot me an exaggerated eye roll as he pulled the front door behind him. I didn't blame him for leaving; my apartment was basically one big room, so there was nowhere to go for privacy unless you wanted to hide in the bathroom. The front stoop was his best bet.

I stuck the dishes in the dishwasher and the leftovers in the fridge, and then reached for my own phone. Emily had created a Facebook album called "First Day at Faire as Mrs. Captain Blackthorne," which was just as insanely cute as it sounded, including a selfie of Simon as the pirate and Emily as his bride, taken early in the morning before Faire had started for the day. There was something about a wide gold band on the pirate's finger that made him look complete.

I'd just finished clicking through the photos and leaving emoji-laden comments, when a text came through from Daniel. He'd sent emojis of his own: three eye rolls. I snorted, and before I could reply he sent another one: **Be back inside ASAP, believe me.** I smiled as I typed a response: **You know where I'll be.** Phone still in my hand, I wandered toward my bed under the eaves, switching on the fairy lights and reclining on my pile of pillows, while the murmur of Daniel's voice filtered in from the other side of the front door. There was something about him, here in my space, that was so comforting. I could get used to this.

Meanwhile, back on my Facebook feed, my high school BFF Candace's baby was now walking! "Huzzah," I said under my breath. She was nearly a year old; should I stop thinking of her as a baby? She was toddling around now—didn't that qualify a kid as a toddler? I had no idea, but I still left a heart-eyes emoji on the video of the kid stumbling through the living room and almost falling on the dog, because even if we were nothing more than Facebook friends these days, I was at least going to be a good Facebook friend. **Spent the day with your little sis,** I added as a comment. **How is she already in high school?! We're getting old!**

A click of a camera shutter startled me, and I looked up to see Daniel in the middle of my living room, his phone pointed toward me snuggled up in bed with my cat and my phone.

"I've pictured this in my head for so many months." A soft

look came to his face as he glanced down at the image he'd captured. "Is this what you looked like, all those times we were messaging each other?"

I hadn't thought about it like that before. "Usually," I admitted. "Sometimes I was on the couch on my laptop, but late nights when we would text just before I fell asleep? I'd usually be in bed on my phone." I patted the mattress. "Right here."

"Hmmm. Right here, huh?" He dropped his phone onto the side of my bed and ducked into my little bedroom space. "I have to say, I did a pretty good job of picturing you . . ." He crawled onto the bed and up my body at the same time, and I clicked my phone off and set it next to his with a grin as he did so. ". . . But real life is much better than pictures. Just like this . . ." He dipped his head down to kiss me, his mouth lingering on mine. "This is so, so much better than texts."

"Mmmm, you think?" I grinned against his kiss, and he responded with a nip, his teeth tugging gently on my bottom lip.

"Oh, I think." His hands glided up my sides, pushing up my tank top, and what do you know, he didn't complain about my squeaky bedsprings this time around.

Later, I reached for his phone and scrolled through to his photos to the one he took of me earlier. "Okay, I take it back," I said, sitting up and frowning at the phone. "I usually look better than this. At least I hope I do. I'm deleting this."

He plucked his phone out of my hand. "Don't you dare. I need that picture. I need more pictures. In fact, I'm going to purchase more cloud storage so that I can have all the pictures of you on my phone that I can take."

"Then take a better one." I pushed the blankets aside.

"Where are you going?" He hooked his hand around my upper arm, stopping me.

"To put on some makeup," I said. "Maybe even do my hair. If you want pictures of me, I want to not look like a swamp witch in them."

"Nope." He tugged on my arm, pulling me back into the bed and into his arms. "You look perfect like this. Your hair's all tumbled and tangled . . ." He ran his fingers through my hair, which had long since come out of its messy bun from earlier. "Your cheeks are pink, and you have the sweetest smile that I've ever seen in my life. I put that look on your face, and I want to document it." He aimed his phone at me, and even though I made a show of trying to cover my face and wrestle the phone away from him, my heart glowed at his words. How could I say no when he said things like that to me? I even retaliated, picking up my own phone and taking pictures of him too, while he laughed and pretended to protest. He looked so comfortable, so right, here in my bed tangled up in my sheets. It seemed he'd always been here. And in some ways, maybe he had.

As night fell in earnest and my little apartment was lit only by the light of the moon streaming through my skylight and the fairy lights above my bed, I nestled into him and he twirled a long lock of my hair through his fingers. "I don't know if I can go back." His voice was hushed, the quiet murmur of a shared secret.

"Then don't." I yawned contentedly and traced the line of his breastbone with a lazy fingertip. "Stay. I'm sure the guys can find their own way to Faire in the morning."

"Oh, I know they can. But that's not what I meant." He shifted under the blankets, settling me just a little more into him, turning his head to brush his mouth over my temple. "I mean later. After this Faire is over and I go on to the next one. When all I have of you are texts and emails. Maybe we can go nuts and actually have phone calls or Skype. But I already know it won't be enough. How can I go back to that after we've had this?" His hand skimmed up my arm, warming my skin.

"I know." An ache rose in my chest. Up until now I'd pushed aside any thought of the end of Faire, choosing instead to concentrate on the good. On Daniel, on how perfect it felt to be with him. Why sully that with the reality of this being just a temporary thing, of knowing he'd be on to the next town as always after just one more week? But it couldn't be pushed aside anymore. "You could always stick around." I said it lightly, a joke I could take back quickly. But my heart pounded in my temples at the thought of it. At the thought of Daniel staying in Willow Creek. With me.

"I'd do that in a second." His arm tightened around me. "I love the small-town vibe of this place."

"Eh, it gets old after a while." I couldn't hide the smile in my voice. "What would you even do in a town like this? Not a lot of bands to manage around here."

"I have other skills, you know. I could . . ." He fell silent, and I waited. "Okay, maybe I don't have any other skills."

"I don't know about that." I put some purr into my voice, and he snorted.

"Marketable skills, then. Ones that would let me make a living here." We were both quiet for a moment. "Then again, you could . . ." His voice broke off abruptly, as though censoring his thought before he could express it.

"What?"

"Oh, no. Nothing." But his heart beat faster under my palm, and the rise and fall of his chest was a little quicker. "It's just . . . I was just going to say . . . I mean, you could come with me. With us." He had that same lightly joking tone of voice that I'd just used. That tone that could easily be serious or flippant, depending on how the words were taken.

"To the Maryland Ren Fest?" I thought about it. "I mean, sure. It's not that far, right? I could go out there on Friday after work and spend the weekend. That could be fun."

"No. I mean, yeah, you're right. That would be great. But . . ." He shifted again, and he wound my hair more tightly between his fingers, leashing me to him. "I was thinking more like . . . long-term."

"Long-term?" I tilted my head to look up at him.

"Yeah." He didn't look back at me; instead his eyes stayed fixed on the lights twinkling above my bed, blinking hard. Blinking fast. "I don't know. It was just a thought I had. I know you don't love your job, and you've been frustrated about staying in this small town. So why don't you leave? Come with me. Come with us. Travel. I think you might like Faire life."

The words hung in the air between us, and he continued to stare at the ceiling, not looking at me.

"I . . ." My heart leapt with an immediate reaction of yes, but my brain froze and I couldn't say the word. Of course, I wanted to leave Willow Creek. But could I leave Willow Creek? The last time I'd tried to leave town my mother had ended up in the hospital. She'd almost died. My mind was filled with that same old image: her colorless face, her limp arm with an IV, the tubes and machines. It didn't matter that it was years ago. It didn't matter that Mom was essentially fine now. There was an irrational part of me that was convinced that the two were linked. If I made plans to leave home again, Mom would have another heart attack. And I'd end up staying here. Again. Probably forever.

While these thoughts whirled around in my head, long moments ticked by, and the silence between Daniel and me grew thicker, his words disintegrating and vanishing in the air. He dropped my hair and slid his arm around my waist. "It was just a thought. You don't have to—"

"No, it's not that—"

"Shhhh." He tightened his arms around me and pressed his lips to my forehead. "It's fine. Don't worry about it."

Saying "don't worry about it" had the opposite effect on me. And on him. He sounded unconcerned, but his heart still pounded under my hand. I didn't know what to say, or how to make the situation better. All joking aside, I couldn't ask him to stay. His life was on the road. And my life was here. All I could do was hold him tighter and pretend I never had to let go.

After that conversation Saturday night, nothing changed between Daniel and me. Dahlia Martin came back to Faire on Sunday, so my time as an overgrown Gilded Lily was over. Daniel and I made a day of it: I terrified him with my lack of ax-throwing skills, and we watched some of the shows we usually didn't have time to take in. It was a hot day, made hotter by sitting on the cheap bleachers during the joust, but we ducked into the relative canopied coolness of the tavern afterward, sharing a drink with Emily and Simon while they were in character. My character was so nebulous at this point that she was nothing but a name, an outfit, and an accent. But still, Beatrice managed to fit in with the Faire just fine.

Daniel spent the night again after Faire on Sunday, and while we spent Monday apart, he texted me on Tuesday just as I was getting off work, inviting me over to his room. He didn't act any differently after our aborted conversation Saturday night, and I didn't know how to ask if he'd really meant it when he'd asked me to come with him. He didn't ask again, and I couldn't figure out a casual way to bring it up, so it was as if that conversation had never happened. As though he'd never asked me to run off and join the Renaissance faire with him. But the more I thought about it, the more I loved the idea. The vendors, the performers, they had their own culture, their own language even, and how many times had I wished that I could be part of it, more than just a few weekends a year? But I had this sick feeling that I'd waited too long at this point to say yes.

I decided to push it down, the way I pushed down other things I didn't like to think about. Like the fact that the last weekend of Faire was coming, and if Daniel and I were to keep this relationship going, we were about to embark on another eleven months of electronic communication to stay together. It wasn't ideal, but it was better than not being together at all.

Right?

Despite all my best efforts at pushing things down, a sort of low-level panic had accumulated in my chest by Thursday, even though on the outside everything seemed normal. I brought Chinese takeout to Daniel's room after work, and we heckled home renovation shows and slurped up lo mein and Cokes from his mini-fridge as if the last weekend of Faire wasn't looming over our heads. But I held on to his hand a little too tightly, and his kiss when I got there had been a little too desperate. We both knew that our time was almost up.

Two DIY shows in, he levered himself off the bed to pour another drink, finally cracking into the small bottle of rum he'd bought a couple weekends ago. But he frowned into the ice bucket. "We're already out of ice?"

"Those things are so small. I'll go get some more." I got up, stretching out my back. It had gotten kinked up from curling against Daniel for the better part of an hour.

He waved me off. "Don't worry about it, I'll go." He took the ice bucket and left the room, propping the door open behind him with the bolt. I channel-surfed for a couple minutes before draining the rest of my own drink, then opened the mini-fridge to see there was only one can of Coke left. I knew I should have brought more. I rummaged in my purse for a few dollars. There was a vending machine near the ice machine; I could just catch up with Daniel and grab a few more sodas.

There was a murmur of voices in the hallway through the partially open door, but it wasn't until I'd opened the door all the way that I realized the voices were Dex and Daniel, a little way down the hall.

". . . do that thing with her tongue? She's pretty good at that."

"Stop it." Daniel's voice was hushed yet vehement. "It's not like that."

A full-body tingle cascaded over me as I realized they were talking about me.

"Not like what? You're banging her, right? I saw you at Faire with her last weekend." Dex looked over his shoulder toward Daniel's room—toward *me*—and I ducked back into the room, heart pounding as I moved the door back into a half-closed position. I shouldn't be hearing this. Nothing good was going to come from listening to this conversation. I should close the door, but I couldn't move. My feet were rooted to the floor, dollar bills clenched in my fist, while the MacLeans talked about, well, me.

"Don't . . ." Daniel sighed, a long-suffering sigh that I'd gotten to know pretty well. He used it a lot when he talked about his cousins. Talked to his cousins. "It's not like that," he said again, his voice almost pleading. "She's special."

Dex laughed, and I flinched at the sound. "I'm not hating on you. I think it's great. I'm just . . . I dunno. Surprised. You could have given me the heads-up that you were gonna handle it that way."

I caught my breath and inched the door open a little more so I could see them better. Handle what? Handle me?

Out in the hallway Daniel threw up his hands, looking angrier than I'd ever seen him. He wasn't an angry kind of guy. "What the fuck do you care, man? You asked me to take care of your problem and I did. Just like I've taken care of everything else for you for the last twelve years."

Dex held up his hands. "Hey. It's fine by me. In fact, I'm impressed. Totally giving you props for the way you did it. Getting her out of my hair. Managed to get a little something for yourself on the side, that's great. In fact . . ."

I couldn't take it anymore. I pushed the door open and stepped out into the hallway. Both men saw me immediately. Dex dropped his hands and raised his eyebrows, but all I could see was Daniel. Wide eyes, stricken expression. He knew I'd heard everything. It had to be obvious from the look on my face.

"I was . . ." My voice didn't work, so I had to clear my throat and try again. "I was a problem?" I drew a shaky breath and looked at Dex. "I was in your hair?"

Daniel opened his mouth, closed it. Surprisingly Dex jumped in, the sudden voice of reason in this conversation. "Naw, Stace. You were great. Honest. We had fun, right?" He nodded encouragingly in response to my own dumb nod. "But then you got kinda clingy last year, sending messages and shit. And you're a really nice girl, so I didn't want to just be all 'fuck off with that.' So I asked Daniel to do it."

"Wait. You put him up to it?" This was new information. I flashed back to almost a year ago. That first drunken message, fueled by a little too much wine and way too much loneliness. How different would everything have been if Daniel had just done what he'd been told? If he'd sent back a nice rejection, letting me down easy. Would it have hurt as much then as it hurt right now?

But something about all this didn't add up. Something about all this made it even worse. I looked back at Daniel. "You said it was an honest mistake. You said you didn't realize the message was for Dex."

"He *said* that?" Dex laughed. It was practically a guffaw, a living thing that swirled around Daniel and me, bouncing off the walls of the hallway while we stared at each other. "Well, he's full of shit. He showed me the message and asked me what I wanted to do about it. I told him to handle it."

"Yeah. You said that already. Handle it." I nodded slowly. "Handle me."

"Well, yeah. You know, let you down easy. He's better with words and stuff than I am . . ." He trailed off, and for the first time in this conversation, Dex looked uncomfortable. He rubbed the back of his neck as he looked from me to Daniel and back again. "That's what he did, right? Told you I wasn't into you like that? He said he was going to . . ."

"Yeah." I cut Dex off. I didn't want to hear any more. Not from him. Not from Daniel, who in all of this hadn't said a word. He just continued to watch me with pleading eyes, as though his house of cards was falling down. "Yeah," I said again. "He knew just what to say." I turned and went back into Daniel's room. My overnight bag was still on the chair, not even unpacked yet, so it wasn't like I had to get my stuff together. That last can of soda was all his. I scooped my phone off the nightstand and tossed it into my purse. There. I was ready to go.

But Daniel was in the doorway when I turned, the ice bucket hanging limply in his hand. "Stacey."

I shook my head hard. "You said there weren't any more lies." I wanted to lash out, to hurt him as much as he'd hurt me, but both of those things required breath, and I couldn't breathe around this stone in my chest. A storm of tears was rising inside me, and I needed to get to my car, ideally to my apartment, before that storm broke. "You promised."

"I know. I did." He looked as miserable as I felt, but I didn't care. I couldn't care.

"So all this time, I was a joke? All those things you said to me, all those months . . . that was you solving a problem for your cousin?"

"No." He closed his eyes, pain etched in his face. "I mean, yeah, okay, at first, yes. Your message was so . . . I didn't want to hurt you."

I had to laugh, but it was a harsh sound, a cry of pain. "Well, good job on that." I looped my purse over my shoulder. "You did great."

He sighed, a deep rush of breath that sounded like it came from his toes. "I know. I fucked up. Again. Stacey, I'm sorry. Please . . ."

"No." I dug for my keys and clutched them in my palm. "No, I've done enough talking. I've had enough of your words." My breath shuddered in my lungs. That storm of tears was getting closer, and I had to get out of there. "It sucked when I thought it was an honest mistake—"

"It *was* an honest mistake, I told you . . ."

I didn't let him finish. "I understood then. At least I thought I did. But this . . . this isn't the same. You were in on it. Dex was in on it. You made me the butt of some little family joke, and I can't . . ." My voice broke, and the first tears leaked from my eyes. "I can't," I said again. "When I thought you were Cyrano, I forgave you. But then . . ."

"What?" His forehead creased. "Cyrano? What are you talking about?"

But I kept going as if he hadn't even spoken. "Then at the wedding, back at my place, I thought . . . I thought you were The One. I thought . . ." I cleared my throat hard. It didn't matter what I thought, did it? "But you played me. You and Dex. You both played me." I pushed past him in the doorway.

"You're leaving?" His voice was both incredulous and defeated. It was the defeat that got to me, and I turned around.

"Give me a reason to stay." My eyes hurt; they were burning with tears that I wasn't allowing myself to shed. Not yet. I made myself meet his eyes, and I waited for him to ask me to stay. To fight for this. For us.

But he didn't. Just like that first night at the bar, he was silent. I drew in a breath, and to my mortification, it was a sob. "Go on to the next town," I finally said. "Maybe you and Dex can find another heart to break together."

"*Stacey.*" His voice was wrecked, but I didn't have it in me to care. This time when I turned to leave, he let me go.

Thankfully Dex had had the good sense to vacate the hallway, so no one witnessed the storm as it broke. No one had to watch me swipe angry, humiliated tears from my face as I made my way to my car and drove home, where I could finally cry in peace. I curled up on my bed and let the tears fall, and soon Benedick was nestled against my belly, my hand in his soft fur, comforting me with his warmth.

Our time was up, all right. Just a little sooner, and in a little more final way, than I'd anticipated.

Twenty

My alarm *went* off the next morning and I swatted at it. Regret settled over me like the worst kind of hangover. I moaned and put my hands over my face as the memory of last night washed over me. Had I overreacted? But Dex's voice echoed in my head, calling me "clingy," saying he'd asked Daniel to "handle" me. Ugh. No. I hadn't overreacted at all.

In a fit of optimism I checked my phone for a text from Daniel, but there was nothing. I took a shower and tried composing a text in my head. First I wanted to apologize, but as soon as I'd composed the perfect apology in my head, I bubbled over with indignant anger, mentally erasing it. I was the wronged party here. He should be the one to be sorry, dammit.

I typed and erased three different texts before I had to leave for work. Once I got there, I put my phone away for the day and tried to concentrate on other things. That went about as well as I expected: by lunchtime my nerves were all live wires, and I dove for my bag before I'd even clocked out.

Nothing. Not a single notification, even from my social media. But I'd been so wrapped up in spending time with Daniel this week that I hadn't posted much, so there wasn't a lot for people to react to. I'd never felt so much despair from looking at my phone. Wasn't he going to apologize?

"What an asshole," I told myself while in line at the drive-through. Only comfort food would get me through this day. "Is he seriously giving me the silent treatment? Me? He's the one who messed up." I took a few deep breaths and pasted a wide smile on my face so I didn't snarl at the poor drive-through girl when she handed me my cheeseburger.

It was midafternoon when it hit me. He was planning something romantic to let me know how sorry he was that he'd betrayed my trust. Maybe I'd come home to my apartment filled with flowers, Daniel in the middle of them begging me to forgive him. I imagined his words, what sweet things he would say to show that he understood how much he'd screwed up. That of course I was worth fighting for, and how he'd do anything to earn back my trust. My heart was buoyed by this idea, so much so that I didn't care that my phone was still notification-free at the end of the day. I drove home with rising excitement; I was barely even mad at him anymore. I couldn't wait to see him, to get this whole fight behind us.

Which was why it was so crushing to come home to find my apartment exactly like it was when I'd left it. Half-empty coffee mug on the kitchen counter, cat snoozing in the same spot on the couch. My place had never looked so empty. I dropped my bag onto the coffee table and collapsed on the couch next to Benedick, who blinked sleepily at me.

Okay. Enough was enough. I pulled out my phone. **What the hell is your problem**—no. I erased that and started again. **Are you really not speaking to me after**—nope. For a long second I stared at the phone icon, my thumb hovering over it. But then I tossed my phone down. We were past texts. Past communicating via screens. If this was going to be a real relationship, we should be able to talk about our feelings, not just write about them. I didn't want to be separated from Daniel anymore, even by a cell phone. We needed to fight this out like adults and move on. And we had to do it face-to-face.

Benedick rolled onto his side for a good long stretch and a yawn as I bounced up from the couch again, grabbing my bag and my keys. I didn't even change out of my work scrubs; instead I drove to the hotel before I lost my nerve, marched up to Daniel's door, and knocked.

He didn't answer.

I knocked again, louder.

Nothing.

I frowned. Maybe he was in the shower or something? That was probably it. I dug in my bag for the keycard he'd given me. He wouldn't have given it to me if I wasn't supposed to use it, right?

I slid the keycard into the slot, but the red light didn't turn green. Hmm. I tried again, slower this time. It still didn't work. I groaned in annoyance after the third try, then headed toward the front desk. Thank God Julian was working tonight.

"Hey, Julian." I slid the keycard across the counter. "This stopped working. Can you rekey it, please?"

"Sure." He hit a couple keystrokes on his computer. "I didn't realize you were staying here." He frowned at his screen. "Uh, Stace? According to this, you aren't staying here."

"Oh, I'm not. I, uh . . ." Heat crept up the back of my neck. "A friend gave me a spare."

"Friend," he repeated. "Uh-huh." His eyebrows crept up and

his mouth twisted in a wicked smile. He knew exactly what kind of friend I was talking about. "Who's that?"

I huffed. How did he not already know? Gossip usually moved so fast around here. "Room 212. Daniel MacLean."

"Oh." His brow furrowed as he shot me a curious look. "But . . ." He tapped at his keyboard again and peered at the screen. He cleared his throat a little nervously. "He's not here, Stace."

"Oh." I looked over my shoulder toward the lobby doors, as though I could see his truck in the parking lot. I hadn't noticed it when I drove in, but I hadn't been looking for it either. "Did he go somewhere? I can wait here for a little bit if you need his okay to rekey the card."

"No. I mean, he's not here. He checked out this afternoon."

"He . . ." I swallowed hard and tried to look pleasant. Normal. Not like my world had just started crumbling around the edges. "He left?"

"Yeah. I thought it was a little weird. You know, since Faire isn't over till Sunday. But he said he was through here and it was time for him to go." Julian shrugged. "Didn't he tell you?"

"What? No. He . . ." God, that made me sound pathetic, didn't it? I groped blindly for my phone in my bag and made a little show of checking it. "Oh my God! No, he totally did, look at that." I flashed the screen in his direction, but quickly so he couldn't see that there was nothing there. "My fault. I should have checked before coming over. I can be such a ditz some-times." My laugh echoed off the tile floor of the lobby, hollow and false.

But Julian had known me since grade school; he knew some-thing was up. His expression softened. "Stacey . . ."

"So I'm gonna go." I backed away a couple steps, my smile manically wide now. "Keep the card, obviously," I added with another little laugh. "I don't need it anymore." That last sentence was a little too true, but I managed to hold it together until I pushed through the glass double doors and back out into the hot summer night. Tears splashed onto my hot cheeks, and I clutched my phone and tried to remember how to breathe.

There wasn't going to be an apology. No romantic gesture. Daniel was just . . . gone.

Emily and I made a terrible pair of tavern wenches the next day at Faire.

Of course we weren't really wenches anymore: we were a pirate's bride and . . . well, whatever I was. But we still walked the grounds together, ducking into each of the taverns at different times of the day to make sure the servers weren't in the weeds. This was the fourth weekend of Faire—the last weekend of the season—and the crowds were still pretty brisk. Well, as brisk as you could be in the mid-August heat.

But the heat wasn't what made us so bad at our jobs that day. We were used to it, for the most part, and swigged as much water as we could and flapped our skirts for some airflow. But newlywed Emily's mind was on her honeymoon, which started the moment Faire ended on Sunday night, so her grin was a little wilder than usual, and her attention span was nil. As for me . . . I was sad. And angry. And then sad again. Every time we walked in the vicinity of the Marlowe Stage, my heart leapt out of instinct and then sank almost immediately, because Daniel had left without even saying goodbye. Part of me wanted to storm over there and ask Dex what the hell had happened. But there'd already been enough of Dex coming between Daniel and me, and I didn't feel right asking him about his cousin's love life, even if that love life involved me.

"Hey." Emily bumped me with her shoulder as we caught the end of the mud show. "Are you all right? You seem . . . distracted."

I wasn't all right. Not in the least. But Emily was about twenty-four hours out from her honeymoon. She didn't need to be worrying about me and my drama. What kind of friend would I be if I burdened her with my troubles right now? A pretty lousy one. So instead I pasted my smile back on my face and kept my voice light, my accent perfect. "Of course, Emma! Everything is fine."

"Hmm." She looked over her shoulder behind us, then turned back to me. "I haven't seen Daniel today. Is he around?"

"I don't think so." My smile was starting to hurt, but dammit, I was going to wear it anyway. "I think he had to leave early."

"Hmm," she said again, a noncommittal sound. "And you're sure you're all right? Because the hot mud guy almost lost his pants just now, and you didn't say a word."

My laugh was a little too loud, but it could be blamed on me staying in character. "Perhaps I am trying to be a little more high-class these days, Emma, dear." I nudged her with my elbow and flashed her a grin. Mollified, she smiled back, a genuine smile that said I had fooled her. As far as she knew, my heart wasn't breaking.

It was exhausting, keeping up that carefree persona for the entire day, but after what seemed like a hundred years we were at the front stage again, clapping along to the final act at pub sing, and then Simon, in his pirate character, was thanking the remaining patrons for coming and the day was finally, finally over. My new bodice was front-lacing, so I tugged the laces loose on the walk to my car in the volunteer parking lot. Once I was home and my breathing was unimpeded, I dug my phone out of my blue leather backpack. If I ordered a pizza now, it would be here by the time I was showered and in comfy clothes. Sure enough, I'd just finished putting on my most comfortable sweats and combing out my wet hair when the pepperoni and mushroom with a side of garlic knots arrived. The knock on the door coincided with a chime on my phone, and for a split second I froze, unsure which to answer first. But food won out, and once I'd gotten a soda out of the fridge to go with my pizza, I picked up my phone. It was an email notification, and the preview was enough to make me almost drop my drink.

> Daniel MacLean: I'm sure an email from me is the last thing you . . .

I very carefully set down my drink, then my phone, since seeing his name made my hands shake. I didn't like the way tears sprang to my eyes at the sight of his name, so I made myself take a couple of good, deep breaths before I went and got my laptop. I needed a bigger screen for this.

There was no subject line.

> I'm sure an email from me is the last thing you want right now. Who knows, maybe you've already blocked my email address, not to mention my phone number. I wouldn't blame you a bit if you did. But here goes nothing.
>
>   I had no intention of misleading you. That may sound ridiculous now, but it's true. You have to know that I don't hang around at all the faires we work. Usually I show up beforehand, make sure all the arrangements are made, and help the guys set up. Then after the first weekend, if everything's in good shape, I don't usually stick around, and I

certainly don't hang out at the faire all day. The only time I do that is when we come to Willow Creek. It's almost comical, the things I do to look busy while I'm there—running the merch, lurking at the back of the show to make sure the guys know what they're doing. But I do it, because the longer I stay in Willow Creek, the more I get to see you.

I'm not Dex. Believe me, that's been drilled into my head my whole life. First by our family, who talked me into managing my cousins once they'd formed a band since I had no real talent of my own. Then by girls who pretend that they're into me so they can get closer to him. No one notices me when he's there, including you. You and I have always been friendly, but he was the one you had your eye on. So I never tried to make our friendship anything more. I've told myself every summer that being friends with you was good enough.

When that first message came through from you on the band's page, I thought you'd noticed me. At last. So I answered you, as myself. Truthfully and completely. Then when you wrote back, you called me Dex, and I realized that I hadn't been on your mind at all. I won't tell you what that felt like. But that's when I passed your original message to my cousin, which was the right thing to do, even though it hurt like hell. And Dex . . . well, he already told you his reaction. He wanted me to "handle it." Dump you, basically, on his behalf.

And I just couldn't hurt you like that. Then it occurred to me that, between Dex's looks and my words, together we made the kind of man you deserve.

I sighed at that point and picked up my glass, wishing my soda was wine instead. "Dammit," I muttered. Simon was right. This really was some *Cyrano de Bergerac* bullshit.

But I kept reading.

I knew there'd be a reckoning at some point. Each time I emailed, or later texted, I told myself that I'd come clean the next time. That it was the right thing to do. But I never did. Because I knew coming clean would mean losing what we had, and I wasn't ready for that.

You asked me to give you a reason to stay. I wish I had one. I've been living on the road, managing this band, since I was nineteen. That's who I am. It's all I have. I don't have anything to offer you but a life on the road. And you made it clear that you don't want that. Of course you don't, and I was wrong to even ask. You deserve so much more than a life like this.

You gave me a second chance, that first day at Faire, and I blew that chance. It would be foolish to ask for a third. I'll see that hurt in your eyes for the rest of my life and hate myself for putting it there.

Of all the things I've said and didn't say all these months, as myself or as my cousin, the most important words I should have said are "I love you." I lied to you about who I was. I even lied to you about why I lied to you. But I never lied about how I feel about you.

I'm not my cousin. I'm not Cyrano. I'm just me. I may not be The One as far as you're concerned. But Anastasia, you were The One for me. You still are. You always will be.

I don't expect you to answer this. I'm not even sure if you'll read it. But I hope that you have the life that you deserve, full of love from someone you can trust. I'm sorrier than you'll ever know that it couldn't be me.

Yours. Always.
Daniel MacLean

It was the first time he'd ever signed an email to me, and his full name at that. I felt the significance immediately. He was saying goodbye.

I swiped at the tears on my cheeks and tore into a semi-cold garlic knot. He'd said his piece, and I could respect that. Most of my anger had dissolved in this latest wash of tears, leaving sadness behind. I could email him back right now, but what would it change? He was off to the next gig. Gone, just like my best friend from high school, just like my job in New York. And I was still here in Willow Creek. Life moved on, and I stayed right here.

I'd never felt so alone in my life. I reached for my phone, wanting to text Emily more than anything. I needed my best friend. But my best friend needed to be happy. She didn't need to be worrying about me while she was on her honeymoon. I couldn't come crying to her with this.

I scrolled through my contacts and stopped, staring hard at April's name. We were friends, sure. Book-club friends. Do-shots-together-on-New-Year's-Eve friends. Laugh-together-as-bridesmaids friends. But I wasn't sure if we were at the "cry on her shoulder because I lost the love of my life" level of friendship. Not yet. Besides, April was the definition of a strong, independent woman, to the point that she was almost intimidating. Knowing her, she'd roll her eyes at my distress.

Social media wasn't the right kind of venue for this black mood either. No, that was only for the happy times: the good things you wanted to share with friends and, let's face it, maybe make them a little jealous of your good fortune. You never wanted to tag your bad memories. I couldn't post anything tonight. Not when my heart was breaking.

No. I was alone in this, and all I could do was sit there with my cat and be alone.

Just like always.

Twenty-One

The *last day* of Faire passed in a blur of hot sunshine, music, other people's laughter, and the pounding of hoofbeats. Emily dragged me to the joust early that day, and I found myself circling back to the jousting field for the rest of their performances. Something about the power in the horses, and the way the costumed knights charged at each other, echoed the hard pounding of my heart and an intense emotion I barely knew how to name, much less express.

I was so caught up in that blur that when I passed the Marlowe Stage, Dex had to call my name three times before I heard him. And when I did, I thought about ignoring him and just walking on by, but I simply wasn't built like that. Instead I plastered on what was left of my smile and turned to him.

"Hey." He paused and looked around, as though that single word was all he had planned to say.

"Hey," I said back tentatively. I wasn't in the mood for Mac-Leans right now, and I had no desire to make this conversation any easier for him. After an awkward few seconds he cleared his throat.

"Listen, I just wanted to make sure that you're cool."

I raised my eyebrows. "That I'm what?"

"You know, that you're okay. You seemed really upset the other night. At the hotel?"

My lips twitched at the question. As if I'd forgotten Thursday night. "That's because I was." That was a hell of an understatement. What on earth was he going to do about it?

"Yeah." He rubbed the back of his neck. Dex clearly wasn't an apology kind of guy, and he was totally at sea here.

But it wasn't my job to help him. "Did you need anything else?" I gestured back to the lane; I really wanted to be on my way.

"Yeah. No. I . . ." He gave an exasperated sigh. "I just wanted to make sure you're okay."

"That I'm okay," I echoed, my voice flat. I was the exact opposite of okay. Would I ever be okay again?

"That you're okay," he repeated. "Like I said the other night, I think you're great, I really do. And if I said anything, or did anything, to upset you . . ." He shrugged. "Well, that wasn't what I was trying to do." His eyes met mine squarely, and I felt a jolt. His eyes were brown, like mine, not the startling green of Daniel's. But there was something in the shape of them, and in his expression, that reminded me: oh, yeah. They were related.

And he really was trying. To be honest, this was probably the longest conversation Dex and I had ever had, even during those summers when we were . . . well, I don't think I could use the word together to describe what we'd been doing. Not anymore. Not when I'd been with Daniel, and truly knew what together meant.

So instead of telling him where he could shove his inadequate almost-apology, I decided to take it at face value. "Thanks," I said. "I'm not doing great right now, but I think I'll be okay." Sure, that last bit was a lie—but he didn't need to know that.

Dex's expression cleared, like a puppy with a short attention span. "Good." He gave me a gentle punch on the shoulder, which was probably meant in the spirit of camaraderie, but really just showed me that he had no idea how to relate to a woman he wasn't actively trying to bed. "I gotta get back." He jerked a thumb over his shoulder. "Show in a few minutes. But good talk, yeah?"

I blinked a few times as he all but bounded away. "Yeah," I said after him. "Good talk." I strode down the lane, away from the Marlowe Stage as fast as my feet could carry me. I needed to get the last day of this topsy-turvy Faire season out of my system; I could start fresh next year. I twirled the dragonfly pendant between my fingers as I walked. Dragonflies meant change, Daniel had said to me last summer. I'd had a little too much change.

At the same time, I'd had no change at all. Back to work on Tuesday. Book club later that week. I'd stayed up late a couple nights finishing the book since I was supposed to lead the discussion, which left me overtired and irritated. The little sleep I'd managed was fragmented and interspersed with dreams that hinged on the plot of the book I'd just read—a woman finding herself and moving on after a breakup. Or were the dreams about me? I was too tired to try and figure it out.

By the time I got to book club that night I'd had three cups of coffee too many and a bad day at work. The last thing I wanted to do was talk about some fictional woman's problems. But I forged ahead anyway, helping Chris's daughter Nicole arrange the chairs in a circle, setting out the wine and snacks as Emily and I always did.

"So, what do we think?" The bright smile on my face belied my churning insides as I consulted the book club questions provided by the publisher. "When Molly chooses to leave her old life behind to renovate the farmhouse in the Midwest, what does that symbolize? Does anyone have any thoughts on that?"

On my right, April shrugged. "I'm not a symbolism kind of person. Can't a farmhouse just be a farmhouse?"

Chris snorted and popped another cube of cheese in her mouth. "I don't know, I could go either way with that. I think I can see where the author was going with the symbolism. Scraping off the old paint as a way of showing how Molly sheds the skin of her old life."

"Right." My mom leaned forward, clearly interested in this line of discussion. "She talks about the house being vulnerable before the new coat of paint goes up. Maybe that's how Molly feels herself, being between relationships? Raw, like a layer of herself has been scraped away? And once she gets into that new relationship, with the guy who helps her put the new coat of paint on the house, she feels strong again."

"But why?" April made a tsk sound. "Why does it have to be a guy, or a relationship, that makes you feel strong? I don't like that message: that a woman can only be strong if she's with someone. Why can't Molly have painted the house on her own?"

"I agree," I said. "What kind of message is that, that you're nothing without a guy? That's crap. There's nothing wrong with being single. In fact, it can be liberating. You're not dependent on anyone else to make you happy, you can just . . . live your life. Right?" I turned to April, who looked a little amused by my vehemence but was also nodding in agreement.

"Well said." She held up her hand and I high-fived her.

"There's also that theme of starting over," Nicole said. "Speaking of liberating. Molly goes to this whole new part of the country where nobody knows her, and she's able to start over, reinvent herself just like she's reinventing that farmhouse. I mean, when I started college, that's one reason I went out of state, you know? I wanted to go to a school where I wasn't going to classes with the same people I knew in high school. I wanted to see if I was the same person when I wasn't around the same people."

That was a really astute thought, and any other time I would have actively engaged her on it, delved deeper into that idea, which was the kind of thing you were supposed to do at a book club. But I was high on exhaustion and caffeine and sadness. So I latched on to the exact wrong thought. "Must be nice." Oh, no. My voice was bitter and there was nothing I could do about it. "Must be nice to just . . . leave town. Start over. Be able to pursue your dreams and chase the life you want, instead of getting stuck, while everyone else goes on and lives out their dreams. . . ." I stopped talking because I realized, to my mortification, that I was crying. Everyone in the circle looked at me with varying degrees of confusion, pity, and what-the-hell-is-wrong-with-her.

"Okay." April plucked the paper with the discussion questions out of my hand. "On to the next question. Weather. What did the freak snowstorm in September represent?" She looked around the circle as I fled to the back room to get myself together. "Other than climate change and we're all doomed, right?"

Mom was silent during the drive home from book club. It wasn't until I turned into the driveway that she spoke up. "Do you want to talk about it, honey?"

"Talk about what?" By then I had my regular smile back on

my face, but for once my false cheer wasn't fooling her. I probably wasn't fooling anyone anymore.

"Is it that boy?" She unclipped her seatbelt, and I had to smile at the thought of Daniel as "that boy." Did Mom not realize I was pushing thirty, and he was past it? Maybe in her eyes I would always be seventeen. "Is he . . . Was he . . ." Her voice trailed off. Mom didn't have the language to ask if he'd been nothing more than a summer fling.

"He was just here for Faire, Mom." My car chirped as I engaged the lock, and I followed her into the house. I was too tired to deal with the steps leading up to my apartment.

"Hmm." Her voice was noncommittal as she filled up the electric kettle. "He was over here an awful lot the past couple weeks for someone who was just here for Faire. Not that I'm judging," she hastened to add. "Quite the opposite. It's about time you had someone over. I was about to give you a vibrator for your birthday."

"Mom!" A shocked, slightly scandalized laugh spilled out of me. Maybe I wasn't seventeen in her eyes after all. I got down two mugs and handed them to her. "I'll have you know I'm all stocked up in that department," I said as primly as I could. "Batteries make a great stocking stuffer, though."

Her eyes sparkled with laughter. "I'll keep that in mind." She added tea bags to the mugs before pouring in the hot water. "Here." She pushed one mug toward me. "Chamomile. It'll help you relax."

"I'm relaxed," I said, a little too petulantly. Okay, maybe she had a point. I took the mug and stared into it.

"You're sure you're all right, then?" Mom asked while our tea steeped. "This really was a, uh, short-term thing?"

I nodded, but then the words burst out before I could stop

them. "He wanted me to go with him, Mom." I wanted to clap a hand to my mouth, take the words back. What was the use of saying them now? That decision had already been made.

"Oh." She sat down at the kitchen table, her own mug of tea in front of her. "You mean out on the road with him? Doing what he does?" Her eyes narrowed. "What does he do, anyway?"

"His cousins are a musical act. He manages them. And yes." I sighed into my own tea. "He asked me to go out on the road with him."

She nodded sagely. "And you don't want to."

"No, I don't . . ." But that was a lie. "I mean, I can't." I sighed and took a cautious sip: the tea was still really hot. "It was for the best that we broke up. Really. His life is out there, you know?" I ran the tip of my finger around the lip of the mug. "And mine is here. He wouldn't want to settle down here in Willow Creek." Neither did I. Not really. But here we were, and I sure as hell wasn't going to say that to my mother.

"Well, neither do you."

"What?" My eyes flew to hers. Had I said that out loud? Had she read my mind?

"You heard me." She blew across her mug to cool the tea. "Listen. I know why you stayed, the first time. And believe me, I appreciate that you did. Your father means well, but it would have been hell without you, that first year or so when things were so bad." She eyed me over her mug as she took a sip. "But you have to know, honey, how much I hated it. You gave up a great opportunity—a career, a life—to stay home in this small town and watch me go to doctor's appointments."

I waved it off. "It's fine, Mom."

"No, it isn't." She set her mug down with a thud, and I sat back in my chair. I'd never seen her look so determined. So angry.

So . . . full of regret. "We asked you to stay, but it wasn't supposed to be forever." She sighed as she looked me over, and I fidgeted a little in my chair. "You were such a happy child."

"I'm still happy, Mom." The response was a reflex, an automatic reassurance to my mother that everything was fine.

"No, you're not. I'm your mother, Stacey. I know you better than anyone. I know when your smile is real, and when it's just for show. But that boy—"

"Daniel," I supplied.

"Daniel." She nodded. "He put your real smile back on your face these past few weeks. And now that he's gone . . ." She shook her head. "I've watched you fade, the last couple years. I figured you needed a kick out of the nest, but I didn't know how to do it. Especially since I was the reason you stayed in this nest in the first place." She reached across the table for my hand. "But don't let me stand in your way again, honey. If you have something—someone—worth leaving home for, don't miss that second chance."

Her squeeze on my hand was strong. Once again I flashed back to her, so weak in that hospital bed, and for the first time it really sank in how long ago that was. Mom wasn't weak. Not now, and probably hadn't been for a long time. I'd stayed in Willow Creek to help take care of her, to be there for her, but she didn't need me anymore. She hadn't needed me for a while.

Somewhere along the way Mom's health had stopped being a reason and had become an excuse. I thought back to that night, Daniel and I wrapped up in my sheets, when he asked me to come with him. I should have said yes. Why hadn't I?

Mom wasn't the only one who noticed my inner turmoil.

Saturday night, there was a knock on my door. I was a mess,

scrolling through Instagram on my phone while wearing leggings and a tank top, but since I was expecting it to be my mom I opened the door without thinking about it. To her credit, April didn't comment on my slovenly appearance. She just peered past me into my apartment.

"Nice place."

"Thanks." I squinted at her. April was one of those people whose sarcasm was so dry that it was impossible to tell if she was serious. But I gave her the benefit of the doubt and waved her in.

"No, I mean it." She walked a slow circle through the main living space, and when she turned back to me her smile was genuine, if a little shy. "This is exactly the kind of apartment I've always wanted. When I was younger, you know? I pictured myself living in the city—New York or Chicago—in a cute little place like this."

"Be kind of crowded though, with you and Caitlin."

She snorted. "Well, I gave up on that dream when she came along." She shrugged. "I got Caitlin out of it though, so I call it a win."

"I would, too." And I meant it. Even though kids weren't high on my list of priorities, I liked Caitlin. She was a good kid with a solid support system in her mom and aunt. Anyone who said that a child needed both parents in order to thrive was going to have to fight me.

"Anyway." April looked me up and down, assessing. "Come on. Get some pants on."

I looked down at my ensemble. "Leggings are pants."

"Nope." She leaned down to give Benedick a scritch under his chin and he closed his eyes in contentment. "I mean real pants. We're going out."

"We are?" Were we at a solo hangout level of friendship? I hadn't realized.

But she nodded, so apparently we were. "It's Saturday night, and you're, what, surfing Instagram in your pajamas?"

"These are not pajamas." That was a weak defense, and I knew it. She knew it.

"Look. I don't know what went down with you and Daniel, but something did, and now you're wallowing." She folded her arms over her chest. "Emily had a feeling that something was up, and she asked me to check up on you while she was gone."

"She did?" That brought a sting of tears to my eyes. I'd been so careful to not say anything, but Emily had still known.

"Yeah. But honestly, after book club I think I would have been over here anyway. You need a distraction that's not a badly symbolized women's fiction novel." April looked to the ceiling, then down to the floor, shifting her weight a little. Reaching out wasn't something she did much, obviously, and that made it even more meaningful. "So come on. Let's go to Jackson's, have some pizza, and watch Mitch hit on girls. That's always a good time."

That brought a smile to my face. "You're on."

My hair was a disaster, so I threw it into a ponytail before trading my leggings and tank for jeans and a hoodie. My makeup could have used a refresh, but I didn't know how long April was willing to wait, and I wasn't planning to flirt with anyone tonight. So I put on some lip gloss and called it good enough.

Once at Jackson's we secured a booth in the back, ordered an obnoxiously large pizza, and settled in for some people watching. The great thing about Jackson's was that even though it was a local hangout, it was close enough to the highway that there were occasionally new faces in the mix.

"So." April reached for a second slice of pizza. "Do you want to talk about it?"

"Nothing to talk about. You're the one who said that pineapple doesn't belong on pizza, and I don't think there's anything I can do to make you see the light."

"There really isn't. It's a useless pizza topping and I'm gonna stand by that." She took a bite and chewed. "But that's not what I asked and you know it. Emily filled me in on . . . well, on what she knew, but there have obviously been some developments in the Daniel situation."

"Yeah." I sighed. "And no. I don't want to talk about it." What was there to say? He'd fucked up, but after his email I was pretty sure I forgave him. But I'd fucked up too, and now it was too late. No, there really wasn't anything to say, but I pulled up Daniel's final email and pushed the phone across the table. April picked it up, squinting at the screen. For an excruciating few minutes we were quiet. I looked around the bar and watched Mitch get turned down by a woman who clearly wasn't good enough for him anyway, while April ate that second slice of pizza and read about my broken heart.

A cough from April brought my attention back to her. "Jesus." She blinked rapidly and pushed my phone back across the table to me. "And you haven't answered him?"

"No . . ." Just as the word came out of my mouth, Mitch plopped down in our booth next to me.

"What the hell are you girls doing back here? No one's going to notice you here."

"That's kind of the point." April's eyes narrowed as Mitch took a slice of our pizza. "No, really. Help yourself."

"Thanks, Mama."

"Mama?" April sat back against the booth and crossed her arms. "Wow. What a sexy nickname. Thanks a lot."

Mitch raised one slow eyebrow. "You want a sexy nickname?"

For a second they locked eyes, and I was momentarily distracted from my own drama by the new potential drama unfolding in front of me. Finally April blinked. "No," she said. "No, I don't."

"Good." He took a big bite of pizza as his gaze traveled down to my phone. "What's this? Did that guy stand you up again, Stacey? I swear I'm gonna . . ." He blinked at the phone, then looked up at me, his brow furrowed. "Daniel MacLean?"

Even hearing his name hurt. "Yeah." My voice sounded rusty, so I cleared my throat and took another sip from my water glass.

"No." Mitch shook his head. "You mean Dex. You were banging Dex MacLean, weren't you?"

"What?" April said, just as I said "No," and Mitch looked back and forth between us, not sure who to answer first.

"Yes, you were." He scoffed. "Last summer. Summer before that too, I think."

April folded her arms over her chest. "How did you know about that?" She sounded put out.

Mitch shrugged. "You want to know the Ren Faire gossip, you gotta join the Ren Faire." She snorted in response, but I wanted to get back on topic.

"I didn't think you knew," I said. "We were pretty discreet."

He scoffed. "Please." But he didn't elaborate. He looked down at the phone again. "So what's with Daniel? I mean, I saw you dancing with him at the wedding, but I didn't realize there was anything . . ." He made a hand gesture that I couldn't even begin to interpret. "You know. Going on there."

"Well, there's nothing going on there now." I sighed. The black mood was back. "We broke up. It's for the best. He travels too much and wouldn't want to live full-time here in Willow Creek anyway." I trotted out the same argument I'd used with my mom.

"Okay . . ." Mitch dragged the word out into about four syllables as he swiped another slice of pizza, taking a bite before setting it down onto my plate. "I mean, that makes sense. You've got a lot keeping you here. Like your career."

"My career?" My eyebrows shot up into my forehead. "I work in a dentist's office. Not exactly my life's dream."

"Hmm." He chewed thoughtfully. "So that's not it. Is it your house? A mortgage can really tie you down." He snapped his fingers. "No. Wait. You live above your parents' garage."

I narrowed my eyes at him. "Yes, I do. You know that."

"Yeah," April chimed in. "That tiny place of yours, you practically live like a minimalist. You could probably fit everything you own in the trunk of your car."

"Or the back of someone's pickup truck," Mitch added with a significant nod. "What does Daniel drive again?" He posed the question to April, who shrugged with a smile.

"I just don't like having a lot of stuff. There's nothing wrong with that." Why were they making me feel so defensive? "You know, you two are not doing the best job of cheering me up right now."

"And your mom's doing okay these days . . ." Mitch still sounded unconcerned as he reached for his beer.

"She really is," April said, talking to Mitch instead of to me. "I see her at Emily's book club once a month. She's had some health issues in the past, right? But she seems to be doing great now."

"Yeah." I thought back to my conversation with her last night. "She's doing really well."

"So." Mitch looked down at my phone again. "Daniel. You love the guy?"

I caught my breath as tears stung the corners of my eyes. "I mean it. Your cheering-up technique really could use some work."

He rolled his eyes. "Do you or not?"

I threw up my hands. "Yes! I do. I really do. But it's too late. He's gone, remember?"

"I don't think so." He gestured to the phone. "Not according to this. What's keeping you here, exactly? It's not your job. It's not your mom. Why aren't you out on the road with him right now?"

"I can't do that." But it was an automatic denial, and even as I said the words there was a thrill in my chest. What if Mitch was right? What if my mom was right? What if I threw everything I cared about into a few bags and just . . . went for it?

April could see that I was wavering. "Does he make you happy?"

"Yes." I didn't even have to think about the answer.

"Would you want to travel with him? Live that kind of life?"

I took the time to think about that. To consider living out of vehicles. Traveling from faire to faire. Living that life, speaking their language.

Being with Daniel.

It sounded perfect. Like the kind of life I'd always wanted, even when I didn't know it.

And I'd said no, because I was too chickenshit. I'd turned him down and let him go.

I groaned and let my head fall into my hands. "God. I really fucked up, didn't I?"

April whistled. "When did you get such a potty mouth?" But when I looked over at her, she was smiling. Why was she smiling?

"That doesn't change the fact that it's too late." I picked up my phone. It was still displaying Daniel's goodbye message, and I traced his name with my fingernail.

"Nah." Mitch drained the rest of his beer. "They're over at the Maryland Ren Fest, right? That's like an hour away, maybe two. They're not going anywhere for a while."

"No, but Daniel is." April's eyes went wide as she looked at me, and I knew exactly what she was talking about.

"Oh, no!" I threw my phone into my purse. "I have to go!" I started to scoot out of the booth but Mitch blocked my progress like a brick wall.

"Go where?" Mitch looked from April to me in confusion, not getting the hint at all.

I punched him on the arm. "Scoot over, I need to get out!"

"Hey, cut it out! What's the hurry?" He looked at me as though I'd lost my mind. And maybe I had. I didn't care.

"I have to get over there. He's gonna leave, and I don't know where he'll be after that." Had he even told me the Kilts' schedule after this next gig? My mind was blank with panic.

"What the . . ." Mitch stood up so I could scoot out behind him. "I just said they're gonna be there for a while."

"But Daniel won't be," April said. "He's only staying the first weekend. He said so, in the email." She squinted up at me. "You know, you could send him an email. Let him know you're coming up, maybe?"

"Okay. Yes. You're right." I fished in my bag for my phone before I remembered. "He doesn't check his email during Faire weekends." I let my head fall back on my neck with a groan. "He was only doing that because I was emailing him, and . . ."

". . . And he doesn't think you're emailing him anymore." April finished the sentence with a sigh. "You could text him, then. You have his number?"

My only answer was another groan. I was so sick of my phone. I was sick of all of it: of emails, of social media, of texts. Of words on screens. I wanted tangible reality. I wanted Daniel's smile, warming me from the inside out. I wanted the feel of his skin against mine. The way he threaded our fingers together when he held my hand. I needed him. Craved him.

Something must have shown on my face, because April nodded. "Okay." She looked around. "Where the hell is our waitress? We need to pay and get out of here."

She slid out of the booth to find the waitress, but Mitch was still watching me. "The first weekend . . ." Understanding dawned on his face. "That's right now."

"And I've already blown Saturday, so that just leaves tomorrow!" Panic rose again in my chest as I scrambled for my keys. I'd been here before. Last time I'd put off my future for my mom, and I lost it all. I couldn't put it off again. Now that I knew the life I wanted, I couldn't wait one more minute for that life to begin.

"Okay." Mitch's large hand closed over mine, both of us holding fast to my keys. "Listen. Take a breath. You're not going out there tonight. You don't know where he's staying, do you?" Off my head shake, he nodded. "So he could be camping, or he could be at a hotel. You'll never find him if you drive out there in the middle of the night. Go home. Send him a text, let him know we're on the way. Get some sleep, and we'll head over there in the morning."

"We?"

"Yeah." He took one more look around the bar and dance floor area as April came back with the receipt in her fist. "Nothing going on here tonight anyway."

"How altruistic of you," April said. "Giving up your valuable hookup time to help out a friend."

"Hey, I'm a giver." He stuck out an arm, ushering the two of us to walk in front of him. "Besides, I think I've hooked up with half of this bar." He shook his head. "I need a new hangout."

Twenty-Two

I *didn't text him.*

I tried. More than once. But the right words weren't coming, and I'd meant it when I'd said I was sick of screens, especially when it came to Daniel. He hadn't fought for me, or done something romantic to win me back, because he thought he wasn't good enough. That he didn't have what I wanted. I realized now that I didn't need a sweeping romantic gesture. Daniel did. So instead I plugged my phone in for the night, telling myself that if for some reason we missed him at the Maryland Ren Fest tomorrow, I'd text. I'd call. I'd do everything in the world to get to him. But until then I needed to find him in person. Do this face-to-face.

The next morning Mitch picked me up in his gargantuan pickup truck—a bright red monstrosity that was roughly the size of my apartment—and we stopped at April's house before getting on the road.

"Thank you so much for coming along," I said from the back

of the extended cab as April opened the passenger door. "Mitch is great and all—"

"Glad to hear it." Mitch's voice was as dry as the Sahara as he adjusted his rearview mirror.

"No problem," April said. "I figured you could use some moral support of the female . . ." Her voice trailed off as she plopped into her seat and closed the door. "You have *got* to be kidding me."

"What?" Mitch put the truck in gear and backed out of April's driveway.

She didn't say anything for a second, just sat back against her seat and shook her head. "You had to wear the kilt, didn't you." It wasn't a question.

"It's a Renaissance faire." He said the words slowly, as though she'd have trouble understanding. "Of course I'm wearing the kilt. Question is . . ." He raised his voice and looked in the rearview mirror, clearly aiming his next words at me. "Why are you wearing civvies?"

I smoothed my hands nervously over the skirt of the sundress I'd worn today. It was still late August: way too hot to spend the day in jeans. Besides, I looked good in this dress. It was the same color as my bridesmaid dress, and Daniel had really liked me in that. The dusty rose shade warmed my skin, and the top of it was cut almost like a bodice, suggesting a period outfit without actually being one. "Because my costume is at the dry cleaners. I didn't think I was going to need it before next summer." I didn't mention my old costume, clean and packed away in the bottom of my trunk. A different Stacey had worn that outfit, and I wasn't that girl anymore.

He shook his head before directing his attention back to the road. "Play your cards right today, and you'll be wearing it a lot sooner than that."

"And a lot more often," April chimed in. "You'll need to get a couple more outfits. You know, if you end up doing this kind of thing full-time."

"Let's not worry about that right now." I took a pull off my travel mug of coffee and regretted it almost immediately. I'd hardly slept the night before, so caffeine had been a must. But my stomach was already jumping around like crazy, and adding coffee just made it churn. I was a live wire. I was a raw nerve ending. How was I going to survive the drive to Annapolis?

It took less than two hours to get there, but it felt like two weeks. Eventually, Mitch's pickup bounced us across the grassy field of the parking lot for the Maryland Renaissance Festival. Three car doors slammed in quick staccato as we got out. For a long moment we looked around at the lot, where we were just one in a massive sea of cars. Patrons who parked in the lot of the Willow Creek Faire could see the entrance when they got out of their cars: a two-dimensional castle façade that some volunteers had put together about five years ago. But not here. Our entire Faire could probably fit in this parking lot, and all we could see around us was row after row of cars. Like parking at Disney World, but without the trams or mouse ears.

"Holy shit." April wasn't part of our Faire, but even she sounded impressed. "Where's the entrance?"

"Up that way." I couldn't see the gates I was pointing toward, but the stream of people told me I was indicating the right way.

"A little bit of a hike, then." April looked behind us, where the grassy lot continued to fill slowly with cars. "Holy shit," she said again. "This isn't a Faire. This is a town."

"Yeah." Mitch had been here before—so had I; if you grew up around here you went to the Maryland Renaissance Festival at least once during your childhood—but even his eyes were a little wide at the vastness of it all. "This place is . . . It's pretty big." He paused. "That's what she said."

I was too nervous to snicker, but April elbowed him in the ribs, and that was good enough.

"Okay. We're going in." He reached over his head for the back of his T-shirt, pulling it off and tossing it into the back of the truck.

April sighed. "All right, Kilty. Naked enough?"

"Look on the bright side." He wiggled his eyebrows at her as he stuck his keys into the sporran he wore attached to the kilt. "I'm not working this Faire. Which means I get to wear this kilt the way it's meant to be worn."

I coughed. I didn't want to think about what Mitch was or was not wearing under there. Which was sad, because thinking about Mitch in a kilt used to be one of my favorite hobbies. The man was born to wear that green plaid, just long enough to brush his knees, leaving a glimpse of thigh when he walked. He wore boots strapped over his powerful calves, and now that he'd doffed his T-shirt that was the whole of his costume. Looking at Mitch in costume had been the best part of Faire for years. My priorities had changed a lot lately.

It took April a beat longer to follow Mitch's innuendo, but I could see the moment when it clicked. She rolled her eyes, shook her head again at him, and then turned to me. "You ready for this?"

Why did she have to ask me that? My stomach rolled, and the butterflies in there took flight, wiggling their way through my bloodstream until everything tingled. I was in no way ready for this. But I sucked in a long, slow breath and wiped my damp palms on the skirt of my dress.

"Yeah." I didn't sound at all convincing. "I'm ready."

. . .

Comparing our Faire to the Maryland Renaissance Festival was ridiculous. If Willow Creek's Faire was a small town, then the Maryland Ren Fest was New York City. The Big . . . Turkey Leg? Whatever. You couldn't compare the two was what I meant.

We joined the masses of people heading for the ticket booth and the entrance. The sounds of bagpipes and drums floated on the air, combining with voices in the distance. Excited expectation surged through my blood. I hadn't been to this Faire since high school, but the sounds were as comfortable and familiar as my own heartbeat.

As we stepped through the gates April stopped in her tracks, her eyes round. "Oh, shit," she breathed. "This is on a whole other level."

"That it is." Even Mitch seemed to need a moment to get his bearings, and I touched his arm to steady myself. We'd walked through a portal into another world. These weren't stages and glorified tents put together by volunteers over a couple weekends. These were *buildings*. Actual, honest-to-God permanent structures that looked like they belonged in a medieval village. My first thought was *What about winter?* Even though there were crowds all around me and the whole scene bustled with life, I wondered what this place looked like in the dead of winter, covered with snow and empty of patrons. I couldn't get my head around the idea that this setting existed all year round, whether there was a faire going on or not.

At the same time, this place felt like home. I knew this place. Maybe not this physical place specifically, but I knew Renaissance faires. I knew the sounds of the people around me, the voices of vendors selling roses and flower crowns out of wagons near the entrance. I knew the sweet smell of deep-fried anything and the savory scent of every kind of meat on a stick, and the sound of our feet shuffling in the dirt of the lanes. Butterflies still swirled all through my body, but my soul felt calm. I knew this place, and I loved this place.

Now all I had to do was find the man I loved, somewhere in this medieval metropolis, and convince him to take me with him. Should be simple.

Beside me, April heaved out a long sigh, a hand on her hip. "So how do we find him? There's so many people."

Mitch leaned over and tapped the map that she'd picked up at the entrance. "This should help, dontcha think?"

She punched him in the arm, which he didn't even register, and shook the map open. She squinted at it, turned it over, squinted at it again. "This thing is ridiculous. There are a million acts and they're scattered all over."

I took the map from her. "It's not that bad. We just have to find their listing, and then figure out where their stage is." I frowned at the map. "Hmm. I get your point." The map only emphasized how huge this place was, and it was hard to figure out which stage was which. But my eyes zeroed in on the Dueling Kilts' listing as if it were printed in bright red, with arrows pointing at it. *Your man is here!*

At least, I hoped he was still my man. And I hoped he was there. What if he'd already left? He could have set them up for the weekend and taken off already. He could be out of the state by now. He could . . .

Enough. There was only one way to find out.

We set off, past the "official" souvenir shop that sold T-shirts and hats, past the booth where people could make wax castings of their hands—why, that was always my question—and I regretted the sandals I'd worn almost immediately. Sure, they looked great with this dress, but how could I have not thought that through? I knew how uneven the terrain was, and how easy it was for minuscule rocks and little tiny sticks to find their way under your feet when you had open shoes on. But I gritted my teeth against the annoyance and soldiered on. The sun was already high in the sky, and it was shaping up to be a hot day. The sundress had been a good call, even though the cotton was already sticking to my back in an extremely unsexy way.

"Oooh." April had taken control of the map again as we neared the stage where the Kilts performed. "There's a bookstore here! I need to tell Emily about that. And look, there's a maze. Near the jousting field. We should—"

"Stay on task, Mama." Mitch plucked the map out of her hands.

She took it back again. "Fine. Their show starts in ten minutes. Do we want to go find him now?"

I shook my head. "No, they're getting ready for the show. I don't want to mess with that."

"Makes sense. We'll just go sit in the audience and watch it?"

"No, we should wait till after." Mitch said. "That would be the professional thing to do, right? We don't want to disrupt their show."

"No," I said. "We don't want to go there after, either. The audience will be leaving, the guys will be selling merch, maybe getting tips . . . we don't want to interrupt that either."

"Okay." April pushed her sunglasses on top of her head and pinched the bridge of her nose. "So we don't want to go before the show, during it, or after. Should we just wait outside the gate till the end of the day?"

"Yes." My nod felt loose, as though I were a bobblehead doll. "That's an excellent idea."

"Nice try." Mitch's hand clamped around my arm as I spun on my heel to go back the way we'd come. The man had a grip like a vise; there was no way I could squirm out. He propelled me forward, which was a good thing because my legs had stopped working.

"Okay, but seriously," I said as he dragged me down the lane, April following behind us in case I made a run for it, "they're about to start a show and we shouldn't interrupt that." Wow, my voice went really high when I babbled.

"It's fine," Mitch said. "We'll sit in the back. They won't notice us."

But I wasn't listening to reason, or anything, really, at that point. "They're busy, you know? They're working. I don't even know where we'd find them. We can't just—"

"Mitch? Hey, Mitch!" The three of us stopped walking and turned around. Mitch dropped my arm and smiled.

"Dex! Dude, how's it going?" He went in for a fist bump, and after that they did that weirdly complicated handclasp thing that men did instead of just shaking hands like normal people. It was a cornucopia of kilted hotness, with Dex in his man bun and Mitch in his shirtlessness. Both with strong, broad backs and powerful legs, and I wasn't interested in either one of them.

"Doing good, man, doing good. What are you doing here? This isn't your Faire." Dex laughed. "Couldn't get enough this summer, right?"

"You know it." Mitch's laugh was a low and easy rumble, because what did that guy have to worry about? "No, we're actually here to . . ." He glanced over his shoulder, and he raised his eyebrows at me. The message was clear: *Should I ask?*

But before I could use my own eyebrows to telegraph something back—like *No, I'm chickening out, get us out of here immediately*—Dex followed Mitch's line of sight and spotted me. Dammit. "Hey, Stace." He said my name easily, as though he hadn't broken my heart outside a hotel room in Willow Creek a week ago, and sort-of apologized for it a couple days later.

"Hey." The word came out as a wheeze, and I wasn't even wearing a corset. I tried again, aiming for casual. "Hey. Dex. Hey. How's it . . ."

"Seen Daniel around?" Mitch cut to the chase. God bless him.

"Oh, yeah." Dex pointed at the stage. "He's back there; just go around to the right to get to the backstage area. But you should go now. Show's starting in a couple minutes." He grinned at me. "About time you showed up. He said he'd never see you again, which is great because now he owes me twenty bucks."

"There you go." Mitch physically turned me around and sent me toward the stage with a little shove in the middle of my back. I walked away just as Dex turned toward April, his eyes alight with appreciation.

"Hey." The word was pure speculation.

"Absolutely not." I could practically hear April's eye roll.

The Dueling Kilts were due to take the stage in four minutes, according to both my phone and the schedule on our map, and even though it was just the first show of the day, most of the benches were full of patrons, fanning themselves with their paper maps while they waited for the show to start. I skirted around the house right side of the audience, heading for a black-curtained doorway. I slipped through the curtain to find myself in a backstage area that was roughly the size of a broom closet. The curtain swung down behind me, obscuring me from the audience, and my breath stopped because there he was, half-bent over a cardboard box of Kilts merchandise. After heartbreak and farewell confessional emails and complete absence for days, Daniel was now barely five feet away from me. It was too sudden. It was too much.

He must have heard the choked sound my breath made, because he turned around and froze, looking as stunned as I felt. The stack of T-shirts in his arms fell back into the box. "Stacey," he said. Or maybe he said. His voice seemed to be as strong as mine, which was to say, not very much at all.

"Hey." My voice worked this time. Better than it had when I'd been talking to Dex, anyway. I should have known; everything about me was better with Daniel than it had ever been with Dex.

"What are you . . ." He shook his head a little while his eyes roamed over me, drinking me in like . . . well, like I was a cold glass of water on a day as hot as today. "How are you here?" he finally asked, his voice filled with something that sounded like wonder. He looked as though he wanted to smile, but didn't know if he could just yet.

Now that the shock of seeing him was over, and now that I knew he wasn't going to throw me out immediately, much of my nervousness fell away. I shrugged, as though I drove across the state to intercept the man I loved before he walked out of my life forever on a daily basis. "Got a ride."

He didn't respond, he just kept looking at me as if I were a mirage that might disappear, and I remembered that I had more to say. I took a breath that was more shake than inhale, but it would have to do. "You were wrong about something."

"I was?" His brow furrowed, and his expression became guarded. I could practically see his shoulders tense up as he braced himself for whatever onslaught I was going to throw his way.

"Yeah." I tried for a smile, but it wasn't coming yet. "You said you didn't have anything to offer me. That I wouldn't want a life on the road with you. But—"

"Look out, coming through!" Dex pushed through the curtain

and bumped me in the back, driving me straight into Daniel. His hands went to my hips instinctively, steadying me, and I barely caught Dex's smile as he walked past us and onto the stage. "Sorry," he said over his shoulder at us. "Gotta start the show."

I watched Dex go and then, as much as I hated to leave Daniel's embrace, I took a step back and tugged on his arm. "Come on," I said, nodding toward the black curtain he'd just come through. "Is there somewhere we can go? Someplace a little quieter, so we can . . ."

"No. We can't." He pulled me back toward him, and I wasn't terribly unhappy about that, despite his words. "The show's about to start. The audience will see us if we try to leave. We have to stay back here so we're not a distraction."

I blinked up at him. "So you were just going to hang out here while the show went on?"

"No. I came back here to grab the shirts for the merch stand after the show. I wasn't planning on being here while the show was going on." He shrugged. "You kinda ambushed me here."

"Oh." I bit my lower lip. "Sorry."

"I'm not complaining." His hand flexed on the small of my back, and a smile teased at the corners of his mouth. My heart soared at that almost-smile. That was how far gone I was for this guy: a hint of a smile was all it took. "But I'm afraid you're stuck in here with me till the show's over."

"Oh," I said again. "Okay." I looked back at the black curtain. "Any other MacLeans about to barrel through here?"

"Nope." Daniel's laugh was a warm chuckle in my ear, and I shivered despite the heat of the day. I'd missed him so much. "The others are out in the house, and they just hop on stage from there."

Sure enough, as if on cue, the sound of a fiddle cut through the murmur of the chatting audience, quieting them down, and Dex's voice rang out from the stage, roughly six feet from where we were standing, the same spiel I heard every summer, every time the Dueling Kilts started a show. That little bit of patter was what drove it home for me. This was what they *did*. Not just at our Faire, but everywhere. This same show, all over the country, all year long. It had to be repetitive as hell. But I still wanted in.

"What were you saying?" He pitched his voice low, since we were only a few feet from the audience, and I leaned in to hear him because there were also loud musical instruments just on the other side of the stage curtain.

Right. I forged ahead. "You said you had nothing to offer me. Nothing I'd want. But you're wrong. This"—I gestured around us, taking in the stage, this tiny broom closet we were in, the entire Renaissance festival around us—"This is it. What you have is what I want. This life. Right here." I took a step toward him, which pretty much closed the remaining distance between us. It was cramped back there. "With you." I rested a hand on his waist; it felt so good to be touching him again.

His breath caught. "Do you mean that?"

"I do." I nodded vigorously. "So, tell me."

He raised his eyebrows. "Tell you what?"

"Tell me," I said again. "You said in your email that . . ." My voice trailed off as the music on stage finally filtered through my consciousness. It had taken a couple verses for me to realize what the guys were playing out there.

Weigh heigh and up she rises
Weigh heigh and up she rises
Weigh heigh and up she rises
Early in the morning

"Oh, listen," I said. "It's our song." That got me another warm chuckle as Daniel's other hand slid from my hip to the small of my back, and the heat of his skin through the cotton of my dress was almost too much to take.

"They don't usually open with that. Tell you what?" he asked again, his voice low and directly in my ear, barely loud enough to hear over the music coming from the other side of the stage curtain.

Now my smile felt real, and not like a mask at all. We should have been somewhere private at a moment like this. But there was something very, very right about telling him how I felt here, in the heat and dust of a Renaissance faire, with his cousins performing a few feet away and an audience just out of sight.

I drew back in his arms, studying his face, loving the light that had come into his green eyes. "No more writing," I said. "No more emails. Tell me to my face. Tell me how you feel. And I'll tell you how glad I am that you aren't your cousin."

His eyebrows rose, and now the smile came full force to his mouth. The joy in his face looked like a sunrise. "You are?"

I nodded. "I'll tell you that I've always had a thing for tall redheads that are on the lean side."

"Oh, really." He would have looked dubious if he hadn't been smiling like that.

"Really," I insisted. "Much, much more than huge, gross, muscly guys."

"Thank God for that," he said, just before he bent to me, and his kiss felt like coming home.

"I mean, eight packs," I said against his mouth. "Ick. Who needs 'em."

"Okay, that's enough." But I could feel his smile against my lips, which only made me kiss him harder.

Out on stage they'd done a couple verses of "Drunken Sailor," and Dex started a brand new one:

Chuck him backstage with a blonde-haired wench

"Oh my God," Daniel said, breaking our kiss. He looked over his shoulder toward the stage, and I burst into laughter, holding on to him more tightly.

Chuck him backstage with a blonde-haired wench
Chuck him backstage with a blonde-haired wench
Early in the morning

"Tell me," I insisted. My smile felt enormous on my face, and this time it was all genuine.

"Oh, Stacey." His kiss told me everything I needed to know, but my heart still soared when he drew back to whisper in my ear. "Anastasia. I love you."

"I love you," I whispered back, but the words were lost in the music and in his kiss.

So, yes, Daniel and I declared our love for each other while his cousins sang a traditional sea shanty roughly eight feet away from us, but I wouldn't have had it any other way.

Epilogue

"You're kidding, right?" Emily looked skeptical.

I shook my head and adjusted my grip on my phone. Dropping her while we were on a video call would be rude. "I am not kidding."

"Yeah, but . . . barf?"

"BARF." My voice was deadpan. "It stands for Bay Area Renaissance Festival. It's one of the bigger ones here in Florida."

Emily covered her mouth with her hand, and her giggle was so strong it made her eyes almost disappear. "That's amazing. I love it. That's so much better than our acronym. WCRF just sounds like a bad radio station."

I grinned. "How's everything back home? Cold?" To my left on the tiny counter, the coffeemaker started making its death-gasp burble, letting me know the pot was finished brewing. I balanced my phone against the dish rack so I could still see Emily while I reached up to the cupboard above my head for the coffee mugs. Space was at a premium in this little motorhome, so there were only two mugs in there. But we only needed two.

"Very." Emily gave a mock shudder. "I'm so jealous that you're down there in Florida in February."

"It's pretty great, I'm not going to lie." I wasn't just talking about the weather. "It's nice to be on the road again, too." I poured milk into the mugs and added sugar to mine before pouring the coffee. I eyed them both before adding more milk to Daniel's mug. One of these days I'd get the proportions right on the first try.

"Yeah? Did you two get hives staying in one place for so long over the holidays?"

"It wasn't too bad." I wasn't lying. We were just coming off the Kilts' downtime, which Daniel and I had split between his family and mine. I'd shared a drink with Uncle Morty on New Year's Eve, and then we'd spent a couple weeks in my garage apartment, which my parents had left available for us whenever we wanted it.

But I didn't want it. Not much. Life on the road agreed with me, more than I'd ever thought it would. Even though every city was different, the festivals themselves felt like coming home every time, and now the days when I didn't have to put on a bodice and long skirts felt weird. Throwing on a pair of jeans to go to Starbucks made me feel like I was going out half-dressed.

"Mom still doing okay?" She'd looked great when I'd been home, but that had been a few weeks ago, and worrying about her was my default state. I couldn't help it. I was glad that I had my bestie there to keep an eye on her, under the guise of book club.

"Oh, yeah," Emily said. "She's great. She misses you, though, I think. She's had Simon and me over for dinner a couple times this month."

I winced. "I'm sorry. You want me to tell her to knock it off?"

"No, not at all." Emily shrugged. "It's actually kind of nice."

The screen door to the RV squeaked open, and Daniel ducked through the doorway. "Truck's gassed up, we should . . . Oh, hey, Emily." He waved at her image on the screen, and she waved back.

"Morning, Daniel! You being good to my girl here?"

"Doing my best." He stepped all the way inside and curled an arm around my waist before dropping a kiss on top of my head. "But I need to steal her back. It's about that time."

"I just finished making coffee," I said with a huff. "That's why I called Emily this early. We were going to have coffee together." He was right, though; my intentions had been good but the timing hadn't worked out today.

"We did." Emily hefted her coffee mug with a smile. "And it's okay. I need to get moving too; the bookstore's not going to open itself."

Daniel nodded. "Thanks for the help with the website, by the way. It looks great."

"Yes!" I said. "Thank you. Did you see that I updated it last week?" I may have been social media savvy, but I was useless when it came to coding. Thank God for Emily; she'd built an actual website for the Dueling Kilts over the winter, so they didn't have to rely on just a social media page anymore. The group's reach expanded exponentially as a result, and Daniel had been able to book lots more gigs for the guys between festivals.

"I saw!" Emily said. "I'm very proud of you. You need to send me one of those hoodies."

I grinned. "It's already in the mail." Daniel had given me free rein, and I'd poured everything I'd learned in college about fashion merchandising into running the merchandise side of things for the band. Until now, they'd just been selling a couple

CDs and a single T-shirt. It didn't take me long to add tank tops and hoodies, as well as souvenirs like beer koozies with the band's logo on them. Then Emily helped me set up the online store, so merchandise could be purchased there as well as at the shows. I rotated the physical merch that we brought with us depending on the location. Hoodies didn't move too fast in Florida, for example. The whole situation worked out well for all of us. Daniel had never enjoyed running the merch; now he was able to concentrate more on booking the band for more gigs in the downtime between Faire weekends.

"Okay. Finish cinching up your boobs and have a great time." Emily shook her head. "Better you than me."

With a laugh, we disconnected the call, and then I did a quick check of the Kilts' business email account. I sighed in relief at the shipping notification waiting for me there. I hadn't ordered enough tank tops, and it was unseasonably warm, even for Florida in February. But now we'd be restocked by next weekend.

"Everything okay?" Daniel reached for his coffee, blowing across the top for absolutely no reason since all that milk made it practically room-temperature.

"Yep, we're good," I said as he took his first sip of coffee and closed his eyes in pleasure. That was one of my favorites of his smiles: that reaction as the caffeine hit his system. It was a sleepy, small smile, and it was all mine.

"Perfect." He sighed and leaned against the counter, downing half the mug in another gulp. "Marry me."

He said that almost every morning while we had our coffee. One of these days I was going to say yes. But today I reached for his hand and he tangled our fingers together. One last moment of peace and quiet before the chaos of the day.

I glanced up at the clock on the microwave. We really did need to get going. "Ready to herd cats?"

Daniel nodded and tossed back the last of his coffee before putting the mug in the sink. "I'll get the baby." But he stopped to give me one more lingering, coffee-flavored, good-morning kiss, pressing me against the counter and making me wish we didn't have to be somewhere really, really soon.

I finished my own coffee and washed out our mugs, leaving them out to dry. Tonight I'd put them back in the cabinet, and we'd do it all over again tomorrow. I laced up my bodice loosely and strapped the wide leather belt around my waist. Everything was loose for now; I still had to ride in the truck to the festival site, and I wasn't doing that in a tight costume. Daniel's voice, a low and indistinct murmur, floated back from the sleeping compartment, and my heart swelled. Sometimes I still couldn't believe he was mine. That this whole life was mine.

I heard a zip, and I turned to see Daniel make his way back to the front of the RV, cat carrier slung over his shoulder by the strap. I bent down.

"You okay in there, Benedick?"

The sound of his name woke him up, and the fat tuxedo cat stretched with a squeak.

Daniel chuckled. "I don't think he even woke up while I was putting him in there."

"Of course not," I said. "He's a professional."

Benedick loved life on the road. After finding Daniel at the Maryland Ren Fest, it hadn't taken me long to go home, quit my job, and pack up my things to meet back up with him to start our life together. I'd brought Benedick with me on a trial basis, hoping he could cope but also resigned to bringing him back to stay with my parents when I went to live on the road for good. To my shock

he turned out to be a cat that was born to travel. He slept most of
the time as we traveled from place to place, and the first time I
tentatively put a harness on him, he took to it immediately. So we
rolled with it. At the next Faire I bought him a little pair of dragon's wings, and he became our little leashed dragon-cat mascot.
He hung out with me during the day while I tended the merch
booth, chasing bugs and butterflies when he wasn't napping in the
sun, and our audiences seemed to love him. I'd already sketched
out a couple different logos with a little dragon-Benedick on them
to sell in the future alongside the official band merchandise.

Now, the three of us got in Daniel's truck. I secured the cat
carrier in between us while Daniel called his cousins.

"Please tell me you're awake."

Dex's laugh came through the speakerphone. "Dude, we're already here, where are you?"

"On the way." He handed me the phone before clicking his
seatbelt and starting the truck. "And don't forget, we get the hotel room next weekend."

"Oh, finally." I let my head fall back against the headrest in
imagined bliss. I loved the little RV, but there was something to
be said for a long, hot shower in a real bathroom, and starfishing
on a king-size bed.

"Yeah, yeah," Dex said. "We'll make the switch during the
week. We still have to flip for it to see who has to give up the
room. I'll try to make Freddy do it, though. You know how staying in the RV throws me off my game. Chicks don't dig 'em."

"God forbid we throw you off your game," Daniel said dryly.
Dex was who he was: the same manwhore he'd always been. But
he and I had settled into an okay relationship, and sometimes I
genuinely forgot that we'd slept together once upon a time. It
was a different Stacey who had done that.

"Hey," I interjected. "I dig it just fine."

Dex's snort was loud and clear despite the cell phone connection. "You don't count."

I gasped and turned to Daniel, my mouth hanging open in mock outrage, but he just laughed. "Okay, we're turning in now. See you in a few." I disconnected the call as the truck bumped over the field where the entertainers parked. After setting the brake, Daniel came around to open my door and help me jump down—trucks like this weren't built for shorter people, and my mobility was already a little limited in this outfit.

"You all set if I run on ahead?"

I waved an unconcerned hand. "I'll text if I need you." I gathered the front of his T-shirt in my fist and pulled him toward me for one more kiss. He smiled against my mouth and nipped my bottom lip with his teeth.

"See you there." He traced the wings of the dragonfly pendant I wore around my neck with his fingertips, and with one more kiss he was off, striding across the lot with those long legs of his. I leaned against the truck and watched him go, already wishing I'd grabbed one more kiss. Oh well, plenty of time later. I set to work cinching everything up: tightening my bodice, settling the leather belt a little more tightly around my waist, and gathering my overskirt up with the skirt hikes I'd bought a couple Faires ago. Much more period appropriate than the safety pins I'd used in Willow Creek all these years.

One last check of the belt pouch at my waist, and I felt a jolt: my phone. I'd left it on the counter in the RV after talking to Emily. Whoops. But I didn't feel the panic I used to feel at the prospect of time without my phone.

I'd realized, sometime around November, that I didn't check

my social media all that much anymore. Sure, I did my yearly Pumpkin Spice Latte Count, made more interesting by the multiple Starbucks in multiple cities as we traveled. (This year's count: seventeen. This was getting ridiculous. But it wasn't all my fault; PSL season seemed to start earlier and earlier every year.) While my online addiction had reached a fever pitch last year, it had never been about the screens at all. It had been about searching for a life of my own, which I now had. And it had been about the man behind those screens. And I knew exactly where he was.

All cinched in, I picked up Benedick's carrier and set off in the direction Daniel had gone, toward the Faire and the Kilts' stage.

Everything I owned these days could fit in two suitcases and a cat carrier. Sometimes I slept in hotels, sometimes in a giant tin can. Sometimes I camped out with my boyfriend, his cousins, and a few dozen rennies. Home was the RV, Daniel's beat-up, rust-red pickup truck, my tuxedo cat wearing a pair of dragon's wings, the smile in Daniel's eyes when he looked at me, and his arms around me when we went to sleep at night.

I couldn't imagine a better home. Or a better life.

Acknowledgments

Books—at least my books—don't get written without the help of some of the best people I know.

My agent, my rock, Taylor Haggerty, I legitimately don't know what I'd do without you. Thank you for talking me down off all the ledges I manage to get myself stuck on.

I'm so glad I get to write these stories with the help and guidance of my brilliant editor, Kerry Donovan. Working with you feels like a true collaboration with someone who really gets my characters. Thanks for your keen insights and your willingness to brainstorm tough scenes with me on the weekend!

All the gratitude to my Berkley Romance team! I can't imagine doing this without the Jessicas—Jessica Mangicaro and Jessica Brock—having my back. Thank you for everything you do to make my life easier! Additional thanks to Colleen Reinhart for a gorgeous cover design—I'm so lucky!

Thank you, thank you to my beloved critique partners Vivien Jackson, Gwynne Jackson, and Annette Christie for cheering me on page by painful first draft page. Thank you for squeeing over the good stuff and saving the real critique until my heart can take it.

Additional, but just as fervent thanks to ReLynn Vaughn, Jenny Howe, Cass Scotka, Trysh Thompson, Ian Barnes, Lindsay Landgraf Hess, and Courtney Kaericher for giving feedback on drafts in various stages of completion, oftentimes more quickly than I had any right to ask for. You all helped make this book better and I can't thank you enough for it.

Re, as always, you are my gif-spiration.

Like Stacey, I've thought about running away and joining the Faire, but also like Stacey, I had no real idea of what that might entail. Thankfully, Nicole Skelly (of The Gwendolyn Show—see her perform at a Faire near you!) was nice enough to give me some insight on the realities of traveling Faire life, and anything I got wrong is on me, not her.

I'm always grateful for the love and support of my Bs: Brighton Walsh, Ellis Leigh, Melissa Marino, Suzanne Baltsar, Anniston Jory, Elizabeth Leis Newman, Helen Hoang, Esher Hogan, and Laura Elizabeth. There's no group of girls I'd rather get stuck on the ice with during a polar vortex.

Finally, I want to thank all of you. The readers who picked up *Well Met* at the bookstore or library, and those of you who are just now joining me on my Ren Faire journey. The bloggers and Bookstagrammers who featured my book on their platforms, the bookstores who hosted my visits, and the readers who came out to meet me. Thank you for your emails and private messages. I've been touched and humbled by your enthusiasm and support. It's a weird feeling to talk to other people about characters who until recently lived only in my own head, but it's been one of the best experiences of my life. Thank you all for going to the Faire with me, and I can't wait to take you back there again soon. Huzzah!

Keep reading for a special preview of

Well Matched

Out now!

The card wasn't addressed to me.

I leaned an elbow on the bar and took a sip of my hard cider. It was happy hour at Jackson's, but I wasn't happy. I wasn't happy at all. And this drink wasn't changing anything. The card still lay there on the bar. It was still addressed to my daughter, Caitlin, and it was still from her father. The man who'd wanted nothing to do with her since the day she was born, or in any of the eighteen years since. It was hard to believe that, after all this time, his handwriting could still strike my heart the way it did. Back in the day, that handwriting had covered pages and pages of love letters. Little notes we'd leave each other on Post-its on the bathroom mirror or near the coffeemaker.

Then our birth control had failed, barely a year into our marriage. The marriage itself had failed not long after that. The last time I saw Robert's handwriting had been when he signed the divorce agreement, terminating his parental rights. Rights that he'd freely, almost eagerly, given up.

Why the hell was he writing to Caitlin now?

Like poking at a bruise, I flipped the card open again.

Caitlin,

I know I haven't been there for you. But I wanted to let you know how very proud of you I am. Graduation from high school is an important milestone in anyone's life. As you move on to greater things, I want you to know that if you ever need anything from me, all you have to do is ask.

With love from your father,
Robert Daugherty

I almost wanted to laugh. *If you never need anything from me . . .* How about eighteen years of back child support? That would be a start. Our daughter had turned out great, no thanks to him. Caitlin was a smart, funny, and respectful young woman and I couldn't be prouder of her. But that had absolutely nothing to do with Robert, who'd been little more than a sperm donor. What the hell was he thinking, getting in touch now and trying to do a victory lap as a father? Fuck that. And fuck him.

I stared at his name, wishing my eyes could burn a hole through this cheap cardstock. I'd been April Daugherty once, for roughly one and a half of my forty years. And if we'd stayed married, my daughter would be Caitlin Daugherty instead of Caitlin Parker. I thought about that for a second, about those two hypothetical Daugherty women, and the life they might have had.

Would Caitlin Daugherty have had an easier time of things? Would April D. and Caitlin D. have worried a little less about affording college, applied for fewer scholarships and grants? I'd sat up a lot of nights with Caitlin P., our laptops side-by-side at the dining room table, filling out forms late into the night. At the time it had felt very feminist, very "us against the world," the way most of our lives together had been. But Caitlin Daugherty would have had a provider for a father. Maybe she would have had to fight a little less. Maybe—

"What're you drinking?"

Oh. I glanced up and to my right, squinting at the guy in a gray business suit who'd taken up residence on the barstool next to mine. He didn't look familiar, and Willow Creek, Maryland was the kind of town where everyone at least looked familiar. He was probably some guy on the way down to D.C.—he had that Beltway look about him. Salt-and-pepper hair with a nice expensive-looking cut, pale eyes, a decent smile. Of course, one strike against him was that he'd just hit on a strange woman at a bar.

I gave him a friendly-but-not-too-friendly smile. "I'm good, thank you." There. Pleasant enough, but not encouraging.

He didn't take the hint. "No, I mean it." He slid his stool a little closer to mine, not quite in my personal space but close enough. I slipped the card back into the envelope and slid it onto my other side. He peered at my drink. "Whatcha got there, a beer? Probably a light beer, huh? I can go for that." He beckoned at the bartender. I wasn't a person who hung out at bars, but I came here enough that I knew her name was Nikki, and she knew I liked the cider on draft.

"It's not a beer," I said.

He wasn't listening. "Another drink for the lady. Light beer. And I'll have one too." His take-charge voice was grating. Maybe he'd sound commanding in a government building in D.C., but in a town like this he just sounded like a dick.

Nikki raised her eyebrows at me, and I shook my head, covering the top of my glass with the palm of my hand. "I'm good. But he can have whatever he wants." I probably should have been flattered. Not bad for someone who just hit forty, right? But I was itching to be left alone. I wanted to be back down that rabbit hole with my thoughts, not dodging advances from Mr. Wannabe Lobbyist over here.

Nikki brought his drink and he held it up in my direction, expectant. What the hell. I raised mine too, and we clinked glasses in a half-hearted toast.

"So tell me . . ." He leaned in even closer, and it took everything I had to not lean away. I had my best resting bitch face on, but this guy wasn't taking the hint. "This can't be your typical Friday night. Hanging out in a bar like this?"

Engaging him in conversation was a bad idea, I knew, but he just wouldn't go away. "Nothing wrong with a bar like this."

"Well sure, but maybe there's something else you'd rather be doing . . . ?" He raised an eyebrow suggestively, and I pressed my lips together. Jesus Christ, this guy was annoying.

"Hey, April, there you are!" Another voice, deep and masculine, boomed from my left, but this time my irritation melted away. I knew this voice. Everyone in Jackson's knew this voice. Mitch Malone was an institution, not just in the bar, but in the whole town. Beloved of the kids of Willow Creek High, where he taught gym, and beloved of most adults with a pulse who enjoyed the sight of him in a kilt every summer at the Willow Creek Renaissance Faire. Mitch was good friends with my younger sister Emily, so by default he'd become a friend of mine, too.

"Mitch. Hey . . ." I'd barely turned my head in his direction before Mitch's arm slid around my waist, tugging me half off the stool and against his side.

"What the hell, babe? You didn't order me a beer yet?" He followed up the question with a kiss that landed somewhere between my cheek and my temple, and I had absolutely no idea which to respond to first. The kiss, or being called "babe." I looked up at Mitch with narrowed eyes, about to give him shit for at least one of those things, when his eyes caught mine and one lid dropped halfway in the ghost of a wink. Ah. Okay. I could play along.

"I didn't know when you were getting here, *honey.*" I punctuated that last word with my hand on his cheek, landing a little harder than was strictly necessary. It wasn't a slap, but it was definitely a warning. *Keep your hands where they are, mister.* "Your beer could've gotten warm, and I know how much you hate that."

"You're too good to me, you know that?" Mitch's bright blue eyes laughed down into mine, and the curve of his smile felt good against my palm. A dimple even appeared under my thumb and I snatched my hand back, keeping the movement casual. I'd been a breath away from stroking that dimple with the pad of my thumb, and that was getting a little too into character.

"Much better than you deserve. I know." Our smiles to each other were full of manufactured affection, yet it all felt so . . . comfortable. In a way that talking with Mr. Gray Suit hadn't.

Mitch stepped closer to me, fitting his body against mine, then glanced over at Mr. Gray Suit as though he'd just noticed him. "Hey, man. Did you need something?" His voice was light, casual, but his arm tightened around me in a not-so-subtle message to the guy on the other side of me. *Back off.*

Mr. Gray Suit got the message. "Nope. I was just . . . y'all have a good night." He fumbled for his wallet, then moved down to the end of the bar, where Nikki was waiting to cash him out. She glanced over at us, shaking her head. I could relate. I shook my head a lot when I dealt with Mitch, too.

Speaking of . . . now that we were alone, I pulled out of Mitch's embrace. "What was that all about?"

"What?" He picked up my glass, sniffed at it, then put it down with a grimace. "I was helping you out. That guy was practically drooling down your shirt."

I scoffed. "I had it handled. I don't need your help."

"You don't have to." Mitch shrugged. "Needing and wanting are two different things, you know. You can want something and not need it."

"Fine." I tilted my head back, finishing off my cider. "Maybe I don't want it either."

Mitch looked up at me through his lashes, and for a split second I forgot to breathe. Damn. Was this what women saw when he really turned his attention to them? I didn't think of Mitch in that way. I mean, sure the man was gorgeous. Well over six feet tall, his physique spoke of lots of spare time spent at the gym, and his golden-blond hair and stunningly blue eyes made him look like a genetically engineered, all-American hottie. He had a smile you wanted to bask in, and a jawline you wanted to run a hand down, to see if it felt as sharp as it looked.

Something must have shown on my face, because his expression shifted. He lifted an eyebrow just a little, and this was nothing like when Mr. Gray Suit did it a few minutes ago. I caught my bottom lip between my teeth, worrying the skin, and Mitch's eyes darkened.

"Liar," was all he said, but his voice had a roughness to it that I'd never heard before. The air between us was charged with electricity, and for the space of a few heartbeats I couldn't breathe. Worse, I didn't want to. I just bit down on my bottom lip harder so I didn't do anything stupid. Like bite down on his bottom lip.

Then I forced out a laugh, breaking the spell. "Okay, whatever." I picked up my glass and dammit, it was empty. I put it down again.

"So what are you doing here, anyway?" Mitch leaned an elbow on the bar. "You're not a 'drink alone at the bar' kind of person."

"How do you know what kind of person I am?" But he just looked at me with his eyebrows raised, and I had to admit he was right. I wasn't that kind of person. I put my hand over the card and, after a deep breath, slid it across the bar in his direction. He flipped it open, his face darkening as he read.

"Her father?" He closed the card and handed it back to me. "I didn't realize he was in the picture."

"He's not." I stuck the card in my purse; I'd had enough of Robert for one night.

"But he wants to be, huh?" Mitch gave me a questioning look. "What does Caitlin think about it?"

"I don't know," I said wearily. "I think she's still deciding." He nodded, and I hated how there was something resembling pity in his eyes. I didn't want pity. "Let me get you that beer." I leaned over the bar, catching Nikki's attention to order a beer for him and a second cider for me. "The least I can do for helping me get rid of that creep."

Mitch accepted the beer with a thoughtful look. "You know, if you really want to pay me back, I know a way you can help me out."

"Oh yeah?" I picked up my cider. That first, icy cold sip was always the best. "How's that?"

He didn't meet my eyes. "Be my girlfriend."

He just wanted a decent book to read ...

Not too much to ask, is it? It was in 1935 when Allen Lane, Managing Director of Bodley Head Publishers, stood on a platform at Exeter railway station looking for something good to read on his journey back to London. His choice was limited to popular magazines and poor-quality paperbacks – the same choice faced every day by the vast majority of readers, few of whom could afford hardbacks. Lane's disappointment and subsequent anger at the range of books generally available led him to found a company – and change the world.

'We believed in the existence in this country of a vast reading public for intelligent books at a low price, and staked everything on it'
Sir Allen Lane, 1902–1970, founder of Penguin Books

The quality paperback had arrived – and not just in bookshops. Lane was adamant that his Penguins should appear in chain stores and tobacconists, and should cost no more than a packet of cigarettes.

Reading habits (and cigarette prices) have changed since 1935, but Penguin still believes in publishing the best books for everybody to enjoy. We still believe that good design costs no more than bad design, and we still believe that quality books published passionately and responsibly make the world a better place.

So wherever you see the little bird – whether it's on a piece of prize-winning literary fiction or a celebrity autobiography, political tour de force or historical masterpiece, a serial-killer thriller, reference book, world classic or a piece of pure escapism – you can bet that it represents the very best that the genre has to offer.

Whatever you like to read – trust Penguin.